Licking the flavor of liquor off his lips, Carrigan mused, *"YOU'RE AFRAID OF ME."*

"I am not," Helena shot back, the fingers at her throat sinking into the cotton ruffles.

"Of course you are. But it's a fear that loves the idea of danger."

The tremor in her voice betrayed her. "That's absurd. I'm not afraid of you."

"Then prove you aren't." He gave her a long, steady look. "Come here."

She hesitated a moment. Stepping forward, she approached the bed. Once at its edge, she released the grip on her wrapper and lowered her arms to her sides. "I've been this close to you before."

Carrigan's voice was seductive and low when he said, "But you and I both know things are different now." Wanting to since she'd come into his room, he brought his fingers around the rope of her hair. He rubbed its silky texture against his thumb and drew her face closer to his by gently pulling on the length. "I told you that I didn't need anyone, but that's a lie. Without you I would have died." Her generous eyelashes fluttered against her cheeks. "But that doesn't mean I have to like needing you." He'd maneuvered her face within inches of his. "And that doesn't mean I won't walk away at the end of the six months." Her startled breath was hot on his chin. "Because I will. . . ."

Books by Stef Ann Holm

Seasons of Gold
Liberty Rose
King of the Pirates
Snowbird
Weeping Angel
Crossings

Published by POCKET BOOKS

STEF ANN HOLM

CROSSINGS

POCKET STAR BOOKS

New York   London   Toronto   Sydney   Tokyo   Singapore

*Fondly for Joe, Michele, and Tara Smaltz,
whose century-old farmhouse in modern-day
Genoa is shared by two mischievous ghosts who
sometimes call Michele's name and have a
penchant for making dishes disappear.*

An *Original* Publication of POCKET BOOKS

 A Pocket Star Book published by
POCKET BOOKS, a division of Simon & Schuster Inc.
1230 Avenue of the Americas, New York, NY 10020

ISBN: 0-671-51047-9

First Pocket Books printing January 1996

10 9 8 7 6 5 4 3 2 1

POCKET STAR BOOKS and colophon are registered
trademarks of Simon & Schuster Inc.

Cover art by Tom Hallman

Printed in the U.S.A.

A Note to ℛ

Genoa was the first town establish
and much has been written abou
Since facts vary, I've altered so
events, and the years in which they
For the sake of my story, I've delayed t
founding to coincide more closely with
Express. This is fiction, after all, and in
the truth sometimes has a way of stretch
suit the writer's needs. . . .

Chapter

→ 1 ←

Genoa, Nevada Territory
April 1860

He called himself Carrigan, and everyone in Genoa figured his mind had to be one cartridge short of a full load for him to prefer a solitary life. Those rare times he came into town with that massive Walker Colt he kept at his side, his eyes were flat and unemotional, leaving to wonder if he'd ever cracked a smile.

Rumors about him abounded, tumbling through Main Street with the sagebrush. Some claimed he'd killed at least two dozen men and was the fastest draw west of anyplace east. Others said he'd earned a haphazard living as a cowboy, a gambler, and an extractor of venom from rattlesnakes before coming to the Carson Valley. However, the tapestry of known facts concerning these professions was threadbare.

All agreed he was unfriendly. For he had chosen to live as a hermit on the eastern slope of the Sierra Nevada, where gold was scattered like raisins on a cake. Carrigan had been holed up there prior to the town's founding. A party of the new pioneers had ridden to his cabin to make his acquaintance, but they had been welcomed with the whine of a bullet. The

1

group left posthaste, and no one who knew he was there had ventured up his mountain since.

Until Helena Gray.

Helena had heard his cabin was built above the northeast section of town where dusk was premature. Ascending the incline spiked with Jeffrey pines, she kept her woolen hem lifted and her gaze downward to concentrate on footholds in the damp ground. She made no effort to keep her approach silent. Talebearers eager to enlighten said Carrigan greeted trespassers with the steel nose of his he-man gun. She had no desire to test that theory.

As she climbed, she recalled their first meeting a year ago. He'd come to her father's general store to trade some pelts for tobacco, a basket of eggs, and a copy of the *Territorial Enterprise.* Impressively tall and broad in the shoulders, he'd been as quiet as a stone wall when she'd waited on him. She hadn't been able to dispute the fact he was an imposing character. Why she hadn't been apprehensive about his presence, she couldn't quite say. Perhaps it was because she understood his need to go off alone. She might have done the same thing had it not been for her mother. Instead, Helena had stayed with her family and knit her torn life into a thin but serviceable fabric.

The smoky scent of a campfire and the aroma of cooking meat wafted through the cool air. Despite her resolution, Helena's heart pounded an uneven rhythm. She stopped abruptly to listen. The faraway squawk of a blue jay and the wind filled her ears. A tin utensil scraping the bottom of a pan pulled her attention in the direction of the sound. She tried to gauge the distance. The breeze through the pine boughs played an eerie tune, and she caught herself glancing uneasily over her shoulder. She wished she could have come before evening, but she'd worried about leaving her sister alone to tend the store. Waiting until after closing hadn't left Helena with much light to guide her way. Inching the woven check shawl higher on her neck to ward off the chill in her spine, she proceeded.

It had rained for a short time in the afternoon, and the woolly violets that littered the bank felt slippery beneath the soles of her shoes as her thoughts drifted back to the past. Now and then, Carrigan had returned to the store to keep up his mild smoking and liquor habit. He never said hello to a stranger—the entire population of Genoa consisting of nothing but, to a recluse like him. The only person he swapped enough words with to be called a conversation was her father. Both men shared a mutual respect for animals. In later months, they'd made arrangements for Carrigan to supply Gray's stockyard with swift horses for their Pony Express station. Few could deny there had ever been a more impressive sight than Carrigan parading that string of high-spirited mustangs down Nixon Street.

Though Helena doubted Carrigan's receptiveness, there might have come a time when he would have shared a supper table with her father. But she would never know. Five days ago, someone killed him. Since then, the fate of Helena and her younger sister, Emilie, had been openly discussed as if they were incapable of thinking for themselves. There was no shortage of eligible men, and she had had several marriage proposals, most of which were based on strong sentiments against their running the station, stockyard, and store alone. Helena had been fending off the bachelors until today. Today the men had done the unthinkable. They'd backed Helena into a situation that forced her to make a decision about her and Emilie's future.

Helena chose to go see Carrigan.

Twirling poplar leaves disguised the noise she made as she came to a copse of saplings, their density screening her. Embers from low flames glowed in the gray sky, illuminating the big and muscular figure of a

3

man. Carrigan sat in an open-sided shelter, its roof sagging in the middle like an old mare's back. There were no chinked walls to hold off the weather, nor embrace the heat and keep warmth cloaked around him. Only the bulky mackinaw jacket covering his torso. He rested a run-down bootheel on the edge of a crate. The crude table at his elbow was low and cluttered with objects—most notably the Walker Colt. He held a bottle of Snakehead whiskey between his thighs, one hand loosely wrapped around the neck. A cigarette relaxed in the corner of his mouth, and he squinted against the smoke to watch his supper cook.

An air of wild and dangerous isolation hung around him, and she sensed the power coiled in his body. When he leaned forward to turn the skewered haunch of some small game, his movements were filled with a restless energy that had Helena's heartbeat thumping madly.

A dog's low growl came from the shadows. Before she could announce herself, Carrigan had picked up the huge revolver and pointed its gleaming barrel directly at her.

"I'll kill you where you stand unless you show me your hands."

Helena's blood ran cold, and she couldn't move or speak as a big black dog appeared with its ears thrown back and teeth bared. The click of the gun's hammer echoed inside her head, loud and reverberating with serious intent. She opened her mouth, and words tumbled forth in a low volume. Her scratchy plea not to shoot was lost on the wind. Somehow, she managed to lift her fingertips skyward before Carrigan made good on his threat.

"Come here," he commanded in a voice icy and exact.

Foreboding numbed her legs. In the cast of firelight, he did intimidate her. His eyes were hooded, the nostrils of his hawkish nose flared and distrusting. Hair the color of pitch was wind-ruffled around his plaid collar. The lines of his rugged face were not put there by the emotions of love and pride; they looked to be the scars of battle.

She walked forward, trying to swallow her fear, but it was as thick as dough. A tremor shook her voice when she said, "It's me, Helena Gray. I've waited on you in the store. . . ." His consuming stare was so unnerving, she momentarily lost her train of thought. "I helped you with your purchases. You know my father. . . ."

Carrigan's brows drew together in a withdrawn expression as he studied her briefly but didn't answer. Removing the cigarette stub from his lips, he flicked it into the fire. "Does August know where you are?"

"No."

"Then go home."

She let his comment pass, though the intensity of his gaze had her pulse spinning. "My father doesn't know where I am because he's dead."

Carrigan was silent, his face stony. The dog snapped his jaws, his sharp teeth biting at the breeze. Carrigan moved his gaze on the animal. "Obsi, lie down."

Helena's arms were tingling. "May I lower my hands?" she asked.

Grumbling, he turned away, and she took his dismissal as a yes. He set his revolver on the table and picked up a long-handled spoon to stir a shallow pan of beans. Afterward, he adjusted the skewer. When he turned toward her, the sharpness in his eyes waned to disbelief. "How did it happen?"

"He was murdered in our store five days ago." Wetting her lips, she continued with a sadness in her tone she was unable to mask. "Our cash box was taken with not enough in it worth killing for." The horror of the scene haunted her sleep and tortured her waking hours, and she thanked God it had been she and not Emilie who had discovered their father's body.

A distilled silence feathered the campfire's smoke before meat drippings hit the flames. Carrigan flinched when loud pops erupted, sending a shower of embers over the sooty containment rocks. He sat quiet and erect, his steely expression diminishing somewhat with the sparks in the wet grass. "Have you eaten?"

"I'm not hungry, thank you."

He removed his meal, fixing a plate for the dog and himself. Then Carrigan proceeded to eat, using a fork and knife. His manners were cultured, unlike those of the old sourdough miners who sat in front of the Metropolitan Saloon. Taking intermittent swigs of liquor, Carrigan consumed his modest dinner and acted as if she weren't there watching.

Helena's leather-laced ankles grew tired from standing on the slant, but she hadn't been offered a seat. Not that there was an extra one. On first glance, there had appeared to be no back to the lean-to. Now she could see that the rear wall was the side of a crude cabin. And on closer inspection, the squat table held a coffee grinder and jars for making sassafras bars, a tobacco pouch, and an assortment of spice tins and oil vials.

"Is anyone searching for the man responsible?" Carrigan's inquiry broke her perusal.

"There is no law or sheriff in Genoa. We're a provisional part of the Nevada Territory. Mr. Van Sickle, our justice of the peace, and Mr. Doyle, our undertaker, are the few men holding legal professions."

"So nothing is being done?"

"I gave my account to Mr. Davis, the deputy postmaster, and to Judge Kimball, but he can't do anything without a suspect."

"Nothing is being done," Carrigan muttered in a caustic tone.

Helena grew perturbed. He made it sound as if she didn't care. "What else can I do?" she asked bitterly.

"There are no witnesses." Her voice clogged with tears she refused to spend. "If I could track the outlaw myself, I would."

Carrigan set his plate aside and stared into the firelight as if the flame beckoned. Lifting the bottle, he took a long swallow, then held out his hand. "A drink will help. Whiskey can be a good cure when there is no visible blood on your wound."

"I don't believe so," she returned, tightening the shawl more closely about her shoulders. "You can't drown your sorrows. They know how to swim."

He apparently didn't appreciate her caution, for he grew as touchy as gunpowder. "What do you want?"

Girding herself with courage, she said, "I want to offer you a trade."

"For more horses?"

"No."

A suspicious line formed at the corner of his mouth. "A trade for what, then?"

She stalled, trying to entice him with the rewards. "You'd be able to select merchandise at the store. Tobacco and liquor. Supplies when you need them. Dry goods. Kerosene. Anything you desire at no cost."

"Everything has a price," he insisted with a sharp edge of cynicism. "What do I have to give you?"

She braced herself for his reaction. "Your name."

"My name?"

"Yes."

"My name isn't worth shit."

Her voice faded to a hushed stillness. "It is to me."

"How so?"

"I would like use of it. In marriage." She took a deep breath and tried to relax. "Our marriage."

The taste of whiskey went sour in Carrigan's mouth. Resting the bottle's end on his leather-clad thigh, he grew intoxicated by his anger. The emotion stabbed at his normally disguised pride. Hostility rushed through him to slip like a greased key into the lock of his resentment.

He didn't like being played for a fool.

At first he hadn't known who she was. The fragrance of crushed violets on her skirts had confused him. He associated the smell of coffee, gun oil, and cheese with her voice. But then he'd recognized the distinctive female scent that was hers alone and had been able to place her. The rose vinegar perfuming her hair had entered him like sweet breath into his lungs.

Ignoring her, he willed her to leave him alone, hoping his silence was louder than the words warring inside his head. Seconds passed. He felt her unwavering gaze on him. Blue. Her eyes were blue and soft and pleading. In that instant he hated her for evoking something within the barren shell of his heart.

"Leave," he mumbled.

"Not yet."

He underestimated her fearlessness. She wouldn't go away.

"My offer is honest. If you become my husband, I'd trade whatever you needed in the store."

Glaring at her, he mentally sifted the rubbish she tossed. He could barely contain his smirk when he found a flaw in her strategy. "As your lawful husband, I would *own* everything in the store."

His satisfaction was enhanced when she nervously bit her lip. "Yes . . . you would. But I was hoping I'd be able to keep running things as they are. I didn't think you'd have any interest in—"

"Suppose I did?" he countered sharply.

"Then we would discuss those arrangements."

He cocked his brow with growing distrust. The transparency of her remark grated on him. Her eagerness to please thinned his forbearance. "There *is* a price. What am I really worth to you?"

"Protection," she said simply and without pause.

8

"People are afraid of you. If I were your wife, they would be afraid of me, too."

Surprise engulfed him. "Am I so crazy to them?" he mused aloud. "I hadn't realized." Stuffing the cork on his whiskey, he put the bottle away.

She wrung her hands together, disregarding his mocking statement. "Nothing need change in our lives. We'd go on the way we have, except we'd share your name. And my house."

Carrigan stared hard, showing no reaction to her proposal. "No."

"Things between us wouldn't be permanent. Just for—"

"No."

She was clearly at her wits' end, her eyes a mirror of desperation. Firelight played across her pale face and danced through her golden hair, which had been confined in a diamond-patterned net. Her features were dainty, but the suggestion of a wholesome figure lay beneath her shawl.

"You don't understand the severity of the situation," she rushed. "They've cut me off. I didn't think they would go that far, but they have."

He struck a match and lit a cigarette, then stood so that she could have his seat. "Sit down. You keep shifting on your feet and it bothers me."

The thick lashes shadowing her cheeks flew up. After a moment's hesitation, she moved toward the crate. The fullness of her skirt brushed against him as she passed. His lids came down swiftly over his eyes, and he sucked in his breath. His senses leapt to life from the heat of her body. It had been years since he'd been this close to a woman. He wondered if she was as soft as he remembered a female to be. If her mouth would burn from his kisses. He could almost taste the dew of violets clinging to her skin, yet his lips had not touched hers.

Blinking, he focused his gaze. An intense longing

flared through him. He didn't want to feel desire for her, but couldn't suppress its potent surge through his veins. Even Obsi was curious about her. The dog sniffed her fingers as she sat. She tried to appear brave but hid her hands in the volume of her dress, out of Obsi's reach. The narrow-striped skirt fanned around her ankles, which were attired in practical shoes. He saw her, and yet he didn't. For the woman he was acquainted with in the store would never have come. She was reserved. A thinker who, like himself, didn't say much. Or perhaps it was just to him she spared few words.

"Why have you really come?" he asked, drawing smoke from his cigarette and exhaling into the same wind kicking the soft curls at her temple.

"I told you. It's business. Ours wouldn't be a marriage in the true sense." She looked downward and murmured, "I didn't think you'd have any interest in consummating—"

"You don't think a lot of me," he interrupted in a patronizing voice that made her flinch. "You strip me of my interests, then you strip me of my manhood—practically in one breath. What would you say if I wanted to take you to my bed? Would we discuss those arrangements also?"

Raising her chin, she parted her lips. He watched the slim column of her throat as she swallowed. "I was hoping you wouldn't . . . but . . ."

"You're doing nothing short of selling yourself to me like a common whore. And for what?" The strength of his voice made the fire shoot sparks. "The nothing cost of my worthless name."

"It's not worthless to me," she rallied. "The name Carrigan commands respect and fear."

His brows arched. "Are you afraid of me?"

"No."

"You're not telling me the truth. I, too, am a liar. So I can recognize the face. What aren't you telling me?"

She lifted her wrist and pressed fingertips to her

forehead as if her head were a ripe melon splitting wide open. "If I don't marry, I'll have to give up the relay station."

"So marry," he said noncommittally. "I'm sure there are plenty of men you can choose from."

Her hand lowered. "But none that would make them cower in their boots if they dared treat me the way they are now!"

"Them, their, and they," he quipped. "A clandestine trio?"

"No. The business owners who have seen fit to inform me two women cannot operate a Pony Express post." Her clarion voice broke. "Since my father died, I have been refused service. I have two horses that need shoeing, but none of the three blacksmiths will shoe them. Mr. Lewis at the hay yard is demanding payment on our account, or he won't give me hay. I already went to his competitor, but he denied me credit."

"What happened to the man who tends your stock?"

"Eliazer."

Carrigan nodded.

"Eliazer doesn't care about his pay as long as he's fed and housed."

"Marry him."

Aghast, she blurted, "He's nearly sixty and already married. Besides, he hasn't the strength or reputation to slight them." Fatigue softened her posture. "They've banded together to shut me out. If I don't have properly shod horses and feed, I'll have to give up everything. What galls me most is, they're right. Emilie and I can't do it alone. I need to hire help, but if I don't have the revenue from the Express, I can't afford to pay a salary."

As Carrigan puffed on his cigarette, his thoughts clouded with the gray smoke in the air. He reflected on private memories, treasures that he kept safeguarded in his mind where they could not be stolen.

Terrible regrets assailed him, and he vowed not to make the same mistakes as he had in the past. No amount of convincing on the woman's part would change his answer.

"I won't be treated in the same manner as those men ridicule the Indians." The determination marking her words splintered his musings. "They can't take away what my father worked so hard for." Her face was flushed but proud. "I have never had to humble myself in such a way as I am to you. But I am asking you to marry me."

He took one last drag before snapping the butt into the fire. "I'm not a rescuer. I can't help you."

She sat in silence, her mouth as pale as her cheeks. The misery surrounding her was so acute, he felt it as a physical pain. A stab of guilt buried itself to the hilt in his chest. He had to do something, say something, to make her leave, or else he would . . .

"Go home," he told her.

Standing, she straightened her shoulders and cleared her throat. "You're right. You are *not* the man who can help me."

She walked away with stiff dignity, Obsi trotting after her.

"Obsi!" Carrigan growled. "Come!"

The dog stopped but didn't yield to his master's command. He slowly sat on his haunches and watched the woman vanish into the dark woods.

Carrigan cursed and kicked the dog's empty plate. The tin made a loud clatter as it bounced off a rock. Obsi ran to the other side of the cabin, out of Carrigan's view. He didn't like losing his temper. When he was alone, he rarely, if ever, did so.

Gazing skyward at the bright flyspecks of stars blanketing the night, he listened to the forest swallow Helena Gray's retreat. Never more than now had he felt so isolated. He hadn't gone in search of seclusion. It had crept up on him as if it were gangrene, eating away at what little tolerance for mankind he had left in his body. Disillusionment with civilization had driven him from populated areas, and he swore he would never go back.

Helena swiftly left the darkness behind, the soft yellow light spilling from Genoa's windows, beacons to guide her home. What could she have been thinking by asking a man like Carrigan to marry her? Had desperation forced her to take irrational measures?

But Carrigan had seemed like such a logical choice. His reputation as a hardened loner who'd closed himself off from mankind because he had a past to hide had been what lured her to him. Like maple leaves in the fall, her past was scarlet, too. They could have formed a common ground and each benefited from a union based on mutual gain. Though Carrigan hadn't seen things that way. He hadn't wanted anything from her.

Perhaps she had been too blunt with her offer. Perhaps she shouldn't have undermined his integrity. She'd made a cold and beseeching proposal to a stranger and had been put in her place. His rejection hurt. Especially when there were others who would leap at the chance to be her husband. But the others would also learn the painful truth about her should she accept one of them. Her mother had taken this truth to the grave, and now Helena's secret was just between her and God. She lived with the weight of her conscience every day.

Helena made her way across Fifth Street, the soggy ground oozing around her shoes. There were few boardwalks to use, the short planks broken by alleys and lots. The streets were not particularly level, as the town was snuggled against the Sierra foothills. Towering pines fanned behind Genoa Street, while Nixon Street cut a direct course through spreading sage as far as the eye could see. Buildings were mostly constructed from native trees, but a few had been made of sun-dried bricks. The mud-colored adobes were a far cry from the neat clapboard edifices of New Providence, Pennsylvania. But Helena found a rugged beauty in the western craftsmanship that had been lacking in the polished carpentry of her eastern home.

"Miss Gray." The masculine voice that called her name was familiar.

Judge Bayard Kimball stood in the illuminated doorway of the courthouse, as always, impeccably dressed in a high-priced suit. His hair was the color of coal without a sprinkling of ashes to indicate his age of forty-six. Thick, prominent brows arched over gray eyes that were astute and bordered on being limned with distrust, given he was a public officer authorized to pass critical judgment. He never boasted of his power, but his authority was evident in the way he held himself. He bore the responsibility of his elected office with stiff dignity and a flask of gin in his pocket. Sometimes he would form an opinion even before the first witness was heard, for he would declare nothing need be said about the case because his mind was already made up.

"Good evening, Judge Kimball."

"I wish you would call me Bayard," he said in a smooth but insistent voice.

Helena didn't feel comfortable addressing him by his given name. He'd requested she do so on several occasions, and she suspected he would continue to press the issue until she acquiesced.

"Are you all right?" His question was filled with genuine concern.

Feeling battered from her encounter with Carrigan, she couldn't answer. She kept her fragile shawl over her sloped shoulders, the crocheted armor inadequate protection against the night air.

"It's too cold for you to be out without a cloak." Bayard slid his arms from his resplendent blue coat and draped its warmth across her back. "Let me walk you home."

She took solace in his presence as he led her toward Main Street. She shouldn't have relied on him, but he had always been there for her family, and giving herself up to his care was effortless.

"Where have you been?" he asked.

Even though she trusted Bayard, she couldn't confide her whereabouts. The whole plan about seeing Carrigan seemed so foolish now that she didn't want to disclose what she'd done. "I've been walking," she half lied. "I needed to think."

His lengthy silence caused her to glance at his profile and see his frown in the dimness. "I'm a judge and I don't have the means or manpower backing me to catch outlaws. Genoa is run on a vigilante system in which I give rulings in accordance with the laws designated for this provisional territory. You know that if the criminal who killed your father is apprehended, I'll sentence him to hang."

"Yes, I know."

"It wounds me that you won't make things simpler for you and your sister, Helena." He caressed her name when he spoke it, leaving propriety behind and becoming more informal with her. "I've given you my permission to keep operating the station if you were my wife. Your grievous circumstances would change under my protection. I could make you happy."

They came to the front of the general store, where a lantern burned in the window behind a drawn canvas shade. Helena didn't have the strength to sidestep his proposal with weak excuses. "I have to go in," she said quickly. "They're waiting supper for me." She handed Bayard his coat. "Thank you for walking me home. Bayard," she added as a small token to show him that she did appreciate his consideration. Then she slipped inside before he could say anything further.

Pressing her back against the closed door, she didn't doubt Bayard would make a good husband. With his political ambitions, he could very well hold a high-ranking seat in the government. But were she to become his wife, she couldn't fulfill the solemn promise of her marriage vows. Pledging herself to Bayard would be a lie.

At least with Carrigan, they'd both know where they stood before the rings were on their fingers. She wouldn't be deluding herself into thinking there could ever be anything more than an impersonal transaction. Because that was what she was destined for should she ever marry.

16

Chapter

⇥ 2 ⇤

Gray's general store sold everything from whiskey to
soothe the soul, to Bibles to enlarge the spirit. The
interior of the rough-hewn structure was a world of
muted sounds and odd mingled odors. Coffee beans
with their rich aroma blended into the leather smell of
boots, saddles, and belts. The lingering woodsy fragrance of Helena's summer herbs distinguished the
area behind the grocery counter. In the fall, she'd tied
the bundles with string and made bouquets, which she
hung upside down from the low-sloped rafters.

Across from the bins of flour, sugar, rice, and salt,
there were bolts of fabric. The musty-sweet tang of
dyes woven into cloth added to the mixture of self-
contained scents. Spring snowflakes had been drifting
from the sky on and off for the past two days, and the
moisture made the chinked logs swell and give off a
damp odor. The puncheon floor was swept twice
daily, but no amount of swishing with the stiff broom
bristles could get rid of the mud.

Helena walked between the crowded aisle dividing
the two counters, which faced one another. Her skirt

17

snagged on a barrel of nails, and she gently pulled the calico free so she wouldn't tear the thin material. Continuing, she went to the rear of the store where a mounted elk head on the wall kept watch over the black potbellied stove. As she bent down, the nights of not getting enough sleep battled to rob the strength in her knees. She felt sore and tired all over from tossing and turning in her bed. There was no option she hadn't considered—yet neither was there a solution she could live with. It would be easy to accept any proposal if she wanted to be subdued by men who thought they knew what was best for her and Emilie. But she wasn't willing to wed herself to just any man.

If only Carrigan . . . No. She wasn't going to think about him. He'd given her his answer and she had to accept it.

Grabbing a piece of wood from the fuel box, Helena added the splintered log to the fire embers. Fresh sparks shot up the pipe as the piney sap burned.

"I'm going to the butcher shop now," Emilie said as she passed through the faded curtains that kept the living area apart from the store. While she walked, she put on her worsted gloves with concise movements that reminded Helena of their mother.

At sixteen, Emilie was developing a figure that was hard to conceal in her girlish shirtwaist and gray pinafore. The hem of her skirt fell six inches below her stocking-clad knees, and though it had been Helena's intention to keep her sister attired in a fashion less mature than her years, the shorter skirt only served to reveal the shape of Emilie's long legs. She wore her yellow-blond hair in two braids that fell to her shoulder blades, but there was no denying the feminine wisps of curls that snuck out to frame her petite face and make her appear more womanly.

Helena straightened and moved around the sacks of potatoes leaning against the counter. She was terrified of Emilie growing up and making the same mistake she had when she was her sister's age. Emilie's desire to wear more mature dresses was a constant source of argument between the two of them. But today, thankfully, Emilie didn't start anything.

Gathering a cigar box from underneath the counter, Helena set it next to the scale. Gone was the shining tin cash box they had once had, and inside it, the daguerreotype of the four of them—Father, Mother, Helena, and Emilie—standing in front of their white house in New Providence a week before they'd moved. Also gone was the half dime Father had been given for the first sale at the store. As a memento, he'd scratched their mother's initials into it, just below Lady Liberty's flag, and kept both the picture and the coin in the pretty cash box. But everything was lost now. Taken by the robber who'd murdered her father. The shock of his death still left a pang in Helena's heart and a void in her life that was almost too much to bear at times.

Helena lifted the decorative El Cid lid; the remnant smell of tobacco leaves mingled with the pungency of petty money inside. Helena counted out several silver coins. "Don't buy a whole quarter. Just a shoulder, and a tail for soup if Mr. Zeckendorf has it."

Emilie nodded and took the money. "Ignacia said she has enough carrots." The coins clinked together as she dropped them in her worn velvet reticule. Glancing at Helena, Emilie smiled weakly. "You've got to try and sleep, you know. I loved Father, too, but you can't keep worrying about what's going to happen to us. We'll still have the store, even if we don't have the station."

"It would be easy to give up, but I won't let Father's dream die." Helena put the money box away and absently fingered a crock of vinegar. "You know how much he wanted to be a part of the Pony Express. It's history in the making, he said. That's why he fought so hard to secure the station for us."

"I understand that, Lena, but he's not here anymore to help."

19

"That's why we have to help ourselves."

"By marrying a man like Carrigan?" Emilie fitted the hood of her heavy cloak over her hair. "I'm glad he turned you down. He frightens me. They say he's killed people. How could you lie in bed at night knowing he was in the house, and at any time could murder you when you sleep?"

Helena sighed. "I'm not sleeping now."

"Don't make fun of me. It must be true, or no one would say such awful things about him." Emilie walked toward the door and lifted the latch. A snap of frosty air seeped through the crack as she turned to face Helena. "Can you honestly tell me you aren't just a little relieved he said no?"

Helena fought the chill with a shiver. "Perhaps I am . . . just a little. But when I think of who else there is to turn to, I'm sorry he didn't say yes."

"There's always Judge Kimball. He's been nothing short of a gentleman from the day we met him. And Father liked him, too." Emilie tucked her hands in the folds of her cloak. "He's asked you twice, Lena, and may not propose again. If you think that marriage is the only answer, you could do worse. Far worse." Fussing with the edges of her wrap, she hid her attire. "I won't be back straightaway. I'm going to visit Mrs. Osterman and her new baby."

The door closed, but the cold fingers of winter's last stand on Genoa dominated the room. Helena didn't readily move. She grew pensive, and allowed herself to imagine what kind of husband Judge Bayard Kimball would be. He had asked her to marry him once before when her father was living, so she knew that his recent offer wasn't purely charitable. A portrait of domesticity with such a man had been clear to her from the moment she met him. He would expect her to be subservient, a pillar of the ladies' community, and serve him well in his political aspirations. That would mean no rides astride the horses, no summer nights spent sleeping on the haystacks, and no swims in the creek wearing her shimmy.

Bayard would want her to be a proper wife. She would have to yield to him on their wedding night, and he would discover what she had sworn deeply never to reveal. The very idea of anyone finding out sent guilt and grief washing through Helena, and she refused to think about what could never be.

Over the course of an hour, customers came and left, their purchases not adding up to the amount Helena needed to buy more hay and to pay for horse shoeing—should those merchants have a change of heart and render her service.

Anxious for Emilie to return, Helena dusted the shelves of patent medicines. The store didn't hold the same appeal for her as helping Eliazer with the stock. She wasn't a woman who preferred the indoors. The lure of fresh air, the vigor of working with horses, and the rewards of physical exhaustion at the end of a hard day were far more alluring to her than minding the till.

The door opened and slammed closed on a gust of wind. Swirling around, Helena tried to subdue the tempo of her racing heartbeat from being startled out of her thoughts.

"Afternoon, Miss Gray." Seaton Hanrahan entered the store with his swaggering presence. A tall and lean man, his stance emphasized the slimness of his hips. He wore his sandy hair cropped short above the ears, with a flashy black hat cocked over his forehead. The rattlesnake-skin band adorning the high crown distinguished him in a crowd during his periodic trips to town. Seaton was a wrangler who worked off and on for the many ranchers in the valley.

As Seaton strode toward her, the jingle of steel spurs rang in showy chorus. He'd fastened little pear-shaped pendants to the axles of his spur rowels. The danglers had no purpose. Their sole function was to jingle-jangle.

"Don't this snow beat all?" he drawled. "It's colder than a crowbar outside."

There was a shrewdness about his voice that never quite sounded sincere to Helena. At twenty-some years of age, he was unsociable, coupled with a sullen charm that went wasted on her. She stared at him, wondering, as she did now with all the roughened customers who crossed the threshold of the store, if he had been the one to pull the trigger against her father. Or had the criminal fled town, leaving her never to know who he was?

"How can I help you, Mr. Hanrahan?"

"I'm just looking around." He wandered through the store, pawing and picking up this and that as if he owned everything lock, stock, and barrel. His tour of the merchandise took him back to the front door, where he glanced at the traffic on the street before heading in her direction. The slanted heels of his calfskin boots scraped over the uneven floor, leaving globs of thick mud. Stopping in front of her, he put both hands on the counter and leaned forward. Brown eyes with flecks in darker hues studied her without blinking once. She didn't shrink away from him, despite wanting to in the worst way. "I'll take a plug of Brown's Mule."

Glad to get out from under Seaton's unnerving gaze, Helena reached for the box of chewing tobacco and pulled out a bar. Red metal tags with teeth, in the shape of mules, were stuck into each portion. She measured out one plug and cut it off. "Would you like it wrapped?"

"No." He slowly slid a coin across the scratched top of the wooden counter with the tip of his forefinger.

She held the length of chew out for him to take. His fingers reached for her offering, but rather than make contact with his purchase, he slipped his hand around her wrist. She pulled her arm back, but his grip was unrelenting.

"You've got soft skin, Miss Gray."

Helena went still, trying to decide if he truly meant her harm or just wanted to scare her.

"I hear you're in need of a husband." His rough-skinned thumb brushed her pulse point, and she was chagrined to know he could feel how rapidly her blood was racing. "Maybe we can work out something between us."

"I don't think so." She attempted freedom again. This time he let her withdraw her hand. "If the tobacco is all you need—"

"No. I'm thinking I need something else." He rounded the end of the counter, and Helena felt panic well inside her. Her gaze darted to the Sharps rifle suspended on pegs above the front door, then at the curtained partition leading to the house. No one was inside. Ignacia had come in earlier to tell her she would be in the yard plucking feathers from the supper chickens.

Helena scooted through the narrow space between the shelves and countertop. "I'd like you to leave."

Seaton bore down on her with nimble feet, trapping her in the corner. Only a few precious yards separated her and the rifle, but she couldn't reach the stock. Seaton pinned her against the glass case containing shoes, his thighs solid and steady next to the fullness of her skirt. "Now, if you've a mind to fetch yourself a husband, I've a mind to show you what I can offer a pretty thing like yourself." His hands cradled her face, tilting her head as he lowered his lips over hers.

Struggling to break free, Helena kicked at his shins and tried to wrench away from his mouth, but the pressure he plied was too domineering to break. His hands holding her cheeks may well have been a vise. Clawing at his nubby coat, she gasped for breath, her throat closing with terror.

Then suddenly he was gone and the space he'd been in was a whirling void. Glass breaking sharpened her rioting senses, and Helena spun to see Carrigan holding Seaton by his fleece collar. Carrigan's large hands rode up Seaton's thin neck, tightening around his Adam's apple. Seaton's arms thrashed upward, clutching at Carrigan's wrists, but Carrigan kept squeezing. The sun-reddened skin at Seaton's throat began to turn white, and his garbled struggle for escape wheezed to near nothingness. His eyes started to roll inside his skull, and his arms dropped to his sides.

"Stop it!" Helena screamed.

The strong veins on the tops of Carrigan's hands bulged as his fingers constricted Seaton's waxen flesh. Every visible muscle in Carrigan's body was strained as his hands jerked and attempted to snuff out a life like an animal going after its prey.

"You're killing him!" she railed in a hoarse voice. "Let go!"

Whether it was Seaton's lack of fight or her desperate pleas, Carrigan released Seaton with a shove. He fell limply over the fabric table, winded and sucking in loud gulps of air that were mingled with coughing spasms. Several bolts of cloth fell as Seaton struggled to regain control of his breath. The color began to return to his cheeks in blotches of red from his panting.

Carrigan stood over him, his face etched in a rage. Without warning, he grabbed Seaton by his collar once again and hauled him to his wobbly feet. Barely able to stand, Seaton snatched his hat. He ground his fingers into the black brim, his eyes watering from the bruising his lungs had taken while fighting for oxygen.

Putting his nose close to Seaton's, Carrigan spoke in a quiet but menacing tone. "If you ever touch her again, I'll slice you with those fancy spurs and the next hard-on you get, you'll be screaming in a soprano voice."

Then he dragged Seaton toward the door and pushed him out the opening. A draft that raised the gooseflesh on Helena's arms was left in Seaton's wake, and the room became as still as the shards of glass on the floor. Carrigan dominated the area as if he were a part of it, dwarfing everything around him. His shoulders and arms, encased in a tanned leather long coat with buffalo-hide trim and fringe on the sleeves, were built like the broad beams of the store's ceiling. The beaded front gapped, and she could see his Walker Colt snugly tied around his right thigh with a thong of rawhide.

Fear absorbed Helena more than gratitude. It was that fear sending a kind of bell to ring in her mind. Carrigan *was* capable of murder. He had threatened to kill her when she'd trespassed on his mountain, and now she'd witnessed his near strangulation of a man.

Helena must have worn her shock and astonishment on her face, because Carrigan responded in a ragged voice empty of apology. "What did you expect? I'm not a saint. He was trying to rape you." Melted snow dripped off the ends of his ebony hair as his fingers dove through the strands to clear them from his vision. "I should have killed him."

"I don't think he was trying to rape me."

"Maybe I should have let you find out."

An explosive silence ran between them like a lit fuse. Seaton Hanrahan deserved to be put in his place for kissing her. He didn't deserve to be put in his grave. He'd had one foot in it and might have gone under body and soul if she hadn't told Carrigan to stop. He was hard-bitten by brutality. Emilie was right about his character.

Without a word, Helena sunk to the floor and began picking up glass fragments from the broken jar of peppermint balls. She felt Carrigan's gaze on her . . . scrutinizing, weighing, deciding . . . what? She couldn't define the meaning behind his stare. Facing him so soon after he'd scoffed at her proposal required much effort.

Carrigan dropped to one knee. The wet leather of his coat exuded a musky scent that rioted her senses. He nudged her hand away to gather the pieces of glass. The brief contact ripped a hole in her cool facade of indifference. She could feel the heat from his body, and the definite arrogance of his sexuality that both entranced and frightened her. Lifting her chin, she met eyes the color of fresh mint and speckled with gold. He looked down at her for a long moment, then said in a voice as rough as the raised calluses on the pads of his fingers, "Get a bin."

She drew herself up straight, glad to get out from under his spell. The aura of mystery surrounding him did funny things to her insides. She didn't appreciate the way she felt compelled to check for flyaway wisps that might have escaped from her hairnet. Or to wonder if the fatigue smudges under her eyes were still as noticeable as they had been this morning. It wasn't like her to be distracted by the state of her appearance.

Depositing her debris in the wooden bin, she returned with it to where Carrigan was crouched. His sinewy thigh strained the duck cloth of his trousers as he pivoted on the ball of his foot to dump the fragments he'd collected. As she noticed the sheathed knife he carried in the top of his boot, her tingling reaction toward him was overwhelming. She quickly turned her attention to the white splinters of candy and the balance of clear slivers that would require a broom to fully remove. She'd do it herself. Later. When Carrigan wasn't upsetting her with his overpowering proximity.

"I'll clean up the rest," she said, and took her place behind the counter, where she felt somewhat safer from the potent magnetism that radiated from him.

Carrigan stood. The thickness of his hair grazed the overhead joists. She realized he didn't wear a hat, nor had he worn one the evening she went to see him. To her recollection, he didn't possess a hat. She fleetingly wondered why, then shook off the thought as trivial and having no bearing on her.

She took a businesslike breath that lifted her breasts and silhouetted them against the black cotton of her shirtwaist. The unintentional gesture drew his eyes. She fought the urge to cover herself with her hands. Before a blush could claim her cheeks, she asked, "Tell me what you need, and I'll write it up."

Unhurried, he crossed his arms over his chest, giving way to an attitude of self-command and studied relaxation. "Have you found a husband yet?"

His question thwarted her attempt to remain unaffected by his presence. She couldn't prevent heat from stealing into her face. "Since you've made it clear you aren't interested, I don't think you're entitled to an answer."

Disregarding her censure, he said with heavy impatience, "Don't play games with me. Just tell me yes or no."

"No, I haven't found a husband." Her composure was under attack, and she felt as if she were quickly losing control of the situation.

"That's all I wanted to know." Carrigan hooked his thumb over the embossed leather of his gun belt, a move that draped the edge of his coat behind his Colt and highlighted his pelvic area. It wasn't a conscious decision, but her eyes lowered.

Then he made a slow, deliberate inspection of the store—something she found slightly annoying. He knew what they had, and where it was located. His purchases consisted of food staples and indulgences such as a newspaper, whiskey, cigarette papers and tobacco, and sometimes a book.

At the fabric table, he bent and picked up the spilled bolts of cloth. Piling them on one another, he lingered over the last roll. The calico had a royal background with a pattern of tiny roses and fern leaves. When it had come in, she'd thought the dye striking, but too vivid for her to wear so soon after her father's death.

Carrigan alternately gazed at her and the predominantly blue material, presumably measuring the hue against the color of her eyes. The intimate comparison caused warm sensations to spiral through her middle. She wasn't accustomed to gestures of such a personal nature from men.

"Did you need help finding something?" she asked, trying to distract him from the fabric.

"Hmm." He made a noncommittal sound that could have meant anything, but proceeded through the path of merchandise. The footfalls of his boots marked the compact weight of his well-proportioned body. At the notions, he ran his fingers across the lace trims and ribbons. That he continued to make a point of examining the ladies' goods had Helena gnawing the inside of her cheek.

At last he walked full circle and stood before her empty-handed. His gaze lifted to a spot behind her, and she turned to see what item he wanted. There was no shelf in that particular section—just a yellowed map her father had drawn of Genoa and nailed to the wall. He'd gotten tired of giving directions to newcomers and found by laying out the town on paper, he could save himself explanation. The map showed the nine streets and the town's boundaries, as well as a large parcel of one hundred and sixty acres on the eastern side he'd bought for her and Emilie under the preemption act. Carrigan focused long and hard on the map, the intensity of his eyes making her wonder what he was thinking.

Helena swallowed tightly as his gaze fell to hers. Without inflection he said, "I'll take a newspaper, and I'll take you for my wife."

The words were out before he could take them back. Carrigan's decision had been made as soon as he'd seen that renegade with an itch in his belly forcing himself on Helena. The scene had summoned a dark spirit whose unheard cries tore into his heart. It hadn't been Helena he'd seen being violated, but an apparition of Jenny. Jesus, how her body and sanity must have suffered. Her death had been a release from her pain, but it had broken him. Though years had dulled the fire of retaliation, today he found out his hatred still burned bright.

He'd wanted to commit murder. To tread over a tombstone and know that the deed had been done. That vengeance was his, and the crime solved. But three years had gone by and the past was trackless, lost somewhere on the frontier. He'd had to ride away from the ghosts, but seeing Helena as a victim made him remember.

His intention had been to walk out of the store with his newspaper and the solitude in which to read it. But he hadn't been able to leave Helena. Ever since she'd come to see him, she'd been in his thoughts. He'd found no peace from her, not even in a sleep induced by long hours of hard labor and the influence of ample whiskey.

When her voice had just been a human sound, he'd been deaf.

When her body had just been a shadow, he'd been blind.

When her scent had just been a suggestion, he'd been unaware.

But that night by his campfire, she'd gotten close enough for him to drink in her essence. Suddenly she became a flesh-and-blood woman with a striking face, passionate voice, and flowery fragrance. He couldn't stare through her anymore. His brain puzzled to cipher some scheme for getting out of staying in Genoa. He was torn between the isolation of his world and the populace of hers, conflict raging in his head as reasons attacked one another. The end result had been decided from a mental flash, except not without gain on his part. He'd trade with her, but the price was going to be a lot more than his name was worth.

"I find no humor in your remark," Helena replied tartly, biting through his thoughts.

"You weren't supposed to." Carrigan felt for the rolled cigarette he'd stashed in the slitted front pocket of his coat. His lips clamped around the twisted end. "I'm serious." He struck a match on the counter and touched the flame to his cigarette.

Her voice rose in surprise. "You can't be."

Waving out the match, he said, "I am." As he drew on the cigarette, smoke curled in his lungs and calmed his churning gut. He stared at her bewildered expression through the haze he exhaled.

"What changed your mind?"

"You have something I want."

Suddenly her face went grim. "What?"

He inclined his head toward the paper on the wall. "Land. The parcel your father told me about. I'd forgotten until I saw that map." His recollection of the day August had colorfully described the lot resurfaced. Out of curiosity he'd ridden across the length of it that afternoon. A belt of the forest covered most of the acreage, with a tributary of water and not too many granite sheets. "I'll marry you in exchange for your land."

"You already have land."

"Not legally." Technically he was a squatter. He'd chosen a secluded spot to make his home a year before settlers began encroaching on his mountain and cutting off his breathing room. By first-come rights, he should have owned the town. But the law didn't see things that way. Sooner or later, he'd be squeezed out by the jaws of bureaucracy, and there wasn't a damn thing he could do about it. "I built my cabin before the town was established. If the boundaries expand to include my land, I won't have jack. I need property with a title. Something no one can take away from me."

The anxious look on her face read like she was thinking of a way out, as if she were having second thoughts about him. "That land doesn't only belong to me. It belongs to my sister, too. My father secured the parcel for our dowries."

"Then you'd be putting it to the right use."

"But our marriage wouldn't be real."

"The certificate'll say it is." A shaving of tobacco sat on his tongue, and he removed it with his thumb and forefinger. The display brought her attention to his mouth.

Awkwardly she cleared her throat. "I would have some terms of my own."

He stared at her in waiting silence.

"You'd have to live with me. Here, in this house. To make it look like we truly were husband and wife." Her sentences were choppy, and she kept rearranging the ink pen and well in front of her. He let her ramble on, taking drags of his cigarette while she talked. "For six months. You'd have to live with me for six months," she repeated as if he were stupid. "After that, you could stay in your cabin, or on your new land. I don't think anyone would question the reason for our separation if you're up there working with horses for the Express. But if I need you to act in my stead as my husband, you'll have to come back sometimes."

"Would I share your bedroom?"

"No," she rebounded quickly. "Bedroom privileges aren't part of the agreement."

"Before, you said that if I wanted to take you to my bed, you'd be willing to negotiate."

Her blue eyes grew darker than the calico he'd compared them to earlier. "It's become a nonnegotiable issue now."

"Six months of playacting as your husband, living

31

with you, but having no sex. Are those the terms you're offering in exchange for your land?"

Hesitation skittered across her face. Hell, he had his own hesitation. He'd be moving out of his mist of silence and desolation. His self-imposed banishment would be suspended for six months. One hundred and eighty days. Christ all Jesus, it might as well be one hundred and eighty years. Six months was an eternity to be straddled with humanity and its habits. Things had changed since he'd left Libertyville. The smallest coin in use back then was a silver five-cent piece. On his several visits to Genoa, he found that if he wanted tobacco, a bag was a quarter. If he wanted cigarette papers, they were a quarter. If he wanted an apple, or a candle, or a newspaper, or enough whiskey to get himself good and drunk, twenty-five cents was the price every time. The current way of doing business in Genoa was nothing short of highway robbery.

"Yes." The fragile whisper of her answer broke into his reverie. "Those are my terms."

Crushing the stub of his cigarette beneath his boot, he talked while he exhaled smoke. "What about a divorce later?"

"Unless you want to be free to marry someone else, a divorce won't be necessary for me. I don't plan on marrying again."

"Neither do I."

The inkwell fell onto its side, and Helena righted the bottle with trembling fingers. "Then I guess we have a bargain."

"No guessing. We do have a bargain."

"Well . . . I'll get Ignacia and have her watch the store so we can go to the justice of the peace."

As she nervously licked her dry lips, Carrigan imagined kissing them to make them wet. Her mouth was full and pink, resembling the petals of a rose. Would they taste just as heady next to the tip of his tongue? He loosely cocked his hip against the counter, needing to release some of the pressure behind the placket of his trousers. "Whatever you say."

Helena was gone and back in less than a minute, returning with a middle-aged Mexican woman who looked thinner than a bar of soap after a hard day's work against a washboard.

"This is Ignacia Perades," Helena introduced. "She's our stock tender's wife and cooks for us."

He had no hat to tip, so he inched his chin up a notch as a form of greeting.

Helena walked toward the counter opposite him while tugging at the wide bow of her apron. The doubled ends knotted, and she jerked on them to no avail. He strode to her and bumped her fingers aside. She froze as he worked the knot free, his knuckles grazing the many gathers of her skirt. The fabric felt soft and feminine beneath his touch. He would have lingered, savored, and perhaps tested the span of her corset-nipped waist with his hands, but she moved away from him with a skittish hop.

"Thank you," she murmured, looping the apron on a hook. He was given a view of her slender back, level shoulders, and the gentle curve of her confined hair resting against her nape. There was no telling how long her hair was, but its thickness was evident inside the net. She didn't miss a step while going for the glass case that contained a small amount of jewelry. Reaching inside for a tray, she took out two rings. "Let me see your left hand."

He held it up for her to examine.

She put the first ring back and picked a second, larger one. Slipping between the part in a doorway curtain, she returned to the store with a drawstring purse on her wrist and bundled in a hooded cloak. "I'm ready. I'll be back in an hour, Ignacia. When Emilie returns, tell her I've gone on an errand."

"Yes, Miss Lena," the woman replied in a light accent.

Pushing himself away from the counter, Carrigan felt the strongest urge to throw himself into a vat of booze and wallow in it until he was pickled. His muscles were hard and bunched underneath his coat, and no amount of stiff breaths could unlock the tension.

He had to remind himself that his new living arrangements were only temporary, and after today, he'd only have one hundred and seventy-nine days left.

Helena opened the door and a gust of chill air slapped him across the face. But it wasn't enough to bring him to his senses. He was on his way to wedlock lane, and there was no turning back.

Chapter

→3←

Helena drove the buckboard to Van Sickle's station, Carrigan sitting next to her on the narrow bench seat. A thin layer of white from the fresh storm dusted the three-mile mountain trail leading to the justice of the peace. With each bump and rut, she and Carrigan were jarred into one another. She tried to give him room, but keeping the reins threaded through her gloved fingers and minding the whereabouts of her skirts wasn't feasible at the same time. Inevitably the fullness spilled onto his knee and thigh in a drape of dark calico. Not once did he make a move to shove the fabric off him.

He hadn't said a word since they left Genoa, frittering away the miles with one cigarette after another. His right foot was braced on the rim of the driver's box, and his left arm settled on the backrest, while a smoke was caught between his lips. The chore of rolling cigarettes in succession was complicated by the motion of the buckboard, but he managed without losing a single leaf of paper or spilling a clipping of tobacco.

A mile out, the wind rolled up like a tapestry rug. The sun came out to soak in the gray haze, promptly melting the snow. Carrigan's eyes narrowed against the dazzling sunlight, and he lowered his head a bit. The road quickly turned into a quagmire under the animals' hooves, and the iron-strapped wheels churned the ground to muck half as high as the hubs.

Helena's hood covered her head, and she snuggled deep into her wrap to ward off the severe spring air. The monotonous jangle of harness tack, and the intermittent snorts of the buckskins, Daisy and Lucy, wore out Helena's thin nerves. Strangers marrying solely for advantageous gain and fixed conditions was bad enough. To have her intended ignore her made her feel snubbed without just cause.

"Where's your hat?" she asked, unwilling to endure the shortage of conversation a moment longer.

"Don't have one."

She waited for him to elaborate, but he kept quiet. Seeing as every man she knew owned a hat, Carrigan being minus one made her idly curious. "Why not?"

"It got swept away in the Carson River last year. I haven't felt like replacing it." His voice had a rasp of embitterment. "Prices are too high to swap good pelts for one."

And yet, Helena thought, he had enough money to support his vices. How he managed to get by without an income other than what he made off the furs he traded, and the payment her father had given him for the mustangs, stymied her. Trying to decide what was worth spending money on, and what wasn't, was something she'd just recently been faced with. She wasn't doing a very bang-up job of robbing the balance in one account to pay the bill for another.

The path became rough and rocky, meeting a steep pitch slathered with mud. Bitterbrush and sage overtook most of the lofty pines. She eased back on the reins and hoped the horses would check their gait. For

Helena, sitting astride a horse was simpler than a first grade primer. Commanding a team was another matter entirely. Her driving skills left much to be desired. Flatland, she could manage passably well, but she wasn't worth a darn on grades.

To keep her mind off the trail's perilous conditions, she asked, "Where's your dog?"

"Home guarding the place."

One of the front wheels hit a chuckhole bigger than a barrel hoop. The buckboard lurched so hard, every joint rattled as if the nails would pop out. Helena's heart jumped, and she suddenly wasn't cold anymore as perspiration dampened her brow. "What was his name again?"

"Obsi."

She glanced at Carrigan, trying to stifle the queasiness in her stomach. "That's an unusual name. What does it mean?"

"It's short for Obsidian." Looking dead ahead, Carrigan's eyes narrowed. "Pay attention to the road."

Settling her gaze forward again, she stiffened. Furious at herself for allowing him to browbeat her, she gave the buckskins some leeway to demonstrate she wasn't an unqualified driver. Daisy and Lucy began clopping along too fast for her comfort, but she didn't want to draw attention to her error. As alarm rushed through her, she squeaked, "What made you think to call him that?"

"His coat is black." Carrigan snapped his cigarette over the side of the buckboard. "Give me the reins."

Helena was loath to let him know she wasn't skilled enough to handle the uneven terrain. His impatient order deflated her pride and made her defensive. "I'm capable of getting us there in one piece."

"Then quit talking and watch what you're doing."

Her head swam trying to remember the instructions her father had given her for this kind of driving.

She kept her feet spread apart for leverage, conscious of the brake handle near her right hand in case she needed to engage it quickly.

She was keeping a modest pace when suddenly Carrigan seized the reins from her and shoved her head on his lap with his hand. Her muffled cry of outrage was lost in the smoky scent of his coat. She heard him holler at the horses to move right, cursing the command through clenched teeth. The traces on Daisy and Lucy strained as they veered sharply in the mandated direction.

Helena struggled to sit up, her palm on Carrigan's knee. After she pushed at him and demanded he let her go, he relented. Righting herself on the seat and flinging the top of her hood from her eyes, she was about to give him a piece of her mind. But the heavy-handed words melted like sugar on her tongue as soon as she saw what had happened.

A telegraph pole had partly given way, the wire dangling dangerously over the road. She hadn't seen it. If Carrigan hadn't taken the reins from her, their necks could very well have been playing cat's cradle with the cable.

Shaken to the core, Helena sat there paralyzed and feeling as small as a grain of sand. She'd made a horrible miscalculation because of foolish indulgence. "I'm sorry," she whispered, her voice breaking miserably.

Leaning forward, Carrigan rested his forearms on his thighs, the reins dangling loosely between his fingers. Sun poured over him, his black hair gleaming in the light. He didn't seem angry. To the contrary, he appeared to be more annoyed than anything else. "I'll drive."

She mutely nodded, grateful he didn't dress her down.

Draping the slack leathers over the box, he turned toward her. "Trade places with me."

Helena stood. There was no way out of putting her ankle between Carrigan's spread legs. Her tapered crinoline made it awkward to maneuver around him, though she tried to do so without touching any part of his body. This caused her to step on his foot, and as she was muttering a quick apology, his hands covered the swell of her hips. She tensed, heat infusing her cheeks. The strength in his fingers was evident even through the starched layers of her underclothes. His unyielding touch elicited a tingle deep inside her that pulsated outward until it reached her every nerve ending. She rarely lost her composure, but she found she couldn't move. If Carrigan hadn't finally slid her over his lap and propped her on the seat next to him, she would have remained there dumbfounded.

She felt his gaze on her, but she couldn't look him in the eye. When at last he slapped the horses' rumps and they were off, she breathed a sigh of relief. Needing to blot out the incident, she closed her eyes and fought off making an inevitable comparison. It had been Kurt who first made her heart dance with excitement. Who first made her senses spin when he was near. He'd been dead for nearly four years, yet there were still times when he stole into her thoughts, and she couldn't help imagining what could have been. Everything changed the year she turned seventeen. There was no going back. Her future was based on a foundation of the past. Love would forever be unattainable for her, and so would a devoted husband.

Carrigan's ability to kindle something within her had her pensively staring at the endless gray scrub. It had to be his blatant masculinity that dazzled her. Everything about him spoke glaringly of his strength, from the way he held a pair of reins in his broad hands, to his indomitable walk.

As Van Sickle's station with its five barns came into sight, Helena felt a confounding urgency to know more about Carrigan. A kind of panic set in as the reality of what she was about to do hit her full force. She was going to wed herself to a man she didn't know beyond what rumor dictated. Just thinking of it nearly shattered her.

"I need to know what your full Christian name is," she said with deceptive calm. "Mr. Van Sickle is going to ask."

"Jacob Henry Carrigan."

"Where were you born and raised?"

"Red Springs near the Yellowstone River."

"Do you have any family?"

"Mother and sister."

"Your father?"

"Dead."

"Just like mine," she said softly, wondering about the circumstances of Carrigan's loss, but not pushing that far. "What made you come to Genoa?"

This time she got a reaction out of him. "You don't question my past, and I won't question yours." Steering the horses up to the front of a large, two-story frame house, Carrigan added without inflection, "It's the present that counts anyway. I could be wanted by the law elsewhere, but you shouldn't hold it against me so long as I'm showing a willingness to walk a straight path now."

She swallowed hard. "Are you wanted by the law?"

"No," he answered in a clipped voice that forbade any further questions.

But Helena wasn't ready to quit. She had to ask one more to lay the hearsay to rest. "Have you ever killed a man?"

His eyes grew contemplative, then he gave her a long, steady look that robbed her of her wits. "Too many to count."

"You married him," Emilie blurted, staring at the gold band on Helena's finger. "Lena, I can't believe you went through with it."

40

"I had no choice." Helena unhitched Daisy from the buckboard and walked her to the stables.

Emilie was on her heels. "Of course you had a choice. You could have given up the station."

"No, I couldn't."

Helena passed through the wide wooden doors. The building's interior was dim and smelled of hay, grain, and livestock. Dust motes swirled down from the high ceiling, stirred by the owls that used the rafters to roost. Horses nickered upon her entrance as she led Daisy to the stall next to Lucy's.

"You keep saying you're doing all this because it's what Father would have wanted," Emilie said, "but I don't think you even loved him."

Helena's steps faltered, and she gasped, "How can you say such a thing?"

"Because you haven't cried for Father, but you cried for Mother when she died."

She had mourned her mother's passing like no one else. But she'd been crying for two graves, when only one marker was visible. Her tears had come from the loss of another life, part of something gone forever. Truly crying over Mother would come when Helena couldn't bear the burden anymore. And tears for Father would come when everything inside her overflowed.

"I do cry for Father," Helena said quietly. "But no one can hear me." She gave Daisy a drink of water, then took the bucket away after ten swallows.

A high bench strewn with grooming accoutrements took up the space behind them. Helena collected a haircloth, dandy brush, water brush, sponge, and comb off it and began to wipe the stiff cloth over Daisy's muddy coat. She had to move around Emilie, who dogged her like a shadow.

"I'm worried about you," Emilie announced while Helena gave Daisy more water. "You don't eat. You don't sleep. You don't grieve. You may think because I'm younger than you that I don't know anything.

Well, I know enough to figure out that you're hurting just as much as me. Not letting go of what's paining you is only going to make things worse."

Sidestepping Emilie, Helena took the dandy brush to Daisy's flank, disconcerted by how close to the truth her sister had gotten. "I'm fine, Emilie."

"Then where is your so-called husband?"

"Gone to pack his things and get his horses."

"You really are going to let him live in our house," came her shocked reply.

"His place is with me." She hung Daisy's harness on an old horseshoe nailed into a post.

Brooms, pitchforks, and shovels lined the outer stall wall. Helena reached into a bin and scooped some oats into the feed receptacle. While Daisy ate, she continued to groom her, using the water brush with its long, soft bristles to wash the feet and legs of the mare.

When Emilie spoke again, her voice held a challenge. "What made him change his mind and marry you?"

Pausing, Helena knew she couldn't tell her sister about the land deal she'd made with Carrigan. Not just yet. Emilie wouldn't see things her way. Right now there was nothing that could be done with the land anyway, but the revenue generated from the Pony Express would bring them relative comfort, as well as accumulating into enough funds to buy a new parcel at a later date.

Helena hoped her tone sounded matter-of-fact when she replied, "He thought it would be advantageous to be married to a store owner."

"Advantageous to get all the free tobacco and liquor he wants," Emilie quipped.

Helena ignored that remark while putting a blanket over Daisy's back.

"Miss Lena?" Eliazer came into the stables. The stock tender was thickset, the complete opposite of his spindly wife. He wore a huge beard and mustache, an old slouch hat, a faded blue shirt, and no suspenders—though he could have used some as the waistband of his pants slid underneath his paunch. Pantaloons of coarse country weave with ample additions of buckskin sewn into the seat covered his stocky legs. The trousers were a dull yellow, and unspeakably homely. He kept them stuffed into the tops of high boots, the heels of which were armed with Spanish spurs. "Which horse do you want to take the western express run today? It's time to saddle one."

"Maria Jane."

Eliazer nodded and went to the next to the last stall to prepare the bay mustang with a heavy black mane.

"Is the afternoon rider Thomas McAllister?" Helena inquired, knowing full well James Whalen was the horseman, but wanting to sway Emilie off the subject of Carrigan.

"No." Emilie's disappointment rang clear in her wistful tone. She had an all-absorbing infatuation for Thomas McAllister that made her face light up whenever he rode hell-bent for leather up Nixon Street. Helena thought her sister too impressionable to be taken by the rider. Not just because his job was dangerous and his life was on the line with each run he made, but because Emilie was too young to know what she was doing when it came to matters of the heart.

"Ignacia could probably use some help with the store," Helena mentioned as she began the same procedure on Lucy as she had done for Daisy.

"I don't have to like him," Emilie said, paying no regard to Helena's observation. "He's a killer."

A lie was on the tip of Helena's tongue, but she couldn't deny the statement. It was true. Verified by Carrigan himself. His flat expression had affected her, for she had seldom seen a face possessing those characteristics. She'd registered a trace of sadness in his features, an underlying complexity that knew a reason and justification for his actions. That inkling of his far-reaching emotional regret had been what allowed her to go through with the marriage ceremony.

"I'll go help Ignacia, only because I want to," Emilie said, then wrinkled her pert nose. "I don't know how you can stand the smells in here. You're just like Father. Sometimes I think he liked spending time with the horses better than he liked spending time with us."

A fond smile lifted Helena's mouth. One of their father's sweetest joys was seeing to the animals, something their mother could never understand.

The stable grew quiet save for Eliazer's efficient movements at the opposite end of the building. Helena glanced to where Emilie had been standing, but the spot was vacant.

With a sigh Helena went back to work, wishing she and Emilie could be the kind of sisters they had been when they were wide-eyed children. Their daily lives had been a shared harmony of picking apples, husking corn, carrying water, and helping their mother cook. They'd gone to bees where they made quilts and strung dried berries. But when Helena turned fifteen, her mother said it was time to stop playing in the fields and quit going to school with Emilie. Helena had had to pull her hair back and start wearing a corset and hoops. No longer was she allowed to run through the meadow and laugh without a care in the world. She'd had to grow up and learn a thousand new things, but it had only taken one wrong turn and she'd fallen. She was scared Emilie would, too. Then nothing of the beribboned little girls from New Providence would exist anymore. And the innocence would all be gone.

After the mail came in, Helena saw to the lathered horse. She spent the next couple of hours in the stables, cleaning stalls, raking the floor, and taking stock of the shelf that contained turpentine, castor oil, copperas, borax, and cream of tartar. Her father had taught her the medicinal benefits of each, as well as the applications.

By the time she finished and ventured outside, the sun was getting low, sinking into clouds of crimson and gold. Its warm hues tinted the flag on the liberty pole in the yard a honey color. Darkness would descend shortly, and Carrigan hadn't returned. She felt a flare of leeriness spread in her stomach. He'd had ample time to throw his clothes in a satchel and string his two horses. There could be no point to him reneging on his part of the bargain. She had what he wanted. But . . . She cast her eyes on the waning sun behind the mountain. She'd give him until five o'clock. If he didn't show up by then, she'd go up there and find out what was taking him so long.

In the meantime, she occupied herself with various chores. She fed the chickens they kept for laying and eating, brought out the crate of paper-wrapped garden seeds and sorted through which ones needed to be planted next, and checked on Esmeralda, the mare due to foal soon. Eliazer worked around her, replacing a rotten post in the corral. He only knew one song and was forever singing it—a ditty in Spanish she couldn't follow. After a while, the melody drained her forbearance, and rather than holler at him to stop singing, she abandoned the yard for the corner of Main and Fifth Streets to see if she could spy Carrigan.

Freight wagons jockeyed for the prime spaces, their oxen and horses sounding off at one another. Shop owners were readying to close their stores, and pedestrians scurried home. But in all the confusion, there wasn't one man who stood out a head above the rest.

Helena turned around and went back to the station, her brisk stride accenting her annoyance. By the time five o'clock struck, she was fairly hopping mad. She left the house with her cloak and set out on foot for

Carrigan's cabin. Her mind raced with the accusations she intended to sling at him for going back on his word.

Feathery flakes of snow had begun to eddy down again, the sky taking on the gray color of an army blanket. The steep hillside had patches of white, but the boughs of wizened trees acted as canopies against the worst of the weather.

As she approached the cabin, she expected to encounter the dog heralding her arrival by his snapping bark. But the lean-to and frontage were sinisterly quiet, and made no more noise than the falling sprinkles of snow. A glance at the stovepipe poking through the rooftop told her there was no fire inside.

"Is anyone in the house?" Helena called out, wanting to alert Carrigan before he came out bearing down on her with his Colt.

No reply came.

Lifting herself up on her toes, she couldn't see through the pane of yellow oilcloth stretched across a high-cut window. She stepped up to the door and looked at the woodpile to the right of it, and the traps stacked in a heap to the left. Nothing seemed amiss. Pine needles from the lodgepole above had fallen on the ramshackle stoop, but didn't appear to be crushed by bootheels. She pounded loudly on the roughly planked door with her fist. Her knock went unanswered, so she let herself in.

The cabin's dusky interior looked as serene as a summer morning, the furnishings orderly. Most everything inside was rudimentary, a hodgepodge of mismatched articles, from where, she couldn't imagine. If Carrigan had been settled here before Genoa became a town, how had he managed to get a cast-iron potbellied stove, the wrought-iron bedstead, and even a big black coal scuttle?

Neatness and organization monopolized the shelves, the items clearly marked. An old chuckwagon box sufficed as the kitchen cupboard and was filled with a large skillet, cooking utensils, and a chipped bowl. On top, there were canisters of gunpowder, tins of garden seeds, and a mold for making bullets.

A bearskin covered one wall, while horns, a ram's head, pegs holding various hemp and rawhide ropes, a saddlebag, concha-adorned chaps, and two rifles were mounted on another. Looking out of place, a roping saddle lay in the middle of the floor. There was a table and a four-legged chair with an oxbow back, but nothing else to sit on except an iron-banded camel trunk. A buffalo hide acted as a spread for the bed, the pillows cased in flour sacks. The red and blue mill brands added a splash of color to the rustic room.

What surprised her was the profusion of books in a makeshift case made out of crates. Aside from many literary volumes written by Cooper, Audubon, and Hawthorne, there was an unabridged dictionary and several almanacs.

The place may have been well stocked and tidy, but Helena found it lacking warmth. Perhaps because she knew the owner was reclusive, and she pictured his solitary figure at the lone table and chair with no one to talk to and only the words in books to speak to him.

A gust slammed the door. Helena started and turned around. The fine hairs at her nape prickled, and she went to stand on the uneven porch. Snow came down harder, penetrating through the dense coverage of tree limbs in drifts. She brought her fingertips to her lips and thought of what to do next. Of where to look.

The lamented baying of a dog seeped through the murky dusk. The eerie cry carried on the wind and sent a sickly feeling winding its way through Helena's blood. She snatched up her hems and ran toward the howl. Branches snapped under her feet, and spindly twigs clawed at her cloak. A compound came into view. It was farther down from the cabin and leading away from town. She hadn't noticed the corral and shed before, having never gone this far. A strawberry roan and stocky bay grazed on the short grass in the enclosure, but Carrigan was nowhere in sight.

A spot of black moved, and Helena recognized Obsi. He sat on his hindquarters, his muzzle aimed heavenward, and let out a wail that tore her heart. Dread gripped Helena as she skidded to a stop, surprising the dog and making him bark and growl. But when he saw who she was, his lanky tail went between his legs, and he hung his head low. He dropped to all fours in front of a wide trough and put his chin on his paws. The long, stiff hairs above his eyes twitched as he followed her approach.

She was more afraid of what she'd find on the other side of the trough than she was of Obsi. As the fearful images built in her mind, she began to shake. The closer she came, the more she could see. An impression of a prone man was cast in white by the sifting snow. She saw the legs, then the outline of a long coat and ample shoulders. She realized, with a shiver, it was Carrigan. He lay facedown, looking like a fallen statue and appearing to be just as cold as marble. She felt the color drain from her face, and wave after wave of shock hit her.

Dear Lord, he looked dead.

Carrigan couldn't move. A dreamless void spun its web about his senses, while the snowflakes wove a sheet over his conquered body. The report of a gunshot replayed inside his head, over and over. Its explosion was deafening, and the echo ringing in his ears seemed endless.

Vague awareness came upon him by degrees, and the pain in his side made him feel like he'd been shoved in a pyre for burial. He shuddered, wanting to clutch at his ribs, but not having the strength to even crook his finger. He couldn't see. Everything was dappled in white stabs of light amid a black canvas. The thought flitted through his brain that he was headed for the hereafter. No wonder he felt hot. The flames were licking at his heels.

He had to get his fingers on the "Doctor" and do himself in. Death by a drawn-out decree wasn't for him. The revolver was the only way out. Only he couldn't move. He just couldn't grasp the implement that could put him out of his misery.

A woman's voice broke into his realm of fire. So sweet and delicate and gentle, he ached. He knew who she was. . . .

Helena.

What was she doing here? A cruel joke sent from Lucifer? To give him the woman at his demise, and to make him want her even in his hour of death. She was talking to someone. The devil himself? If it was, Old Scratch had a Spanish accent.

Sudden spasms of pain took him, and he groaned with anguish, filling up the night with elaborate profanity. Hands held his legs and shoulders, jostling him onto a hard plank of wood. Goddammit! He wasn't dead yet and they were putting him in a stinking pine box! He raved like a maniac, threatening to shoot whoever was moving him but not having the capacity to draw his gun.

A soft palm touched his cheek, and he desperately tried to see her, but the confines of blackness shut him out. If only he could discern a shape . . . if only she would say something to him.

"I'll take care of you," she whispered, the huskiness of her tone lingering in him like sensual pleasure. She took his hand in hers and held on tightly. Then he was being bounced in the back of a wagon, having the marrow beat out of every bone in his body.

His last conscious thought was, hell had an angel.

Chapter

⇒ 4 ⇐

Helena, Eliazer, and Ignacia wrestled an unconscious Carrigan upstairs. Despite their efforts to move him gingerly, he ranted at each tread they took upward, and made delirious utterances that practically dislodged the chinks out of the log walls. Emilie was so horrified, she could only stand at the base of the steps with a dumbstruck expression on her face and watch.

The hallway was narrow, making it difficult for the three of them to navigate in sync. With each run-in with the wall, Carrigan mumbled an oath. As they walked his suspended body toward the featherbed in August's room, Helena wished she could take off the colorful quilt her mother had made. But there was no time, and worrying over its ruin wasn't going to help matters. She needed to keep a level head.

Once Carrigan was on the mattress with his back to the testers, he began to shiver. Though Helena had covered him with a blanket on the ride home, the snow on his clothing had melted and left water on his coat and trousers. Unclasping her cloak, she covered his long legs with the leftover warmth in the fabric.

She had to work fast and opened the front of his decorative coat. The odor of spent gunpowder clung to him. Blood tainted the right underarm area of his flannel shirt, its crimson bloom spreading high over his chest. Flakes of unburned gunpowder had been forced through the hole in the coat's leather and looked like ground pepper around the matching hole in his shirt.

Holding her breath, she slipped the shirt buttons from their holes and slowly parted the sticky fabric. Dark specks tattooed the edges of his red-black wound, while blood smeared his right nipple, and the surrounding skin. She'd witnessed her mares giving birth and had wrapped enough brush-scraped hocks on her Express horses not to cower at the sight of blood. But the scorched smell of Carrigan's clothes, and the violent path the iron had taken in his body, upset her stomach. She had to swallow her discomfort.

Her gaze roved over his torso, looking for further damage. He was well built, with an upper body that spoke of exercise through hard work. His flesh tone seemed naturally tan, the kind of brown her face took on in the summer when she neglected her bonnet. He had a smooth chest, small nipples, and an abdomen corrugated with muscle. His physical appearance would have been flawless were it not for the copious scars and nicks marring his skin. The vague impression of a horse's hoof was beneath his last rib, and what could have been the result of a knife fight left a lasting mark on his shoulder. Other than the healed cuts and old bruises, he had no fresh wounds.

Helena looked helplessly at Eliazer. "I don't know anything about tending gunshots."

Leaning over Carrigan and gazing at the damage, he commented thoughtfully, "In the war, I saw such wounds. I don't know if the bullet is still inside him. If it is, he's as sure as dead."

A tremor shook Helena's courage. Carrigan wasn't

going to die. He couldn't. He was too strong to let go of life.

"But if the bullet came out the other side," Eliazer continued, ruffling his beard with stubby fingers, "he might have a chance. No way to tell until you turn him over."

"I'll need to undress him. You're going to have to help me with his coat." Her next move wavered between continuing to assess Carrigan's condition and warming him to stop his chills. Seeing his teeth rubbing together from cold, she knew the wet pants took precedence. But she couldn't slide them over his knee-high boots, so they had to go first.

The muddy heel was slippery, making removal difficult. Helena had to give it a reluctant pull that dislodged the knife. The sheathed blade fell out of his boot as Carrigan's low groan tormented her. She hated to cause him more pain and knew the worst was yet to come. Glancing at his face, she took some relief in the fact that his eyes were still closed.

After shedding both boots and his damp stockings, she wiped her dirty hands on her skirt. "Ignacia?"

"Miss Lena?"

"Heat some water and bring me a large basin." Helena's voice lowered along with her gaze. "With plenty of towels. And while you're downstairs, tell Emilie to tear a worn-out bedsheet into strips."

Light footfalls signaled the cook's departure.

Carrigan wore two belts—one threaded through the loops of his waistband, and one slung low on his hips. Helena carefully withdrew the weighty Walker Colt from its holster, keeping the end of the barrel trained on the floor as she walked to the bureau across from the bed and set the gun on top beside his knife. Returning to Carrigan, she unbuckled both belts, easing the length of the empty holster out from behind his hips. She bit her lip, her hand falling to his navel. He felt hot against her knuckles as they grazed his skin while she undid the placket of his pants. Dark whorls of hair filled the widening wedge, evidence he wore no underdrawers. She wasn't going to be a prude about things. It wasn't as if she hadn't seen this part of the male anatomy before. And Carrigan was her husband—even if in name only. But she felt excessively aware of being observed by Eliazer while she came to the last few buttons that stretched over Carrigan's sex.

Brushing aside her modesty, Helena turned to the stock tender. "Come here and try and lift his hips a little while I pull off his pants."

Eliazer nodded and they were able to remove Carrigan's pants as swiftly as possible. She tried not to look at what was cradled between his legs. Her eyes were drawn for several seconds before she arched her gaze to his face. He seemed so vulnerable lying there, unlike the virile man who'd sat by a campfire cooking his supper. She got a blanket from the trunk at the end of the bed. Draping the homespun over his middle, she tucked the ends around his legs.

"Now we have to do his coat," she said, wishing there were a simple way.

Eliazer absently scratched his temple. "I'll roll him on his side, and you take out the arm nearest his wound so we don't have to make him lie on it."

"All right."

With a subtle rotation of Carrigan's upper body, Eliazer held him while Helena gently freed his arm. Carrigan swore incoherently, his jaw clenched and nostrils flared. For a moment he opened his eyes, and she froze. But he looked right through her. His green irises were all but obscured behind the black moons of his dilated pupils.

"I don't mean to hurt you," she murmured apologetically, but he was unconscious again. While Eliazer still held Carrigan, she removed his shirt on that side as well. After that, taking his left arm out of his other coat and shirtsleeve was relatively easy.

Eliazer perused the wound, then shifted Carrigan

slightly so he could see his spinal area. "Ah, it's good. Come, Miss Lena. I'll show you."

Helena drew up to Eliazer's side. A puddle of blood crept from the exit wound in Carrigan's back, and Helena pressed a hand to her throat.

"It looks like," Eliazer commented attentively, "the hole sealed itself when the bullet exited. The cartridge entered him just below the nipple line. Had the bullet been larger and not ricocheted off his rib and gone down and out, there would be a lot more blood. Instead, it seems his vital organs have not been hit." Eliazer ran his hand lightly across Carrigan's swollen flesh. "I think the damage was done only to his muscles."

"What should I do? Sew him up?"

"No. Just put a poultice on the wound and wrap him with bandages." Eliazer slipped the brim of his hat higher on his forehead and said in a solemn voice, "He is lucky to be alive. Whoever shot him intended to kill him by the angle of the entry. They were aiming for his heart."

Helena hadn't had a spare thought to wonder who could have wanted Carrigan dead. But having two men connected to her be shot within the span of a week undid her nerves.

Ignacia returned with the water basin and towels slung over her arm. She put the items on the bureau. Helena gave Eliazer the muddy boots. "Take these to the kitchen, and I'll clean them later. There's mustard seed in the larder. Ignacia can show you where. Make up a plaster."

Nodding, Eliazer went with his wife.

Alone with Carrigan, Helena began the process of bathing him. She dipped a cloth into the warm water, wrung it out, then ministered to his chest with a butterfly touch. Repeating the process until the basin turned pink, she was able to remove the gunpowder residue and control the flow of blood. His breathing remained somewhat ragged. Drops of moisture clung to his damp forehead, and she wiped them away with the towel. Her fingers paused. An impulse to smooth the swath of hair from his brow took her, and she acted.

His hair was coarse, but felt silky. The length fell past his collarbone, making her wonder how he managed to cut the ends himself. They were even and nearly blunt, save for the shorter locks that teased his forehead. He kept them shoved away from his eyes, but she had noticed they came forward to aggravate him.

She gave his face a lingering look. The granitelike features softened in his sleep, though the troubling lines around his mouth and at the corners of his eyes had not diminished. Complexities surrounded him. She guessed his wounds went beyond superficial and doubted she would ever know the true extent of his pain.

With each soft, drying stroke of the towel, Helena's sympathy for Carrigan increased. She took his broad hand in hers, studying his fingers. They were lean, the pads tough. His fingernails were short and clean, the crescents of white on the ends cut straight. She found it difficult to connect the wedding ring on his fourth finger with her. But as their fingers meshed, the bands of gold were an identical set. To be taking care of her husband seemed surreal. Nothing had prepared her for the nurturing tendencies she was feeling now, and they frightened her. She gave his joints each a massage before placing his arm at his side.

Eliazer came up to her with a bowl of the plaster and sheet strips. He handed her a vial. "Rub some sassafras oil over his skin before you use the mustard. Bind him tight enough to stanch the blood, but not so tight as to chafe."

Helena applied the hot poultice with Eliazer's help. They wrapped the bandages around Carrigan and changed the soiled quilt for a laundered coverlet, bringing the edge halfway up his chest.

"Leave the plaster on for ten minutes, then take it off and apply some of this salve." Eliazer took out a tin from his pocket. "I make it with beeswax."

"I'll need your help again."

"I will help you." He turned away and headed for the door. "I'm going to go down and tell Ignacia to steep some pine nut tea. That will medicate his insides. And I'll get the laudanum."

She watched him go, then turned her focus back to Carrigan, who seemed to finally be resting comfortably. A flicker of hope fueled her stamina as she thought of the long night ahead. If only he didn't wake up in torment, she could cope.

Ten minutes later, she and Eliazer completed the process of dressing Carrigan's wounds. She thanked Eliazer for his help and told him to go to bed.

"You should eat, Miss Lena. You didn't have any supper."

"I'm not hungry."

He comforted her with his palm on her shoulder, gently squeezing. "I think he will live. Everything will be all right."

Nodding mutely, Helena felt tears standing in her eyes. She wasn't an overly emotional woman and had no tolerance for those who couldn't hold their own in a crisis. But the stress of the day caught up with her. Fighting the urge to cry drained her energy, but she resisted. As soon as Eliazer left, she brought a chair in and positioned the legs close to the bed where she'd set a kerosene lamp on the floor rather than the stand. The wick was turned low and burned in a haze of tranquil light. Folding her arms across her middle, she settled into the hardwood chair that was to be her bed for the night.

At first, the slightest inconsistency in Carrigan's breathing made her alert. But after a while, she caught her chin dropping to her chest and had to snap it up. Widening her eyes, she shook off her fatigue.

Sometime around midnight, she couldn't fight her body's need for rest and dozed off.

Her empty slumber was short-lived. Without warning, her pulse leapt to life at the sound of Carrigan's voice. As she was pulled from her sleep, anxious trepidation zipped through her brain. Carrigan had bolted upright in the bed, his eyes flashing.

"Where's my Colt?" he hollered, clutching at the vacant spot on his hip. "I want my gun! That son of a bitch is out there, but I can't see him! Got to get off a shot before he shoots again!"

Alarmed, she braced her arms on his shoulders and tried to settle him back, but she was hardly a match for his strength—even diluted from his injury. "Please," she said firmly. "You have to lie down. You'll hurt yourself."

He caused a wild hubbub, demanding that big revolver of his. She had stored it in the bureau drawer after taking the bullets out, never thinking he would go crazy for it.

"Where the hell is my Walker?"

"You don't need it. No one is going to come after you here."

His leg left the bed and it looked like he would try and stand. She barred his move by sitting on the mattress and leaning into him with all her weight. "You're in my house and you're safe. Do you know who I am?"

Miraculously, his struggles subsided, but he swore a world of oaths that nearly singed her sensibilities.

"Do you know who I am?" she repeated, and eased off him a bit so he could see her face.

He stared at her, his hair untidy, and replied in a scratchy voice, "Helena."

"That's right. I'm not going to harm you. There's no one else in this room except me. No one's coming after you." She wanted to reassure him with a consoling touch, but wasn't sure how he would react to her comforting him while he was cognizant, so she refrained.

He blinked. "Helena?"

"Yes," she whispered in a soothing tone.

"Did you save my life?"

"Yes."

"Why?" he mumbled, then closed his eyes to exhaustion and was lost again.

For a long moment, she couldn't take her gaze off him. He may, or he may not, forget the incident, but she never would.

Why didn't he think himself worth saving?

Hell hadn't burned him to ashes, nor had someone come down from the Holy Road to get him. Fate had let him stay on earth. This, Carrigan realized as the blackness unfolded from his sight and a log ceiling came into his vision.

He hadn't felt what hit him, the lead plug deadening the muscles it had ripped. But he was hurting now. The tear in his side felt like a hundred sharp needles fighting to get inside the bullet hole at the same time.

There had been no warning, the ambush consisting of a single shot that had taken him down. Whoever had gunned him had hidden in the brush with a clear view of his activities, waiting for the perfect instant to shoot. Though Carrigan hadn't seen who fired, he had a hunch who the assailant was.

Jesus, his ribs hurt. He figured at least one had to be cracked, having had them busted before. The dregs of pine nut tea stuck to his tongue. Licking his dry lips, he tasted laudanum. The dosage he'd been given had softened his head to jelly. He'd slept with a hair trigger, his mind churning with unfinished dreams.

Lowering his gaze, he took in his surroundings. He was alone in an unfamiliar room. The walnut furniture with its marble-topped dresser and washstand looked too heavy for the delicate walls lined with muslin—one even embellished with a floral paper. Etchings, an old-fashioned oval portrait, needlework pictures, and daguerreotypes hung on gold hooks. And from the unfiltered sunlight pouring in, he guessed there to be a real glass window.

He couldn't recall how he'd gotten here, but he remembered talking to Helena sometime during the night. She wouldn't give him his Colt. His fingers itched next to the vacant spot at his hip. He wasn't used to being without his gun. Even in bed. He flattened his palm into the mattress, feeling a plushness to it that came from feathers stuffed in the ticking. His own bed was filled with curly bison hair and had a firm shape this one didn't have.

Shifting his leg, he became aware he wasn't wearing any clothes and wondered if Helena had been the one to strip him raw. If she was the kind of woman who could view a naked man and not blush to her toes. Coyness didn't seem to be in her.

That he'd had to depend on her charity not twenty-four hours into their marriage rankled him. For three years he'd taken care of himself and had survived. He had never been too sick not to cure his ailment with herbs, or been too broken up not to set his bones. However, this time the man-made offense to his body was something he couldn't have fixed. He would have had to call on his fortitude and used the "Doctor"—a backwoods name he'd given to his gun since there wasn't a real doc around who could fix broken legs should he ever be thrown off his horse bad enough to bust both of them. Yesterday, if he'd engaged his Colt before being found, that remedy would have put his lights out for good.

But Helena had saved his life.

Why she'd done so was perplexing. She didn't owe him and might have been able to run the station on a widow status alone. But maybe not. Hell, he guessed he was worth more to her alive than dead, and that was incentive enough. Not since Jenny had someone done for him. A woman taking care of him felt strange and burdened him with a debt to return the favor.

Female voices sounded outside the door, which had been left ajar. While he distinguished Helena's, the other's was unrecognizable, but her identity became apparent as their conversation progressed.

"I don't see why you had to put him in Father's bed. Why couldn't you have put him in your room?"

"Because he'll be using Father's room for the duration of his stay here," Helena replied.

"But he's your husband. You mean you're not going to really be his wife. I thought that since you went through with it, you'd at least make the best of things."

"The particulars of my marriage aren't important right now, Emilie. Getting him well is what matters."

"So you can parade him around town and have everyone see that we're not alone."

"I doubt he would let me parade him anywhere."

"Then you got a loveless marriage for nothing," Emilie stated flatly. "The sacrifice wasn't worth it. I wish you could see that."

"And I wish you could see that it is."

The hallway grew silent for a long moment, then the door creaked inward and Helena entered the room. Her head was down. His gaze fell on her, and he wondered why she was denying herself happiness. He didn't find martyrdom noble, nor indispensable to a strong character. Suffering never gained him a damn thing but misery.

The heavy lashes that shadowed Helena's cheeks flew up as she raised her eyes to find him watching her. "You're awake."

"Were you expecting a corpse?" he asked with disaffection for his weak tone, which bore the parched dryness of fall leaves.

"What a thing to say," she chided. "Of course not."

The dark and drab poplin of her bereavement skirt modestly swayed as she walked toward him. He allowed himself to picture what she would look like in a blue the color of violets that grew on the mountain. Her eyes would mirror the hue and bring a spark of eroticism to her face that was suppressed by the somberness of her weeds. At least she'd twisted her golden hair into a loose knot on the top of her head instead of trapping the curls in a net. Unbound tendrils softened her face, but didn't lessen the strength of her demeanor.

She stood over him and put her hand on his forehead. His stomach muscles tightened from the unexpected contact. A woman's touch wasn't something he'd experienced in quite some time. The fragrance of wild roses filled his nostrils and wrapped around his sex. He was practically eye level with the side of her breast, its high lift formed by her corset. For years he'd annihilated his desires for women, and in doing so, he'd annihilated his manhood. His gratification had languished under the drowning stimulants of whiskey—a poor substitute for sipping love from a breast.

"You don't feel too warm," she claimed optimistically, then withdrew her hand.

He could have taken issue with her, for the heat within him equaled the bake of summer. The excessive bedclothes suddenly grew sweltering and oppressive. Longing for a smoke, he asked, "How did I get here?"

"Eliazer and I moved you." Helena backed from the headboard and stared at his bare chest where a crimson-stained bandage was wrapped around his torso. Her intense, exploring gaze on him was not purely curative, and he took satisfaction surmising she found his body attractive.

"I vaguely remember being lifted. My side hurt like hell."

Her eyes shifted to his face. "Did you see who shot you?"

"No." He was having trouble picturing a set of facts

61

that would screw on straight. Recalling the details of the shooting while the residue of laudanum polluted his brain only frustrated him. "No," he repeated, his annoyance spilling into his tone.

"I don't want you to think about it if it's going to upset you." She turned to the bureau and collected some strips of white cloth. "I have to give you a fresh dressing. I'm going to get Eliazer to help me sit you up."

"I can sit up myself."

"I don't think you're well enough—"

"I'll sit up on my own," he growled, unaccustomed to someone dictating to him.

A pregnant pause stretched between them. He brooded over his state of incapacity, while she frowned at his adamant refusal. At length, Helena was the one to relent. "It won't do you any good to get upset. If you think you can sit up yourself, then try. In case you do need assistance, I think I should have Eliazer here—"

"No."

Putting her hands on her hips, she glared at him. "You're not a very cooperative patient."

"It's a damn inconvenience being laid up."

"Being sick is never convenient," she said without sympathy. "You'd better accept you're going to be in this bed for at least a week."

His lack of sleep, the fiery stab of pain shooting through his upper body, and the ring of truth to her statement pulled a presumptuous remark out of him. "I'd consider staying in it if you joined me."

"Don't be absurd."

He gave her a slow, lazy smile even though he didn't feel like smiling. "I wasn't."

Riveting his gaze on her face, he got her to blush. "I don't see the necessity for this conversation, as the subject was already discussed in our agreement. You knew perfectly well what the sleeping arrangements would be before you married me."

"That doesn't mean I have to be satisfied with them."

"If you're implying you'll be after me to change my mind," she said as she laid the bandages, salve, and a pair of scissors next to him, "I can assure you, I won't."

"We'll just have to see."

An arched eyebrow indicated her ill humor, but she said nothing to the contrary. She sat next to him, the edge of the mattress dipping slightly under her weight. Taking the scissors in her fingers, she shifted her energies to his wound. "Rather than unwrap the binding, I'm going to cut the fabric away layer by layer. It will be far less painful for you that way."

Without asking him his opinion, she leaned forward and snipped the knot free, then lightly pulled one of the strips until she was able to get a scissor blade beneath it. As she began to cut, there was no place for him to put his gaze except on her. Her movements made him notice a tiny gold cross undulating from a thin gold chain around her neck. If she'd worn the crucifix before, he couldn't recall. He wondered if she was a devout listener and follower of Psalms and exhortations.

"Do you drop down on your knees on Sundays?" he asked in a voice fringed with a rasp as her fingertips touched him.

"No," she replied without pause from severing a soiled band.

Complete surprise hit him. "You're wearing a cross."

"I didn't say I was a disbeliever in God. My sister attends the church. I don't. Our systems of faith may be different, but we both pray."

Her ministrations were slow and drawn out like foreplay. He felt the blood pumping through his veins and heard his heart beating in his ears. "Did you pray for me when I was shot?"

"Yes."

"You think that's why I didn't die?"

Keeping her chin down, she stole a glance at him. Her blue eyes shimmered with the light streaming from the window. "Do you believe it's a possibility?"

"I was raised on Proverbs, if that's what you're getting at." He made no attempt to hide the fact he was watching her. "I guess I'm like you. I don't need to stand on any prayer carpet to say what I've got to say to the man upstairs."

"Then we have two things in common. Our views on religion and the deaths of our fathers."

She left the observance open-ended, as if she were waiting for him to elaborate on how his father had died. The day it happened seemed far off, and as recent as yesterday. Hundreds of years could pass, and he would still think of the times that could have come.

Closing his eyes, he transported himself into the spirit of the past so he could see the man he used to be: infinite in his desires, in union with the soul of another, and laughing at the riddles of humanity. But Jenny's death didn't leave him the same. The world spun a groove of change into his life. Each revolution seemed to decay his old character until he became unrecognizable even to himself. No change in his surroundings could repair the defect, for living alone hadn't blotted out his past. Solitude had only given him more time to let the horrific scene embed itself into him deeper than roots.

Ensconced on his windy mountain, he soon realized that no possession, no sunset or sunrise, no hill or valley, no constellation, no river or body of water, and no choir of birds was gratifying without a companion. But he accepted this as his forfeit and was reconciled to living alone until his hair grew as silver as a birch, and he became as petrified as a stone.

Then Helena came to him, her offer of matrimony ruining his plans. He became starved for human contact. Not only in a physical manner, but the exchange of thought and the contagious need to trade gestures and voices. Though he clung to the security of his freedom, each subsequent day in her company, he'd soak up every drop of her to hold him through the years to come.

"Are you in any pain?" Helena's subtle voice broke into his guarded thoughts.

"No," he murmured, his eyes still closed. Breathing in until his lungs were filled, he let the scent of a woman flow into him like a river through the woods. Helena's fragrance was exceptionally delicate and fine, akin to the bouquet of roses. She seemed unaware of the poignant affect she had on him.

He slipped his eyes open, needing to utilize his other senses or else he would throw his arm around her neck and bring her down to his mouth.

Lines of concentration deepened along her brows. "I'm almost finished."

She was nearing the end where the cloth wasn't as thick. The natural heat from her hands diffused across his chest, and the snip of the scissors sliced at the tension in his ribs. Like a summer storm, the touch of her hands on him was all too brief. She stood and visually examined his injury. He followed her gaze to the ugly pucker of flesh around a hole the size of his smallest fingernail. Having never been gunshot before, he muttered his disgust under his breath. The scar would be nasty, but he figured the ones on his body were nothing compared to the hidden ones of his heart.

"It actually looks better today."

"Then I'm glad I didn't see it yesterday."

"You'll have to sit up a little now so I can get the bandages out from behind your back." Her hand supported his shoulder to help guide him.

Seeing as he'd been lying in bed so long, he called to mind the strength that should have been revitalized by now. Only it didn't answer. He found this out as he inched his way off the pillows and immediately flopped backward. In a fit of swearing, he condemned the beads of sweat that had popped out on his brow.

Helena's mouth thinned with displeasure. "Blasphemous use of the Lord's name isn't going to do you any good."

"Saying it makes me feel better," he grumbled, refusing to acknowledge his weakened condition. Willing his muscles to work right, he tried again. Once more, failure seemed intent on breaking him. But he gritted his teeth long enough for her to remove the dirty bandages and tell him he could lie back down.

Girding himself against the stroke of her fingers across his skin as she gently applied salve to his wound, he kept his focus straight ahead on the high collar of her bodice. The vertical row of jet buttons that safeguarded exposure of her pale throat marched downward between the pinnacles of her breasts. He'd forgotten just how tiny a woman's fasteners were. A man had to have a fair amount of patience and dexterity to master them with one hand.

"You'll have to lie on your left side now," Helena said.

Carrigan complied, suffering the irritation of his pain and aspiring for an intermission from it—no matter how short.

"You can rest for a moment, but then you're going to have to sit up so I can get fresh bandages around you."

He wouldn't anticipate the torment while she arranged the strips of cloth. Though the notion of sitting up for such a length left him cold. His weakness indicated dependence. And dependence went against the grain of his mind.

Helena studied him with hesitation. "Are you sure you don't want me to get Eliazer? He could—"

"I'm sure." Using the muscles stretched along his belly, he rose to half sitting and slightly lifted his arms. Through a grunt, he said, "Do it fast."

Nodding, she nimbly set out to work.

"It's not snowing outside today," Helena commented as if to sidetrack him. "Maybe spring will come after all. The sun is shining and melting the snow."

"I want to go outside."

"You can't."

"That doesn't make me stop wanting to."

"You'll adapt to the bed. You'll see." The faint smile on her lips was shot with bygone thoughts. "When I first arrived in Genoa, my petticoats were like my mother's. A mass of lace—frills upon frills. I found out pressing ruffles was too much ironing with so much else to do. So now I make my petticoats with just a single deep ruffle to hold the starch."

Carrigan tilted his brow in amused wonder and momentarily captured her eyes with his.

She laughed, the sound singularly affecting. Its depth was throaty, and as sweet as music. "I hope I don't shock you talking about my petticoats."

"No."

"Good. Because I'm just trying to tell you how one makes adjustments when they have to. On our journey through the states and then the territories, I also learned how to make rice pudding without eggs. That may not be thought-provoking for you, but it was a learned accomplishment." Her sleeve brushed his sore ribs as she made another pass around his rigid torso. "Rice pudding without using my eastern recipe calling for eggs, plus a vague understanding that petticoats ought to be plain, was all I knew about conquering the West."

"I don't need a simple petticoat to conquer going outside."

"I should hope not," she replied, biting on her

lower lip as she gave him her full attention. He craved the mellow taste of tobacco to blot out thoughts of his mouth tasting hers. "But you need strength, and right now yours is on the mend. So don't have any rose-colored expectations about getting out of bed before you're able."

As she tied off the bandage in a neat little knot, the blankets slipped below his navel. Since he was bracing himself up with his arms, he couldn't let go of the mattress to readjust them. He monitored her expression.

She didn't bat an eyelash.

"If you're waiting for me to swoon," she ventured, "I'll have to disappoint you. I have no patience with mock modesty." Rising to her feet, she plumped his pillow, then anchored the bedclothes to his chest. "You may make yourself comfortable again. I'm finished."

Easing back into the feather softness, he asked, "Were you the one who undressed me?"

"Eliazer and I."

"Nothing you saw shocked you?"

She paused, her eyes fixed to his. "Your wound distressed me terribly, your scars made me wonder how you got them, but viewing you in your altogether didn't traumatize me into a fit of vapors." On that note, her brusque tone closed the subject.

Lying motionless, he asked, "Where's my gun and knife?"

She gave him no reply as she put up the salve and leftover bandages.

"Where did you put my Colt?"

"It's safe."

"I want my gun in the bed with me."

"There's no reason."

"My saying I want it is."

Gazing at him, she apparently thought on the subject for a while, then concluded he wouldn't give in. Pivoting, she opened the bureau's bottom drawer and extracted his Walker by the walnut butt.

He took the weapon and checked the cylinder. The bullets were missing. "It's no good without ammunition."

Not saying a word, she dumped the six cartridges into his outstretched palm, and he fit them into their respective chambers. "I won't go shooting up the place unless it's absolutely necessary," he said wryly, flicking the cylinder closed with a snap of his wrist. Then he hid the Colt beneath the covers.

"I assure you, it won't be necessary." Trying to discreetly stifle a yawn, she inquired, "Are you up to eating something? I could make you some corn-flour porridge and more pine nut tea."

"Did you sleep in the chair all night?"

"Yes."

"You shouldn't have."

"Well, I did. Now, would you like the porridge?"

"Hunger isn't plaguing me. A headache from the laudanum is. Don't slip me any more."

A wisp of hair teased her ear, and she smoothed it back. "But you need something to help you sleep."

"Get me some whiskey."

"If you think that's a better alternative."

"It's what I'm used to."

Shrugging, she started toward the door.

He called after her. "Where's my dog?"

She turned around. "In the barn with your horses. Eliazer said they weren't eager to follow his lead. What are their names?"

"Boomerang and Traveler."

"I'll tell him. He likes to call the animals by their names." Ready to leave, she asked, "Is there anything else?"

"You could bring me some papers and tobacco when you get around to it."

Her hand was on the tarnished knob when he spoke

her name. "Helena?" The gentle syllables were pleasing to his tongue, and the temptation to repeat them was there.

She gazed at him over her shoulder. "Yes?"

"Thanks," he mumbled.

She waited a moment, then said, "You're welcome," before letting herself out.

Chapter

→ 5 ←

Carrigan was a difficult patient to tend. Being bedridden for the past six days put him in a chronic state of crankiness. The only thing that mollified his sore disposition was an unlimited supply of cigarettes and whiskey. When Helena visited him, she had to squint through the haze and throw the window sash up to purge the gray cloud from the room. She had no aversion to the smell of tobacco. Her father had smoked a cutty pipe. But when she walked down the hall and got a whiff of the masculine habit seeping underneath the door crevice, it disoriented her. She'd have to remind herself that her father wasn't in his room, another man was.

Her husband.

She hadn't slept in the chair by Carrigan's bedside since the first night. When she brought him weak tea later that evening, and began to move the uncomfortable seat to settle into, he told her to leave it be. He refused to sleep with someone watching him. The need for a decent night's rest stole her arguments, and she didn't disregard his wishes.

From that moment onward, his attitude soured. He expressed his dissatisfaction about not being able to go outside each time she brought him a meal tray and changed his bandage. If she'd had a free hour to spare from the stables and store, she would have insisted he let her sit with him to take the tedium out of his day. In lieu of that, she brought him a history book to read, but he claimed he had no concentration. All he did was brood and smoke. And continuously ask for his dog. She had to tell him animals didn't belong in the house. Swearing became a part of answers, especially when she had to deny him. She would have reprimanded him on his language, but felt she was already holding too much authority over his daily life. She didn't like keeping Obsi away, but she had strong convictions that pets had their place—outside, where their fleas and other small bugs that tagged along in their fur couldn't invade the household and its occupants.

Carrigan was up only for the essentials, and even then he complained bitterly because it meant she knew he was human and had to answer nature's call. Despite his grumbles, he slowly continued to improve each day. The edges of his wound had pinkened. Today she would remove the dressing and leave it off so the area could scab. But even though the outside was healing, she saw he was still in terrible pain. Each move he made with his arm brought him anguish. The muscles inside were damaged in such a way that no matter how he lifted his arm, he struck a cord in one of the damaged tendons. She hadn't realized until she saw Carrigan struggling to hold a fork, how connected side muscles were to the body, and how crippling the lack of their full use could be. But he wouldn't let his weakness overcome him.

This morning when she'd brought him his breakfast, she'd caught him with his Colt in his right hand. It had taken her several stunned heartbeats before she realized that he wasn't pointing the gun at her. He was using its weight to exercise his arm.

"I think it's unwise to be doing that," she said while setting the tray down.

Ignoring her, he held the grip, lifted the revolver to his chest, then lowered it to his side. His brow was washed in a slick sweat, and his square jaw so tense with agony, she feared he would cause himself further injury.

"You're expecting too much, too soon."

But Carrigan was not the type of man who took criticism, no matter how well intended. He had said nothing. She'd left him alone, feeling an ill temper rise in her beyond measure. For all the hours she'd put into fixing him, there was nothing she could do to prevent him from doing what he wanted in that bed.

Three days ago she'd found out he had already packed his belongings the day he'd been shot, and they were in a satchel near the shed of his corral. With two horses not running because they lacked proper shoes, with one mare ready to foal, and with measuring out frugal portions in their last haystack, Eliazer hadn't been able to get away to retrieve the bag.

Helena had had Ignacia launder Carrigan's trousers and clean his coat, but the shirt hadn't whitened even when left under the sun to bleach, so it was now a member of the rag pile. The pants and freshly polished boots had been put in Carrigan's room, while the buffalo coat was downstairs on a hook next to her cloak, looking out of place.

"Helena?"

Helena was pulled from her thoughts by her sister's voice. "Yes, Emilie?"

"Mrs. Doyle just said she requires two pounds of pearl barley." Emilie stood behind the store counter opposite Helena's, giving her a searching stare. For the past six days, they'd been civil toward one another, but the relationship between them had clearly been strained by her hasty marriage to Carrigan and his presence in the house.

"Of course," Helena replied, turning to the bins of dry grains. She grasped the scoop and began to fill a sack, wanting to be anywhere but in the store under the concern-filled gaze of Mrs. Doyle. But the crisp, clear morning had brought in a steady flow of customers, and Emilie had required the assistance.

"It's such a tragedy about Mr. Gray," Mrs. Doyle lamented into her handkerchief. Her dress was a volcano of brown and ecru eiderdown, the sunbonnet on her round head so stiff, the brim would have snapped in two separate pieces under pressure. "My George laid him out in such a very fine manner, you know."

And Helena had received the unrestrained bill as proof. Not that Mr. Doyle had been disrespectful when he'd given it to her, but his services weren't frequently needed, and when he did get a client, he had no choice but to overcharge the bereft party. Though Helena doubted it was actually Mr. Doyle setting the high prices. Mrs. Doyle took in ironing to sustain them during hard times, and Helena suspected the woman's chagrin at having to do so was what drove her to making up the charges, for it was a slanted feminine script on the statement.

Helena brought the sack to the scale, the barley coming up short so she had to add another scoopful as Mrs. Doyle went on.

"That was a quality silk lining, you know. The box was of the finest hardwood."

"And the headstone was real marble," Helena said, tying off the top of the burlap with a piece of twine. "I know, because it came off my dressing table."

Mrs. Doyle's full cheeks colored like two apples the sun had ruddied. "My George would have used a marble headstone, but they are so difficult to have sent out here. Other than that, you can't find fault in the services you were rendered. Paying homage to a departed loved one should be worth any expense—"

"Is there anything else?" Helena queried shortly, irked by the woman's lack of sensitivity.

"Well, yes, there is." She gave an indignant little sniff, her pointed nose out of joint. "But I think I'll have your sister get it for me. She's such a dear little thing. And not in the least bit impertinent."

In her voluptuous skirts, Mrs. Doyle squeezed through the merchandise to the other side of the store. Helena had never gotten along with the townswomen. But Emilie did. Helena's interests were vastly different from embroidery, sewing, tried-and-true recipes, and light tittle-tattle.

Helena counted the minutes until noon, when Ignacia would be finished with boiling and hanging up the laundry and could come help Emilie. Then she would be free to escape outside. A sudden knife of commiseration jabbed her, and she knew what Carrigan felt like trapped upstairs in bed. She vowed to tread more lightly with him, even if it meant he overextended himself.

The patron door was opened, and when Helena glanced toward it, Bayard Kimball had entered. Worse than knowing she had to spend hours more in the store was the prospect of encountering Bayard. She'd been avoiding him since her wedding, not wanting to have another conversation with him like the one they'd shared on the boardwalk. His talk of marriage was fruitless and served no purpose. She'd break her new status to him, and everyone else, when she was ready. Emilie, Ignacia, and Eliazer had had to promise her they wouldn't reveal her secret. She was holding out until Carrigan was well enough to make his presence in her life known. For that reason, she'd taken off her wedding ring.

Her days of going without adequate supplies were growing; she didn't know how much longer she could last. But Carrigan would be a far more dangerous opponent when he had his strength back. Only then could he take command of the situation with one glaring gaze and a voice booming in authority, stopping cold those proprietors withholding their services.

"Judge Kimball," Mrs. Doyle greeted, exuberantly. Bayard was respected and well liked for his no-tolerance approach to defilers of the law.

"Mrs. Doyle. Miss Gray." Bayard's gaze strayed to Helena, and the warm smile that he gave her was proof of his pleasure. "And the other Miss Gray. What a nice surprise to find you inside, instead of outside in the stables."

"I'll be there soon enough," Helena replied over her beating heart as anxiety settled in her breast. She didn't like deceiving Bayard. His friendship had been the one constant in her life that she could count on.

Bayard strode toward her. "Be that as it may, I'm delighted to find you here."

Mrs. Doyle made a phlegmy noise in her throat. "Judge," she imposed, "have you ferreted out any culprits in Mr. Gray's killing?"

"I've been left with an empty plate, Mrs. Doyle. No leads, no suspects, no criminals." Bayard plucked a piece of lint off his dark sleeve. "It's very frustrating."

"I think the whole incident is bad for Genoa," Mrs. Doyle sniffed, the ruffle on her bonnet crackling. "We have our ruffians, just like any other western town. But murder. Murder is not to be tolerated." Expressing her sorrow with a cluck, she sighed, "And two young girls left alone to fend for themselves."

"They wouldn't have to be alone," Bayard said quietly, and Helena felt her stomach twist into a knot. "I would gladly take care of them both. Perhaps, Mrs. Doyle, you could convince Miss Gray to marry me."

"Why, that's a splendid idea!" Mrs. Doyle trapped Emilie's hand in her pudgy fingers, Emilie's eyes widening with surprise. "Dear Emilie would make a wonderful wife!"

"All due respect to Miss Emilie," Bayard said with

some embarrassment, "I was referring to the other Miss Gray." He drew up to the counter.

For once, Mrs. Doyle was speechless. She switched her attention to the yard goods Emilie had been cutting for her. Briefly Emilie's eyes leveled on Helena, but Helena was unwilling to confront the controversy in them and shied away.

A smile remained on Bayard's handsome face as he spoke in a soft tone for her ears alone. "You see, I have no qualms about publicly airing my desire to marry you. I won't give up, Helena."

His words were the voice of his heart, but they pierced deep into Helena's. The artillery to fend him off graciously and without compromising his feelings failed her.

Though the width of the counter acted as a barrier between them, Bayard inclined himself in such a manner as to be close to her without being ungentlemanly given the general store was occupied. Helena could hear the muffled ticks coming from the pocket watch in his suit coat as he studied her face. The admiration in his gray eyes worsened the entire calamity she found herself entangled in. "Forgive me for taking the liberty," he ventured, "but I've inquired into your accounts at the farrier and at the hay yard. You're past due at both establishments. Let me help you."

"Judge Kimball . . . I . . ."

"Bayard," he corrected in a hushed tone. "If you're worried about the true measure of my sincerity, I can only blame myself for not being forthright enough. The extent of my feelings toward you is far greater than you realize. I can assure you that I—"

A commotion erupted from behind the curtain that led to the house. There was a loud thud and a stumble on the staircase. Then a vile curse. Helena's breath left her, just as dread settled itself in her every thought. A large fist gathered the cloth of the partition, and the center was swiped open. Carrigan filled out the narrow area, his mane of raven hair tumbling over his furrowed brows. The dark stubble on his chin made him appear swarthy and lawless. Tall as he was, he had to dip his head. Knee-high boots molded his calves, trousers hugged his legs, and that infamous holster with its gargantuan gun in residency rode low on his hips. He wore no shirt. The breadth of his smooth chest was openly displayed, the white strip binding his wound a flagrant symbol of his recent ill health.

"Oh my heaven!" Mrs. Doyle screeched, a vermilion stain blotching her neck. "It's that uncivilized native from the mountain!"

"If I don't get outside and feel the wind on my face," Carrigan blazed in a voice gravelly from plentiful smoke, "I'm going to go crazy. I want to see my dog and horses."

Helena went to Carrigan and willed him to retreat behind the curtain with a furious plea in her eyes, but he ignored her. The slight wobble in his stance wasn't solely from descending the stairs. Liquor had done its fair share.

"I'm not going back up there until I see my dog and horses."

"Please," she petitioned. "We'll talk about this later."

"No." He let go of the curtain and started through the store, his steps heavy and awkward. His gaze fell on Mrs. Doyle and Bayard, who stood in the aisle. "Get out of my way."

Helena quickly met Carrigan and laid an imploring hand on his naked back. The gesture resulted in a brassy cough from Bayard. Carrigan flinched, swung around too quickly, and had to use a tabletop as support. She should have remembered he wasn't accustomed to being touched and immediately withdrew her hand. His eyes said she couldn't talk him out of going, so she reconciled herself to letting him go.

"Do as you wish," she ground out, "but you're

headed the wrong direction. This is the street exit. Go through the house."

She stepped aside when he did as she asked and disappeared beyond the closed curtain. Only then did Helena turn and face Bayard with a silent apology.

"What is that man doing here?" he asked in disbelief.

She had no choice but to respond, "He's my husband."

Mrs. Doyle sounded as if she were asphyxiating. Emilie's gaze on Helena held a morsel of sympathy. Disappointment was grim at the corners of Bayard's mouth.

"What shall I offer?" His judicial voice faded, losing some of its steely edge to the unexpected blow. "I suppose congratulations are in order, but I'm unable to give my best wishes."

Carrigan's ill-timed entrance rang through the room like a sullen bell. Terrible regrets assailed Helena that Bayard had had to find out this way. She valued his friendship, and although he would have balked at the news even if it had been offered to him prior to today, her chances of retaining any kind of friendship with him would have been far greater.

Glass broke behind Helena, muffled by the recesses of the living area from where the sound had come. She couldn't explain anything to Bayard right now with Emilie and Mrs. Doyle present, so she excused herself.

Slipping inside the narrow corridor that led to the body of the house, Helena grabbed both her cloak and Carrigan's coat from the horseshoe hooks without missing a step. She passed the side table at the base of the stairs. Carrigan had tipped the unlit globe lantern over, spilling the precious kerosene. Cloying fumes rose from the planked floor, seeping in between the cracks. An oily puddle of kerosene advanced, and it would take her hours to scrub the damage out. Lifting her skirts, she proceeded, mindful of the mess.

A glance in the sitting room didn't turn Carrigan up, so she continued on. She caught him with his hand gripped on the jamb as he passed underneath the doorway into the kitchen.

"You shouldn't have come downstairs," she said, confronting him on his haphazard route.

The cooking area was the largest in the home, with few solid objects to help him maintain his balance. A trestle table where Ignacia prepared the meals took up the center, while a battered pine table with four chairs sat on the opposite side. The butter churn in the corner served as an extra chair in a pinch. Besides the cast-iron stove, pie safe, an open cupboard holding mismatched dishes, and a pantry with the front made out of blankets that had worn thin, there was nothing else.

Using the trestle's sanded surface a moment, Carrigan said, "I'm going to see my dog."

"You're drunk."

Through the hair impeding his vision, his green eyes drank her in. "What of it?"

"If you're looking for sympathy, you've got mine. I'd hate being confined to that bed, too. But pouring liquor down your throat out of self-pity isn't going to help you get better faster."

"It makes me feel better," he growled, grabbing hold of the rawhide latchstring and lifting the stout wooden bar on the door. The light of day flooded the opening, and Carrigan squinted into the brightness as he stepped down onto the large, flat stone that served as a doorstep.

Helena shoved his coat at him, then covered her shoulders with her cloak. Though the sun shone in a dazzling brilliance devoid of clouds, a chill leftover from the early morning freeze clung to the air. The northern sides of the buildings and troughs were white with a mantle of frost. Deposits of old snow banked the footings and sleepers of the cabin's floor supports where the sun hadn't been able to melt it yet.

Carrigan managed to ease his coat on, but left the front to hang open. As he walked, his gaze took in nuances of the yard, and he seemed to be taking inventory of things. The rain barrel, smokehouse, lye-making vat, springhouse, and root cellar. What was left of the pathetic haystack, the ten-foot-high posts comprising the stockade gates, the zigzag rail fencing, and the feed bucket Eliazer had left next to a heap of snaffle bits.

"Reminds me of . . ." Carrigan mumbled, but didn't elaborate, leaving Helena to wonder.

At the entrance to the stables, Carrigan raked his hair off his forehead and proceeded into the interior. Sunlight pierced thin beams through minuscule gaps in the roof beams. Eliazer had gone to the lumberyard to buy replacement shingles and had been doing some cleaning earlier in the morning. A manure fork was lying on the hard-packed floor among hinges, bridles, and wagon grease.

Traveler and Boomcrang were in the fore stalls where the gates met immediately left and right of the slated wall separating them. They stuck their heads out, and nickering in low rumbles, signaled their want of Carrigan's attention. As he moved closer, their ears came forward. He ran his good hand over their noses and jaws, giving each equal regard while his hoarse whisper reassured them. The bond between him and his animals was evident as their twitching nostrils caught his scent. One corner of Carrigan's mouth pulled into a slight smile.

It was the first time Helena had ever seen him come close to smiling.

Turning toward her, he asked, "Where's Obsi?"

"I'm not sure. I didn't want to tell you, but the night we brought you here, your dog disappeared. After two days, he came back and I fed him."

"He probably went to the cabin." Carrigan fixed his concentration on the horses again. "He must think I'm dead."

"He hasn't run away since, though he does vanish from sight for most of the day. Sometimes he'll follow Eliazer, but only when he rewards him with a lump of sugar. And the dog never eats it from his hand. Only if Eliazer drops the cube on the ground."

Carrigan leaned against the stall door, grimacing. Exertion did a moderate amount of good when a man was fit, but Helena knew he wasn't up to this. The exercise may have improved his spirits, but it had taxed his strength. He'd pushed himself to the point of severe pain, but he'd never admit that to her. Rather than chide him for it or convince him to return to the house—both efforts a waste of her breath—she took the opportunity to speak about what had been troubling her the past few days.

"I blame myself for your being shot."

"Yeah? Why would you say that?"

"I've had six days to think about it. There's only one person who had the motive. Seaton Hanrahan." She waited for Carrigan's reaction, but he had none. "If you hadn't come into the store that day and thrown Seaton out, I don't think you would have been shot."

"Maybe. Maybe not. Blame is a hell of a load to carry around. It gets heavier as the years go by. I suggest you drop it now."

There was an implication to his words she waited for him to define, but the plaintive sound of a dog at the wide stable entrance caused them both to turn their heads. Obsi sat in the dirt, his black body quivering. The wag of his tail swished the scent of mud into the building.

Carrigan pushed off from the stall and lowered himself onto one knee with a stifled groan. "Obsi. Come."

The dog ran to Carrigan, licking his hands with excitement, then raised himself on his hind legs to reach Carrigan's face. One eager paw pushed into the cloth binding where the main point of the wound was located. Carrigan went down on his buttocks with a roar and curse that sent Obsi scurrying backward several feet.

Instinctively Helena rushed to Carrigan. She reached out and lightly rested her hands on his shoulders. Not caring that he wasn't used to someone dictating to him, she said, "I was afraid something like this would happen. You're going back into the house right now."

A bead of sweat rolled from beneath his hair, curving down his temple. There was a spark of some undefinable emotion in his eyes. He didn't wholly want to be left alone.

"I can help you up," she offered in a quiet voice that sounded strange to her ears. The revelation that he may actually crave her company had her realizing that it wouldn't be easy to be indifferent in her marriage.

"I'll get up myself."

"Don't," she whispered, shaking her head. "You don't have to be so strong. There's no one here but us, and I don't care that you have to use me as a crutch."

His hands came up to grip her sensitive wrists in a display of strength that took her off guard. He held her hard enough to cause some mild discomfort. "I don't need a crutch. I don't need anyone."

She whimpered, and the pressure of his hands on her wrists instantly lessened. Pulling away never entered her mind, for it wasn't fear that kept her still. It was the false note in his voice contradicting his words. There was a deeper significance to their visual exchange than she cared to acknowledge. Suddenly she felt ill equipped to face him. She knew what was coming and said nothing. Did nothing to stop him. She couldn't escape his compelling stare even as his head lowered. His mouth descended toward hers and would have caught her lips had Obsi not stuck his head between them.

The cold wetness of the dog's nose was a sober

awakening. One that Helena wished she'd had the foresight to give herself. Carrigan held her at arm's length, then let go. Obsi's long hair brushed her fingers as he tried to climb on Carrigan's lap and seek overdue affection from his master.

Helena disentangled herself and stood. Smoothing her skirt and cloak with trembling fingers, she called herself every kind of fool. Her behavior was an unbecoming weakness that proved she'd learned nothing from her past experiences.

She heard Carrigan struggle to stand, but she didn't aid him. Once he was safely on his feet, she started for the yard. He followed with a stiff gait, and so did the dog. Obsi trotted close to Carrigan's heels, darting this way and that with little yaps. At the kitchen door, Helena let herself in and waited for Carrigan. He came inside. Obsi put his front paws on the threshold as if he'd be given free admittance now that he was reunited with his owner.

"Not you," she scolded. As soon as she closed the door, Obsi began to scratch on the panel.

She didn't have to look at Carrigan to know he was angry. So was she. He'd made it known it wasn't just her companionship he craved when he'd almost kissed her.

Heaven help her, this union in name only wasn't as impersonal as she thought it would be. Wanting anything more from Carrigan in return would be fatal. Sometimes a woman couldn't be driven out of a man's arms, even if she didn't want to be there.

And she was an awful driver.

The Genoa courthouse was one and a half stories high with whitewashed clapboards in front and rough boards standing up endwise on the sides. It had shakes for a roof, at the peak of which full water buckets had been strategically placed in case of fire. The building had once been a livery, and Judge Kimball held sessions of court in the renovated loft.

Helena held on to the rickety banister as she ascended the outside steps to Bayard's office, hoping to find him in at the supper hour. She'd delayed her own meal, wanting to put things in order between her and Bayard before the day passed.

Raising her hand to the door, she knocked lightly on the upper pane of glass. After a moment, the door was answered. Bayard stood in the doorway, looking the worse for wear. He'd unknotted his silk tie, which he was usually very fastidious about. The ends hung unevenly over his lapels. His vest was unbuttoned, the fob of his watch dangling against his trim waistline.

"Helena." Her name was spoken with bittersweet fondness.

"Have you a moment?" she asked. "I'd like to talk with you."

Silently he stood aside and allowed her entrance.

The ceiling was high, the rafters exposed and blemished from previous rain damage. Remnants of grain and horse left a scent in the wood despite not being in residence for quite some time. Parted, dusty portieres spilled their abundant hems to the floor, framing the large picture window that looked down on Main Street. Spittoons, splattered tobacco residues, and heel marks monopolized the floor in front of the bench—which was really just an ancient chair where Bayard enthroned himself to dispense justice and sarcasm in equal parts. She'd witnessed him in action once. He made short work of lawbreakers, imposing high fines and lengthy jail sentences. Despite his eccentric ways, his judgment was unquestionable. He had the full confidence of the townspeople.

Bayard went to his desk, sat behind it, and offered her a seat opposite from him. An engraved silver liquor flask shone amid the stacks of documents, and he made no move to hide it from her view. Apparently he'd been drinking. And she was the obvious cause.

"I'm sorry you had to find out about my marriage the way you did." She kept her purse fixed in her lap, her fingers entwined nervously with the silken cords. "I was going to tell you, but I was waiting until my . . ." Not comfortable saying the word "husband," she paraphrased, "Waiting for Carrigan to recover."

Bayard's eyes betrayed his brittle anger. "What happened to him?"

She wasn't anxious to divulge the extent of Carrigan's injuries. Since foul play suspiciously clouded the incident, she wanted to keep it to herself. There would be enough talk circulating without the added information. "He had an accident."

"What kind?"

"He fell off one of his horses and hurt his ribs." Bayard's frown caused her to hastily add, "It really isn't important how he was injured."

"It's important when I've made my intentions clear. Despite the stability and protection I offer you and your sister, you insult me by marrying a man you know nothing about." Shoving a pile of papers to the corner of his desk, Bayard pressed, "My God, Helena, what made you do it?"

She looked at her lap and absently twisted the circlet of gold around her fourth finger. There was no longer a reason not to wear the ring. "He had something I needed."

"It couldn't possibly be money. He can scarcely scrounge enough to sustain himself."

"It wasn't money I was after." Lifting her chin, she met Bayard's gaze. "It was his reputation."

"His reputation?" Bayard spat with incredulity.

Though Bayard would have understood the absolute truth better than her waxed-over interpretation, she couldn't tell him any more.

"I'm so very sorry for having hurt you," she said with real regret. "I never meant to. Our family has been close to you since we arrived in Genoa. I'd hate to lose your friendship over this."

Bayard seemed to be weighing her words for merit, and considering his options. After a length, his features softened, though the lines of remorse didn't lessen around his mouth. "Regardless of what's transpired, you can always come to me for advice."

Her sigh of relief was nearly audible, the pressure in her breast lightening to a certain degree. "I appreciate that."

She quietly stood, gave him a consoling smile, then left the office without making a sound as she closed the door.

Bayard remained motionless after Helena left. Lifting the flask to his lips, he drank a generous portion. Helena had meant everything to him. She was all that a politician's wife should be, and then some. He had been modestly courting her from the moment he'd met her. Losing her to a man like Carrigan was galling.

Good Lord, what had she been thinking? He would have done anything for her. Anything. Except let her continue to run that Pony Express station once they'd been married. A wife of his couldn't have had manure beneath her shoes. But she was a wife he couldn't have now, and it was killing his hopes.

The coming months without her would harm him. He needed a decent woman by his side if he was to be in the running as a candidate for governor. Congress was in the process of appropriating twenty thousand dollars a year in greenbacks for its support of the fledgling territory. A paltry amount, but Bayard would see the funds well spent. He did an exemplary job as the chief justice of a one-man court. The governorship should rightfully fall on his shoulders.

Bayard knew there were those who would call him a hard-nosed judge for his harsh rulings and edicts. He was but a man, swayed like other men by vehement prejudices—though he would never call it corruption. Heaven sat in judgment of him, and what did Heaven care how he secured his happiness? His one and only fault was loving Helena Gray with all his heart. Without her, the principle foundation of his future crumpled.

Movement in the curtains caught Bayard's eye. Glancing toward the distraction, he said in a flat tone, "She's gone. You can come out now."

Chapter

⇒ 6 ⇐

The dog's whines woke Helena from a sound and heavy sleep. A crescent moon lit her bedroom. Shadows flitted across the wall, the source a poplar tree outside being disturbed by the breeze. Tired as she was, she hugged the blankets, rolled over, and drifted off for a scant second before Obsi's cries intruded again. She opened her eyes once more. Resentment never made a good bedfellow to wake up to, for at this moment, she resented that dog with every muscle she reluctantly stretched. Yawning, she rose and put her feet over the side of the moss-filled mattress.

Her thighs were tangled in the hem of her nightgown. When she stood, the lawn fabric floated to her stockinged feet. She grabbed her plain wrapper from the end of the bed and slipped her arms into the sleeves. As she descended the stairs, the sound of claws scratching on the kitchen door carried through the house. For the first time in six days, Obsi was making a pest of himself. It had to be because he'd seen Carrigan in the yard today.

Helena wasn't averse to dogs. In fact, the family had had one when she was a little girl. But dogs had their place. And their place was outside to let the occupants inside know if there was an intruder on the property. Obsi's cries now were not ones of warning. They were quivering begs to see Carrigan. Well, she was absolutely not letting Obsi in. And she was absolutely not going to let him keep her awake.

Helena released the latchstring from its position of being pulled in at night for security's sake, then lifted the bar. Obsi's nose poked into the crack before she had a chance to fully open the door. Shoving her knee through, she kept him at bay and slipped outside to reprimand him. The wind went right through her clothing, causing her to shiver.

Obsi barked once, and scudded away. He instantly came back to sniff her.

"It's not your master, if that's what you were hoping," she said, holding her wrapper together. "I'm not letting you in, so you can save your barks."

A half howl, half yap was his response.

Bending down, she lightly tapped Obsi on his nose. "Be quiet. Bad dog. You're going to wake everybody up."

Apparently Obsi didn't take being disciplined seriously. He lowered himself onto his hindquarters and stared. Crossing her arms under her breasts, she studied him. The name Obsidian suited him. Beneath the silver moonbeams, his long-haired coat shone a glassy black. His ears were pointed, but there was no curl in his slender tail. Those long, stiff hairs above his brows tweaked with his eye movements. He watched her just as intently as she did him.

No longer wary of his bite, she gave him the last word. "Just be quiet or you'll get no more sugar lumps from Eliazer." She let herself into the kitchen. But no sooner had she closed the door than the mournful cries started in again.

* * *

There were times when Carrigan was dreaming that he'd begin to jump, feeling the bullet hitting him. If he moved his arm the wrong way, that sudden searing pain felt like the slug still entering and moving in him. He would wake in a cold sweat and be unable to return to sleep.

Lying on top of the rumpled bedclothes in the room hallowed by the moon's majesty, he propped his back against the pillows with one leg bent, and a cigarette dangling between his lips. The bottom of a whiskey bottle rested on his knee, the neck in his grasp. Intoxication wasn't a part of his daily habits. He never got so drunk he spoiled his health or clouded his mind. The whiskey helped him return to sleep. Though at this hour, it wasn't working. For he had done nothing tiring the whole day except visit his horses and dog.

And almost kiss Helena.

Carrigan took a thoughtful drag of his cigarette. *She* was the root of his insomnia. The woman saw him as a trump card and would discard him in six months. Knowing what was expected of him, he had no problem with that. He'd be well compensated for his time. What bothered him was the element lying hidden in the contract. A magnetic attraction toward her.

The stairs creaked, signaling Helena's return. He'd heard her go down a few minutes ago, no doubt to lecture Obsi on his midnight serenade. As much as Carrigan wanted his dog with him, he wouldn't go against the rules of the house. Respect was a serious thing to him. But that still didn't mean he had to give way to Helena's way of thinking. She was wrong. Dogs and men belonged together at all hours.

On the other side of his door, the footsteps paused. Then the door slowly rasped inward and Helena peered around its edge.

"Don't sneak around on my account," Carrigan

said as he crushed his smoke in a chipped dish on the quilt. "I'm awake."

"So am I. No thanks to your dog." She remained where she stood, obscured by the door except for her head.

"Now that I've been resurrected in his eyes, he wants to be with me."

"You know I don't approve of dogs in the house."

"So you've said plenty of times."

"Well, just so you'll know." Then she let the door open all the way, and Obsi shot out like a streak from behind her. He pushed his muzzle into the hand that Carrigan was resting on the covers. Obsi's tail moved side to side in a half circle.

As Carrigan buried his fingers in his dog's thick fur to stroke his ears, he lifted his gaze to Helena. She was an ever-changing mystery. "What made you give in?"

"A greater need to sleep tonight rather than stand on ceremony."

Obsi smacked his tongue like he was licking his chops, then he jumped onto the foot of the bed, sprawled out, and put his chin on his paws.

Though the light was not the best, Carrigan could make out Helena's distinct frown. "If he makes one sound, if he piddles on the floor, if he brings fleas and cockleburs into your bed, I'm holding you accountable and will assume you'll correct, clean, or change it. Posthaste," she added with a prudish squaring of her shoulders.

"Are you henpecking me?" he queried in a humorous tone she was too worked up to appreciate.

Night drew her blond hair down in a thick braid that tumbled carelessly over her right breast. The softly curled end reached the curve of her hip. Her pale nightgown and billowing wrapper kept the exact dimensions of her figure from being seen.

"I don't find nagging an admirable quality in a . . . a wife," she replied. "It's just that—"

"Helena." He didn't let her continue. "I was kidding."

She stared at him. "You aren't the type of man who jokes."

"You don't know me." Carrigan set the whiskey bottle on the candlestand next to the head of the bed. Lowering his leg, he felt the stubble on his chin. Earlier he'd bathed from the washbasin, but hadn't had a razor to shave. He grew a thick beard, and the lower half of his face was rough with a week's growth.

"I know that you abhor men forcing unwanted aggressions on women," she said. Her discreet attempt at sudden modesty by way of a hand lifted to her high-neck collar didn't escape his attention. "That you say and do things no matter the consequences just to make yourself feel better. And that you've killed people."

"Men, not people. People would include women," he corrected, but other than that, he didn't defend himself.

"There was a reason you killed those men."

"Yes."

"Will you tell me?"

"No."

Licking the flavor of liquor off his lips, he mused, "What can I say in return about you? You're independent, yet you know your limitations. You hate to admit you're wrong, but you will. And you're afraid of me."

"I am not," she shot back, the fingers at her throat sinking into the cotton ruffles.

"Of course you are. But it's a fear that loves the idea of danger."

The tremor in her voice betrayed her. "That's absurd. I'm not afraid of you."

"Then prove you aren't." He gave her a long, steady look. "Come here."

She hesitated a moment. Stepping forward, she approached the bed. Once at its edge, she released the grip on her wrapper and lowered her arms to her sides. "I've been this close to you before."

Carrigan's voice was seductive and low when he said, "But you and I both know things are different now." Wanting to since she'd come into his room, he brought his fingers around the rope of her hair. He rubbed its silky texture against his thumb and drew her face closer to his by gently pulling on the length. "I told you that I didn't need anyone, but that's a lie. Without you, I would have died." Her generous eyelashes fluttered against her cheeks as he continued bringing her toward him. "But that doesn't mean I have to like needing you." He'd maneuvered her face within inches of his. "And that doesn't mean I won't walk away at the end of the six months." Her startled breath was hot on his chin. "Because I will."

His last words were smothered on her lips as he took possession of her mouth in a kiss burning with intensity. The exchange was like a homecoming. Kissing conveyed joy and sorrow, the sealing of promises, and the receipt of fulfillment—emotions he'd run from. The long dormant feelings had no less affect on him now. Rather they seemed stronger and more stimulating than he thought possible. His senses indulged in the pleasure, while his mind marveled at the harmony.

Releasing Helena's braid, his hand cupped the back of her smooth, ivory neck to hold her head immobile. Like a man parched from endless days in an arid desert, he drank in the sweetness of her kiss. Three years had been too long to go without touching a woman's petal-soft lips.

Helena's palms clutched his bare shoulders in protest when his tongue slid between her lips.

"You don't like this?" he murmured.

"It's just that . . . it's been a long time."

"For me, too." The implication of her words didn't immediately register. When they did, a firebrand of jealousy ignited in him. "You were married before?"

She carefully kissed him back, a sure sign she was dodging his question.

So be it, then, and to hell with answers.

He deepened her efforts, wanting to obliterate her memory of any other man's kiss. His own secrets haunted him, so he could find no fault in hers. It was safer to remain silent about the history of one's heart. The ghosts of old loves were merely apparitions that vanished into smoke at dawn.

Capturing Helena on his lap, Carrigan secured a free arm around her waist, mindless of the discomfort to his injury. He was putting more into this moment than was wise. Repercussive thoughts and negative reasons fled.

"We can't . . . I can't . . ." She struggled to lift her head, and he reluctantly released her. "This isn't part of the bargain."

With his hand on the small of her back, he pointed out, "You said no sex. Kissing is merely an ingredient. Like fruit without sugar, it can be consumed and enjoyed on its own."

"You have your definition, and I have mine." Helena rose and fell back a step. "Kissing is the prelude to intimacy. And I can't be intimate with you."

"Why not?"

She gazed at him with moonlight shimmering in her eyes. "You wouldn't understand."

"I can't understand what I don't know."

"It's impossible for me to tell you. I think it's best if we remember our living arrangement is only temporary, and anything beyond a noncommittal attitude toward one another would be inadvisable." Retreating to the door, she paused. "I meant to remove your bandages tonight, but my mind was otherwise occupied. I'll take them off in the morning."

"I can manage on my own."

With a final glance in his direction, she left.

The only noise was Obsi's contented sniff, and the

unevenness of Carrigan's breathing. He'd gone over the line, knowing full well the boundaries. He never should have kissed her. Because now he wanted to kiss her again.

Helena had concealed the markings of Carrigan's kisses with corn silk powder. Though the rosy blush on her sensitive skin from his beard was greatly disguised, she still worried it could be seen. As she entered the kitchen, she hoped no one would be perceptive enough to notice at the breakfast table.

Ignacia was at the stove flipping griddle cakes, while Emilie set out the syrup crock and covered butter dish.

"Good morning," Helena said self-consciously.

Heads turned toward the direction of her voice, Ignacia smiling and Eliazer pausing from refilling the fuel bin with kindling.

"Good morning," Emilie dutifully replied, and put a bowl of applesauce with raisins next to the cream jug and sugar basin. Though in disagreement, the sisters conducted themselves with a strained cordiality when in the company of others. Helena knew she couldn't convince Emilie that her quick marriage had been the right thing to do, so she didn't try to explain herself further. If Emilie saw how Carrigan's commanding presence would help the Express station run smoothly, it might help her understand.

Automatically Helena headed for the cupboard and began to bring down the plates.

"I didn't see the dog in the yard this morning," Eliazer commented while lumbering to his feet. "Maybe he's taken off for good this time."

Arranging the flatware, Helena said, "The dog's in Carrigan's room."

The three of them stared at her, but it was Ignacia who spoke. "You don't allow animals in the house, Miss Lena."

"I had to make an exception if we wanted to get some sleep."

Ignacia and Eliazer lived in a bunkhouse on the property and probably hadn't heard Obsi's cries, but Emilie remarked, "The whines woke me up for a minute, but I went back to sleep. I assumed the dog gave up."

"Well, he didn't." Folding a towel, Helena retrieved the coffeepot from the stove and deposited it on a decorative iron stand on the tabletop.

They sat down to eat, and no one added anything further to the subject. Helena felt oddly out of place for the first time in her own house while she listened to Ignacia and Eliazer talk about what they had planned for the day. Emilie added her thoughts, the most enthusiastic concerning Thomas McAllister. He was the scheduled rider this afternoon.

A bite of the doughy flapjacks stuck to the roof of Helena's mouth, and she took a sip of sugared coffee to wash the lump down. Her appetite was poor, but she forced herself into finishing what she'd been served. While those around her chatted, her mind kept straying to Carrigan.

Of course, she'd known their kiss had been coming. What had happened in the stables yesterday had presaged the inevitable. She couldn't let herself fall into his arms again. If she did, she'd lose her upper hand in the marriage. But his kiss had been the kind she'd wondered about. Filled with a passion so furious, it pinpointed every emotion and thought she had into one dazzling spear of focus: his mouth on hers.

She didn't know how long it had been since he'd kissed a woman, but she could reassure him he hadn't lost his talent for it. Carrigan expertly monopolized the situation to his advantage, making her weak and wanting. Making her nearly forget her resolve.

"I went up to Mr. Carrigan's property first light this morning and found his satchel," Eliazer said, breaking into Helena's thoughts. "The cloth was damp, so I put the bag near the stove to dry. I think everything inside is free from moisture."

"Thank you."

Emilie lifted her head and addressed Helena with earnest fear in her eyes. "Have you given any thought to the possibility that whoever shot him may come gunning after us since we're harboring him?"

Helena hadn't told anyone about Seaton Hanrahan's assault, not wanting to add further tension to the household. Though her suspicions about Seaton had merit, she couldn't be sure. If the gunman had been committing a random act—of which thievery generally was the intention—why hadn't Carrigan's cabin been ransacked? "There's no good reason why anyone would want him dead," Helena hedged. "I'm sure we're safe."

"I hope so." Emilie set her fork down. "I'm frightened, Lena. Not only for us, but for you." The tone of her voice was grave. "I don't want to see you get hurt."

"No one's going to hurt her or anybody in this house as long as I'm in it."

They all started at the resonant sound of Carrigan's voice coming from the doorway. His unexpected appearance put Helena at odds, while his state of undress embarrassed her. She should have had the foresight to at least give him one of the shirts from the store so he wouldn't have to continuously go without.

True to his word, Carrigan had removed his bandages. The fresh scars on his chest didn't diminish his appeal. He looked like he lived and worked hard. The flaws and that .44-caliber Colt of his had him resembling a fearsome figure out of a sensational blood-and-thunder story.

Obsi heeled at Carrigan's boots, but as soon as Carrigan strode toward the table, he trotted after him. "I'm not an invalid. I'll eat my meals here instead of in bed." His gaze searched for a vacant seat. The extra one was the butter churn they put a braided rug over, but Carrigan wouldn't know that.

Eliazer stood and relinquished his spot. "I was finished. You can sit here."

Carrigan fell into the seat adjacent to Helena. She rose almost immediately and went to the stove to get his belongings. She held out the bag as Obsi lay down. "If you're going to eat at the table, I think you should put on a shirt."

He eyed the satchel and took the handles. Opening it, he rummaged through the contents and selected a wheat-colored muslin. As his arms slipped through the sleeves, he caught the attention of Emilie, who hadn't uttered a word since his entrance.

"Morning," he said, looking directly at her. "We haven't been formally introduced. I'm your sister's husband, Jake."

"I know who you are," she returned, her voice small. Pushing her chair back, she stood without clearing her dirty plate from the table. "Excuse me."

Helena looked at her lap, then at Ignacia. "Could you fix him a plate?" To Carrigan, "Do you want coffee?"

"Black."

She poured while Ignacia set the pancakes in front of him. After staring at the three of them in turn, he picked up his fork and began to eat as if his presence hadn't all but silenced the room.

"You didn't tell me you'd be down for breakfast," Helena said while Eliazer kissed Ignacia's thin cheek, then set out for the stables after removing his slouch hat from the peg by the door. Ignacia gathered the dishes and stacked them in the dry sink.

Carrigan gazed at her from underneath the dark lines of his brows. "We didn't get around to discussing that last night."

She couldn't prevent her cheeks from becoming warm, but she wouldn't give him a response. "What do you propose to do after breakfast?"

He took a bite of pancake, chewed, then swallowed with a gulp of coffee. "What you got me here to do. Raise some hell with the hay yard owner. I saw the sorry state of your feed pile yesterday." After consuming the last portion, he shoved his plate away and hooked his finger through the handle of his coffee cup. "You can forget the blacksmith's services. Just buy the shoes, and I'll nail them on the horses myself."

Helena left the table and brought Ignacia Carrigan's plate. "You've shoed your own horses before?"

"Mine and several hundred."

"Where?" she asked, more anxious to know about his background than his credentials.

"Red Springs. Split Rock. Libertyville."

"Who taught you?"

"A man named Hart." He weighed her with a critical squint. "You wouldn't know him."

"I don't suppose I would."

Leaning back in his chair, he kicked up his bootheel on the seat opposite him. "You want to know how I learned to handle horses? Flat out ask."

Helena glanced at Ignacia. Her face was expressionless as she took up a bucket and let herself outside to pump wash water for the dishes.

Resting her hands flat on the table, Helena decided she'd play showdown with Carrigan. He was in a mood this morning, the root of which probably stemmed back to her staving off their kiss. "You're very good at cat and mouse."

"So are you. You never answered my question about having a husband before me. The way I recall it, you distracted me with your kiss."

She wouldn't comment on that because he was right. But she could say, "On the day we got married, you said that what we did in the past was our own business."

"True. But when a woman kisses the way you do, it's only natural for a man to be curious." He eyed her over the brim of his mug. "Now, you could either be a widow, or a former lift-skirt. Which one do you want me thinking you are?"

Fury almost choked her. "I'm neither."

"Then that does make the plot interesting." His foot came down hard on the floorboards, causing Obsi to relocate onto a rag rug by the pantry. "You were someone's mistress."

Her breasts rose and fell with mortification. "How dare you!"

"I can dare anything I damn well please."

Helena wanted to hit him. She'd never had the impulse to strike a human being in her entire life, but Carrigan had gone too far in his assumptions. White with indignation, she pushed away from the table and turned her back on him. "You will not manipulate me into losing my temper. You're mad because I didn't let you kiss me."

"You did let me kiss you."

"I don't believe I had a choice."

"Don't you go making me out to be a profligate who forces himself on women. I've never had to. I never will."

She whirled around, not wanting him to dredge up his sexual indiscretions. "What happened last night won't be repeated, so there's no sense in our discussing it."

Carrigan downed the last of his coffee and stood. His fingers caught her chin. He turned her head from side to side, examining her mouth. "Next time I'll shave."

Horrified that he noticed, she felt her breathing hitch. "I told you there won't be a next time."

"Don't think I'll shave right now," he mused, scratching his jaw with blunt fingertips, totally disregarding her. "We could use the beard to our advantage. I look rougher-edged with it. And the whole point is to make Lewis jump like he's stepped on raw eggs."

"You remembered his name." Helena had mentioned Mr. Lewis to Carrigan only once—the day she asked him to marry her.

"I remember everything anyone tells me." Carrigan's voice grew distant. "Or does to me and my family."

There was a double meaning to his words that ran far deeper than the generalization on the surface.

Carrigan started for the hall. Helena and Obsi followed. It seemed a plan was in the workings and Helena had no part. She stated her case to Carrigan's broad back. "I thought before we went, we should discuss the terms of my account with the hay yard. I should fill you in on the details of my business dealings in Genoa so you can tell Mr. Lewis I've always paid my bills and—"

"I don't discuss," Carrigan broke in. "Action gets results. Whatever you've got to say, tell me on the way." He snagged his coat from the hook and shoved through the curtains to the store.

Emilie, who was readying the merchandise for opening, glanced up at their intrusion.

"We're going to see Mr. Lewis," Helena said, keeping pace with Carrigan's long stride while putting on her cloak. "We'll be back shortly."

When Carrigan was out the front door, Emilie raced to Helena and whispered, "Lena, he looks positively bloodthirsty."

Helena replied with quiet but desperate firmness. "I hope he is."

Heavy hauling between California and Virginia City packed Main Street with wagons and teams. Sometimes horses, mules, and oxen were tied to the wheels of their wagons to feed overnight because stable room was not available.

Helena wondered what Carrigan must think of it all, having not been exposed to such a density of man and animal for so long. At certain times, it was almost impossible for a pedestrian to walk the street without risk of getting his head kicked at.

The running of the two buhrstones from the flour mill on Mill Street lent the scene a rumbling background hum. A different sound, but no less potent, came from the sawmill irons operated by flutter wheels and an upright sash saw. The building was located at the mouth of Mill Creek Canyon—the town's source of drinking water by way of being diverted in little ditches that spread beyond the city's limit to irrigate the fields, farms, and ranches. This source was also what kept the many deciduous trees flourishing, in addition to rotting the boardwalks in places. Especially in April when the rains came and flooded the channels.

A roar of vulgar laughter erupted from the open two-paneled door to the Metropolitan Saloon. The split-log benches sheltered from the sun by awnings were vacant, indicating the shiftless group was inside having a grand old time. Shad-bellied nags with their cinches loosened were butted shoulder to shoulder at the hitching rails. An odious smell rose from the ground, which had become a gumbo of droppings. Offended, Helena put a hand to her nose and mouth without veering her gaze to investigate the raucous jug-house. She'd never once tried to steal a peek inside.

But Carrigan was interested. He stopped and glanced through the smoke-filled doorway. "This the favorite watering trough?"

"It's one of two, but seems to be the most popular."

"Hanrahan ever come here?"

"When he has money in his pockets, he goes on wild sprees. But his paydays are always numbered."

"Why do you say that?"

"There are a dozen or more ranches in the valley that he can work on, but from what I've heard, he never stays long on one before he's let go. Usually for fighting." She pondered Carrigan's motives. "If you've got a mind to look for him, I wouldn't know which way to direct you. You'd pretty much have to ride out to each ranch individually, and that would take you days."

Carrigan moved on, Obsi trailing. Helena noted Carrigan took in the fine elements of his surroundings. His right arm bent slightly at his elbow, the fingers on his hand spread wide. Ever wary of strangers, he'd pushed his coat back so no one could mistake him for being unarmed. She didn't blame him, as she often looked into the faces of unfamiliar pedestrians, wondering if one of them had killed her father.

Blatant stares and shocked expressions landed on Helena from those who knew her. Word of her marriage must have blazed like a prairie fire, scorching and consuming those who got an earful. She didn't care. None of them had ever professed any loyalties to her. Not all, but some, lived for gossip and fuel to feed their cracker-barrel conversations. Well, now they had fresh news to jaw about. Carrigan was an imposing figure, a man who'd never ventured this far into their town. His walk down Main Street took merchants and customers by surprise. Doorways filled with gawkers, while movement on the boardwalk stopped as they walked past. By this evening, she and Carrigan would be the topic at many a supper table.

Helena chewed on the inside of her lip, putting up a front of nonchalance she didn't necessarily feel. "I wanted to tell you about my accounts with Mr. Lewis."

Carrigan jumped down to the muddy thoroughfare after her as she dodged vehicles and veered up Carson Street.

"For as long as my father was alive, we've had credit. Not once have we disregarded a bill and not paid it. But after my father's death, suddenly I was denied service. Though Mr. Lewis never came out and said so, I believe it's because I'm a woman."

"Can't fool him there."

She gave Carrigan a glance. "What's your point?"

"I have no point."

"And?"

"Neither does Lewis. Within the hour, you'll have feed." Carrigan gazed at the sights, his brows drawn into a frown. "Where's the hay yard?"

"There." She motioned to the stout-framed establishment four doors down.

Carrigan took her by the elbow and guided her to the weathered building with double-wide doors. They entered the barnlike cavern where dim light filtered through windows hazed by grain dust and the dormant webs of spiders. The wall was twenty feet on the sides, soaring to a near twenty-five in the center where the roof peaked. Hay and straw bundles were stockpiled one on top of the other. The scents of alfalfa, clover, and grasses clustered in the air. Scythes, cutters, and various plow tools lay in the front of the building, while to the immediate right was a framed-in office with a single entry door.

Helena proceeded, but at the open threshold, Carrigan put his hand on her shoulder.

"No disrespect," he said, "but I'll go in first."

Staying back, Helena let Carrigan pass. Then she stepped in behind him. Carrigan's unannounced intrusion had the desired impact on Mr. J. H. Lewis. His mouth fell agape; he was shocked by the sudden appearance of the man all of Genoa knew nothing about—but feared worse than the plague. Lewis rose from his chair on quaking legs and smoothed the wrinkles of his checkered trouser legs. As he removed his spectacles, his eyes went wide and traveled the inordinate length of Carrigan's tall stature. Then of Obsi, who was displaying his canine incisors.

"Lewis," Carrigan kicked off before the man had a chance to make an inquiry.

"Y-Yes?" J.H. stuttered in a voice strewn with hesitation.

"Jake Carrigan."

Helena nervously wet her lips. Feigning innocence, she directed her gaze to the windowsill. A battalion of dead bottle flies and one solitary wasp were aged casualties of entrapment.

"I understand you're refusing service to my wife."

Lewis swallowed hard, his throat bobbing. "I've had some resent reservations about rendering her service . . . yes."

"Has she ever not paid you?"

"I . . ." Sweat popped out on his face, and he drew out his handkerchief to blot his ruddy skin. "No."

"Then what seems to be the trouble?"

Lewis's hands were jittery as they lifted to refit his eyeglasses behind his ears. "When Miss Gray's . . . er, Mrs. Carrigan's father died, I grew concerned about the risks of doing business with a woman. Without the sensibilities of a man's head—"

"What do I look like?"

"Look like?" he muttered, clearly confused by Carrigan's remark. "Well . . ."

"I hope to God you say a man, because anything else is going to insult me."

"I didn't mean to—"

"No," Carrigan interrupted. "I'm sure you don't mean to waylay that shipment of feed to our stockade. I expect you'll have it there by noon."

J. H. Lewis glanced at the dozen notes pinned to his wall, and the calendar that was penciled in with various job orders. "That would be impossible today—"

"'Imposible' doesn't exist in my vocabulary. I suggest you make the arrangements." Relaxing his finger around the trigger of his revolver, Carrigan tilted his head. "Are we clear?"

"Yes, sir," Lewis spouted stiffly. "Very clear. I'll get Billy right on it."

Carrigan turned to leave, then stopped and faced

off with Lewis again. "You owe my wife an apology for the way you've treated her."

J.H. cleared his throat. "I'm sorry, Mrs. Carrigan, for any inconvenience you may have suffered."

Helena silently accepted his atonement.

"Let's go," Carrigan said flatly.

She followed his lead, her astonished thoughts leaping ahead of her legs as she stepped outside with Obsi at her skirts.

"Which blacksmith do you use?"

"Wyatt's across the street."

A wrought-iron sign hanging from the front eave was inscribed with: *Wyatt & Sons, Blacksmiths.* The clang of a hammer against an anvil pealed through the street, while the heat of a forge being fanned by the bellows lit up the inside like a blooming fireflower.

"Wyatt treat you like Lewis did?"

"Yes."

"Come on."

On the way over, Helena tried to subdue the quickening in her ribs. She had encountered many stalwart men during her years in the West. Salty drovers, gritty settlers, and stoic bluecoats who settled their disputes with physical force. But none made such an impression on her as Carrigan's performance with J. H. Lewis. Contrary to Carrigan's opinion he wasn't a man of discussion, it was his tough words that demanded she be given due respect.

To her amazement, Helena acknowledged being in awe of her husband.

Chapter

→ 7 ←

As he headed back to the store, Carrigan's ears rang with the ceaseless clink of hammers, the buzz of trades, and the hum of drums and flywheels. His muscles were tense, the slightest noise causing him to flinch. The only place he'd been accustomed to had been Gray's general store and stockade—visits he could count on one hand. He'd exiled himself not a mile from the teeming streets, but he may as well have been in a foreign country. On his journey through the center of town, he'd instantly become aware of his ignorance of things he'd never seen before and never felt enough interest in to read about.

Though there had been stares directed at them, the entire population went on as if he and Helena had not existed. People pushed and shoved. No one stopped to view the majestic panorama of the mountains behind the storefronts, nor the impressive tones of Carson Valley's desert sage and grasses below.

He wasn't used to walking over a sidewalk of boards that were more or less loose and inclined to rattle when trod upon. The variety of stores influenced his desire to buy unessential items and whetted his appetite. Bread the shape and size of cheese wheels was available to purchase without the bother of baking it himself. Boarding and lodging went for ten dollars for a week—a ridiculously excessive amount.

But some things never changed. The rowdy Metropolitan Saloon mirrored the types of bars he'd bellied up to in the past. Swearing, drinking, and card playing were the order of the day, with an occasional fight thrown in for variety. He'd searched for Seaton Hanrahan while taking a look around, but had come up short.

Genoa's populace was composed of different types of characters, but the image that stayed with Carrigan was that of the Washoe Indians, who were tolerated with blind eyes even though they stuck out like sore thumbs. Donned in cloth of loud black and gold stripes, they were squalid in appearance and languid as consumptive forty-niners. Blighted hope dimmed the pride from their eyes, their complexions sallow like yellow jackets.

Helena wasn't as offending as most who passed by the sorry souls, but she was just as ignorant of their plight. What would she say were she to learn his mother's Choctaw blood flowed through his veins?

"Thank you for speaking with Mr. Lewis and Mr. Wyatt," Helena said from her place at his side.

"Don't thank me." He surveyed the walkways on both sides of the street, keeping an eye out for a glimpse of Hanrahan. As he'd only been face-to-face with him once, Carrigan's picture of him wasn't entirely clear. But he'd recognize that decorated black hat amongst the mostly rough-used ones on the men in town. "Don't make out what I did to be a gallant act. I want my land. As long as I'm living with you, I'll earn my keep to get it."

"Here he comes!" came a rousing shout to Carrigan's right. Instinctively he shoved Helena behind him, drew his Colt, and crouched to the balls of his feet. Obsi set off into frantic barks and snaps of his jaw.

Shaken, Helena gazed at Carrigan as if he were crazy. "What are you doing?"

"Who's coming?" His only thoughts were of some imbecile bent on taking potshots at him.

"Thomas McAllister," she explained. "The eastern-bound Pony Express rider."

Carrigan narrowed his eyes, glanced every which way in the cleared road, then slowly rose to his feet. "Obsi, shut up."

On a last snort, Obsi whined.

Reholstering his gun, Carrigan scowled. He felt like an idiot. "Why the hell are they yelling about it?"

Taking him by the bulk of his sleeve, Helena hurried across Nixon Street in a flurry of skirts. "I forgot you've never seen the exchange of horses." They went up the curb, and she let go of him. "Look down there."

Coming across the continual plain of the southern valley, a black spot materialized against the horizon. The naked eye could see it obviously moved. In a second or two the speck grew more readily defined as a horse and rider, rising and falling with the tempo of the animals swift gait. The duo swept toward town. Nearer and nearer, the tremble of hooves came to Carrigan's ear. In another instant, a whoop and hurrah erupted from the crowd as man and horse bore down Nixon Street, heading directly for him. The facility and pace at which they traveled was a marvel to Carrigan. A horn blew as the rider brought the instrument to his mouth, then he gave a coyote yell.

With his broad slouch hat brim blown flat up in front, and leaning gently forward, Thomas McAllister seemed to be a part of the horse. He burst past Carrigan like a gale. Silver-mounted trappings decorated both man and beast. McAllister wore a uniform with plated horn, pistol, scabbard, and belt. Flowerworked leggings, a gaudy red shirt, and jingling spurs added to his distinctive costume.

He couldn't have weighed more than three fifty-pound sacks of flour, but no finer-looking man ever rode a horse. The pony was a splendid specimen of speed and endurance, dashing toward Gray's relay station speckled with foam and with nostrils dilated. Excitement brightened Emilie's eyes as she waited, her hands clasping the strap of a canteen. Eliazer held the reins of a fresh mount, which Carrigan recognized as being one of the mustangs he'd caught for August.

Helena ran to the corner. Caught up in the spectacle, Carrigan went after her and stopped just short of Eliazer and Emilie.

Reining to an abrupt halt, McAllister dismounted. Carrigan could smell the horse's coat reeking with perspiration while his flanks thumped with every breath. Standing straight as an arrow, Thomas McAllister had a determined expression. He took the water from Emilie with a wink. Her cheeks blushed a fair rose as he drank deeply to sate his thirst.

There was only a second or two delay as Helena ran from the corner and threw a saddlebag with four locked compartments over the modified saddle of a fresh mount. McAllister tossed Emilie a round package no bigger than a fist and tied at the top with string. Then he stuck his foot in the stirrup and leaped into place. With a dig of Thomas's spurs, the horse darted away like a telegram. McAllister's gauntlet-covered hand lifted in a wave good-bye, and soon his figure was reduced to a mole on the undulating body of terrain to the east.

Carrigan had never witnessed such an event in his entire life.

"It's an orange!" Emilie exclaimed, holding up the thick-skinned fruit for Helena to see. The packaging was stuffed under her arm as she clutched an envelope in her other hand. "And a note. He wrote me a note." Her voice softened with a tender passion so plain, even Carrigan took notice of it. The letter, she didn't share with Helena. Instead, she dreamily walked up the steps of the store, her nose buried in the sheet of thin paper.

Eliazer walked the exhausted horse to the stables, but Helena remained on the street, misgivings clouding her gaze. It wasn't hard for Carrigan to deduce her thoughts.

"You don't approve of your sister being in love with that rider."

Helena's chin came up. "Leave Emilie to me."

He'd apparently hit a sensitive mark. "Is that why she dresses like a child? You won't let her put on a corset? If so, you're not fooling anyone. I can see she's nearly a woman."

"She's only sixteen."

"Woman enough."

"To make a mistake," Helena finished.

"Sounds like you're living her life for her." Carrigan shook his head. "I can tell you now, it won't work. She'll end up hating you for it."

Helena bit her lower lip. "Emilie would never hate me."

"Don't give her a reason to. Let her grow up."

"I'm her only parent," Helena reasoned.

Carrigan recalled August telling him in passing he was a widower, but Carrigan didn't know the circumstances and for how long. "You're her sister. Not her mother."

Helena gazed at him as if she were taking his comment into consideration. Then she frowned. "In the future, I would appreciate it if you kept your opinions about my sister to yourself."

He no longer felt the need to argue with Helena. She believed she had her sister's best interests at hand. What did he have to gain by contradicting her?

Helena went into the store, while Carrigan opted to stay outside a moment longer. He leaned against one of the shady awning posts and lit a cigarette. Blowing smoke through his lips, he gazed at the street, which had returned to normal. He was an outsider and always would be. He no longer fit in with society, for his view of life far differed from that of those around him. He put a high priority on nature and its gifts, but the beauty went unobserved by this bustling throng. It was no wonder he rarely came down from his mountain.

His eyes searched once more for Hanrahan, but there was no conspicuous black hat in the sea of dingy crowns. Exhaling, he crushed his smoke beneath his bootheel and readied to return to the store. Turning, he detected a silvery light from the upstairs window across the street.

The prominent name on the building front read COURTHOUSE, but it had been a livery at one time. Paint from the old sign was just visible enough for him to read. The gleam came again as an object behind the glass caught the sunlight. Carrigan squinted to make out an image, and was able to define the silhouette of a man. Whether he was watching him intentionally, Carrigan wasn't sure. But the mere fact that he'd been observed while enjoying his smoke had him suddenly longing for the privacy of his cabin.

Carrigan had to be made of rawhide, because he was just as tough as leather.

The next morning Helena heard him ask Eliazer for a loan of the buckboard. An hour later, he reappeared with his saddle, chaps, and a toolbox. Helena was helping Eliazer align snares in the stockyard garden when the wagon pulled in. Carrigan hadn't told her where he was going, and she hadn't asked. Their discussion yesterday about Emilie and Thomas had upset her. Her anger had abated somewhat, but its warm glow was still on her mind.

She didn't pause from her task, hearing Carrigan before she actually saw him. The jangle of spurs came to her ears, and she lifted her gaze. He strode toward her in glove-fitting boots to which long-shanked spurs where attached and kept on with broad, crescent-shaped shields of leather laid over the insteps. The big sunset rowels dragged on the ground when he walked. Pliable calfskin vamps fit tightly over the top of his feet, giving the appearance he'd poured his calves into his boots. He'd changed into a pullover yoked shirt in a striped hickory with a row of four buttons spilling down from the collar. A buckskin vest, rather than his coat, didn't restrict his freedom and was an effective buffer against the temperature, which was brisk, but not penetrating.

He stopped in front of her, and she tilted her chin upward. The brim of her straw hat shaded her eyes from the deep blue sky above. Carrigan's voice melted down to her. "You said you've got two horses that need shoeing. Get 'em."

"You want to shoe them now?"

"Yes."

"I appreciate your offer, and Lord knows I desperately need them shoed, but you haven't had enough time to mend. I can manage awhile longer now that I have feed."

"I know my limitations, and I'll be damned if I'm going to sit in the house like a cripple."

Helena thoughtfully gazed at the young cabbage shoots, which already had been nibbled on by rabbits. She didn't like humdrum jobs like setting traps, hoeing, planting, and weeding. But she did them just the same because Eliazer couldn't do it all. Horses, however, were another matter. For anything involving them, she'd lay down her spade with pleasure.

"All right." Standing, she clapped the damp soil from her hands and stretched the kinks out of her legs. "But you'll need help."

"You got a resister?"

"I wouldn't call Columbiana a resister. She just knows what she likes and what she doesn't." A revealing smile caught Helena's mouth. "And she doesn't like getting new shoes."

The twine and stakes in Eliazer's hands dropped to the seed box when Helena said, "Come on, Eliazer, looks like we won't be having rabbit stew for supper tomorrow."

Fifteen minutes later, Carrigan had built up a makeshift forge in the yard and set out his equipment: picker, tongs, heavy hammer, and light pincers. Wyatt's had delivered two sets of fullered shoes.

While Carrigan began work on the shoes, Helena put a halter on Monarch and led him out of the stables. He was a six-year-old gelding who had a fine disposition. Though moodiness sprang up in him every once in a while, he was pretty reliable.

Carrigan's back was to her as he set the hammer down on a tree stump. In lieu of a hat, he'd tied his hair with a piece of thin rawhide to keep it from his eyes. The gathered length of glossy black fell between his shoulder blades. The sight made her want to touch his hair . . . and pull the string free so she could sift every strand through her fingers. It was only when Carrigan pivoted toward her that she returned to her senses with a dry-eyed blink under his order of, "Hobble his fore feet."

"No need to," Helena replied. "He's so gentle, you could stake him to a hairpin. He's fast, but he's a sweetie." Her hand smoothed the bay's coat.

Monarch tolerated Carrigan's management with hardly a grumble. Utilizing a punch, Carrigan dragged the old shoes off with the short rod of steel, then he used the pliers, and employed a drawing knife. Helena had to swallow her trepidation, having seen the handiwork of too many smithies who thought cutting the horn low was the key to preventing rocks from embedding into the sole. But Carrigan knew to remove just the brittle areas and create a smooth, even surface.

He situated the plate of iron, and hammered the nails in the hard horn's wall by slanting them outward, so as not to puncture Monarch's toe or foot. Rather than trim the sharp protrusion of the nail points, he slipped a tiny washer over each one, then lightly tapped them down against the hoof.

Eliazer put his finger on the brim of his hat and tipped his head at Carrigan. "I've never seen that before."

"Washers cut out weakening the horn from the groove formed by the clinched nail."

Even Helena was impressed. None of the Wyatts knew this trick.

"Where did you learn about the washers?" Eliazer asked, adjusting the tension on his suspenders. "No one in these parts practices such a method."

Crouched and fixing the last shoe in place, Carrigan spoke around the nails between his lips. "Ranch near Cheyenne."

Eliazer fingered his beard. "I heard it told, cattle up there are bigger than bears."

"I wasn't herding cattle back then." The tap of the hammer intruded on his words. "Sheep."

Puzzlement furrowed Eliazer's brows. "Sheep?"

"Working for cow outfits was what I did first and last. The sheep came in the middle."

Helena listened with interest.

"I can fence, brand, buck hay, bronc, and punch, but where I was headed, there were no cattle. Just stinkin' sheep." Fitting the washers, Carrigan kept talking as if he were unaware of enlightening them with a slice of his former life. "I wanted out of Red Springs fast. Range-lambing five hundred ewes was the quickest exit. I'll admit, it was a job no true cattleman in his right mind would ever take. But I wasn't in my right mind."

Not once had Carrigan revealed so much of his past, and Helena was hanging on to his every word.

She was dying to ask him questions, but he'd risen to his heels and was handing her the reins.

Using the back of his hand to wipe the sweat off his brow, Carrigan said, "Get me the other one."

Complying, she returned Monarch to the stables. The gelding was tenderfooted from the forge. Helena still wouldn't be able to run him or Columbiana, but by the week's end, the station would be in full operation again with rotation horses.

After putting a hackamore on Columbiana, Helena came out with her. Columbiana was a spirited mare, and Helena's best mount. She often reserved her for Thomas to ride.

With ears pinned back and nostrils wide, Columbiana was truly a resister of everything. But Carrigan didn't flinch at the horse's headstrong display when Helena deposited the rope in his hand. Skittish, Columbiana bumped into him. He shoved her away with a hard push. "Get the hell off my foot."

"She's the fastest horse I've ever seen," Helena said. "She's also a pain in the ass."

Carrigan gave her a double glance. "That you, Helena, who just said ass?"

"I did," she replied evenly, unable to contain her smile. "Sometimes a good, mouth-filling oath is the only way to describe Columbiana. Just wait until you try and shoe her."

"The animals that Hart and I used to ride were violent when it came to shoeing. The only way I could subdue them was to throw a rope around each foot and stake them out. I'd have Hart on the head and another man on the body while I trimmed the hooves and nailed on the iron. Those damn horses would squeal and bite all the time I was working with them. If I can shoe those devils, I can shoe this one."

The skin on Carrigan's face was baking a dark brown from the high sun, enhancing the green of his eyes, which matched the spring buds of the cotton-woods leafing out. He took a black neckerchief from his pocket and tied the ends around his forehead to keep his perspiration at bay. She regretted his not having a hat and promised to rectify that by the day's end.

He pointedly looked at her; his studied gaze carried a hint of admiration. What for? she wondered. Just because she was willing to do dirty work? Her senses whirled, and pleasure radiated outward to her smile. She was impressed with the obvious confidence he had in her, though baffled as to why she should take his quiet appraisal to heart.

"Ready?" His smoke-roughened voice held a challenge.

Helena gave him a firm nod, and she and Eliazer did what Carrigan told them.

By late afternoon, every muscle in Helena's body ached as if she'd been dragged through the yard on the end of a lariat. Columbiana wasn't to be shoed easily, and Helena would have the nasty bruises to prove it.

When Ignacia rang the supper bell, Helena hobbled to the door. Outside was a tin washbasin on an overturned barrel where she kept a piece of yellow bar soap. She rinsed the grime from her hands and face. An unrecognizable tier of ruffle from her dark blue eastern dress hung from the eaves as a towel. The trailing skirt had been utterly impractical for the West, its train wearing holes within a month. Helena was glad when the dress finally wore out so she could cut it up for better uses.

She dried her skin with gentle pats, appreciating the cool water. Despite the protection of her straw hat, she felt the sting of sunburn across the bridge of her nose.

At the table, Helena barely tasted the venison, boiled potatoes, dried fruit, and sourdough bread Ignacia put in front of her. Bone-tired as she was, she nearly fell asleep in her chair.

Emilie retired immediately after supper.

an was going to be tempted to pump the
ch so full of holes, he wouldn't float in

ng soak, Carrigan rose from the tub, dried
ipped on the fresh pants he'd brought
. He was just finishing emptying the tub
e open door when Emilie came into the
s soon as she saw him, she froze. Her sunny
in its usual dual braids, but she'd changed
hite nightgown several inches too short for

use me," she murmured. "I'll come back."
need."
anted some tea . . ."
straightened and put the bucket on the workta-
I'm finished, and the kettle on the stove is half-
You might as well use the water while it's hot."
autiously she went to the cast-iron range and
gged a cup from the cupboard next to it. Without
glance in his direction, she began to steep an
rbal-smelling brew.

Bathwater pooled in scattered puddles on the
iamond-dyed floor. Bunching up his soiled shirt, he
mopped them up. Then he put the tub back into the
pantry.

Emilie acted as if he weren't in the room.

His arms crossed over his bare chest, he gazed at
her speculatively. "You don't like me, do you?"

She said nothing, her profile unchanged.

"You don't have to." Carrigan collected his boots,
dirty pants, and gun belt. "Because you don't know
me from shit."

"Shit smells. You don't."

Sincerely amused, Carrigan couldn't control his
burst of laughter. "Hey there, little sister, you're some
wisdom bringer."

She faced him. "I'm not little."

"No, ma'am," he assured. "My mistake. But you

Waiting for Ignacia to wash and put the dishes
away, Eliazer and Carrigan spoke in muted tones
about the day's events. When Ignacia was finished,
she told Eliazer she'd rub some black birch liniment
on him. Helena made a note to do the same on her
battered joints.

Everyone had called it a night except for Carrigan,
who still sat at the table lingering over his coffee and
smoking. And Obsi, who was dreaming with paws
twitching at his feet. After the immense help Carrigan
had been, Helena felt obligated to stay and hold on to
her yawns.

"You have to be feeling a lot worse than me."
Helena wasn't embarrassed to admit her discomfort.
"How's your wound?"

"Still there."

"That's not what I meant." Her fingers toyed with
the red-edged wheel of a white doily Emilie had
crocheted as a centerpiece. "Does it hurt bad?"

"Not much."

She studied his eyes, the corners creased by tense
lines. "You're lying."

He merely shrugged and crushed his cigarette in the
saucer beneath his cup. "You got a bathtub?"

"I have a hip bath."

"Where is it?"

"The pantry."

"Mind if I use it?"

"No . . ." Helena was deflated by the prospect of
having to drag it out and fill it up. Boiling enough hot
water to make the bath soothing would take almost an
hour. She stood and refrained from rubbing the knots
in her spine. "I'll add more fire to the stove and put
on a kettle." Just the thought made her shoulders
slump.

Carrigan scraped his chair back. "I can heat my
own bath."

The relief that flooded her was a welcome tide. She
went to the pantry and slid out the metal tub toward

the opening. Carrigan stepped next to her, his hand covering hers. He'd ducked his head to accommodate the low slant of the ceiling, and his mouth was within inches of hers. He claimed a short kiss on her lips— just long enough to say that he was in charge, not her . . . and he'd kiss her if he felt like it. When he raised his head, she collided with his powerful body. Her mouth longed for the contact of his. A whirl of sensations swept through her stomach. She wanted him to kiss her again, but she didn't want him to . . .

When he pried her fingers from the tub's rim, she refused to acknowledge her disappointment. "I'll do it myself," he said. "Go to bed."

Her pulse had quickened in response to him, and her unsteady voice betrayed her feelings. "G-Good night, then."

She was on her way out of the kitchen when Carrigan called her name. "Helena."

"Yes?"

"You held your own out there today. That surprised me." His handsome face was reserved. "And very few things ever have."

Christ all Jesus, Carrigan hurt. Everywhere. He hadn't shoed horses in years. His own went without. All he did was trim their hooves every eight weeks. He hated to feel pain for something he should have been able to do without any effort. But his insides were still chewed up, and he'd pushed himself too far.

The warm water worked over his indignant muscles, seeping into his bones. He began to relax even though his legs were bent nearly to his chest. Leaning his head against the curled-under rim, he closed his eyes and reviewed the scene at his cabin earlier that morning.

Upon entering the room, the first thing he'd noticed was the coil of rope thrown to the floor. The hemp reata normally rested on top of his trunk. When he lifted the lid, he could tell someone had rifled through

the contents. The o[...] Carrigan was attache[...] had taught him the [...] Carrigan had made a [...] handsome carved mahog[...] just under a year to com[...] pocket pistol that took [...] sufficient and accurate bulle[...] it was gone, and Carrigan's [...] the man who'd stolen his valu[...]

Nothing was misplaced or [...] outside. Having a fair idea wh[...] hidden, he investigated an exagge[...] looking for tracks. The melted sn[...] ground into a sponge of moldering [...] were unreadable. When he came to[...] he'd been shot, wild grass grew in a c[...] and his search turned up nothing.

What puzzled him was the fact his w[...] was three-quarters empty. He refilled it [...] to compensate for evaporation. Even in [...] the rain and snowmelt should have kept th[...] higher than they were.

On further investigation, he found a tiny ho[...] side. The water level was dead even with it, a[...] ing for the leak. He rolled his sleeves and subm[...] his hand into the murky water. His fingers dre[...] across the bottom, disturbing sunken leaves and s[...] but his hunch paid off. He came up with the bl[...] whistler that had punched through his body.

From the size, Carrigan determined the bullet to be a .36-caliber. It could fit in a variety of models, but the lead plug did narrow down the list of shooters— anyone owning hardware that housed a wheel of .36s.

Pocketing the bullet, Carrigan had taken satisfaction that this one hadn't sent him to Heaven hunting for a harp. Sooner or later Hanrahan would show up in town—and if Hanrahan had been his would-be assassin because he'd come to Helena's aid in the

don't have to worry about McAllister making the same one."

That remark brought a gleam to her eyes. "What do you mean?"

"I saw him looking at you. He knows who you really are, and Helena can't do a damn thing about that no matter how hard she tries." Carrigan nudged Obsi with his bare toes. "Get up, dog. It's time to turn in." Then to Emilie. "McAllister's a man I wouldn't mind knowing. 'Night."

He left Emilie in the lantern-lit kitchen to ponder his words. The climb upstairs tested his waning endurance. After closing the door to his bedroom, he dragged his feet to the bed and lowered himself onto the mattress edge with a tight-lipped oath. His clothing fell from his lap to the floor.

"To hell with it," he muttered, not bothering to even kick them aside.

He would have lain down, but there was a dove-gray hat on the pillowslip. When he picked it up, buckskin thongs dangled from the underside. They were anchored through a jet glass bead.

Helena.

He didn't know what to make of a considerate woman, and he found himself in debt to her. Again. Pride was one of his vices, but he supposed, like laudanum, in a small dose he could swallow some.

Tonight he'd touched his lips to hers because one kiss was better than any words he could have said. Respect for her stamina had provoked him into kissing her. She'd all but consented with the half-moon look in her eyes when their fingers had touched, so he'd obliged because there was nothing more he wanted to do at the moment. He was in need of a woman to take his mind off aches and pains before hunkering into a tub full of relaxation.

Examining the hat under the natural light of the moon, he mused that only one other woman had filled his thoughts the way Helena did. Jenny. But it was still too hard for him to think about his first wife.

Carrigan put his forefinger in the crown and twirled the brim. Hats were a personal thing, but this one appealed to his taste and suited him fine. He tried it on.

The brim was stiff and flat as a cow pie, the band not feeling right around his wet hair. But after a few weeks, the fit would be better. A hat's wearability improved with age like a vintage wine, its beauty and service never fading in the owner's eyes. When this one was stained with his sweat, disreputable in appearance, and kneaded into diverse shapes, Carrigan would have a constant to remind him of Helena.

Lying down with his gun at his side, he pushed the brim over his eyes. Obsi put his chin on Carrigan's belly and waited for his master to stroke his ears. On a tired sigh, Carrigan complied until he began to drift off.

He slept with the scent of store-bought newness filling his nose.

Chapter

→ 8 ←

Over the next four days, Helena worked side by side with Carrigan. There were mornings and afternoons when she had to help Emilie and Ignacia in the store or with kitchen chores, or she had to look over the ledgers and pay out accounts, but she merely went through the motions. Her mind was on the mailbags, managing the horses, keeping the equipment in good order, and the news that the Paiutes had held a council at Pyramid Lake in which they'd recited their grievances and were in favor of war. Shortly thereafter, a small party of warriors had attacked Williams Station, killing two of the operators.

The latter had her greatly concerned because the winter had been a difficult one for the local Washoe Indians. As scanty as the Paiutes' supplies were, she feared they would raid more of the outlying stations for food. She'd received a dispatch from the Pony Express firm of Russell, Majors and Waddell initiating a policy to supply the Indians with rations should they approach a station, not only to keep them friendly but as an act of humanity.

Genoa was a pretty hurrah town with a growing population. She doubted the Paiutes would declare war on a settlement that couldn't be easily overtaken. Gray's stockyard was merely a swing station—one in which the riders made horse changes and nothing more. But the home stations where the riders finished their runs were spread out in the open-range counties across the territory. They would be prime targets, as the smaller number of occupants would be poorly protected.

Helena tried to keep her anxiety at bay, focusing on the turn of events in her own life. With Carrigan's assistance, the station was functioning as smoothly as it had been when her father was overseeing its management.

While she and Carrigan handled the Express ponies and kept up general maintenance of the stockade, Carrigan reserved his speech, expressions, and mannerism for moments in which they would have the most impact. The longer she was around him, the more she picked up on the idiosyncracies of his uncommunicative nature. His inclination for few words was born from years of having no one to talk to.

His tough mask would crack on occasion to display an unexpected smile and laugh. When a black and white magpie stole food from Obsi's plate, Obsi tried to climb the old cottonwood to chase the bird. Carrigan's baritone laugh seemed to make the sunshine feel warmer, and Helena had had to pause from feeding the chickens to relish the sound. The other incident that stuck out in her mind was when Carrigan had come to the breakfast table the morning after she'd left the hat on his pillow. He'd eased his mouth into a fragment of a smile to show his thanks.

For her part, their fraudulent marriage was increasingly becoming a troublesome one. Each night she would hear Carrigan moving in the room next to hers. Rather than sleep being a welcome relief, she dreamed of Carrigan. Things she would never admit to herself would surface in slumber. She would relive his kisses, and invent others in vain fancy. Upon waking, she'd brush the hair from her eyes, sit upright in bed, and vow to put him out of her head. Even if the marriage were real, she could never give him the gift a wife bestows on her husband. Only a fool would think she could make him happy.

And she was feeling foolish lately.

She'd begun to worry overmuch about her appearance, taking care to wear a clean apron and keep her shoes polished. Her hair was in place at all times, even when she was mucking the stalls. Hands that were usually chapped from scrub water were given special treatments of rose glycerin.

Helena didn't like what she'd become, and she somewhat resented Carrigan for making her aware of being a woman again. If she could, she'd run away from herself. Just as she had when Kurt had died. But there was no place for her to go now. Genoa had become home, and she could no more leave it than she could her own skin.

On a Monday night, Esmeralda went into labor. Since Eliazer had sprained a muscle in his back earlier in the day while lifting saddles to the racks, the task of the mare's care fell to Helena. Normally Esmeralda was quite capable of foaling on her own and made it perfectly clear she preferred to be left alone. But her labor had been going on long after supper and nothing was happening. After examining her, Helena had no reason to suspect a breech foal, so she decided to give Esmeralda another hour before revaluating her. Since the mare would prolong delivery if Helena kept a vigil by her side in the stall with a lantern, Helena chose to wait on the haystack where she could be near without intruding.

The night was cool, but clear and bright. Snuggling into the rotund haystack on its leeward side, Helena breathed in the grassy scent and felt comforted. An eternal roof of quietness above garnered her stare. The stars reminded her of candle flames flickering to a radiant glow, then sputtering to a wick point of near nothingness. Unnumbered sparks of light shone down on her from the serene and silent space, and put Helena into a maudlin mood. Sorrow was beginning to win the battle inside her. She knew no cure for grief other than to be active and let time cleanse it away. But she was losing the race.

She missed her father so much, she imagined seeing his shadow next to hers. When she was younger, she used to sneak away from her mother and Emilie in their sewing circle to be with Father in the barn. He would tell her stories about the Old Country and his family while he rubbed the tack into supple leather. It was her father who taught her to load and shoot a Sharps rifle . . . her father who had taken her on fishing trips.

Helena brought her knees up and spread her skirt hem over her shoes. Her mother had always told her, out of suffering emerged the strongest souls. But that wasn't true. She was weak. And she was so lonely, she hurt.

A tear rolled from the corner of her eye, and she wiped the droplet away with her sleeve cuff. But another one followed. Then another. Until she was sobbing quietly. All the memories of her parents flooded her, and she couldn't stop the flow of grief from coming.

Helena yielded the weight of her conscious with a tearful release necessary for the elevation of her spirits. Time passed, as if the grains in an hourglass stood still. She mourned in her dark hiding spot where no one could witness her frailty.

Out of the night, Obsi trotted to Helena and sniffed her skirt with a sneeze. Startled, Helena sat straighter and quickly dashed the tears from her cheeks. Where

Obsi was, Carrigan wouldn't be far behind. And she didn't want him to see she'd been crying.

Cigarette smoke drifted to her nose as the outline of a dark figure and a red glow approached. Carrigan stood over her like a towering spruce. She wasn't really surprised to see him roaming about. He didn't sleep much either. Instead, he prowled the confines of his room, and sometimes the yard, smoking half the night.

Carrigan lowered himself to his heels. "You ever pull a foal out before?"

"Once," she replied as he sat back into the hay, somewhat dismayed that he'd decided to join her. The crisp rustling that resulted from his crushing weight sent delicious gooseflesh up her arms. "My father made me. My mother watched and threw up."

"The West is hard on women," Carrigan remarked, grinding his smoke beneath his boot sole. "Maybe your mother wasn't made for it."

Quietly Helena replied, "She wasn't."

Carrigan grew silent, not prodding her for details. Perhaps his lack of pressure was what made her want to tell him. "My mother never made it to Genoa. She died of diphtheria in Nebraska Territory on the crossing from Pennsylvania." Helena pictured the monument Father had staked into the hard prairie earth, made from the wood of Mother's prized organ. They'd piled flat stones on the mound to keep the wolves away. As the Conestoga rolled on without Mother, the forlorn marker and mutilated remains of the lacquered instrument were a blur in Helena's tear-filled vision.

It was the loneliest land for a grave.

No one understood the devastation Helena had felt leaving her mother there with the scattered skeletons of animals. Not even Father, who'd never spoken a word of love to his wife, but had broken down and wept for forgiveness at her burial site because he'd made her go on a journey she hadn't wanted to. That night he drank himself into a great state of inebriation.

Were it not for Helena, her mother would have refused to leave New Providence. But Helena had done something that forced her mother into giving up the home that made her happy.

Mother had taken care of Helena when she'd needed her. But Helena, despite unfailing hours of effort and energy, hadn't been able to save her mother. Buffeted by the winds on the western trail, Johanna Gray's frail body broke. She'd been a woman of culture and refinement, but the travel made her hollow-eyed, tired and discouraged. Helena would never forget the look in her mother's eyes when they first saw the plains of endless grass. Without a word, she stood very still and looked slowly around her. Then something within her seemed to give way, and she sank upon the ground. She buried her face in her hands and sat that way for a long moment without moving or speaking. Never before had Helena seen her mother give way to despair.

Nine days later, they buried her.

Helena didn't want to think about her mother anymore. Instead, she asked Carrigan, "Where are your mother and sister?"

"Red Springs, last I knew."

"You don't correspond with them?"

He gave her a dubious scowl. "Now, how would I do that?"

"A letter."

"Before this town was here, there was no way to post one."

"There is now."

Carrigan fixed his gaze on the stars. "Been too many years to start up writing."

"But what if they think you're dead?"

"I've been dead for a long time, only my body just doesn't know it."

His cryptic statement sounded ordinary to Helena when it should have made her pale. She never used to think about dying. But seeing how fleeting life could be had made Helena aware that every moment on earth deprived people of a portion of life and advanced them a step toward the grave. When she was five, she thought her mother and father would live forever. That she and Emilie would never grow up and be old. Until her father sat her down and explained mortality. She hadn't wanted to believe there was a gate in Heaven for her to walk through and had cried. It was only after she first experienced death—one of the Sully girls had drowned—that Helena accepted the truth. What Father hadn't explained was what it meant to lose everything dear to your heart and feel like your soul was dead, only you were still breathing.

Helena knew exactly how Carrigan felt.

Fingering the hay beneath her hand, Helena absently twirled a piece. "What are you going to do on the land when I turn it over to you at the end of the six months?"

"Same as always. Sit and be alone."

Helena looked at him. "But do you really want to?"

"Really want to what?"

"Be alone?"

Carrigan kept his eyes forward. "Obsi's there to keep me company."

At the sound of his name, Obsi came. For the first time, he went to Helena and laid his chin on her knees for her to scratch him. She'd always been watchful of the dog, but now she put her hand in his fur and gently stroked his ear.

"Where did you get the furnishings in your cabin?"

"People leave things behind when they attempt to pass over that mountain. It's not as easily conquered as they think." Carrigan turned his head in her direction. "Why do you ask about being alone?"

"Something happened to you to make you run

away." Her voice lowered. "That's why you're alone. Because you're afraid."

His gaze riveted to hers. "I'm not afraid of anything."

"You're afraid of yourself."

"What makes you such an authority?"

"Because I'm doing the same thing, only I can't leave my sister. So I stay and feel alone even though others are around me." After the words were out, she couldn't believe she'd made such a confession to Carrigan, of all people.

Carrigan stared at her for an eternity without speaking. Then he lifted his hand to her hair, and she involuntarily froze. Obsi nudged her fingers with his cold, wet nose, but she couldn't move. When Carrigan withdrew his arm, he held a strand of alfalfa he'd plucked from her hair. "Looks like you've been rolling in the hay."

His lack of any outward emotion or comment that verified he'd heard her compelled Helena to say, "You are afraid. Admit it."

"Fear doesn't know me."

"You're lying."

His work-toughened fingertip slipped across the curve of her cheek. "Seems we're going to be accusing each other of that. Maybe we better stop fooling ourselves."

Her pulse tripped. She knew what he was implying and what was to come. She couldn't go through with kissing him again. Not if she wanted to keep her objectives from getting clouded by irrational feelings that served no purpose.

As his head came closer to hers, she tried to stop him. "Don't. You're going to leave, so there's no point to this."

"But I'm here now."

"In six months you'll be gone and I'll be alone again."

"You said you were already alone." He caught her

chin in his fingers. "So am I." Then he brought her mouth to his in a show of arrogance that announced he didn't care what she said.

The kiss wasn't demanding and burning like the time before. His lips were lingering and lazy, coaxing her out of her demur.

"I want to see what your hair looks like without a net or braid." The vibration of his murmured voice on her mouth flared through her. "Is it as curly as the little ringlets that tease your brow?"

"Yes . . ." The mastery of his kiss was drugging, making her languid and immersed in her rioting senses.

"Take it down for me."

If she did, her resolution would come tumbling down with the curls. She'd be defenseless and unprotected by her dispassionate facade. "I can't."

His fingers worked through her confined hair, massaging her scalp and easing the tension that enveloped her. When he found the whalebone comb that kept her curls firmly arranged in a net, she felt his smile sweetening her lips. "Then I can." The comb's teeth were slid free, and the heaviness of her hair was released to her shoulders as soon as the net was free. If she sat up, the remainder would flow to her waist.

Carrigan put his hand on her shoulder and pulled her next to him, pressing her breasts into the hard strength of his chest. The fullness of her hair curtained them, falling onto his shoulders in a seductive ornament of her femininity. If she had suppressed her first desire to kiss him, she wouldn't be encountering the yearnings that followed.

It wasn't of her own accord she surrendered. She knew she should resist him, but couldn't when his mouth worshiped hers. The longing to be needed by somebody overrode her better judgment. She so wanted to be loved and be in love. To be the wife she should have been. Would have been if only . . .

The tip of Carrigan's tongue stroked the seam of

her lips, and she gave him intimate entrance. A low groan flowed from her throat, dissolving against him. He brushed her mouth with his tongue as his fingers bunched her hair into his large fists. She heard his intake of breath as he brought his face to the bundle of curls in his grasp.

"Your hair smells like rosebuds before they petal." He kissed the line of her jaw, then higher to her ear where he whispered, "Fresh and sweet. Just like from a summer garden. Long after I leave, the scent of roses will haunt me."

Rolling her back into the rustling bed, he put the bulk of his weight on his knees, which were on either side of her thighs. With the iridescent skylight behind him keeping his face in near shadow, he looked bigger, broader, and more powerful. "There's no gown that would become you more than your hair. Even in your weeds, you can't hide the allure of it." He dipped his head to steal a timeless kiss that sent a thrill through her trembling body.

When his hand rose to the swell of her breast, he deepened the kiss, snuffing the sharp intake of her breath. Her heartbeat throbbed in her ears as his fingers discovered the soft curve beneath his palm. The decision to relax and sate the need building within her came as he teased her nipple into a peak despite the layers of fabric comprising her bodice. Instinctively she arched toward him, casting all caution to the wind. She told herself making love with Carrigan would be a purely sensual experience and nothing more. When he was gone, she could forget him. She could forget everything.

Giving in to abandon, Helena circled her arms around his neck. She kissed him back with all the emotions raging in her heart and soul. Their breaths fused together in hot, moist clouds that filled the night with sighs.

Obsi gave a tight bark, and had Helena been alert,

she would have realized someone was approaching. It was Carrigan who tore his mouth free and broke the kiss. He put her at arm's length just as eye-opening kerosene light spilled onto them.

Surprise widened Eliazer's eyes at seeing Helena and Carrigan lying wantonly in the haystack. "Ah . . . I'm . . . sorry, Miss Lena," he mumbled, embarrassment wavering in his tone. His posture was stooped. The strain on his portly figure was a visible discomfort. "I couldn't sleep not knowing about Esmeralda. . . ."

Carrigan stood and extended a hand to Helena. Overcome, she could only stare in speechless horror. Reluctantly she took his offering and allowed him to pull her to her feet. Her heartbeat was frantic, her face surely a hue of sunset red. Once she was standing, she hastily shoved her hair behind her back and brushed the hay from her skirt. "I checked on her less than an hour ago and she was progressing, but the labor was slow."

"I'm going to go in."

Helena nodded and watched the wire-framed lantern in Eliazer's grasp bob with his awkward steps.

Unable to look Carrigan in the eye, Helena composed her racing pulse and willed herself to regain her detached composure. With the cool night air embracing her, the feelings of wanting she'd felt in Carrigan's arms swiftly scattered. Hard reality set in. So did the shame. If she'd lain with him, he would have asked questions. Questions she wasn't prepared to answer.

Needing to flee from the complications Carrigan's presence evoked in her, Helena made a move to follow Eliazer. Carrigan put his hand on her shoulder and turned her to face him. "Now who's the one running away?"

"I have to see Esmeralda—"

"Stay." His eyes were compelling, his voice a husky whisper.

"I can't." She bit her lip, tasting Carrigan on her mouth. "And after the six months are up, you won't stay either."

The winds moaned like a human wail against Bayard's office window. Dust clouds blew across Main Street and its intersections. They flitted in rolling billows of hats, tin signs, sagebrush, shingles, and doormats. Vacant lots were stirred into a batter freckled with dirt particles and weeds. The rushing howl that shook the walls and roofs of businesses didn't let up long into the night.

Bayard checked his watch and noted the time of three-twenty. Calling it a night—or rather, morning—he left the Metropolitan Saloon with the cheer of gin warming his blood. Hunched over in his dusty coat, his eyes blinking against the grit, he walked to his modest residence on Poplar Street.

At the corner of Main and Nixon, he paused in the shadows of Mayhew's butcher shop. Across the street was Gray's station. The stockade gates were thrown open, the white skeleton of an ox head on the high bar above giving off an eerie shine. A darkly clothed figure moved through the opening, his tall shape recognizable to Bayard.

The man disappeared for unmeasurable seconds, then horses materialized. They were herded out of the stockyard by encouraging slaps on their rumps. Bayard counted twelve head and one new foal.

The wind muted the sounds of the horses with its shrieks as the mustangs impulsively ran up Nixon Street and headed for the wilderness of the Sierras. When the last one vanished from view, the tall figure closed the gates and was gone before Bayard could approach him.

Eliazer blazed into the kitchen with perspiration circling the underarms of his shirtsleeves. With his hand bracing his lower back, he announced, "Someone let the horses out." Then he looked directly at Carrigan. "All of them but yours."

The three at the table gazed across their breakfast plates at Carrigan. Helena felt a sickening dread work its way up her spine.

"What do you mean? Is the gate closed?" she asked, unable to believe that all twelve horses and one colt had broken loose.

"The gate is closed and the stable is shut tighter than a miser's purse." Eliazer kept staring at Carrigan. "Someone had to have opened the stockade gate, the stable doors, and the stalls in order for this to have happened."

Carrigan shoved his plate away in a jerking motion. "Are you accusing me of something?"

"It is suspect that all the horses are gone but yours."

Helena put her hand to her forehead, where she felt an instant headache blossom. Her horses . . . gone. It couldn't be true. She needed those animals. Without them, she had no means to stay in business.

"Why didn't we hear anything?" Helena said, panic in her voice. *No, no, no!* There had to be a mistake! "My window looks out at the yard; I should have heard something."

"The wind, Miss Lena," Eliazer reminded. "When the zephyrs blow, they distort sounds. Whoever let them out must have known the wind would disguise the noise."

Helena's heart stopped for agonizing seconds. Was it possible Carrigan could have done it? She didn't want to believe he was capable of trying to ruin her, but if she didn't have a station to run, he wouldn't have a reason for being here. . . . No . . . no! He couldn't have . . . not Carrigan. Not to her. But still . . . "Why are only your horses in the stables?" she asked, anger, disappointment, and hurt clashing in her tone.

Carrigan pushed out of his chair and glared at her. "I want the land you promised me. Letting out horses would be a sure way not to get it."

"What land?" Emilie asked, but her query was disregarded.

"You can't deny it's suspect that only your horses are left," Helena said.

The fire of his temper pulsed at Carrigan's neck. "You can think whatever you want."

"If that dog had been outside, he would have barked," Helena shot back. She was placing blame where it was the easiest to pin, even knowing her accusation was unfair without concrete proof against him. "This is why animals don't belong inside."

"If I did rustle those horses out, Obsi wouldn't have barked at me. So you can think that over." Collecting his hat, Carrigan smashed it on his head. "But no one has thought to go after the horses before they get too far into the high country I caught them in."

Carrigan walked past Helena and down the hall. The fall of his boots hit the stairs hard as he climbed them.

Helena was so upset, she couldn't move. Ignacia, who had departed from the kitchen in the heat of the argument, returned.

"Miss Lena, Judge Kimball was knocking on the store window. He says he needs to speak with you. I let him in."

Putting her hand on her brow, Helena waved Ignacia off. "I can't talk to him now."

"He said it was urgent."

Raising her chin, Helena choked on her sigh.

Emilie set her napkin on her plate. "What land was Carrigan talking about, Lena?"

"I can't go into that at the moment, Emilie. I have more pressing things on my mind." Helena left the kitchen and went to the store, her nerves unraveling. What was she going to do? No horses meant she'd have to shut the station down. Temporarily. Because she'd get her old horses back, or she'd get new ones. There was no way she was quitting. But in the meantime, she'd have to send a message to Friday's station and the Carson City station, telling the masters their riders were going to need to keep the same horses through Genoa. The loss in revenue was going to gum up her finances worse than they already were.

"Judge Kimball," Helena greeted quickly as she went behind the counter. "I don't mean to be rude, but I've got a problem that needs my immediate attention."

Bayard doffed his hat. "I can guess what it is."

"Can you?" She was in no mood for games, her thoughts tripping over one another to oversee everything that needed to be done.

"Your horses have disappeared."

Their eyes met as surprise ran through Helena. "How do you know about my horses?"

"I saw who let them out."

Her stomach clenched tight. She wanted to know the answer, and she didn't. "Who?"

"Carrigan."

Helena had to grip the counter for support, her worst fears confirmed. "You saw him? When?"

"Last night when I was leaving the saloon. I saw a figure herding them through the gates."

"Why didn't you wake me?" she blurted.

"I was rather inebriated and in no condition to knock on your door."

Welcome doubts set upon her. "If you were so drunk, how can you be sure it was Carrigan you saw?"

"He was the same height. The same build. There are no other men in Genoa who have his composition." Bayard's expression looked truly regretful. "I'm sorry. The horses fled so quickly that even if I'd come to you right away, you couldn't have traveled at night to round them up."

Helena was numb with increasing shock.

"Horse thievery is a hanging offense, Helena,"

Bayard informed her gravely. "I could take him into custody right now."

"No." An oddly primitive warning sounded in her brain. She didn't want Carrigan dead—even if he did steal her horses. There had to be an explanation. Carrigan denied his guilt, but at the same time, Bayard had identified him. She'd known and trusted Bayard for years. He wouldn't lie to her.

"Thank you, Bayard," Helena said woodenly. She went to the door and unlocked it. "I appreciate you telling me. But I'll handle the matter on my own."

Bayard glared at her as if she'd lost her mind. "Helena, you don't realize what an error you're making. The man has committed a serious crime. He should be hanged. You need to be safeguarded from him."

Wanting desperately to believe Bayard could be mistaken, Helena put off making any rash judgments. "I don't want to make a decision I'll regret later." She opened the door. "I need some time to think things through. But I really do need to see about getting my horses back before it's too late."

Bayard was barely on the boardwalk when she closed and locked the door behind him. Helena picked up her skirts and sprinted up the stairs. She found Carrigan in his room, packing his satchel.

"I want to make one thing clear up front," she said, her breath rapid. "I'm not a woman who craves heroics. In fact, I prefer my life to be quiet and orderly. I like having a routine that I go through each day, knowing what's expected of me from sunrise to sundown. But in this instance, I'm compelled to leave the norm. I have no choice." She lifted her shoulders. "I'm going with you."

"The hell you are."

"I am. I need those horses back the quickest way possible. Two riders would do the job faster."

"Send Eliazer with me."

"Even if he could tolerate being in the saddle, I

wouldn't let him go. I can't leave my sister here without a man's protection. Eliazer stays."

Carrigan stared Helena down, but she was unflinching.

"I'm not a physically breakable woman. I can handle a horse a lot better than I handle a buckboard."

"You don't trust me to go alone."

She wouldn't lie to him. Despite the probability he had lied to her. "Not entirely, no."

Tossing a pair of trousers into his satchel, he snorted, "At least you're honest about it."

"I can be honest in a pinch."

"So can I." His green eyes bored into her. "I'm leaving in fifteen minutes. You want to go, be ready."

Chapter

➔ 9 ◄

Carrigan held a light rein on Boomerang as he steered the horse through the two-foot-high sagebrush. Keeping as lax a hold on his poor disposition was something he had to constantly remind himself to do. Helena making it clear she thought of him as a suspect in the emancipation of her horses had put him in a foul mood he couldn't shrug off.

He could feel her blue eyes on him. Steadily. Through the remote ramparts, ribs, and gorges. Her unwavering gaze harassed his irritable side. He was close to yanking her out of the saddle and shaking some common sense into her. She'd undermined his integrity. The dark and treacherous reputation she thought he had was a figment of her imagination. Character was something that lived inside him, and he wasn't the sort of man who double-dealed. At least not without just cause. And in this case, there was no reason for him to commit the crime.

If she put as much energy into objectively piecing together the whys for the horses' disappearance, she wouldn't be stewing over his possible involvement.

Somebody apparently wanted to shut her down other than the obvious two, Lewis and Wyatt, who had been taken care of without further confrontations. There was someone else. An unseen party. Her father's death had been no random robbery shooting. Carrigan had come to that conclusion not an hour out of town. The logical choice for a suspect would be a person who could benefit by Helena not having the Express station. But Carrigan knew from past experiences, logical choices were never logical. If answers were simple, questions wouldn't spring up.

Obsi ran ahead, a blur of black through the drab scrub. Boomerang would have spooked if he were a young green-broke with unpredictability still in him. But the strawberry roan had seasoned and wasn't quite as reckless as he'd been four years ago.

Lifting his nose, Obsi read the scent messages in the air—most notably the gray squirrel clinging to the side of a pine and noisily scolding their intrusion. The dog snorted, as if trying to discern food, friend, or foe. Low on his paws, Obsi took off for the upcoming ridge, apparently deciding the squirrel wasn't worth his trouble.

Bunchgrass grew between the crevices of rock and sprouted through sand, while greasewood gave way to a dense growth of dry manzanita chaparral. Carrigan knew this land well, having hunted not only game, but horses, in the varying terrain.

"Are you sure you're headed in the right direction?" Helena asked. "We've been on this trail for over an hour with no signs of my horses."

Carrigan glanced behind him. "You want to lead this search?"

Sitting astride Traveler, Helena met his gaze with one just as imposing as his. "You know I don't have the knowledge."

"Then quit bothering me." Carrigan faced forward, his legs hugging Boomerang's girth snugger than he should have. He was still trying to register the significance behind the Sharps rifle Helena had housed in a scabbard over her pommel. Had she brought the weapon to threaten him? If so, he could tell her she was in serious trouble. A gun barrel aimed at him would only make him want to avenge himself. Woman or not. He'd tussle her to the ground if she so much as lifted that Sharps his way.

The wind rose with the altitude. Carrigan's hat shaded his eyes, the wide brim a welcome respite against a sun he'd been looking sideways into for nearly a year. Given the strain in his and Helena's supposedly cut-and-dried relationship, he hated to admit he would have been half-blind by the sunlight without the hat. Surveying the slide damage to the north where an unsightly scar upon the mountain's front left a vast, treeless patch, he noted the landmark hadn't been there the last time he'd come up this way.

Conversation between them ceased as the high, mountainous country required a rider's full concentration. Carrigan was glad for the quiet to give his thoughts over to reflections other than the woman whose stare into his back was becoming a real grievance on his part. The sun-bright summit reminded him of his boyhood. Of the high hill in Red Springs that he and his brothers climbed to the top of to mingle with the sky.

Jesus, he'd been eight or so. It was the year his mother inherited some horses from a relative of hers. His father sold most of them off to support his liquor habit, and his poor business sense left the family at the mercy of creditors. They'd had to open their small house up for boarders. His mother never lived down the shame of it.

Willie, Robert, and he used to sneak off when the old man got roaring drunk and was in a mind to unleash his belt on their backsides. On the property, there was a small creek to play in with cutbanks some fifteen feet deep. They would escape to its shore and tie hooks to twine and harpoon a piece of salt pork to catch crawfish. They'd build up a good fire, cook and eat the tails. The other hunting skills they'd developed were gathering the mourning doves that didn't nest very high. Pilfering the fat squabs just about to leave the nest was as easy as throwing a two-day calf.

The three of them had a collection of small reptiles and animal skulls decorating the room they shared. Their sister, Sarah, would raise holy hell when they took a mind to tease her by putting rodent bones beneath her pillow.

But all that was before the Mexican War had gotten in the way of good times, and he'd moved on afterward to pursue the other avenues he could take to mold himself into a man. In his absence, death had taken both his brothers.

The heartsick chord that suddenly struck Carrigan was unexpected. Lost years of his youth should have been something he accepted by now. Childhood days behind him. What was gone . . . was gone.

Carrigan began searching for signs when he reached an overhanging, wall-like ridge of rock that projected from the earth. It had been here he'd first found traces of the herd from which most of Helena's stock came.

"Do you see something?" Helena's hopeful query went wasted on him.

Ignoring her, Carrigan dismounted and walked a small area until he found horseshoe imprints in the soft-rock ground. No wild band would have been shod. Crouching down, he ran his fingertips over a clean print. "Which one's your lead mare?"

"Columbiana."

"She's been here." The deeper depth and defined impression of the shoe said it was new iron. Carrigan stood and gazed at Helena. "But the track isn't fresh. Your horses have gone farther than I wanted."

Helena met his eyes, her face protected by the brim of a straw bonnet. She didn't employ a sidesaddle as he would have guessed. But Helena was no ordinary woman. When she had an objective, she took the most prudent course to achieve her goal. A lady's saddle would have slowed her down. But ever the lady, she hadn't donned britches.

She straddled the horse, the fullness of her dark-checked skirt bunched on Traveler's bay rump without the hindrance of a wooden hoop. Her slim legs were exposed only to her knees where the weave of her black stockings, and just barely a hint of white petticoat, was available for his view. Too bad it wasn't more. But like him, she'd forgone a heavy coat. A short cape covered her arms and shoulders, with just enough of her enticing form on display to distract him.

"You can still get them back, can't you?" Helena asked with a faint note of urgency.

"I got them once before," he replied, not liking her tone. "I can get them again."

With a fluid swing of his leg, he mounted Boomerang and gave the horse a light nudge in the ribs. Despite the chilly air, the sun beat down on him in simmering rays. His annoyance increased. Her doubt ate at him. Now she was questioning his capability of rounding up the runaway animals.

For the next several hours, Carrigan pushed Helena to ride hard. Somewhat to his irritation, she proved she knew what she was doing in a saddle, keeping up with him and guiding Traveler with a precise hand. She didn't complain about navigating the grueling slopes and precarious ledges, nor did she look the worse for wear. In fact, he'd never seen her look better. The wide-open space seemed to do her good, bringing forth a slight color to the bridge of her nose where the sun caught her skin when she lifted her gaze skyward every now and then to assess the time.

He stopped on occasion to sparingly water the horses, and at noon so they could eat a quick meal. Less than fifteen minutes after Helena brought out a round of bread, cheese, and pumpkin chips, he told her to saddle up. With narrowed eyes, he watched her for signs of fatigue. None were apparent in her walk to indicate her behind was saddle-sore. The only difference in the sway of her skirt was, she'd forgone a crinoline for the journey. He wanted her to feel the effects of the trail because she didn't trust him. And somewhere in the back of his mind, he chose to make her trip a little hellish for it.

Carrigan pursued the multiple tracks over the northwestern rim of the Sierras. The rock beneath his horse was crumbly like a baked potato, making travel cautious and slow. Just before sunset, he took a high mesa where the hoofprints ran upward and disappeared. Helena reined in tight next to him, following his gaze to the valley below. A gathering of solid-colored horses were cropping meadow grass, but they were too far away for Carrigan to number.

"Do you think they're all there?" Helena asked, her voice exuding optimism.

Turning toward her, Carrigan noticed her lips were slightly parched from the wind. The only sign of her discomfort. But rather than feeling satisfaction, he wanted to caress her mouth with balm to ease its dryness. "I reckon they are. But no way to tell until we get closer."

The light breeze was against them, and Carrigan wove his way through the towering pine until he was within counting distance. On a visual estimation, there were all twelve head plus the furry colt Esmeralda had delivered the day before.

Helena's impatience had her giving Traveler some lead. "Let's go get them."

"Not now." Carrigan bristled, tugging on her cape to keep her back. "I have no place to put them."

Obsi made a low growl in his throat, his eyes fixed on a magpie pecking at a nut.

"Obsi." Carrigan warned the dog, who went still, but continued to emit a noise from deep in his throat. "Stay and be quiet."

The horses picked up on the subdued sound. They

lifted their proud heads and discovered him and Helena in the brush. Columbiana arched her tail and took off in a run. The herd galloped behind her.

Carrigan urged Boomerang after them in a wide circle, not as a chase, but to see where the thundering mustangs would go. The animals only traveled about a mile or so before halting. They rolled their noses and waved their manes.

Helena drew up to Carrigan, winded and with the ribbon of her hat around her neck. The hat itself had fallen down her back. "What are they doing?" she whispered as curls teased her brow.

"Sizing us up."

"They know who I am. Can't I just call them?"

"Isn't likely they'll come." Carrigan leaned his forearm on the saddle horn. He felt the stretch in the sleeve of his red mackinaw jacket. "You didn't have them long enough for them to forget about the good life. No saddles, no riders . . ." He lifted his mouth in a sarcastic smile. "No geldings. That flashback alone would make me run for the high road."

Helena saw no humor in his remark. "You said you need a place to put them. Where? What do we do?"

"Nothing tonight."

"Nothing," she mumbled incredulously.

"No." Carrigan wheeled Boomerang around. "We're going to make camp. Our horses aren't fresh enough to give any of them a run tonight. Besides, I've got to find a spot that I can make a corral. Don't know if all those horses will take a string or not. I'd rather be prepared if they don't."

The sun was getting low, and the breeze diminished as they made their way over the back hills. Clouds of every color from the deepest purple to the palest pink hosted the twilight sky. In the midst of the puffs, the sun sank in a halo of bloodred light. Over the next ridge, Lake Tahoe flooded the panorama. It looked like a golden sheet between the deep gray banks and clumps of spruce.

He heard Helena's intake of breath as she got her first glimpse of the picture. The lake was a vast oval walled in by a rim that towered above it. The water lay there with the shadows of mountains brilliant upon its still surface.

"You've never seen it before?" he asked over his shoulder.

Helena shook her head. "My father intended to take us girls, but Emilie doesn't like camping and didn't want to come. It seemed like there never was a spare moment for just Father and me to go."

Carrigan kneed Boomerang to higher ground were the grass wasn't too turfy. A wall of rock presented itself in a natural indentation caused by the wind.

"We'll camp here." He swung his legs down and began to unload the bacon, sack of beans, small bag of coffee, sugar, flour, some tin cups, a coffeepot, and frying pan he'd carefully packed in canvas. Helena's horse was carrying the hackamores and ropes, as well as an ax and saw in case he had to make an enclosure.

Carrigan made no offer to help Helena remove the gear from her horse. He tended to his own, unsaddling and ridding Boomerang of his sweat blanket. From a glance, he could see Helena was doing the same. He had no qualms about her taking good care of Traveler. She was kindhearted toward horses, never abusing or neglecting them. And she was strong, too. It took a great deal of strength to handle the heavy saddle, but she did so without a hard struggle.

As soon as Carrigan had Boomerang picketed for the night near a seep spring and plentiful grass, he set out to gather firewood, keeping within hearing range of where he left Helena. Obsi trotted along, exploring the brush with his muzzle halfway hidden in the grass and leaves. No longer the victim of Helena's stare, Carrigan walked at ease. But the night was going to be a real short one if she kept on with her dedicated vigil on his person. He'd clue her in quick that no one messed with him.

When Carrigan returned, he noted Helena had lined up all the equipment in military rows. Her bedroll—with the Sharps at her saddle pillow—was made as neat as a bakery pie. The waterproof tarp enclosed by a couple of sugans was strategically placed next to where he assumed she wanted the campfire to be. She'd arranged a ring of bleached riverbed rocks.

Carrigan strode into the camp and deposited the rough-barked and twisted boughs of sagebrush into the pit.

"I'll fix supper," Helena offered.

"I can do it." Carrigan preferred to cook the meal himself. He wasn't accustomed to being waited on. Taking his meals with the rest of them at the station without lifting a hand didn't feel right to him. He'd done for himself too long to give up his independence when it came to a skillet. He could hold his own and prepare a passable dish. Years of experimenting, with spices adding flavor to his meat and vegetables, had turned him into a veteran cook. He even bet he knew a few tricks Helena didn't.

Helena put her hands on her hips, the level of her shoulders not so straight as they'd been in the saddle. She was running out of energy. "What should I do?"

"Get me some water." He handed her the coffeepot. "Don't get it from the lake. Use the spring. And maybe you better take that Sharps with you. Wild animals could chew you up." When she made no comment, he added, "That is why you brought the rifle?"

"I brought it for protection." Her expression veiled any thought she was holding. "If something were to happen to you, I'd need to defend myself."

"Nothing's going to happen to me unless you point that gun in my vicinity. Then I can see a problem. Is there one?"

"No."

"I'm glad to hear that."

Without a word, she went off, and he figured they'd cleared up the matter of the Sharps good enough. She knew he wasn't blind to it, so he better not hear the weapon going off for no good reason.

In Helena's absence, Carrigan arranged the wood and struck a matchstick. The end burned azure, then budded into a lusty flame to light the fire. As the wood caught and brightened to a yellow-orange, he grew mesmerized by the fire's beckoning snap. Ghosts of the past rose with the waves of heat. Of its own accord, his mind drifted. He would never understand how Jenny could have wanted death this way . . . by burning. By suffocation and . . .

The crackling pop of dry tinder belching forth had Carrigan cringing. To him, fire was dangerous and cruel, but he wasn't in a position to slight it. His life depended on its heat source. But little sparks grew demons that had the power to assume the figure of a woman. Jenny. For each time the fire's entrancement caught him, he could see her. The visions used to literally cause him to retch with sorrow, but that had passed over the years. Now the fire just preyed on his heart, squeezing his ribs with a fiendish, convulsing smile of glowing red.

"I said, here's your water."

Carrigan slowly lifted his gaze. He had no idea how long Helena had stood there, her hand extended with the coffeepot. Muttering his thanks, he took the handle from her.

Over the next half hour, he formulated a simple but palatable plate of skillet cakes with portions of the hickory-flavored bacon. With Helena contributing some of the cheese Ignacia had sent, and piping hot coffee, the mixture filled and satisfied his empty stomach.

Helena ate without saying a word, her gaze periodically taking in the scenery. From their spot, they had an open view of the lake. As the stars came out, the diamondlike points were reflected off the water.

After supper, Carrigan cleaned up and covered a skillet of pinto beans with water to soak overnight for tomorrow's supper. That completed, he leaned into a boulder still warm from the departed sun and smoked meditatively in the sedate hush. With the mollifying whispers of trees calling to one another, he could forget about his agreement with Helena and the months he had left on their marriage contract. But he couldn't forget about the haystack. His thoughts always went back to that night.

After Helena had retreated for the stables practically on Eliazer's heels, Carrigan had left as well. Needing a chilling bracer to douse his hot state of arousal, he'd combed his hair away from his face with icy water from the basin at the back door. He'd been consumed by Helena, wanting her, but all the while he'd told himself he could be an impartial participant. The act of sex was nothing more than the gratification of his body. He could be detached and think solely of the pleasure copulation brought a man.

Carrigan flicked the butt of his cigarette into the fire with a frown. There was no sadder contradiction for his sorry line of thought. With Helena, nothing came without complexities.

"How are you going to build a corral?"

Helena's question registered in his musings, and he looked at her. She sat on top of her bedroll, one of the wool-batted quilts over her bent knees. The fire's gleam highlighted her coiled hair, making it shine like new coins out of a rich man's pocket.

"Don't think I'll build one just yet."

"But you said——"

"I changed my mind." The clink of his spurs intruded on his words as he straightened his leg. He one-handed the fasteners, undoing each strap and setting them aside. "I'm going after Columbiana first.

152

The others may surrender more easily once they see I've got their leader."

"If that doesn't work?"

"I'll make the enclosure."

Sipping coffee to a noisy serenade of coyotes, neither commented further on the subject of horses. Carrigan had his own thoughts competing for his preoccupation, and from the roundabout interrogation he'd gotten from Helena, so did she. That blanket of distrust she had for him could very well have kept her warm until morning.

After a spell, he banked the fire for the night. When he glanced at Helena, he saw she'd drifted off while half sitting and with the cup in her hand. He went to her and took the unfinished coffee, flinging the cooled contents into the grass. Then he gathered the edge of her sugan and brought it to her chin. Before he could walk away, he paused and stared at her.

The sweep of her eyelashes shadowed her cheeks. Exhausted, the adventurous woman had found well-earned sleep. Seeing her so peaceful, and without her courageous expressions, he wondered when she ever did anything for herself. People needed moments to appreciate their good qualities and do something they enjoyed. He knew Helena loved horses, but that wasn't a womanly thing to take pleasure in. Country dances, new dresses and ribbons, and tea socials were the choice frivolities of females. Why had she deprived herself of such diversions? Of letting her sister grow up?

It would seem the intricacies of Helena's past rivaled his own. Had she ever been in love? Who was the man who'd given her the kissing lesson? Not knowing the answers was the best way to keep his distance from her. But of late, he found himself trying to figure her out. Trying to understand why she'd hidden herself away behind the counter of a store, and the door of a stable. Of course, he could never fault or condemn her for it. He'd done the very same thing on his mountain.

Unable to leave her as she was, Carrigan pitched the empty cup toward his cooking gear and bent down to arrange her proper. His hands lifted her limp shoulders and slid her down into the warmth of her bedroll. Saddles made poor pillow cushions, so he shrugged out of his mackinaw, wadded the fabric, and placed it beneath her head. The silkiness of her hair teased his fingers, but he left the pinned curls alone. The next time he took down the thick tresses, he wanted her wearing absolutely nothing else.

Tucking in the quilt that encompassed her, he stood back and continued to watch her sleep for several minutes more. She hadn't made a sound when he moved her, and he didn't think anything could intrude on her deep slumber. If only he could deaden his mind in such a way.

Carrigan left Helena and settled into his own pallet. Obsi soon made himself at home in the covers.

In due time, Carrigan felt himself getting tired enough to sleep. The shore's lapping surf had a lulling sound he found soothing. But it was difficult to get into that dreamless state when he was frequently disturbed by Obsi, who stretched and braced his feet against the length of Carrigan's back. The dog shoved, grunted, and being relatively warm and cozy beneath the blanket, he pawed Carrigan to express his contented comfort.

Just as Carrigan was finally dozing, Obsi began dreaming of the chase—no doubt a heated pursuit of the magpie. He tugged and bit at Carrigan's hair while barking softly in his ear. When an elbow nudging his belly didn't cease the dog's twitches, Carrigan snapped his eyes open with disgust.

For a long time after, he charted the tortoiselike movement of the three-quarter moon as it inched toward a morning sky. He had many regrets in his life. But foremost at this moment was having a dog with spiny stickers in his fur lying next to him instead of Helena.

The next morning, Helena and Carrigan ate breakfast in a mutual quiet, then left camp just after daylight streaked the sky in a swath of russet. Refreshed after a night of near-uninterrupted sleep, Helena felt up for the long and hard ride ahead.

Carrigan covered ground quickly, heading toward the same mesa as yesterday. Her gaze kept falling on his broad back, and the crown of his gray hat where his hair flowed underneath the brim. Sometime in the middle of the night, he'd put her blankets on and seen to it she was snugly inside her bedroll. She barely remembered falling asleep.

To think he could be so generous toward her, yet sabotage her station, was perplexing and very upsetting. Wayward suspicions continued to occupy her mind. But they were less and less aimed at Carrigan. More were directed toward Bayard. Not that she thought him responsible for her trouble in any way. Bayard wasn't a disreputable character. He wouldn't commit robbery. Especially not against her.

But some nearly intangible feeling that resembled a deep-seated loyalty to Carrigan wasn't wholly convinced by Bayard's story. His account of Carrigan's guilt hadn't won her over as it immediately should have. Uncertainty niggled at her. Before she passed a final verdict, she would watch Carrigan closely. Size him up and put him through the challenge of regaining her lost horses—but not challenge him with her Sharps. That had been a bad idea . . . and an unnecessary one because he'd seen through her plan like glass.

It was almost high noon when they cleared the foothills and Carrigan began to track the prints that were reasonably clear. Over the edge of the mesa the grassland was vacant, and Helena's heart dropped in horrified panic.

Her voice faltered when she asked, "Where are they?"

Carrigan adjusted the brim of his hat, keeping his eyes in gray shadow. His mouth was discernible, as was the slightly crooked line of his nose. A brown tan deepened the color of his skin. "Probably over that next ridge. This might have been their late grazing spot."

At least as they progressed through the valley, Helena was able to identify the tiny prints of Esmeralda's colt. Just beyond the edge of grass, a line of trees marched in almost a succinct break, as if they'd been intentionally planted that way. Shading themselves beneath the resplendent poplars, the herd sighted them. Rather than bust out of the mottled leaf canopy, they slowly started on with ambiguous reservation. Columbiana led them, the dun mare raising her tail and throwing her ears back. She obviously intended to take them to a more peaceful territory.

"Turn around," Carrigan cautioned while reining back. With an easy command, he wheeled Boomerang in the opposite direction of the herd.

"Why are we leaving?"

"To have dinner."

"Dinner?" she parroted incredulously. "The horses are right here. We can get Columbiana."

"I want her to think we can't."

Carrigan trotted away, Obsi running alongside the strawberry roan. Helena had no choice but to follow. She was fuming, not at all understanding Carrigan's rationale. The horses were here. They were for the taking, and he was going to ignore them. Did he intend to get them at all? She wondered about his involvement anew.

Ahead, a south-sided bluff was washed in sunlight. Carrigan rode to the top of it and dismounted. Tethering his horse, he stood at the edge of the precipice and smiled. She couldn't figure out why. There was nothing funny. It was only after she'd wound Traveler's reins around a scrub and walked to Carrigan that she could see what he was so smug about.

They had a perfect view of the herd. Columbiana kept her head high, nose lifted to scent them. But she couldn't. The wind was on their side. After a while, she lay down on the grass and began to roll as if she hadn't a care in the world. Helena wanted to yell at her their friendship was over. When she thought of all the sugar lumps, carrots, and apples she'd treated that horse to . . .

"Who does she think she is?" Helena said under her breath.

Carrigan let out a low-pitched laugh, as if he were in on a joke she wasn't. "She's a female. And I'm going to best her."

Helena thought this over while they fed their horses a small amount of oats and took in a meal themselves. But Helena was too excited to eat much, even though Carrigan said she'd be sorry for it later when her stomach was growling. In the early part of the after-noon, they remounted, and Carrigan moved into motion.

"I want you to stay back," he cautioned while slipping on a pair of rawhide gloves. "If they stam-pede, they'll run you down and kill you."

She said nothing.

"You hear me, Helena?" he repeated in a stern tone that bristled. "I said to stay out of the way."

"I will," she snipped.

"You do as I say." Then he gave the dog a talking to. "Obsi. Sit."

The dog slowly lowered into position, his tongue lagging to one side of his mouth in a brisk pant. For most of the day, he'd been hunting lizards and birds.

Carrigan sat taller and unhooked a sturdy lariat he'd draped over his saddle horn. With great dex-terity, he fashioned a big loop. Helena watched him with interest, noting the efficient manner in which he readied himself. He knew exactly what he was doing, his movements precise.

As a current of air ruffled his sleeves, she couldn't help being favorably influenced by his showy expertise. He cut a dashing picture in his buffalo-hide chaps of a shotgun style with fringe down the sides, striped vest that hung open in the breeze, and a blue cotton shirt. Drawing the bead upward on the thongs of his hat, he anchored the moderate crown firmly on his head.

"I'll bring her back with me," he promised while putting a double half hitch in his rope, securing the end to his saddle horn.

Rather than approach the herd quietly, Carrigan bore down on them full speed. His strong arm raised, he shook out the rawhide rope. He made a whooping noise and whistled. This put the herd in disarray. They churned the earth with their hooves and took off running at a stiff-legged pace. Riding close as they charged, he kept right on top of Columbiana, calling on Boomerang for all he had.

Faster than Helena could see, Carrigan had the rope around the mare's neck right behind her ears where she would choke quickly and wouldn't pull as much as if he'd caught her low on the throat.

Obsi began to bark excitedly, but didn't defy his master's order.

Columbiana began pulling and kicking in a little circle, trying to get loose from the rope. But the more she pulled, the more she choked. Helena put her hand to her throat, feeling sympathy for the struggling mare.

Carrigan jumped off his horse, dug his spurs into the ground, and held the rope tight while the horse fought him. With his free hand, he reached for the hackamore he'd slip-tied to his saddle.

Pretty soon Columbiana lost all the air she had and fell. He yelled at Boomerang to give him slack, then rushed up to the mare's head and loosened the rope so she could get air. Before she attempted to regain her feet, he slipped the hackamore on her and fastened the throat latch. Then swiftly he took the lead rope on the hackamore and hurried back to Boomerang, where he untied the lariat from the horn.

Columbiana caught her breath and came up pawing, those soft ears of hers thrown all the way back to California. Carrigan swung into his saddle as she tried to run. He let Boomerang go a distance with her for a few lengths, then he turned her around in the direction where Helena waited.

Obsi wiggled, his tail swishing back and forth. He gave a few frantic barks, then rose to all fours as Carrigan progressed with a triumphant grin on his face.

"One down. Eleven and a half left to go," he said, cocksure of himself as he passed her by with a mock salute that had more brass to it than a roomful of high-ranking military officers.

Chapter

⇸ 10 ⇷

Jumping into the lake's freezing water, Carrigan let out a chilled howl. Wearing only duck pants, he disappeared under the blue depths. Ripples ringed the disrupted surface left in his wake. Helena sat on a nearby rock and observed him, thinking he was an idiot to subject himself to such an icy bath. But he'd said he couldn't stand the grit and sweat on his skin, and no inconvenient temperature was going to stop him from getting wet. She would have liked to jump in, too, but wasn't about to strip to her underclothes. As soon as he came out, she planned on freshening up at the water's edge.

Carrigan's head broke the surface. He shook the water from the ends of his long hair with a yell. "It is *cold* in here!" He walked toward her, the broad expanse of his shoulders and chest revealed to her with each step he took. "Throw me the soap."

Helena got off the boulder and found the small bar next to the heap of his discarded clothing. She tossed the cake to him, and he caught it in his left fist.

While he worked the soap into a lather he spread

160

across his skin, she resumed her spot on the rock. Hugging her knees to her breasts, she crossed her legs at the ankles of her scuffed shoes. As Carrigan washed his hair, she noted he still favored his right arm. He didn't lift it as high as his left. Over the distance between them, she couldn't assess his injury. She was sure he'd healed on the outside, but it would take weeks for his muscles to mend and return to their original strength. Though him admitting to such was unlikely.

Helena felt out of place and intrusive by keeping an eye on him as he went through his ablutions. But there was nothing for her to do. Carrigan had made it plain that he was cooking supper again, and the mouth-watering aroma of bacon-seasoned pinto beans wafted to her nose. He'd put a lidded skillet over the banked gray ashes of the campfire. As the mixture began to simmer, her hunger rose. She'd never expected a man to prepare her a meal, much less her husband.

Resting her chin on her knees, Helena wondered if there was anything Carrigan couldn't do. He'd proved himself skillful at many things in the brief time she'd known him. If their marriage hadn't been founded on conditional terms, she might have allowed herself to feel more than appreciation for him and consider what other attributes he may have that she'd find to her liking. But there was no purpose served in romanticizing their relationship. It wasn't realistic.

In regard to her horses . . . she'd come to the conclusion she had to follow her honest convictions. Belief was a matter of choice. And at this point, she chose not to believe Bayard's account of what happened. He had freely confessed to being under the influence of liquor, and drunkenness wasn't a supporter of accuracy. If Bayard had mistakenly identified Carrigan, then the question was left open: Who had let her horses out?

Mr. Lewis and Mr. Wyatt hadn't taken being put in

their places too kindly. Either one of them could have done it. But physically, neither was even close to resembling Carrigan. She supposed one or the other could have hired someone for the dirty dealing. Perhaps Seaton Hanrahan. But whatever had transpired, Helena couldn't come up with a pat suspect.

The caw of a jay made Helena glance over her shoulder. Obsi paid it no mind. The dog was stretched out on Carrigan's bedroll sunning himself in a late afternoon snooze. A bit to the east, Columbiana had been tied to one of the spruce trees in front of the camp where they could keep an eye on her. She had access to the sinkhole, and Carrigan had given her a ration of oats. Earlier, Helena had reacquainted herself with the brooding mustang, who, albeit very slightly, seemed happy to see her.

Carrigan ducked beneath the water briefly to rinse the soap from his hair and body, then he came up. As he exited the lake, tiny droplets glistened on his upper body. His nipples had puckered, and she could see he was fighting not to click his teeth together. The buttons on his trousers weren't doing their job at keeping the waistline taut without a belt. Wet cotton sagged at his navel where a thin line of dark hair trailed downward. The sensual image of what his pants cradled came to her mind. She had told herself gazing at him in a state of undress when she'd taken care of his wound was nothing to lose her head over, but she hadn't forgotten. Carrigan had the kind of build a woman could never disregard.

"Grab me one of my blankets."

Helena went quickly to get one, but seeing as Obsi was dead to the world and in no mood to budge, she had to use a blanket of her own. As she handed it to Carrigan, their knuckles met in a light touch. The blameless contact set off a responsive shiver through her. She was dismayed by the currents and hastily averted her eyes from his chest. Looking down, she stared at the water that ran off the hems of his trousers. His bare feet were coated with coarse, brown sand.

When she raised her gaze, their eyes met and an inexplicable sense of intimacy came over Helena. She became aware of him in ways that were impractical. He shouldn't have made her want to pin hopes on the future. Carrigan would never love her, nor could she ever allow herself to love him. She had to distance herself from futile thoughts such as affectionate husbands and dedicated wives.

For the lack of anything better to say, she remarked politely, "Your supper dish smells good." Though suddenly hunger wasn't the cause of her ribs pressing down on her stomach.

Taking an unsteady breath, she retreated like a coward for the shore and kneeled on an overhang of rock that tumbled into the water. Her murky reflection greeted her. She looked an awful sight with her hair windblown and flyaway curls framing her face. A dirt smudge left an imprint on the hollow of her cheek, and her lips were pale from dryness. It was *good* she didn't need to impress him, because in her disheveled state, she couldn't impress the dog.

Without looking to see if she was being watched, Helena proceeded to wash her hands and face with the soap Carrigan had left. On a whim, she took her hair down and smoothed some order into it with water on her palms. When she was finished, she walked up the embankment to the campsite. She noted Carrigan had strung a rope between two trees and draped her wet blanket over the line and was standing behind it. In a swift rummage of her saddlebag, she found her brush and ran the bristles through her tangles. With nimble fingers, she fashioned a fat braid and bow-tied the end with a short length of black ribbon.

Moistening her parched lips with some balm, she sat on her bedroll to wait for Carrigan to dress. All she could see was his naked legs from beneath the blanket's edge. The well-shaped definition of his lightly haired calves was soon taken from her view as first one, then the other, leg slid into butternut-colored fabric.

He came out barefoot and with his gun holster draped over the shoulder of a soft ivory shirt. From the center of the small, fold-over collar, pearly buttons fell to midway down his chest. She vaguely recalled carrying such a ready-made shirt in the general store, but she couldn't remember selling one to him.

Carrigan sat on the lower edge of his pallet, mindful of Obsi's tail. After lighting a cigarette, he kept the end between his lips as he put on a pair of socks, then his boots. It was daunting to watch him dress in such an unhurried manner. She would have frantically been trying to cover her exposed feet. But he didn't seem the least bit bothered that she could see his toes.

Gazing at her through a curl of smoke, he arched his brows. He talked around the cigarette while he said, "You're staring."

Helena flushed to the roots of her hair. "I didn't mean to."

"Stare all you want. I don't care." With splayed fingers, he combed damp hair from his eyes. Then he removed the holster and laid it and the Walker on his pillow within easy reach of his hand. Picking up a long fork, he slid the tines underneath the handle of the skillet lid to lift it. Beans bubbled in the bacon juices. He gave them a stir with a spoon. "Can you wait ten minutes more while I mix some biscuits?"

Helena made an effort to keep her gaze anywhere but on Carrigan when she nodded. To her thorough embarrassment, he laughed at her.

"Does this mean you're going to stop looking at me?"

"No." Then to prove her point, she stared him in the eyes. Which was the wrong course of action to take. His eyes always undid her. They were too layered with keen observance. He could probably read what she was thinking about him. Then he'd surely be laughing again when he figured out she was forever preoccupied by thoughts of him.

Thankfully, he broke away to get the flour sack and a box of staples. The slow-burning cigarette still dangled from his mouth when he asked, "Can Columbiana take a command without having a fit?"

His query threw her off, and she immediately pondered his motives. "Thomas has never complained. She's an independent horse, but she's well trained."

"You ever ridden her?"

"No."

Carrigan abruptly let the subject go with the pitch of his cigarette butt, but Helena wasn't so easily swayed. "Why do you ask?"

"It doesn't matter."

"Yes it does. You need me to ride her."

"I can get the rest of the horses without you riding her."

"But it would be faster if I did."

He remained silent, rolling the top of the flour sack down and pouring water directly inside. With his free hand, he began to squeeze the sack. This unusual method pulled at her attention, but she didn't immediately comment on it.

"But it would be faster if I did," she repeated.

"Yeah." He concentrated on kneading the lump of flour and water without taking the mass out. "It would be. But I'm not going to set you on a horse you don't know."

"I know her," she disputed. "Better than you."

"Which is precisely why I won't ride her."

"And which is precisely why I will."

Carrigan gave her a good going over with his steadfast eyes. Then he dumped some baking powder, salt, and a spoonful of lard into the bag. "You don't even know why I want you to ride her."

"She's the lead mare and the others are more apt to follow her than they would Traveler," Helena replied with uncompromising satisfaction. That temporarily out of the way, she had to ask, "What are you doing to that flour?"

"Mixing biscuits."

"In the sack?"

"It's less messy this way and only uses the amount of flour I need." He brought the smooth dough out in his palm and showed it to her. "If you get bucked off that mare tomorrow, I'm liable to shoot her."

"I won't." Helena felt a smile growing at the corners of her mouth. "And if you get any ideas to shoot her, you'll have to shoot through me. She's fine horseflesh, even though she's capricious."

Carrigan put the biscuits on and lit another cigarette. He lazed on his side, indolently enjoying his smoke. It occurred to her, he was minus a vice.

"You're not drinking."

"Having a case of alcohol dementia isn't going to help me round up the horses these next few days." Lying on his back with his head propped on the arch of his saddle, he took a puff and exhaled the smoke in a slow ribbon. The creases at the edges of his eyes deepened with devilment. "But I did bring the whiskey in case either of us got hurt." He bent his leg and kicked up his bootheel onto the top of his knee as he turned toward her. "You want a taste?"

"No."

"Didn't think so."

In the cooling of a red sun making way for evening stars, Helena reserved her speech to appreciate the colors. Real sunsets didn't visit Genoa. The quiet camaraderie between herself and a man was a pleasure long since past for her. Idle talk and yarn spinning around a campfire as a carefree couple was something she'd only experienced once. Sitting this way with Carrigan reminded her of that. But what was missing were the anecdotes and their outlooks on a shared life ahead. The gently spoken words of admiration, heartfelt laughs of amusement, and the soft touches of reassurance—these were the missing elements in their doomed relationship. In less than six months, their perfunctory involvement would end.

This bothered Helena when it shouldn't have. When she thought of the many things Carrigan had accomplished in so short a time, she couldn't help but think about his additions to her life. Though she would never admit, not even a little bit, she was feeling more for Carrigan than was wise. And these feelings ran a close second to a profound and deep affection for him.

The biscuits were soon ready to eat, and Helena accepted the offered plate of food. Obsi woke to the delicious smells and sat up to beg. Carrigan tossed him a chunk of bacon. The single bite didn't appease Obsi, who turned to Helena with large brown eyes. She held out a portion of her bacon.

"You'll have to take it from me if you want it," she said, coaxing him with a slight pulse of her hand. Obsi dipped his head low, raised his chin, sniffed, then moved backward a few steps. "Come on. You want it. You know you do."

"He won't take it from you." Carrigan used his biscuit to sop the bean juices.

"He'll take it if he wants it bad enough."

Obsi came forward, his tongue coming out to smack his chops. Ever closer, he was practically drooling when he reached her hand. He whined, bent his neck low, then she felt his teeth very gingerly remove the meat from her fingers.

"I'll be damned." Carrigan's brows rose as Obsi returned to mooch more bacon from him. "You'll have to wait until I'm through with my tin before you can have a plate to eat off of. Go sit."

Obediently the dog complied.

Helena's triumphant smile was mixed. Even though she'd set out to conquer the dog's fear of taking food from anyone but Carrigan, it also meant she was becoming fond of Obsi. She hadn't had a desire to have a dog since she'd lost hers as a child. People outlived animals, and it was a hard thing having to bury a beloved pet once a person was attached to it. From now on, she'd better shy away from the dog. When Carrigan went, Obsi went with him.

From her first bite, Helena realized she had a wolfish hunger after all. The flaky biscuit melted in her mouth, and she helped herself to another later in the meal. As soon as supper was eaten, Obsi fed, the dishes cleaned and put away, Helena lifted the flap of her saddlebag and dug into the side containing a deck of cards. She brought them out and held them for Carrigan's view. "Are you a cardplayer?"

Night had fallen, and with it came a chill. When Helena had covered her shoulders with her cape, Carrigan had stoked the fire. Its flames cast enough brightness to see by, and also put his face in a complimentary light. He sat directly across from her, the fire pit at their respective left and right knees as each sat cross-legged.

"Depends on what game is being played."

"Seven-up."

"Sure, I know Old Sledge."

"Would you care to play it? I thought it might take some of the tedium out of the nights, so I brought the cards."

Lighting a smoke, he said, "All right."

"Where did you learn to cook?" Helena asked, while dealing.

"On the range, and by trial and error."

"I can't imagine you as a cowboy, much less a sheepherder."

Carrigan drank black coffee from his cup. "Don't know why not."

"Because you're a solitary man, and driving cattle takes teamwork."

"I wasn't always a loner."

"I sense there's a story in that."

"Many."

"Would you tell me at least one?"

Carrigan's circumspect expression told her he was weighing the consequences of her request. "If you're specific, I might."

She had more questions to choose from than she did the six blue-backed playing cards on the blanket in front of her. The foremost: Who were the men he'd killed, and why? But to get him to answer a hard and direct question like that, she'd have to be careful how she phrased her inquiry. For now, she stuck to one that she was fairly certain he would respond to, and that would perhaps tie into the one burning on the forefront of her mind. "What was it that made you leave Red Springs so fast and take the sheepherding job?"

"Not what."

"Pardon?"

"It wasn't a what. It was a who." Carrigan didn't handle his cards. Tapping his right forefinger over the tops of them, he clarified, "The who was a woman."

Helena wasn't so sure she wanted to hear any more. Jealousy wasn't a common emotion in her, but suddenly it sprang out of nowhere and crawled into her lap. Unbidden, a petty query took over her voice. "Was she pretty?"

"Very."

Of course. Any woman who could turn Carrigan's head would have to be beautiful. Helena turned up the final card for trump and left it on top of the deck. Her concentration had been shot the moment of Carrigan's answer.

Picking up his cards, Carrigan flipped one over the trump. "Her name was Kate Hisom. She came to town the year I signed up with my first outfit. Her father opened a grocery store and turned a nice business."

Helena played on Carrigan's discard.

"I'd just turned twenty, and I thought I knew everything there was about life. I figured I was ready to make a commitment to a woman." Carrigan followed suit with a club, then tossed his cigarette into the fire. "Her family allowed me to call on her, and I did for a few months. Then I asked her to marry me."

Helena's throat went dry as sawdust. It had never occurred to her that Carrigan might have been married before.

"But she turned me down flat. I thought she was interested in me, only she was interested in seeing what it would be like to be courted. She said she wasn't going to marry a man punching cattle and smelling like horse sweat. She'd set her sights on the banker's son." Carrigan swallowed another gulp of coffee. "Milton Grimes smelled like money."

"What an awful girl," Helena commented, feeling guilt over her relief that Carrigan hadn't been married previously. She had no right to wish that he hadn't, because she'd almost had a husband herself. But there was something special in not having spoken vows to anyone prior to each other.

"After being made the brunt of many jokes between the other punchers, I didn't want to stay in Red Springs. The constant reminder of Kate turning me down had me resentful, and I didn't want to take on any of my father's ornery traits."

Her brows rose with curiosity, but before she could say anything, Carrigan was shaking his head.

"No. One question. And I answered it." Drawing his legs in tighter, he arranged his cards and gazed at her over the tops of them. "You never talk about yourself."

Her heartbeat picked up speed. "There's nothing to tell."

"You're full of secrets."

She only had one. "I am not."

"Who was the man in your life before me?"

"There was nobody," she lied.

Carrigan shrugged with indifference, winning the trick. "I'm not going to make you talk about him." If Helena had been paying attention, she could have discarded one of her hearts. "Tell me about August, then. What happened the day he was killed?"

Helena recalled the incident with an overwhelming sadness and had to prod herself into speaking of it aloud. "It was a normal day, just like any other. Father had opened the store, sent Emilie on an errand, and I was getting ready to help before the morning rider came. I heard a gunshot and ran to see." Grief doubled back to Helena and ambushed her with the threat of tears. "I . . . I found my father on the floor. He'd been shot in the stomach. Our cash box was stolen."

"Was there money in it from the day before?"

Helena shook her head. "Not much. Nothing to kill over."

"Was money the only thing in the box?"

"There was a picture of our family. And a special coin."

"A special coin?"

"It was a half-dime and had my mother's initials— J.G.—engraved on it. Father scratched them on the surface of the coin we took in for our first sale." She blinked, fighting against crying.

Carrigan's eyes narrowed to hard flints. "You weren't robbed for the money. A robber would have waited until the end of the day when the till was full."

"But maybe—"

"No. Whoever shot your father had a reason other than wanting money," Carrigan said, eliminating a card. "Why hasn't that judge approached you with any information?"

Try as she might, she just couldn't condemn Bayard. He'd said he would make sure her father's death was avenged if a killer was caught. That was all she could demand of him, especially now, given the set of circumstances surrounding their strained friendship.

"Judge Kimball doesn't have any suspects, but he's not a sheriff. He can only prosecute criminals, he can't apprehend them. If he had the means, I'm sure he would. I know he would," she reaffirmed. "Why do you ask?"

"Because I have a suspicion, whoever shot your father is still in Genoa. It's the same man who let your horses out."

Carrigan's words awakened her hope. She'd so wanted to find her father's killer, but apprehending a suspect without witnesses, nor presumable reason for the heinous crime, seemed very unlikely. Not wanting to torment herself, she'd nipped any optimism she'd had in the bud before it had a chance to bloom. "Do you have any idea who? Mr. Wyatt and Mr. Lewis . . . Do you think it was one of them?"

"Wyatt and Lewis want you to fail. But neither of those men is clever enough to arrange a shutout. They're acting on orders from another source, though I doubt the man who freed the horses is the one giving the orders. He's a hired gun. Could be the same man who shot me."

Definitive answers rested on the identity of the man who'd let the mustangs out. If she went on Bayard's interpretation, she was looking at one of the culprits. But Bayard had misnamed Carrigan. So who, then, matched Carrigan's height and build? There were many men who could fit the description if she stretched the measurements a little. Trying to discern which one was guilty would be nearly impossible. Confessions weren't easily wheedled out, and there was no way she could think of to incriminate them.

"I don't know how to find a guilty man amid a town full of citizens who could have had a part in the murder. I can't ask them all if they did it. No one would tell me the truth."

"You don't ask." Carrigan flipped his final card to the stack, winning the game. "You make yourself invisible, and you listen. I'll try and find the man who killed your father. But it may take me some time."

"I have time." Then a telling chord struck her heart. "But you don't."

His gaze was penetrating, his voice firm when he replied, "Whether I'm in Genoa or on the land, I'll keep looking for leads in both shootings. His and mine. I liked August. It isn't right that his death is being swept under a carpet. I don't give a damn if Genoa has a lawman or not. Justice doesn't need a tin star on its lapel to get the job done."

As Carrigan added the points, Helena contemplated the prospect of actually being able to confront the responsible parties. She wanted to hold out hope that Carrigan could find her father's killer. But even if he couldn't, that he was willing to try meant more to her than anything. What he offered was beyond what anyone else had. And for that, she was grateful beyond words.

It took Carrigan another five days to gather the remaining horses. The next day out, he'd taken Esmeralda and her colt with relative ease while Helena rode Columbiana. He hadn't found it necessary to halter the colt, which Helena had named Jake on the spur of the moment, for some damn reason. Jake ran alongside his mother, bawling for her teats.

By Sunday evening, Carrigan had added Daisy and Lucy, the team horses, to the string he'd staked back at camp. Monarch and Maria Jane were caught on Monday. Maria Jane, a blood bay, hadn't come peaceably. His rope had slipped, and he'd caught her by the forefoot instead of the neck. He'd had to come up behind her on the ground and put his knee on her withers.

The line was full up on Thursday night with grazing horses whose mud-dappled coats were in need of brushing and currying. None were resisting the ropes, and all were taking water, so he hadn't had to build an enclosure, and they'd saved valuable time.

Everything would have gone smoothly if he hadn't been bitten this afternoon by the last horse to round up—a mare Helena called Dolly. She was a dun-colored thing, and she'd gotten him on his left hand just when he was putting the hackamore on her. There wasn't an opportunity to bind the wound, and by sundown he was smeared with blood.

Since he'd sent Helena ahead to divide the last of their oats and feed the twelve and a half head, her face went white as a sheet when he rode into camp. On a glance, he saw that the bright blood had splattered his pants leg and Boomerang's shoulder, making it hard to detect where exactly he was injured.

On his approach, Helena dropped the open-lidded coffeepot she'd been holding. Water splashed her skirt, marking the fabric with blotches. She ran toward him, her fingers over her mouth as if she were stopping a scream.

"What happened?" she gasped.

Carrigan swung his leg over the pommel and hopped down from the horse. "She bit me in the hand when I was putting the bridle on her. At least it wasn't my roping and gun hand." Fisting the reins, he led Boomerang and Dolly—who was attached to a rope on the saddle horn—toward the other horses.

Helena and Obsi trailed after him. "You need that looked at."

"I've got a horse to cool down first, and one to tie up."

"But—"

"Don't fuss over me, Helena." Carrigan was tired and didn't want to stop before he finished his day. Ducking slightly beneath the sprawling boughs of a wind-gnarled pine, he approached the tranquil herd and began unlooping the knot that kept Dolly from going anywhere. As soon as the mare was reunited with the other mustangs, she began to nicker and swish her black tail, as if she were happy to be back. Carrigan could have smacked her in the muddy rump.

He immersed himself in the grooming of Boomerang, and only when he'd completed the task did he notice Helena had left. Since he hadn't been paying her any attention, he couldn't be sure when she'd taken off. He hadn't meant to be short with her, but he was weary to the bone and just wanted to put things to order so he could clean up. As he walked toward the campfire, he saw her sitting there with her back to him. She was stock-still. In fact, the coffee was boiling over, and she made no move to yank the pot off the fire.

Bending down, Carrigan grabbed a frayed towel, snatched the pot away from the low-burning flames, and set it on the scorched rock he used for hot pans. "You daydreaming?" he asked, rolling up his shirtsleeves with the intention of sinking his throbbing hand into Lake Tahoe's numbing water. "Helena?"

It was then he noticed her shoulders were quaking. He lowered himself onto his knee, the leg of his chaps pressing around his thigh. Turning her to face him, he saw that she was silently crying. Her tears hit him in the gut as surely as if she'd slugged him.

"What's the matter?"

She shook her head and clamped her lips together to imprison a sob. She covered her face with her hands, her voice a choked whisper when she implored, "Don't look at me."

He disregarded her plea and grabbed her wrists to lower her arms. Her eyes were rimmed with moisture, the fullness of her lashes wet from tears. He would have never taken her for the kind of woman to fall apart for no apparent reason. She could handle anything and had proved herself many times over. "Helena, why are you crying?"

"It's just that . . . when I saw the blood . . . I . . ."

He caught and held her gaze with his, trying to read what she was saying in the depths of her sky-blue eyes. They were clouded with sorrow and a pain that ran deeper than he could explain. "What, Lena? What are you so upset about?"

She took a shuddering breath, looked at her lap, then at him. "I've lost my mother, and I've lost my father. As soon as I married you, I almost lost you, too. I couldn't bear it if I had to bury another person I was close to. I just couldn't do it. I'm not strong enough."

"You thought because of the blood, I was going to die?"

Her lashes lowered, and a tear fell onto the billow of her drenched skirt.

Without conscious thought, Carrigan drew her into his arms and held her tightly to his chest. "I'm not going to die. It would take a lot more than that damn horse's bite to put me in an eternity box." His hands ran over the trembling length of her spine in a reassuring massage. "Don't ever waste your tears on me again. I'm not worth it."

"But you're my husband."

"Not really."

Her soft crying quieted, and she spoke in an equally sedate tone. "In my heart you are, whether I want you there or not."

Carrigan didn't know what to do with her declaration. He had none to give back to her. At least none that made any sense. His emotions were mixing into a storm of uncertainty, and he felt out of his element and out of place in this conversation. "Been a long time since I was in somebody's heart."

Helena's cheek lay softly against his shoulder when she whispered, "That doesn't mean I love you."

The indirect endearment rocked through Carrigan. "Didn't think it did."

"It just means that I feel connected to you because I'm your wife. If something were to happen to you, I'd feel responsible."

"Nothing's going to happen to me." He should have released her, but he couldn't. The braid cuddled against her neck smelled like the fresh mountain air and faintly of the pungent campfire smoke. She'd never before come to him for this kind of intimacy. The union of body touches for the sole purpose of comfort and understanding was an option long since past for him. As soon as he'd been given a taste of it, he wanted more. His forearms circled her waist in a soothing hold that kept her close.

"It already did. You were shot . . . just like my father." Her voice thickened. "Only I never got the chance to take care of him. All I could do for him was bury him decent."

Carrigan rested his chin on the top of Helena's head and closed his eyes. He knew what her frustration felt like. There were two faceless men from his past he couldn't identify either. The lure of fury's never-ending trail had obsessed him for a while. He'd pursued leads through the Cheyenne Territory until the tall grass shifting in the winds obscured his quest with its trackless stalks. His thirst to exact revenge had gone unquenched, but the insatiable hunger was still there. Always. And him not knowing if the men he'd sought were dead or alive.

Helena lifted her cheek and pressed herself away from him. "I shouldn't have bothered you with my melancholy silliness. I don't know what got into me. I'm not a weepy woman." Wiping beneath her moist eyes with her fingertips, she took in a shallow breath.

"A scare got into you." Carrigan's hand rose, and he used his forefinger to blot a tear on the high point of her cheekbone. "Nothing wrong with being scared sometimes. You just had to cry yours out."

"Well, I'm over it now, so you can let me go."

Her pink lips were damp from the salty tears she just licked off. The compelling temptation to give her a thorough kissing knocked the wind out of him. But that one kiss would be all it would take for him to make her his wife in every way. The night on the haystack, she'd been willing until Eliazer had come.

But afterward, she'd stuck to her resolve with embarrassed blushes that hadn't fully convinced Carrigan she was relieved they'd been discovered.

Since then, Carrigan had had some time to think about the consequences of an affair between them. While he would merely be fulfilling a physical desire, she would be left to pick up the pieces when he left her. But those pieces were the very same ones that were tumbling down around them now. Whether Helena wanted to admit it or not, they were headed in a direction she was desperately trying to veer away from.

Carrigan needed a bath and a smoke. A minute to get away and clear his head. He was too dirty to be putting his hands on her. The left shoulder of her dress was now smudged with the blood from his cut hand. Jesus, there was also a vague hint of it on her cheek where he'd touched her. "Do you have a clean dress?"

Following his stare, Helena looked at her bodice. "Yes."

"You better put it on." The fabric of her skirt was still wet from the water she'd spilled on herself. "Might as well do it right and take a dunk in that lake."

Her eyes widened. "It's too cold."

Carrigan rose to his feet, his gaze fastened to the noticeable rise and fall of her breasts. "It's not cold enough." He unbuckled his chaps and let them fall where he stood. Without a backward glance, he picked up his soap and a blanket, and brought them to the water's edge. Removing his holster, he kept the Colt within a comfortable reach. Slipping his arms from his vest, then unbuttoning his shirt, he had a decision to make. Either he could take a bath in a half-assed manner—as he'd been doing—or he could strip down all the way. Seeing as she'd already seen him raw, it wasn't a lengthy debate.

The waning sun was still warm in a sky burgeoning

with great masses of gold and purple clouds. As soon as his boots and socks were off, he flicked the top button of his trousers free with his thumb. The succession of five other flat disks followed, then he shucked his legs out of his pants. Naked, he bent to pick up the soap cake. Walking without self-consciousness, he went to the boulder and climbed on top. Then he plunged into the frigid water and drowned his carnal thoughts of Helena jumping in after him without a stitch on.

Chapter

⇒ 11 ⇐

Helena stared in disbelief at the taut muscles of Carrigan's backside. How could he walk so unabashedly in his altogether? The tight swells of flesh were paler than his back, which was a honey brown. His upper body was naturally darker in skin tone, but his bare behind proved, not by much. When he dove into the lake, she blinked out of her stupor.

The moment regained clarity again. She'd shown him her weaker side by crying in front of him, and it was painfully humiliating. But seeing the blood on Carrigan and not knowing the extent or seriousness, she'd thought he was gunshot again. She didn't want to lose him. Not because he was responsible for making Mr. Lewis and Mr. Wyatt treat her in a professional manner rightfully due any customer, and for saving her from ruination. That thought hadn't crossed her mind. The reason for her overemotional state was that she cared about him. He was family now. Her name would forever be linked to his, even when he wasn't living with her. She'd always be Mrs. Jacob Henry Carrigan.

Splashing water drifted to Helena's ears. She hadn't had a proper bath since leaving town. Daily she'd been soaping her face, hands, and the private parts of her body with a cloth. And each night she slept in a clean change of clothes. She'd brought a poplin skirt, two shirtwaists, and one dark dress. The blouses, she'd washed out, and they were fresh, but not ironed. After she'd shaken the dust from the gathers, the skirt was in good shape. The dress she had on now wasn't fit for another minute. A full body bath with her hair washed would be heaven. But Carrigan was in that lake, and she wasn't going near it.

Being in his arms had a dangerous appeal—one that would be deadly to her adamancy about upholding all aspects surrounding their premarital agreement. But she wasn't blind. She could see what was happening. She'd absorbed the looks passing between them and felt the friction of his hot touch. She'd heard the comforting tone of his low-spoken words meant for reassurance. The fundamentals of courtship had been there tonight when he'd held her whether she wanted them to be or not.

Helena thoughtfully chewed the inside of her cheek. She was a woman who'd listened to her heart once. She should know better than to become entangled a second time. Generous impulses and sentiments had no place in her anymore. And yet . . . chance kept whispering in her ear. *He's different . . . he won't care about what you did in the past. Take today for all your lonely tomorrows. . . .*

They were here alone, and no one would know. Emilie could never guess. She'd seen that Carrigan had his own bedroom at the house and that they weren't living as husband and wife.

Helena hadn't given Emilie much thought since she'd been away with Carrigan. Knowing she was safe with Eliazer and Ignacia had been a source of Helena's peace of mind. But that didn't make up for the fact she hadn't paused once to worry about her sister's welfare. Perhaps it was something Carrigan had said to her about letting Emilie grow up or else she'd hate her. Maybe this was a start. Maybe it was time for Helena to try and begin living again herself. She was painfully aware of how reserved she'd become over the years. How boorish and matronly in her conduct and speech, when she was barely twenty-one. Her smiles were infrequent, her laughter dusty. Why had she allowed such a thing to happen to her?

As soon as Carrigan started for the bank, Helena averted her gaze from him. When she detected his approaching footfalls, she turned her head. He'd wrapped the blanket around his middle and was going in the direction of the screen he'd put up. She came to her feet, the beat of her pulse thrumming swiftly through her body as she clutched the full blanket from off her bedroll. "I'm going in," she said in what she hoped was a casual tone. "Could I borrow your soap? It would seem mine is used up."

"I left it down there." Water dripped off Carrigan's hair. He shoved the raven locks from his forehead with one hand, the other holding the gap in the makeshift towel together.

Helena nodded and walked to the lake. She didn't want to think about what was going to come later, because there would be no going back now. Only forward.

After picking up the soap, she chose a secluded area that was hidden from Carrigan's view. Here she undid her braid and disrobed. Her soiled dress pooled around her bare ankles, and she was left in just her shimmy, drawers, and petticoat. Since she only had these three pieces available, and since she would never commit to going into the lake naked, she held her breath and quickly ran into the icy water with her underclothing on. She made fast work of lathering her body and hair, vigorously scrubbing the curls until her scalp tingled. Her underclothes got a laundering while she was wearing them. Gooseflesh broke out on her skin, and her teeth chattered. With a final dunk, she rinsed herself and was back on dry land just as the sun settled over the mountain peaks for the night.

Huddling into the warmth of her blanket, Helena gathered her clothes and walked back to camp feeling better and cleaner, but more nervous than ever. Before she could re-dress, the chemise, petticoat, and drawers would have to dry. That meant sitting by the fire for a length and allowing its dry heat to evaporate the moisture from her lawn garments. But she'd known this before getting into the water. The internal battle was hard-fought, but she'd closed off the argumentative side of her mind. With her decision came an impulsive nature she'd thought was all but gone from within her.

Carrigan looked up, but said nothing when she deposited her clothes in a heap next to her saddlebags. He'd put on trousers and boots, but nothing else except for a black neckerchief wound and tied around his left hand.

"Does your hand hurt?" she asked with genuine concern, though there was a forced nonchalance to her tone so he wouldn't comment on her state of dress—or rather, undress. She kept the blanket securely around her chemise-strapped shoulders and gripped in front with her shivering fist.

"As a matter of fact, it hurts like hell."

"Is there anything I can do?" Cold water ran down her neck and tickled her between her breasts. Her nipples were tense, and not just from the icy lake.

"No."

"Maybe the whiskey would help."

"This being our last night out, I'd be tempted to get dead drunk." His lean fingers felt his chin and made her notice he'd shaved in her absence. "And you don't prefer me drunk."

A faint dizziness claimed her. Since when did he care how she preferred him? Before her legs buckled, she sat down. She felt her heart hammering beneath her breasts while a host of thoughts tumbled through her brain. Had he guessed she'd changed her mind? Was he waiting for her to tell him outright that it would be all right if he made love to her?

After brushing off the sand that clung to her feet, she tucked herself neatly inside the blanket and used the excess corner to rub her hair. Trying to keep a note of calm in her voice, she asked, "What are we having for supper?"

"Whatever you want," he drawled in the darkness.

His response undid her. There were only several food items on their list of a possible menu. But there were many others to choose from off a different kind of plate. And none were edible. Unless she counted nibbling on Carrigan's mouth or the flesh curving his sinewy shoulder.

"Leftover biscuits would be fine," she replied, unable to meet his gaze.

"That's all?" His breathing was slow and heavy.

The blanket in her hand felt like lead. "That's all I want."

"Is it?"

Helena lifted her chin, her hair falling next to her cheek. She couldn't find the voice to speak her feelings aloud. Her stomach pounded with tension.

"Is it?" he repeated, his persuasive lips beckoning her.

Her heart lurched. Carrigan was going to make her say it, and she hated that he was trying to coerce it out of her. The chords of her voice were rough and scratchy in her answer. "No."

"What else?"

Raising her eyes to his, she wouldn't allow his strong and potent presence to disarm her. "You. I want you."

Carrigan leaned forward. His unruly hair fell over his forehead, the top of his dark brows set in a questioning furrow. The lines bracketing his mouth were no longer so cutting, making his lips appear firm and tantalizing. Extending his brawny arms to either side of her bent knees, he brought his face within a whispered breath of her ear. "I can't hear you."

He was breathing more rapidly, his lips hovering next to her earlobe while awaiting her reply. She drew in a shallow breath of her own when saying, "I want you."

"That's what I thought you said."

His lips touched her, moving upon her flushed cheek and downward over the arched column of her neck. He kissed her, his nose against her skin as if he were consuming her very scent.

The blanket fell as Helena's arms stole around his neck, keeping him close. She had never touched him with a lover's hand before. His body was familiar from her doctoring, yet unfamiliar to her exploring caress. Cool and warm at the same time, his skin was smooth as fine marble. The stirring kisses he gave molded her lips to fit his as his practiced mouth roused the passions she'd suppressed for so many years. His tongue swept rhythmically into her pliant mouth in a hot, erotic way that made each pleasure point in her come alive. She became lost in the heated kiss, in the way his mouth ravenously took hers. Nothing would be slow and savored tonight. Things had gone beyond that. An urgency for a long-sought gratification was what drove Helena.

With his mouth burning an imprint on hers, he laid her down atop the bedroll as his seeking hands slid down her shoulders. The blanket fell open in the front, and the air against her wet clothing caused her to shiver. Carrigan brought his weight on top of her, searing his body heat into her breasts and pelvis. His fingers explored her well-defined curves with featherlight strokes that caused a cascade of tingles to radiate from her every nerve ending. Of their own accord, her legs parted when his wide hands splayed over her rib cage and scooted her upward a notch.

His mouth separated from hers, and he caught her

nipple in a light grate of his teeth. The combination of clingy, damp cotton over her breast mixed with Carrigan's tongue as he drew the bead into the heat of his moist mouth brought Helena to a full-fledged arousal she fervently wanted to complete. Her breasts grew tender with slight prickles where Carrigan continued his assault through her chemise. She would have unfastened the buttons herself if he hadn't done so. His tongue gently flicked over her swollen nipples in turn, laving her until she squirmed beneath him. Her fingers kneaded his flexing back muscles, the nails lightly digging into his flesh. All sounds ceased in her ears except for the choppy sighs coming from her throat. She could no longer hear the fire popping softly or the horses whickering, or the water beating against the shore.

Opening her eyes, she stared at the brilliance of stars in heaven's throne. They were on safe ground here . . . where no one could judge either of them for giving in to their bodies' needs. It was the only way Helena could rationalize her behavior. The sensuality of nature in Carrigan's world on this mountain had called her . . . and she let herself be taken in by it.

His hand swept over her slim waist, bunching the sodden gathers of her petticoat into his strong fist. When he found the cord on her drawers, he pulled the end and undid the bow. She helped him rid her of the cleaving garment, kicking her feet out of the legs until she was free of it. Rather than bring her petticoat down, Carrigan left the wad of cotton resting on her pelvis, the most intimate part of her exposed for his perusal. She felt accessible and unsure. Carrigan had undoubtedly had sex with countless women, while she had only experienced one man. Would he find her too eager . . . or too lacking in knowledge?

She had no time to ponder her uncertainties as Carrigan dexterously stripped his trousers and kneeled over her. His erection was thick and firm . . . flawless. Sex had never been anything she'd been afraid of before, and she told herself there was nothing to fear. She knew Carrigan. He was her husband. But the other time she'd fallen into passion's arms, she'd been in love. And love's emotions had orchestrated what she would do. Now she had to act on brazen desires, putting all thoughts aside other than this man's body inside hers. With Carrigan, sex would be for the passion of it and nothing more.

Her arms stretched out for him, and he fit into her embrace. She held him tightly, burning her face in the arc of his neck and pressing kisses along his skin. She could taste the cleanliness of soap, and a salty trace of perspiration teased the tip of her tongue. Willing and eager, she forgot about everything in her life but this one moment. She clung to him as he dove into her. Her responding gasp was soft and lost in the hoarseness of his groan. His next thrust was deep and earthshattering. She felt herself tightly closing around him as if she'd never known a man before. He moved with strong, smooth strokes that had her lifting to meet each one. She began to throb where he joined her. She looked up at him and saw his forehead bathed in a sweat of forced control. He continued the rocking movements, each lunge of sexual pleasure driving her to the brink of climax.

Her palms limply held on to his shoulders, then lowered to her sides as tingles swirled in her fingers. Carrigan caught her hands in his, entwining them, squeezing them . . . bringing them over her head where he held her still. All the while he kept on in a pace that soon grew frantic and rushed, his breath a broken moan. Helena couldn't hold back any longer. She surrendered to the raw power of his body, focusing on the pounding length of him as his tempo culminated into pulsing release. He'd pushed her over the edge, and she fell right alongside of him, reaching out to take all she could, knowing this may be the last time she'd ever know him in this way.

Carrigan's chest crushed her as he pressed himself

over her breasts, spent and damp with satisfaction. She felt his heart beating against her own as they caught their breath. Sliding her legs over the backs of his knees, she kept him inside her. Savoring and reveling in the vibrating release that still had a hold on her. She'd missed being in the arms of a lover . . . missed the amorous nights and the soft laughter afterward.

"Who was he?" Carrigan's sudden husky voice came to her ears.

She'd known he'd ask. The time had come when she could no longer avoid the truth. "Kurt," she said quietly. "His name was Kurt von Shiller."

Carrigan rolled onto his side, taking Helena with him so that her face was even with his. His arm reached over the dip of her waist, the tickle of his hair caressing her bare shoulder. He grabbed the blanket and draped it fully over her, making sure she was snug. Giving her a brief but tender kiss, he waited for her to elaborate. A tale she would have to expound on now.

"I met him when I was fifteen. My mother said it was time for me to stop playing like a child and going to school with Emilie. I had to wear my hair in pins instead of braids. Mother made me new skirts and dresses that reached the floor and would accommodate my hoops and a corset. That was the year Emilie and I began to drift apart. I didn't want it to happen that way, but I was five years older than her and was expected to find a husband, marry, and set up my own house. I wasn't allowed to run wild through the fields anymore or make daisy chains for my hair with Emilie."

Carrigan's fingers worked over her shoulder, then downward until he touched the chain around her neck. The gold cross hugged the curve of her right breast where her chemise was still parted and left her naked. She made an attempt to at least button the top button, but Carrigan touched her wrist.

"Don't hide yourself from me," he said slowly. "I've waited too long to look at you."

Helena let her hand fall to Carrigan's and their fingers meshed. "One evening I was invited for supper and to spend the night at Preacher von Shiller's house for spiritual affirmation. There were several von Shiller brothers in the home, and a half dozen other students from the Bible class besides myself had been invited. After a pleasant supper, the oldest von Shiller boy excused himself from the parlor and went to smoke a cigar on the porch. In a minute he was back. There was an excited animation on his face when he announced Kurt was home." Helena recalled the moment with crystal clarity. Nearly every face in the room had blanched. Not at all the kind of reception she could have imagined for a returning brother. But she instantly found out the reason for their reservations. "Kurt, I learned, was the black-sheep brother who had run away to California when he was twelve years old. The family hadn't seen him for nine years."

Obsi came over to them, his chin dripping water from a recent drink. He walked a tight circle at Carrigan's feet, then curled into a ball and put his muzzle on his outstretched paws.

Helena continued with her story while the hoots of an owl interloped on her words. "Preacher von Shiller made him come into the house, where we were able to get a good look at him. He wore a sombrero and chaps. We girls were not impressed. We thought his appearance was outlandish. But his face was beautiful, and he was big and blond with fair skin." A contrast to the coloring of the man she lay next to now. She didn't want to compare them, because there was no comparison. The two were miles different in character and mannerisms, but each was a fixed part of her life. "I remember he was rather silent and ill at ease with all of us staring at him, talking politely around him . . . waiting for him to explain his sudden presence at his family's home. But he didn't, and no one asked. He soon excused himself and said he was going to bed. In the morning we found out Kurt left the house very early before any of us were up, and I didn't see him again for a year."

Carrigan tucked a curl behind her ear and stroked the side of her neck with a soft, complacent touch. That he said nothing while she spoke made her wonder what he was thinking. He didn't interject his opinion or ask any questions. Rather, he allowed her to control the one-sided conversation in whichever manner she chose. She appreciated his leniency and decided to take things slow.

"After he was gone, I did find out the reason he'd left in the first place. His parents were high-minded people who thought their first duty was to the Lord and church, not their children. I learned that when Kurt was younger, his mother was too busy with the parish to give him much attention. And so, much of the time he'd been left in the charge of his older brothers, who were allowed to punish him. He resented their abusive ways, and that was what had made him run away." Helena paused to search Carrigan's eyes. They were devoid of emotion, the fire's light mirrored in his pupils. She had to ask, "What are you thinking?"

"I'm not thinking anything." His head was supported by the hand of his bent arm. "I'm listening."

"I probably wouldn't have seen Kurt again if his father hadn't taken ill. Since there was no doctor, the neighbors took turns tending Preacher von Shiller. I was sitting up with him one night when Kurt returned home. He was taller than I remembered, his eyes bluer than cornflowers. For many nights after his arrival, we sat up together by his father's bedside or talked quietly in the next room. In those talks, he told me much about his early life, and one thing he said that I will always—" She was on the verge of saying "cherish" when she stopped herself cold. She didn't want to intentionally wound Carrigan. "Always remember. He said that he had never known any pleasure in his home until I was in it. He told me that he'd made up his mind never to marry, but that I'd changed it. He was planning to start a cattle ranch in the Kansas Territory, and asked me if I would be afraid to share that kind of life with him. I told him I wasn't, and we became engaged soon after his father died."

Helena grew extremely aware that she was revealing a part of herself that she'd tucked away. With the wedding gown of corded silk and tulle-ruche trim wrapped in paper on the bottom of the trunk in her bedroom. She felt open to attack. Though she didn't think he would, Carrigan could pass a harsh judgment on her when he heard the rest.

"I don't think I should go on. . . ." she whispered. "There's nothing really left to tell."

"There's everything left. Continue."

Helena swallowed, biting her lower lip. After she composed herself with a deep breath, she went on. "My family didn't approve of the match. Not because Kurt wanted to take me out west—my father was encouraged by this news, as he'd been wanting to leave New Providence and seek his fortune where the sun sets for quite some time—but because of Kurt's wild reputation. Kurt left for the Kansas Territory to view prospective sites for our ranch. Six months before my seventeenth birthday, he sent for me to show me where I would be living to make sure I could be the wife of a rancher. Traveling alone was out of the question, so an aunt of the von Shillers accompanied me as a chaperon.

"When I met Kurt, I was amazed by the vastness of the land and embraced the wide-open space. My chaperon didn't fair well on the journey. She took ill in Topeka and died three days later of pneumonia."

Prickles coursed through Helena's hand, and she brought her arm down and rested her head on her inner arm. "Until other arrangements could be made, I was on my own and alone with my fiancé."

This admission garnered an expression out of Carrigan. His face was as dark as pitch, and fraught with a distinct hardening of his eyes.

"Shall I stop?"

"No."

Licking her lips, she pledged to be careful how she worded what happened next. "We left Topeka after sending word to my family that I was in need of a traveling companion home. When I had my first view of the ranch, I knew I'd made the right decision. I could easily feel at home in such a place. There were several hands on the property, and an Indian girl cook—the first Cheyenne woman I'd ever met—who didn't live in the house. They were quartered in bunkhouses. Even though Kurt and I shared the same roof, he and I lived respectfully. But . . . it became increasingly difficult for us to refrain from acting on our feelings."

"You were in love with him."

"Very much." Of that, she would not lie or lessen the extent of her feelings. But what was to follow caused her to close her eyes so she wouldn't have to see Carrigan's reaction when she revealed the first part of her deepest secret. "I am not proud to say we consummated our marriage before we were lawfully wed. At that time, I was so in love and knew that we would marry, the lack of a certificate could not stop me."

Unbidden, tears gathered as she slowly opened her eyes. She'd thought she was over crying.

Carrigan's mellow voice drifted to her. "Love makes people do things they normally wouldn't." He sounded as if he knew of what he spoke.

"My father came for me and took me home," she said in a rush, blinking back the moisture clouding her vision. "Arrangements were made for a Christmas wedding. I wanted desperately to confide in Emilie. When we were younger, we told each other everything. But what had happened in the territory was too personal. Emilie was only twelve and so very impressionable. I couldn't tell her. It had been scandal enough that I traveled without being married.

"The week Kurt was to arrive in Pennsylvania, his partner rode into New Providence alone." Helena could not stop the tears from spilling. "He bore news so horrible, the room spun when I heard what he had come to say. Kurt had drowned in a river crossing on his horse. . . . It had been raining and the current was . . . It carried him away. By the time he was rescued, he was . . . dead."

Carrigan's thumb caught the tears that rolled down her cheek and on the side of her nose.

"My grief was so strong that I couldn't eat and became very sick. A sickness that lasted for weeks and plagued me worse in the morning."

"Lena . . . no."

A sob hitched in her throat as the second most private part of her past was about to be revealed. "My mother asked me if I was with child. I'd seen her go through the sickness with the baby she'd lost, and suspected it could be true. I had to tell her I thought I was. It was utterly humiliating, and I wanted to die of shame." Helena fought for air, her heart breaking. "My father had wanted to move for a long time, but my mother put him off. As soon as she learned about my condition, she told Father she would go. She only relented because of me. Because we couldn't stay where people knew us. When I would start to show, Mother said we would tell Father and Emilie the truth. And to anyone who inquired, we would say I was a widow.

"We weren't far into our journey when I suffered a miscarriage." She quietly wept for the child she couldn't hold. The children she would never have.

"The pain was so bad, I knew it was God's way of punishing me. You see, this is why I can't go into the church."

"Yes you can."

"I can't. Not ever again." She shook her head. "My mother took care of me, and told me it was God's will and for the best. But I secretly wished I'd been able to carry the child. For Kurt. Father and Emilie never knew about my pregnancy, for Mother had told them my illness was due to the rough traveling." Helena wiped her tears with her hand. "My mother lied for me. She never lied. And she never would have died if it hadn't been for me. She would have been in New Providence where she wanted to be." Fingering the cross at her breast, Helena held on to the icon. "This is my reminder. It was my mother's. And every day I burden myself with its weight because I have to. Because it's *my* punishment for what I did. And so now you know. We're the only ones who do."

Carrigan surveyed her without any glare or conclusion that said he thought less of her. "This is why you shelter Emilie."

"I have to."

"She's not you, Lena." His features were deceptively composed, offering no clue to his emotions. "Give her the same chance to grow up that you had."

An easy defiance allowed her to challenge him. "But she fancies herself in love with Thomas McAllister. What if she does what I did? Her life will be forever ruined."

"Yours isn't."

"But it is." Her misery was so acute, it physically pained her. "An unborn child wasn't the only thing I lost that day. I lost any baby I could ever hope to have." She pulled the blanket closely around her, wrapping herself in anguish. "When we reached Fort Kersey to buy fresh supplies, my mother took me to the military surgeon. His examination was thorough, and he told me I had a lot of scarring inside because I hadn't had complete bed rest after my miscarriage. He said that in his estimation, it was very unlikely I would ever be able to conceive another child."

A dead silence layered the night, Helena sick at heart to think about everything she'd just disclosed. Sacrificing herself to the truth was her undoing. To put herself in a position wherein she had to relate what had happened to her was unforgivable. She'd sworn never to tell a soul. Never to let any man, much less Carrigan, know what he was getting—or rather, not getting—when he married her. The secret was why she'd been so adamant about no sex in their relationship. Now that he knew the echo of sadness from her past, simplicity in their arrangement would be nothing more than a bygone sentiment. Exposing herself in such a way to him gave Carrigan a powerful advantage over her.

Carrigan's next words were saturated with censure. "Is all this why you sold yourself to me in a loveless marriage?"

"What decent man in Genoa would want me if he found out I couldn't give him children?"

His voice dropped to a condescending tone. "Self-pity doesn't become you."

Her left arm swung out at him, catching the side of his neck. But Carrigan took hold of her wrist, flung his weight over her, and pinned her beneath him. "I may not be a decent man you could have lived respectably with, but you still should have told me the truth before that ring was on your finger." His mouth was hot inches away from hers. "Just to reassure you, I don't need children. I don't care whether you can have them or not. But I do feel relieved that I won't have to worry about leaving you pregnant when I go."

Scalding tears seeped from the corners of her eyes. Immobile against his unflinching grip, she hissed, "You're heartless."

"No I'm not. I just don't pretend to be someone I'm not." He lightly grazed the fullness of her lower lip with a damp kiss. "You knew what you were getting when you married me. What makes you think another man would make you happy?" He kissed away a tear on her cheekbone, then pressed his lips to hers. The salty taste on his mouth was hers as he coerced a response out of her. "You need someone to take you as you are." His bracing hold on her wrist lightened. She somewhat relaxed, though wary of her body's traitorous stirrings. "You came to me once, Lena. Come to me again."

Carrigan's lips were hard and searching and more persuasive than she cared to concede. Her mind relived the velvet warmth of his kisses . . . the way he'd made her feel when his fingers and mouth had burned over her skin when he'd brought her to fulfillment.

"Come to me again," he murmured, his tongue slipping inside her mouth. His hungry kiss left her weak and confused. Twisting in his arms and arching her back, she sought to get free so she could think without being distracted by his undeniable magnetism. But while her efforts were valiant, her heart was not so heroic.

She wanted him. Again. As soon as the softness of her breasts molded to the contours of his lean chest. As soon as his uneven breathing filled her ears. As soon as his mouth fused to hers. She locked herself into his embrace, burying her hands in his thick hair and bringing him to her.

Once again, she gave away her determination to the downpour of fiery sensations. Under the forbidden cloak of night where nothing was bright and true as day, Helena made love to Carrigan simply because she wanted to.

Chapter

→ 12 ←

Carrigan didn't want to love Helena. It wasn't as if he didn't have the capability to. He just didn't have the willingness to live with her. As she lived now. This was never more evident as he sat in the lean-to off his cabin, a smoke clamped between his lips as he viewed low clouds in a sky that threatened rain. As soon as he'd gotten away from town, the songbirds' notes of serenity had overpowered the rasp of hammers, the clink of metal on anvils, and raised voices in greeting and in argument.

When he and Helena had been by the lake, he'd forgotten about the strain on his ears made by Genoa's ever-continuing nuisances. The rowdy streets never slept. By day they were clogged with the sounds of freighters and their whips, wagon chains, and tradesmen wielding their professional tools. By night they gave way to the din of drunks, fiddles, and an occasional weapon discharged at the moon. Or no moon. It made no difference.

Never were these penetrating noises more unbearable to him than this afternoon when they'd rode down from the mountain onto Nixon Street with the string. One minute he'd been enjoying the honks of geese as they flew overhead; the next, the hollers of teamsters at an impasse over who had the right of way in the road had taken over the song of the birds in flight.

Carrigan had closed off his mind to the ruckus, and in doing so, closed off himself. Getting the horses into the stockade had been a priority. Once inside, he'd shut the high gates—hoping to shut out some of the racket—and begun the long process of checking each animal into its stall. He did all this with few words to spare. In the coming days, there would be much work do to with the horses. Their shoes and the nails would have to be checked, soles cleaned of rocks and gravel, each tail, forelock, and mane combed, quarters scraped, and washings given with warm water. But for today, since it had been late afternoon, the best Helena, Eliazer, and he could do was see that the animals were comfortably in their stanchions with the proper feed for the night. That done, Carrigan had left the station for the temporary seclusion of his cabin to fortify his staying power.

It hadn't felt good walking away. In fact, the departure brought a bitter taste to his mouth. Though this was where he wanted to be, he had to figure out how to be alone again. His mind was adrift in this picturesque and remote surrounding that was the only home he'd known in three years of his self-imposed banishment from society. Everything around him was the same, but he wasn't.

Last night had been a delicious fantasy. A feast for his senses. His every thought, touch, and taste had funneled in on Helena, and how she'd made him feel. He'd turned a deaf ear on the voice inside his head warning of the repercussions and visions of a future without her. His opinion of this dangerous entanglement with a woman who'd made him forget about his simple existence had been cast aside for his body's

many were making a wild dash for
would be no ground to stand on un
put out.

rusting the door to Gray's general store
igan found the interior deserted. He pushed
ugh the curtain partition, then ran through the
se and slammed out the kitchen door. Obsi ran
t to him in a considerable state of excitement, his
nzied barks filling the vacant yard. The horses had
eady been driven into one of the outlying pad-
cks. From the stables, frantic shouts arose. Then
azer, his wife, Emilie, and Helena came out with
oden buckets in each hand.

As soon as she saw him, Helena stumbled but kept
r balance and went straight for one of the watering
oughs. The wind blew cinders in showers. "Help
e," she pleaded. "We're going to wet the roof of the
able down so it doesn't burn."

He put his hands on her shoulders, gripping her
ith imploring fingers. "It won't do any good if that
re gets on top of you."

She broke free of him. "Don't say that." Dipping
first one, then the other, bucket into the water, Helena
struggled to hold the handles while moving briskly
toward the ladder on the side of the lofty building.
"Get water! Quickly!" she told the others.

Precious seconds ticked by, and Carrigan anxiously
gazed at the sky, which had grown thick with smoke.
"You won't have enough water, and you can't climb
that ladder with the weight you're carrying."

"Don't tell me no!" she screamed in a moan, water
sloshing the sides of her skirt. "I have to try!"

"Then try," he yelled, snatching one of the buckets
from her hand. "I'm going to make sure that fire
doesn't have the chance to burn you out. But it
breathes one spark into that rooftop, swear to
you'll run!"

She defiantly said nothing.

He roughly caught her elbow, taking her unawares

---

short-lived pleasure. Throughout a night of slow,
exploring lovemaking, his feelings had varied. So he'd
thrown them all to the wind and damned his promise
to put nothing more into it than physical necessity.
But the delusion had been dispelled by his awakening
with her in his arms. With her sun-golden hair a cloud
on his chest . . . her slumbering breath a rose's blush
on his cheek, he'd had to face the stern realities of his
life. In five months he would go. And she would stay.

He would become another painful memory to her,
shelved next to the man and child she'd lost. Her
admission hadn't tainted his view of her, nor had
beastly jealousy come to nip at him. Everyone made
mistakes. He wasn't faultless. Far from it. But it took
a strong person to realize the sins of the past, put a
name to them, and beg the mind for forgiveness.
Whether or not a soul wanted to accept atonement
was up to the individual, for he hadn't the same
power as Helena to speak of his aloud. His own
misjudgments were packed lock, stock, and barrel
beneath his ribs, stored safely in that organ of his
called a heart. If indeed the damn thing still worked.
Every now and then he could feel the chambers
pumping, but was it blood that flowed through him
. . . or ice water?

Carrigan rose from the crate he'd been sitting on,
and with a jerk of his wrist, projected his cigarette
into the cold fire pit at his feet. He went to the door of
his cabin. The porch was thick with unswept brown
pine needles and evidence of squirrels. Webs of spiders glistened in his rabbit traps with a tapestry of
gossamer threads. Already the place looked deserted.
Pulling the latch, Carrigan let himself in with Obsi at
his side to investigate.

The lackluster interior was filmed by the dirt that
had settled from the roof. His wrought-iron bed was a
dull gray. Even the red and blue pillows that normally brightened the coverlet were faded by dust from
lack of use. There were a couple of dead bees on his

tabletop, and a black ant crawling on the globe of his hurricane lamp.

On a whim, Carrigan removed his hat and tossed it toward the horns on the wall. The hat plummeted to the floor. He walked over to retrieve it, then took a few paces backward and tried again. The brim plunked off the chinked wall and wobbled on its crown in front of his trunk. Bending down, he dusted off the hat on his thigh and resettled the band around his head. He'd been able to perform the trick with his old hat. Guess he was rusty. Or he guessed he wasn't used to Helena's hat yet. The reminder of unfamiliarity didn't bode well in him. Not even his hat felt like it belonged here. Without her.

Carrigan glanced at the table again. It looked plain and ugly. Not like Helena's where the center was filled with pinecones and wild rose berries for decoration on top of the red-edged crocheted pieces. This room looked cold and bare with no flowered paper on the walls, nor etchings or portraits. Helena had silver candlesticks on the stone mantel in the sitting room. Carrigan had a pipe-stove with no adornments. Her floors were diamond-dyed brown and oiled so they wouldn't show grease spots. His were splattered with discolorations.

Seeing the cabin through the eyes of a man who'd just spent nearly a month in civilization, he admitted that there were certain aspects of city life that could be deemed agreeable. After years of only seeing wildflowers, he'd been treated to windowsill tulips and daffodils in boxes. There were lawns at certain residences that looked a lot better than the sunbaked, barren grass in the low country. The trees even had some good points. Their deep, peaceful shade could be enjoyed while sitting on a swing beneath them. And indoors, he could account for two things that this place lacked: high ceilings that seemed a damn spacious relief after the low log roof of this cabin. And closets. Helena's place had closets.

Jesus . . ." Carrigan muttered. "V___ ster, ___inking like this?" He needed to ride ___ there All one hundred and sixty acres of it. ___ was that was what he wanted. That that ___ would be happy.

Carrigan called for Obsi, who'd disa___ the bed. The dog came out with an elk b___ his teeth.

As Carrigan closed the door and ste___ porch, the odor of smoke reached his nos___ thought the smell was from his smolderi___ But when he checked, the butt had burne___ Sharp apprehension coursed through him ___ cles of his forearms tensed beneath his s___ hands hardened into fists. His heart began ___ madly as his gaze searched the treetops in ___ tion of Genoa. Over the lofty spires of gree___ of gray smoke slithered skyward.

Carrigan instantly set out in a run down h___ tain. He was seized by the terror surging in hi___ The fire serpent was deadly, for it had bitten h___ before. Flames were a worse enemy to him t___ soldiers he'd fought in the Mexican War. Beca___ took no prisoners, consuming everything in its ___ And God help him, with the wind in this dire___ Helena was in the road.

Carrigan pushed his legs to their limits in a ___ race down the center of Main Street. His lungs bur___ from the breakneck pace. General confusion reign___ among the men who blocked his way. He shoved pa___ a group of onlookers onto the boardwalk, sprintin___ over half barrels of merchandise and anything els___ that obstructed his path. Women, some holding ba___ bi__ and children crying fearfully were gathered on ___ t__ front entry walk of the Express station to watch ___ e blaze. The fire hadn't gotten this far, but was on ___ he opposite side of the street devouring the fourth ___ building from the corner. Rather than fight the mon-

and fiercely yanking her toward him. "Swear it, damn you!"

"This is everything I have!" she cried.

"You're everything I have," he shot back. "I will not lose another woman to a fire fiend. Do you hear me? I won't let you kill yourself. Swear it!"

Her mouth quivered, and the blue of her eyes widened. The tone of her voice came out in a barely discernible whisper as she said, "I . . . swear."

He shoved her away, firmly told Obsi to stay, then fled the stockade, still holding the bucket.

Pandemonium had broken out in the street, but someone had had the brains to at least form a bucket brigade. As Carrigan drew up to the conflagration, dust and hot ashes blew into his eyes. He squinted, staring into the burning blaze, momentarily blinded by its consuming power. The first building to go had been Wetherill's barbershop. Constructed of wood with thin paper covering interior walls, it had ignited as easily as newspaper in a woodstove. A column of fire shot through the roof, which was in imminent collapse. Glass fell in shards from the windows, as if giving the flames the right to enter. Samuel Paster's bootery shared a common wall with the barber's, and the smell of burnt leather was heavy in the air the moment smoke began to seep beneath the door.

Carrigan fell into the line of sweating men who were passing the buckets. No sooner had he tossed his container to one of the runners who were making passes to the water source than he received a full one in its place from the fellow behind him. In a handoff to the well-dressed gentleman in front, Carrigan barely made eye contact with him, but was given as stern a staring in return as the brief time would allow. Carrigan didn't remember the man and could see no reason for the hostility in his gray eyes.

Sparks flew like explosive celebrations out of the boot shop's chimney, which was nothing more than a barrel chinked with mud. One of the fire bugs caught in the rubbish pile on the side of the building, spreading to a mound of iron castings, where the red glows mercifully fizzled out. The business next door was Noonan's grocery. Built of wood, it was extremely dry and ripe for a fire. Within five minutes, flames had reached the roof and were bursting through the front windows.

"Get back!" came the hollers as glass sprayed the sidewalk.

The man with the gray eyes turned on Carrigan. "Move back, will you!"

Carrigan had already taken several sizable steps to the rear, so the reprimand was unnecessary. Had he the opportunity, he would have asked the man what the look was for. As it was, the wind was fanning the fire straight for the stockade. There was only a narrow alley, Mayhew's butcher shop and the expanse of Nixon Street keeping the wave of destruction from hitting Helena. The one hope Carrigan could see to keep the flames at bay was to outrun them by dousing Mayhew's. They could climb the stairway on the side of the building and water the roof.

A blast roared from the grocery as some type of contained chemical ruptured from the heat. Men scurried away, the brigade temporarily forgotten. Carrigan tried to stop several men and yelled, "Leave the grocery! We can't save it. Get to the side of the next building! We'll water it down!"

The man who'd been in front of him scoffed at the idea. "That won't work! The place is going to go up in flames. Keep trying to put out Mr. Noonan's, everyone!"

"Noonan's is gone," someone said as the roaring fire fed on its awning and posts. "I think Mr. Carrigan is right, Judge Kimball. We can't save anything here. Let's try and hold it off so it can't burn anything else."

Kimball. Carrigan took a hard look at the judge Helena said was powerless at finding her father's killer. This man had the appearance of a growling bear with a sore toe. He had the power.

"Hell yes to that!" seconded a third party. "It's my business we're talking about, and I'll do any damn thing I can to save it!"

"You're Mayhew?" Carrigan asked, pulling his thoughts from Kimball.

"I am. Can you help me?"

"You bring me enough hands and I can."

Mayhew hollered into the streets for volunteers. Carrigan led a group of men up the outside stairway, while a handful of others stayed behind to follow the judge's advice. In the confusion, Carrigan didn't have a moment to read Kimball's expression further, but he felt those steely eyes on him as he retreated. Windborne fire carried pieces of roofing, swirling great clouds of dust and ashes for Carrigan to dodge. He quickly put Judge Kimball at the back of his mind.

Taking the stairs by twos, Carrigan ran halfway across the roof. A sheet of flames from the grocery rose heavenward and danced about. An abrupt shift in the wind, and he felt his hair singed from the heat alone. The orange eyes of the serpent stared holes right through him. Momentarily frozen in his steps, Carrigan grew transfixed by his mighty opponent. He despised fear, and never more than now did he feel it working through his blood. This is what had taken Jenny's life . . . bringing her into this hell. Roasted alive in a blazing inferno was not his idea of glory . . . nor a way out of sorrow. He'd never go this far to be released from pain. Never. If only . . . if only he'd been there to stop her.

The water buckets soon flowed, and Carrigan, being in the front of the line, had to snap out of his flashback to dash toward the wavering flames beckoning from the adjacent rooftop. He was momentarily lost in the smoke, coming back out again, choking and coughing, only to handle another bucket and return to battle the insidious enemy before it leaped across the building.

The water brigade did keep the flames at bay for a while, but didn't quell them. Fire beads shot through the sky, raining down on Carrigan and the men who were struggling to keep Mayhew's from ruin. There was no way to increase their efforts. Each one was pushing himself to the limit, and water could not come any faster. It looked to Carrigan as if they would have to abandon their cause. His only thought was Helena and what was at stake for her. With a quick glance, he tried to see her on the stable roof. Eliazer was there, his bulky figure not suitable for the kind of energy walking swiftly across a pitched roof demanded. Before Carrigan could see who would follow the stock tender, he had to return his gaze to Mayhew, who stood behind him, and grab a fresh bucket of water.

Droplets fell on Carrigan, wetting his shoulders, but he couldn't immediately discern the source. At first he thought they came from Mayhew's water bucket. Only when he turned, Mayhew wasn't holding a bucket. It was delayed farther down the string.

"Did you feel that?" Mayhew asked, lifting his gaze. "I just felt it again!"

Carrigan tilted his chin, aiming the flat brim of his hat skyward. First one, then a second, drop splashed on his face. The thickened sky, like a dark ceiling, stood still . . . but from it came the kind of refresher that makes itself known in spring. Rain. Plump drops fell from the hooded clouds, dissolving the tiny sparks that bounced at Carrigan's feet.

"It's raining!" Mayhew screamed, passing the word down the line. "Rain!"

The moisture began to fall in a large downpour. Pools filled in the dimples of Mayhew's rooftop as dirty men stared at each other with mouths agape in disbelief. In prior weeks the lot of them had cursed the rain for mucking up the streets. Now they embraced and blessed it with wide, welcoming arms stretched toward the heavens.

Like a river, rainwater filled the gutters of Mayhew's. The firefighters began filing down from the building and congesting the streets. The shower prevente the fire from spreading, cooling hot ashes and putting out many of the spot fires in the fallen structures. Smoke damage from scorched wood filled the air with a putrid smell.

With his sleeves blackened by soot and a multitude of tiny cinder holes in his shirt, Carrigan stood with the others and surveyed the smoke and embers of the surrounding ruins as they hissed and steamed . . . slain. The blaze had taken half a city block. Smoldering and charred remains left the ground black and reeking.

"I want to thank you," Mayhew was saying to Carrigan as rain steadily plummeted around them. The butcher had reached out and encompassed Carrigan's hand with a tight squeeze. "The place would have been at least half-gone."

Carrigan saw the light of indebtedness in the man's eyes. He didn't like it. Not wanting anyone to feel like he owed him anything, Carrigan shrugged out of Mayhew's grasp with an affirming nod and began walking toward the stockade.

His ruined shirt was soaked through, and his pants stuck to his legs. Water fell in rivulets from his hat, wetting the back of his neck where his hair rested on his collar. Helena stood in the opening of the stockade gates, rain droplets streaming over her pale face. Obsi was at her side. Rather than go to her, Carrigan veered away and the dog came after him. Out of her sight and to the side of the high wall encompassing the Express station, Carrigan took in wavering gulps of air, swallowing the bile that rose in his stinging throat. With one hand leaning on the rough timbers for support, he emptied his stomach.

* * *

After the fire had been put out, an emergency town meeting had been called at Singleton's Hall in the Nevada Hotel. The townspeople had converged in the room indiscriminately used by the preacher, several debating clubs, the ladies' auxiliary, and at least one prisoner. On that occasion it had been before the courthouse had put in a cell, and a man accused of swindling had been chained to the printing press of the *Territorial Enterprise*. That was before the newspaper operation packed up and moved to Carson City.

Helena had gone to the meeting. So had Emilie, Ignacia, and Eliazer. But Carrigan was nowhere to be found. Helena hadn't seen him since he'd stood in Nixon Street just before disappearing around the side of the stockade without saying a word to her. She'd worried about him those long, interminable minutes before the meeting got under way. Once it did, her thoughts were taken by the startling news.

The fire had been started by the Paiutes. Ned Sanders had seen them on ponies in the sagebrush behind Main. They'd ridden pell-mell down the alleyway, shooting off several burning arrows into the buildings. There had been only a handful of the Indians, so Mr. Brown, the Indian agent, had discounted the possibility that the episode was a war party. In his estimation the incident was one of young warriors blowing off steam. But still . . . Genoa being attacked in broad daylight made Helena afraid.

"I tell you, people," Mr. Brown stated over the rain hammering on the ceiling, "I will inform Carson City of the events and request troops be brought into Genoa as soon as possible to dissuade any further trouble."

The room grew into a buzz of voices, then Mr. Mayhew rose from his chair. "I'd like to thank the Lord for the rain." Seeing the crestfallen faces of Messrs. Noonan, Paster, and Wetherill, he added, "And I'll be the first to pitch in and help my neighbors

rebuild." Nods of agreement followed. "But it has to
be said, I'd likely be burned down, too, if it hadn't
been for Mr. Carrigan." Shading his eyes with his
hands, Mayhew searched the crowd. He saw Helena.
"Where's your husband, ma'am?"

Helena bit her lip. "I'm not sure."

"Well, I think the town ought to know how he saved
my shop." On that, Mr. Mayhew related the events,
and a chorus of applause rose from the crowd for the
hero not in attendance. Helena graciously acknowledged their cheers, thinking that Carrigan should
have been here to receive his congratulations.

"Before you go handing out accolades for Miss
Gray's husband," Bayard said from the front of the
room, "I think you ought to know the truth about
him."

The room fell still, Helena's heart with it. She
stared at Bayard—albeit a ragtag version in his soiled
suit of clothes and face darkened with soot—seeing
the familiar figure of a man she'd known and trusted.
Counted on more times than she had fingers. Been a
confidante to, and loyal to the bone. What he was
going to say made her nauseated. He would slander
her husband. And in front of the town.

"As you know, Miss Gray's horses were let out on
the evening of May the ninth." It didn't go unnoticed
by Helena that Bayard didn't address her by her
legally married name. "I was a witness to their
release."

A rush of astonished voices passed through the
crowd, and gazes fell to Helena. She kept hers fastened on the man who commanded the room. The
man who commanded Genoa with his judicial presence. Her friend. Her betrayer.

Bayard's watch fob caught light of the high lanterns
hanging from ceiling chains. "I had the misfortune to
see Carrigan letting her animals go. Such an offense is
a hanging one."

Gasps rose; so did Helena. She angrily twisted the

front of her apron in her fingers. "I asked my husband about the incident, and he claims his innocence. I believe him. All the animals were rounded up—with his help, I might add—and no harm was done. I will not press any charges against him. I don't believe the law permits a wife to testify against her husband anyway."

Bayard's face went red with rage, and for the first time, Helena was scared of what he could do with the given authority of his appointed office. Could he impose a sentence on Carrigan, even if she wouldn't accuse him of the crime in question? Bayard's attempt to slander Carrigan was nothing short of getting back at her for marrying someone else. Perhaps she was due some of his scorn, but she hadn't intentionally scandalized him in public, as he'd just done to her. What he'd said was cruel, and she wouldn't readily forget his insensitivity.

No one dared say anything against Judge Kimball, but neither did they back him up in his quest to see Carrigan taken into his custody and hanged for an offense he didn't commit. Thankfully, just after Bayard's announcement, the discussion returned to the Paiutes, and the meeting broke up without any further mention of Carrigan. Bayard tried to cut through the throng to get to Helena, but she artfully eluded him, using the side aisles to make her escape.

She couldn't speak to him right now. Not with the way she was feeling about his duplicity. Once outside of the Nevada Hotel, Emilie linked her arm through Helena's. They walked with hurried steps in the rain to the general store. Helena's mind was not at all trained on her stride, but rather on where Carrigan had taken himself off to. As she stepped over a puddle, she tried to piece together why he'd left without an explanation.

"I need to know something, Lena," Emilie said through the downpour, drawing Helena from her troubled thoughts of Carrigan's disappearance. "The land your . . . Jake . . . was talking about was the parcel Father bought for us. Wasn't it?"

Helena couldn't flat out lie to her sister when Emilie was stating the truth. "Yes."

"I thought as much," she replied dismally. "How could you do it, Lena?"

"I had to. It was the only way he'd marry me. I'll get us other land. I promise. The station will bring in enough revenue for an even better parcel." Helena wrapped her fingers around her sister's arm, wanting desperately to make peace with her. "Believe me. Please believe me when I say I would never hurt you, Emilie."

Emilie stared at Helena, her youthful face looking wiser than her years. "I believe you, Lena. Just stop treating me like a child."

Helena found no ready reply to give her, no easy rejoinder that would dismiss her sister's worry of forever being a young girl in Helena's eyes. Rather than make any false promises, she said nothing.

Once at the station, everyone cleaned up and ate a cold supper before retiring early. The stressful exhaustion of the day had taken its toll on them all.

Everyone except Carrigan.

He hadn't come back, and the hour had grown late. The rain had increased, its deluge turning the streets into muddy streams. Had the weather permitted, Helena would have put on her clothes, taken a lamp, and walked to Carrigan's cabin. She couldn't help reliving the day she'd found him shot.

How could he make her worry so about him?

When they'd returned from the lake, she'd been filled with anxiety over where he would sleep tonight. But if he didn't come home, she wouldn't have to wonder anymore. Things had changed between them, but the elements of their marriage had not. At least not here. In the house, their relationship would have to remain the same. There was Emilie to consider. She would not embarrass her sister in such a way. And she could not put herself in Carrigan's embrace again. It was too difficult to leave it. But right now she would have gladly thrown her arms around him if he walked through the door unharmed.

The patter of rain fell on the boardwalk in front of the general store. Helena had come into this part of the house to wait for Carrigan. The rhythmic sounds of torrential water seemed to chant his words: *You're everything I have. You're everything I have.*

The litany confused her already unsettled thoughts. Did she really mean something to him? Or had he spoken to her in the heat of the moment, needing her to promise she'd leave if the fire came too close? Either way, he'd said them, and she couldn't forget.

In her nightgown, robe, and stockings, Helena stood at the store's window inconspicuously looking between the frame and the drawn ivory shade for a sign of Carrigan. The intersection was near pitch-dark, as lights from the four corner businesses were all but extinguished. A velvet yellow spilled from beneath the batwing doors of the Metropolitan Saloon. Talk of the fire would undoubtedly fill the rest of the night's drinking conversations. She'd welcome Carrigan being in the bar getting drunk with the rest of them. As it was now, she hadn't a clue to his whereabouts.

Blinking her weary eyes, she kept a vigil while shifting her weight from one foot to the other. In a moment she'd make a pot of coffee and bring it back to the window. And wait. And look. And hope.

Chapter

→ 13 ←

Carrigan was dying.

The mother of all hangovers had made itself known in his brain and was hammering mercilessly at his blood vessels until he swore they would rupture from the pressure. Lying on the rumpled bed in his cabin, he fixed his gaze on the ceiling timbers. It had to be daybreak because he could see sunlight beaming through tiny cracks in the corner joints. Staring so long, his eyes grew dry. Carrigan blinked. His vision blurred. Then he closed his eyes again and went back to sleep. For what length of time, he had no idea.

When he woke, he was as cold as an outhouse seat on a January morning. Slipping first one, then the other, eye open, he attempted to lift himself onto his elbows. His head spun like a top out of control, and he had to lie back down until the spasms of dizziness subsided. When he was able, he pushed himself up and glared at the yawning front door. He must have left it open all night long.

Rainwater puddled on the flooring in front of the

door. Damn, he was freezing. He hadn't slept with a blanket on that he could recall. Mustering his energy, he rose to sitting. Instantly he clutched his head before it split wide open. He sat that way for quite a spell, then by small degrees, inched his legs over the side of the bed. When he stood, he had to grip the bedstead for support. Slowly making his way to the door, he held the jamb and leaned on his side before proceeding outside.

The sun was blinding, and were he able to hit a mark right now, he would have thrown his boot at it to shut it off. Walking to the rear of the cabin, he relieved himself in the blue building, then went back inside and closed the infernal cold out.

He needed to get warm and opened the door to his stove, hating that he had to turn to fire so soon after yesterday. His hangover left him incapable of judging how much wood to put inside, so he pitched in three huge wedges and slammed the door.

Obsi lay in the corner, his head lifted from his paws as Carrigan stumbled about.

"What are you looking at?" he snapped.

The dog lowered his chin and watched his master make an ass out of himself.

Carrigan rifled through the trunk by his bed, searching for another bottle of Snakehead. He knew he had one around here somewhere. Surely he couldn't have drunk the place dry. He needed a bracer to take the edge off this damn headache. Finding a bottle buried in the folds of the bedclothes, he popped the cork and took a burning swallow, thankful he couldn't smell the smoke anymore.

He'd come to his cabin after the fire and stripped out of his clothes, plunging into the trough in the corral and scrubbing the stink off his body until his flesh stung. But he could still smell it. The reeking scent of smoke and charcoal. It had upset his stomach, and he'd gotten sick once more. When he couldn't take the smart of lye soap anymore, he'd walked naked into the cabin and dressed in clean clothes. But the permeating stench had gotten inside him. He'd had to turn to liquor to get rid of the odor. To fog his mind enough to pass out.

He'd had a dream last night. A vile, sickening dream. That he'd been chewing on the end of his gun and . . . Jesus, he couldn't summon any more than that. But it was enough to make him want to jump out of his skin. During his cattle days when nights were spent around a campfire discussing philosophy, Hart had told him that every man had some peculiar train of thought that he fell back on when he was alone. For years that deliberation had been on Jenny and her death. That, and the unknown troopers who'd raped her. But last night's dream had him scared. The normal course of mourning had gone over the edge the moment he'd had to encounter that fire and saw firsthand the jailer who'd kept his wife captive while she perished.

After hearing from the Libertyville sheriff that she was gone, there had been that split second when he'd thought about joining her. But the idea passed so briefly before his eyes, it was never really there at all.

Until last night in his unconscious. In the shadow of his mind where dreams were fatal. He should know they were nothing but pure imagination. Had he not imagined making love to Helena before he actually did? Giving way to a drunk had put too much stress upon a dream that he would never act out.

Obsi growled, rising to his paws and stealthily going toward the door. Carrigan groped for his Colt, but wasn't wearing his gun belt. In a sloppy search, he brushed his fingers across the butt beneath his pillow. That the revolver had been so close to his head had him breaking out in a cold sweat.

Training the Walker on the door as it moved in with a creak, Carrigan clicked the hammer back. Helena came into view, and Obsi ceased his low rumbling. Wagging his tail, he nuzzled her hand with his nose.

Carrigan fell back a step, his balance not worth a flying eagle cent. Neither was his accuracy, so he was rather relieved it was Helena come to call instead of Hanrahan or some other bastard come to put a slug in him.

Helena's cheeks were the color of strawberries poured with cream . . . a delectable blush of sweetness. Though the look in her eyes was anything but. Sour. The blue was as sour as an unripe fruit on the vine. And dusted with dark smudges beneath as if she hadn't slept. Wearing a cloak and the same dress she had on when she'd first come to his mountain, she put her hands on her hips. She had nice hips. He liked them pressed flush against his. And he loved her scent. Like sage honey. So desirable and feminine . . . he could barely stand to be in the same room with her without his body inside her and staying there forever.

"To what do I owe this pleasure?" Carrigan asked in a wry tone, grabbing the bottle by its neck after depositing his Colt on the banded trunk's lid.

"What are you doing here?"

"Now, that's an asinine question." He raised the Snakehead whiskey in a toast to her. Her gaze narrowed. "I'm enjoying the spectacle of an outraged woman."

She closed the door, making no comment. With a fluid motion, she unfastened the closure at her throat and took off her cloak. She hung it next to the door.

"Why is it so hot in here?" she asked.

"I'm preparing for hell."

She flashed him an icy stare. "It looks to me like you're wallowing in a suffering of your own making. Though whatever for, I don't know."

"I can wallow in whatever I want."

Her back turned on him as she went about tinkering in his kitchen stuff. Carrigan slumped onto the bed and kicked his feet out in front of him. Why had she come? He didn't like being in her company when he was feeling nasty. It wasn't her fault he'd gotten drunk, but he was in a mood to take it out on whoever was nearest him.

Soon the aroma of strong coffee wafted through the damp air.

Carrigan took a slight drink of whiskey, but the taste didn't settle his stomach as it should have. "What are you doing?"

"I'm going to offer you a drink."

"You got whiskey hidden on you?"

"No. Coffee."

"I'd rather not."

"But you will because I insist." She turned toward him, a steaming cup in hand, and brought it to the bed. "I'll take that so you can hold on to the cup without spilling on yourself."

With an arch of his brow, he relinquished the whiskey and took a sip of the hot coffee. Then another. And another. Admittedly, the dark brown liquid was effective in tamping the throb at his temples.

Helena pulled out the chair at the table and sat, her hands clasped in her lap. "You didn't come home last night."

"I know that."

"I was worried."

"Don't worry about me."

"I couldn't help myself. I stayed up nearly all night watching for you. I feared you'd been shot again."

"Nobody's going to shoot me again."

"Why didn't you come home?"

"I am home."

She appraised him with a slighting gaze. "You know what I meant." Her punctuated sigh filled the room. "I was very worried," she repeated. "All night, my mind went around and around what could have happened to you. I almost thought that Bayard Kimball had taken you into custody and—"

The name inspired a recollection. "Bayard Kimball, the judge?"

"Yes."

"Why would he take me into custody?"

Helena grew visibly distraught, her teeth catching her lower lip. "It doesn't matter now."

"It does when you bring something up, then don't finish what it is you were going to say."

She was clearly torn between silence and revealing the rest of her thought. When she looked at him, reluctance marked her gaze. "The morning Eliazer told us the horses had been let out, Judge Kimball came to me and said he saw you herding the mustangs from the stockade the night before."

A streak of anger lit through Carrigan. "That's a crock."

"I didn't believe him."

"You sure as hell did."

"Perhaps a little." Her eyes were guilt-ridden. "But I realized you couldn't possibly have done such a thing to me."

"Damn right." Carrigan let the coffee sober him. "So why is this judge pursuing the matter? What's he want to do—charge me with horse thievery?"

Nodding, Helena slowly said, "I don't think it's you he really wants to hurt. It's me."

"Why would he want to hurt you?"

"Because I married you instead of him."

Carrigan took a swallow of coffee, the heat melting his throat. He didn't like what he was hearing. "Is this judge in love with you?"

"I don't know." Helena's gaze fell to her lap. "But he did ask me to marry him. Twice."

The green-eyed monster took a satisfying mouthful of him, just when he thought he was immune to it. No wonder Kimball had glared at him with deadly intent. "Why didn't you?"

She met his eyes. "Because I couldn't. It wouldn't have been fair of me to do so. You know why."

"Then you have feelings for him?"

"Yes . . . no." Her cheeks flushed a rosy color. "I . . . That's not the point."

"Either you have feelings for him or you don't."

"I did . . . do think of him as a trusted confidant. He was our closest family friend when my father was living. I know that's he upset with me, so . . ." She shook her head. "It just doesn't justify what he said. Right now it's not important what my relationship is with him because I'm not sure myself." She leaned closer, lowering her tone to a lacy-soft whisper. "I need to know, could Bayard find out about the men you . . . killed, and do something to you because of it? Did you serve jail time? Or could he impose another sentence on you?"

"No one can sentence me for something I haven't done."

"But those men . . ."

Carrigan's brain was sloshed with a mixture of coffee and liquor, but he did know that he was beginning to see her meaning. "If anyone wants to find the men I killed, they'll be looking for an unmarked graveyard."

"I don't understand."

"First of all, the men can't be traced back to me. Secondly, at the time of their deaths, they were shooting at our side, as much as we were theirs. I fought in the Mexican War and was attached to E Company, First infantry, for ten months. I was seventeen. It was my duty and obligation to my country to take up firearms against the Mexicans. I couldn't give you an exact body tally, but there were too many to count."

"Why didn't you explain this to me before? Why did you let me believe—"

"Your stock tender is of Mexican descent, and once your father told me Eliazer was a soldier in the war. Do you think Eliazer would like knowing the enemy was living on the very property he was?"

"But that was twelve years ago."

"Men never forget the battles that take their brothers." Carrigan finished the coffee and handed the empty cup to Helena for more. "You saw how quick Eliazer was to accuse me of letting your horses go. I'm an outsider to him. He may be tolerant of me, and even see the benefits of having me help with the horses, but there's no trust there. Trust is earned, and in his mind, I haven't proved myself yet. I was right in keeping my military background from you. From him. Disclosing it would have served no purpose."

"But I believed that you killed men, though I told myself there had to be good reason."

"And there was. So that's all that needs to be said on the subject."

Helena came back with a refill and resumed the chair. "Is there anything else you haven't told me about yourself? Anything you've implied, but isn't necessarily accurate?"

"Is this the hour of confessions?" His headache came back in a full swell of beating drums. It was hardly worth him discussing his past if he couldn't reconcile it in his own mind. "Have you others yourself that you need to enlighten me on?"

Now there was more anger on her face than concern. "I have nothing else. Unless you want to count the flaws of human nature. I'm not perfect, nor do I profess to be."

"My character is far from impeccable. But that was one of the reasons you married me. You wanted a disreputable man."

Helena studied him, reflections of light in her eyes. There was defiance in her expression, as well as subtle challenge. She'd laid her cards on the table when they'd been at the lake. Now it was his turn to call. But like Helena, he'd never spoken a word of what happened in his past to a soul either. How could he tell her he was a failure? A man who couldn't avenge his dead wife, so he'd boxed himself away from everyone and everything, ashamed and disgusted by his inability to attain justice.

The black silence lingered between them, Carrigan uncertain how to pull the story from his hardware of rusty keepsakes.

"I'm leaving." Helena gathered her skirt to rise. "You obviously have no faith in me. In us. Sham that we are. No convictions—"

"I had convictions." His loud and emotion-filled voice stopped her. "Only they were forged in a bonfire of confused romanticism. I thought . . . I thought love was forever. But it's not." With a jittery hand, he combed the hair from his eyes, then took another swig of coffee to sharpen his vision. "There are many things about me you don't know. Things that I wish even I didn't have to live with. But I do. And so I have. Until you came into my life. Then everything looked different. Felt different. I became different."

Helena quietly gazed at him, her face half in sunlight. The murky rawhide film that covered the window only bestowed a muted brightness to the room. "Why did you run away from me yesterday?"

"It wasn't you. It was the fire. The smell of it, the feel of it, on me and in me. I couldn't stand to be in my skin and had to get out."

"Tell me," she gently asked. "Please."

Carrigan drew a deep breath inside, feeling the heat of the room bearing down on him. "I have to start from the beginning."

Helena poured herself a cup of coffee and waited for him to speak what he'd never spoken before. "You know that I thought I was in love with a woman named Kate Hisom."

She nodded.

"But that was not love," Carrigan disputed. "It was my obligation to find a wife. Much like yourself, the same things were expected of me. My mother, Malissa, was a convert to the Free Methodist way of thinking. My father used to say, 'Free to do almost

nothing. No smoking, drinking, dancing, or singing.'
A hard message to live by when my father had
abandoned religion, being a mean and ornery drunk. I
didn't know what they valued in each other to make
them take their wedding vows, until I was older and
could calculate for myself that I was conceived before
they were married. I have to give the old man some
credit for making an honest woman out of her. She
brought a wealthy dowry with her into the marriage.
Saddle horses, blankets, and skins. She was part
Choctaw." He waited for Helena's reaction, some
skitter of shock or loathing to betray her thoughts
about his ancestry. But none came. "You have no
comment?"

"What would you have me say? That I find it ap-
palling your mother was an Indian? You'll not get that
response from me. I know you for who you are, not
what you are. It makes no difference to me, and I'm
insulted you would think otherwise."

She'd put him in his place faster than a gallop. "I
wasn't sure how you'd feel about it," was all he could
offer in his defense, then wisely continued before she
could make him feel like a bigger jackass. "After I
graduated from school, I traveled and followed the
wheat harvests to earn some money for the family. I
read everything I could get my hands on and put up
with a lot of ribbing because of it. Being the son of a
onetime cattleman, I wasn't supposed to like books.
But I did. English literature mostly."

Helena's gaze landed on the case of novels that
lined the lower half of the wall. "I like to read, too.
But it seems like I never have the opportunity."

"You should make the time. Reading enriches the
spirit. And it makes a man forget about his own life."
Carrigan nursed the coffee in his cup, now cooled to
the temperature of the warm room. "Two years later, I
returned home for the burial of my younger brother,
who had been fifteen at the time of his death. He died
of a disease the doctor hadn't been able to diagnose.

Once back at home, I saw that things between my parents hadn't improved, but rather, deteriorated. I wasn't there long before the bickering made me move on once again. I left my sister and other brother behind for the gold fields of northern Idaho. The inhumane conditions of the mining camps were enough to make me enlist in the army to fight in the Mexican War. That is an entire story of blood and gore, one that altered my outlook on life, and one that I will not discuss with you. I was discharged in July.

"The year I turned twenty, my hometown of Red Springs had grown to a moderate size. It's then I met Kate Hisom, and you know that much." He drained his cup, thirsting for another. "If you don't mind, pour me one more."

Helena rose and refilled the cup. He watched her gentle motions, thinking he was every kind of fool for spilling his guts to her. He hadn't spoken so many detailed sentences to another human being in well over three years. She came back with his coffee, but remained silent. Her thoughts were anyone's guess. He could no more read her expression than he could next month's newspaper.

After taking a deep drink of the hot brew, Carrigan went on. "Kate's refusal had me moving on. From sheepherding, to cattle once again, I ended up in Libertyville. I was a man who felt the itch in his feet so strong, I couldn't settle anywhere for long. But I liked the town enough to stay. I got a job breaking horses for a cattle company. It's there I met Hart, the fellow I told you taught me about shoeing.

"Libertyville wasn't on the beaten path, but it was built up enough so that a man could buy himself a drink and a woman every Saturday night after he got paid." Carrigan paused, wondering how much he should candy-coat, and how much he should just plain come out and state. Seeing Helena's unflinching gaze, he opted to hold nothing back. "There was one whorehouse, The Exchange Club, that caused quite a stir one night when the madam, Glory, announced the arrival of a new girl. She was rumored to be a Shoshoni princess. Curiosity got the best of every man, myself included, and the place was busting at the seams to get a look at her." Carrigan need a moment to bring Jenny to his mind first, picturing how she'd looked that first time he'd seen her. Dressed in doeskin regalia with beads and feathers. Her skin had been a burnished brown, and her unbound hair a lustrous raven. The large, sad brown eyes that softened her face were not downcast. Pride lifted her chin, but her shoulders trembled. The man next to Carrigan boasted Jenny had been sold to Glory for an outrageous price by two packers who'd found her wandering in the mountains after her family had been killed. The madam claimed Jenny was a virgin and would expect top dollar for her.

He'd taken his pleasure with the whores with little conscience, for he'd known they were in a profession of their own choosing. But Jenny had been sold into it. As the bidding had begun, he hadn't joined in. Rather, he sought the company of one of the other girls, eager to please.

"Go on . . ." Helena's voice hurtled Carrigan back to the present.

"Her name was Jenny, and she was a beautiful woman." That was all he would elaborate on. The portrait of Jenny was on a canvas in his head. Like a selfish artist, he didn't care to share its fine details. "I never touched her when she worked there. One afternoon, two weeks later, she cut herself. A bunch of us filed into the brothel, and we saw Jenny laid out in a filmy dress with a towel on her face. She'd tried to disfigure herself by that heathen Indian custom of cutting off her nose. She would have succeeded if Glory hadn't stopped her. But the damage was done and Glory was sure her best girl would be scarred and so tossed her into the street." Carrigan cringed, clearly seeing in his mind's eye Jenny lying in the dirt, holding a towel to her face, neither crying or moving. Jesus, he'd known she'd been violated in that house, but interfering with a madam and one of her boarders was not something a man did unless he felt like having the crap beat out of him—or worse—by the house watchdogs.

"My friends went into the saloon. So did I. I needed a stiff belt to erase her face from my thoughts. But I couldn't forget. When we left the saloon, we found her. She'd crawled to the opening of an alley and was barely conscious. My friends moved on, but I was rooted to the spot. She opened her eyes and gave me a soulful gaze that shot right through me. I couldn't walk away, no matter how badly I wanted to."

The rest of her recovery was a painful time for Carrigan. Moments he didn't want to divulge. But he was helpless not to relive them right now in his own head. Jenny had allowed him to pick her up, perhaps because he'd been the only one never to touch her before. Since he couldn't keep her at the bunkhouse, he'd taken her just outside of town, ridden back to get his gear, then put up a camp in which to tend to her. She never said a word. She just stared at the campfire. Day in and day out. After the fifth day, she spoke, but in the Shoshoni language of which he had no experience. She made gestures for him to allow her to do the cooking. He'd figured as soon as she was well, she'd leave. But she didn't.

"Did she die?" Helena's gentle query sent sorrow through him, like the dart of an arrow, piercing deep.

"Not then . . . no. I took care of her, and she stayed as my companion through the winter. Just my companion," he restated. "Nothing more. I'd built a crude little cabin for us with Hart's help just in time for the first snow. With a combination of Shoshoni and English, Jenny and I were able to communicate with one another. I never made contact with her in an intimate manner. But as the long months wore on, her faith in me turned to trust." Meeting Helena's eyes,

Carrigan took no pleasure in saying, "One night she crawled into my bed and our relationship took on a new meaning. That spring I realized I'd fallen in love with her. I decided to marry her, seeing as I was enjoying all the comforts of a husband."

"You were legally married?"

"Yes."

He saw that this saddened Helena. It wasn't his intention to cause her grief, or to make their own marriage look more invalid than it was. But she'd wanted the truth, and this was it. No holds barred. "I wrote to my parents and told them about Jenny. To my surprise, my father came to Libertyville, announcing after thirty years, he'd split the blanket with my mother and gone on his own way. He also informed me my other brother had died of pneumonia that winter.

"It wasn't an easy life. My wife was taunted when she went to town, but she never let them know how much they hurt her. That summer, Hart and I and a dozen of the men were sent on a mare roundup some miles away. I left Jenny in the care of my father and was gone for a month. When I returned . . ." Carrigan's voice dried as if it were parchment blowing in an arid desert. He felt pain slicing in his chest, a wound reopened. Raw and aching. "I returned and found out a week prior to my homecoming, my wife was attacked and raped by two cavalrymen who were in Libertyville with their company on reconnaissance. My father tried to stop them and had taken a severe gash on his forehead before being knocked unconscious."

Helena put her hands to her lips and shook her head. "I'm sorry . . . so very sorry."

Carrigan couldn't afford to absorb Helena's comfort. Like a man confessing on a witness stand, he had to go on before he changed his mind. "I found her sitting beside the hearth, mesmerized by a blazing fire. The season being early summer, it was hotter than Hades in the house. I didn't understand why she needed to be so warm. She wouldn't respond to me. She refused to speak about the incident and merely stared at the flames with a transfixed gaze. My father told me she hadn't said a word since the attack.

"The sheriff in Libertyville said he wasn't about to dispatch a posse after one of the army's own." The company name replayed in Carrigan's head. Detach D, Ninth Infantry U.S. Cavalry Indian Scouts. "They were men who served their country . . . not animals who raped women, the sheriff told me. It was all bullshit, and I wasn't about to let the crime go unpunished.

"My father wasn't able to describe the two men to me, his memory having been faded from liquor. Never more than then did I resent his fondness for the bottle. But I wouldn't be put off. I meant to hunt them all down, and if need be, slaughter the whole damn company.

"I tried to reassure Jenny that I would find and kill the men responsible for hurting her. She didn't speak to me. She'd withdrawn in the same manner as when I'd found her in The Exchange Club. I should have known. . . . I did know. . . ." Carrigan felt the sting of tears biting the backs of his eyelids. "All I could do was hold her in my arms and tell her that I loved her. I packed my gear early the next morning.

"The time frame being what it was, I had no fresh trail to follow other than the mention in Libertyville that Detach D was headed into Cheyenne Territory. I was gone for over a week and found nothing. It was as if their tracks had been swallowed by the plains of grass. Fury devoured my insides. I couldn't eat or sleep. My desire for revenge was so strong, it threatened to break me. But it was a futile chase, and I turned my horse around and headed for home.

"The afternoon I returned to Libertyville, I found the cabin in ashes." The scene of destruction haunted him until this day. Smoldering ruins. A fireplace standing alone. Walls blackened and fallen. The ground putrid and reeking. "I rode to the sheriff's and was informed my wife had died in the fire the prior day. My father was barely alive at the doctor's office. I went to him. . . ." Even now, it was too painful to imagine the state his father had been in. Like a breathing corpse . . . dark and stinking of smoke. "My father's dying words were spent on telling me she'd done it on purpose. She'd sat on the bed and burned the place around her. He'd tried to get her out, but couldn't. Jesus, God Almighty, she killed herself, and I knew she was suicidal before I left, but I wanted to avenge her so bad, I didn't acknowledge that she needed me more."

Helena had left the chair and sat quietly on the bed next to him. She took the cup from his hand and held his fingers. "Don't do this to yourself," she said in a soothing voice. "Don't . . ."

He glared at her, unable to accept the consolation she was giving. "I might as well have started that fire myself and killed them both."

"You didn't."

"I left that goddamn town the day I turned twenty-seven. I had become so disillusioned with civilization, I wanted to get away from it before I lost my mind. Even the thought of tracking the bastards who'd violated Jenny became a numbness in my head. I tried to pick up their trail once again, but there was no hope for it. At a stage stop, I heard that most of the company had been slaughtered in a raid near the Bighorn River."

Drawing in a shaky breath, he nailed the last spike into his coffin and laid the final piece of his past to rest. "I wandered south for a year, searching for a place to live in solitude. A place where no one would find me and I wouldn't have to deal with people. I found this mountain. I encountered some sodbusters near Pierce Town—the last folks I spoke with for a long time. They put me up in their barn for the night. Before I left in the morning, they gave me a pup. Obsi." Carrigan smiled at the dog, who lifted his head at the sound of his name. "I wouldn't have made it without him.

"My first year of true isolation, I nearly died of starvation. The cold, lack of someone to talk to, and my grief killed my spirit. I survived on the wild berries I'd picked in the summer and small game I trapped. I was never so happy for a thaw in all my life. I built this cabin the spring and summer of 'fifty-eight. In doing so, I accepted that I would never go back to where corrupt men's rules governed the law of the land." His gaze rose to hers. "But they found me . . . the settlers who came to this town. And I was lured by the prospect of a newspaper and its information. Fresh eggs. And the things I'd taken for granted. Not only that, but conversation. Jesus, talking to Obsi or my horses . . . they don't talk back. But your father did. And we shared a common interest. Horses. Then you came, and now things are different again. Your place reminds me of my working days at the ranch and how much I'd liked it. I have no use for that now, but getting myself to admit it is hard."

Helena let out a long breath, her fingers stroking the top of his hand. He wasn't used to caring gestures, soft words, and remorseful sentiments echoed in his behalf. This was a new experience, and he wasn't certain what to take from her and what not to. Helena knew how to give genuine comfort, knowing just how to soothe, how to reason, and how to understand. She could sympathize with him. She had a past of her own. Now they both had given a part of themselves to each other. Not unlike the symbolic gold bands on their fingers that had originated out of false adornment. Beyond the gold was a silent token of trust. And faith.

It amazed him that what was to have been a

marriage in name only was turning into more. By trading thoughts and emotions, they'd superseded the physical need and release between a man and a woman. There was a deeper bond now. One that he had neither expected or sought. He had feelings for her. Deep-seated in his heart. But those very feelings were his worst enemy. Because he constantly fought them, unwilling to give up his way of thinking that he was better off alone.

What he could concede was that he wanted her arms around his neck, her hair against his cheek. There was nothing sexual in his want. It was a purely affectionate craving. Wanting her body, he could rationalize as a man desiring a woman. Wanting her friendship, he could not readily define. Friendship didn't come easy for him. He'd been a roamer for most of his life, wherein friendships were born out of necessity to stay alive. A man had to count on his fellow puncher to keep the cattle in line, or else they'd all suffer the consequences. But once at the end of the trail, those hasty friendships that had been formed usually dissolved.

Just like this relationship would in October. It seemed a fair amount of time away. Too long a span to be together with Helena without feeling something for her.

Without saying a word, he held open his arms and she came into them. Her hands fell softly on his shoulders. She didn't embrace him with false abandon, nor touch him with personal indifference. Her body compliantly met his. The stubble on his chin caught in her hair, and he smoothed the few golden skeins with the flat of his palm. She'd worn the curls twisted and pinned at the nape of her neck. He had no thoughts to remove the confining pins from her hair. This was a moment of tender expression, one in which he took just as much pleasure as he did in sex. In this, the coupling of arms where warm clothing met warm clothing, he could admit there was more to his emotional frame of mind when he was near her than just the desire to bring her to his bed.

Holding a woman and enjoying her feel, smell, and breath on his neck without needing passion was the beginning of love. And no man was ever cured of love once he discovered its hidden riches.

Chapter

⇒ 14 ⇐

Helena decided she was going to start thinking of Carrigan by his given name, Jake. The name Carrigan was nothing more than a front to a man who was no longer someone she thought of as a recluse with a hefty Colt that kept people at bay. Jake's character came from within and wasn't cut of stone. He had many sides to him. There were still some elements of the Carrigan she'd first met—the man with a pensive side who was, more often than not, silent and brooding. Yet she had seen that he felt pain, laughter, joy . . . love. That was Jake.

He had loved his first wife. That much was very evident when he spoke about her. Oddly, Helena didn't feel cheated that he'd been married before. Nor was she angry at him anymore for not coming home and scaring her half to death. She felt saddened he'd had to lose Jenny in such a horrible way. The circumstances surrounding the people they'd once loved were tragic, and it was those knowing feelings that had them holding each other for unchecked minutes after he'd finished telling her why he'd come to the mountain. Never more than then had she felt so right in a man's arms. Not even with Kurt had she sensed such a profound closeness. Was it unfair of her to feel this different kind of kinship with Jake? She didn't want to do anything to lessen the joys of her magical first love.

Love. The irresistible impulse toward it after the night she and Jake had spent at the lake had seized on her suddenly and without warning. She had to remind herself this was no charming romance in which picnics, poems, and presents were the order of the day. Love could not endure indifference. She had to stop herself before she magnified her emotions into a vast deal of nonsense and no sound common sense.

It was just as well when they left the mountain together, with Obsi sprinting every which way, there was no more touching. Not even a joining of hands.

"I found out the fire in town was started by the Paiutes," she told Jake while minding her steps. "Mr. Brown, the Indian agent, is going to call in troops from Carson City."

"You shouldn't go far from the station, then," Jake said as he bent a branch back to let her pass. "No more coming to my cabin."

She wondered if that meant he'd be frequenting his former residence more often. Though she didn't question him.

"If you have to go anywhere in town, take me or Eliazer with you."

The name of her stock tender brought forth a recollection. "I'm going to talk to Eliazer." Helena lifted her skirt and petticoat a notch higher so the hems wouldn't bead with rainwater from a cluster of violets. "I want to make him understand that you had nothing to do with the horses being let out. I don't want any animosity in the house when there's no reason for it."

They reached the general store and entered through the front doors.

"I've got fences to finish repairing," Jake said, and continued on with Obsi trailing after him.

While Helena walked between the aisles, Emilie glanced up from the female customer she'd been waiting on and gave Jake an accusatory stare. Another person Helena was going to have a talk with. Emilie would have to accept that the land their father bought them was gone, and it wasn't Jake's fault that it was. Helena had traded it to him without any pressure. She could have said no. Emilie needed to believe that Helena would get them a better parcel when they got back on their feet.

"Eliazer was looking for you," Emilie mentioned. "It's time to saddle a horse for the morning rider. It's Thomas McAllister, you know," she added with a smile she couldn't keep back.

Helena knew, but hadn't a moment to ponder how to handle the budding romance between her sister and Thomas. No sooner was Helena outside than the morning and afternoon were taken by the demands of the Express station. She found a few minutes to slip away and offer the victims of the fire free mail service for as long as they needed it. That was all she could do for now. Had she the money to spare, she would have donated some to the fund. But even without her currency in the pot, both Mr. Lewis and Mr. Wyatt had seemed genuinely impressed. They'd been among the group of men standing in front of the damaged buildings assessing the repairs and talking about the cost of lumber to rebuild.

Just as long, cigar-shaped clouds formed off the eastern slopes of the Sierras, forecasting dust devils, Helena took shelter in the stable and set up the candle-making equipment for beeswax dipping tomorrow. With no one else in the building, she lit a lamp and hung the wire handle on a nail above her head. She went to work by laying out the plaited cotton wicks and sorting through the strong stems of cattails she used as molds.

One of the double doors pushed in, and Helena turned to see Emilie approaching. Her sister's smile hadn't faded since Thomas's speedy departure some hours before. She held a fancy, printed circular in her hand. Helena knew what it was and went back to measuring lengths of wicks.

"Is supper almost ready?" Helena asked as Emilie drew up to her side.

"Uh-huh." Emilie knit her slender fingers behind her back and watched with a forced interest that Helena was able to note without much trying. "I closed the store a little early. With the wind picking up the way it is, I didn't have a single customer the past half hour. I don't understand it. People won't come out in the wind, but they will on the first day of the week. Last Sunday we sold over two hundred dollars worth for cash. I don't like doing business on the Lord's time, and it seems sacrilegious we do so well on a day intended for church reflection."

"Tending store on Sunday doesn't mean you can't conduct yourself in a Christian way."

"Hmm." Casual as could be, Emilie asked, "Are you going to make candles now? It's rather late in the day to start."

"I'm dipping them tomorrow."

"Oh." The paper in Emilie's hand ruffled.

Helena didn't say a word about it. "I'm glad you came in, Emilie. I wanted to make you understand why I gave Jake the land."

Emilie's face pinched.

"It was only fair I compensate him with the parcel to seal our bargain. He didn't force me into giving it to him. I was backed into a corner to get married because of the town's refusal to give us service. Two unmarried sisters couldn't have operated this station without being shut down. One of us needed a husband."

"I could have married Thomas," Emilie said quietly.

Helena gazed at her sister. "You're only sixteen."

"Mother was sixteen when she married Father."

Unable to dispute that, Helena made no comment. "I just don't want you to dislike Jake."

"Why not? You don't like him."

Helena was shocked. "Wherever would you get an idea like that?"

"Because you don't share a bedroom with him. You don't love him, Lena. You can't pretend you're happy. Is he going to stay in Father's room forever?"

Helena bit her lip. That was a difficult subject, but one about which Emilie would know the truth sooner or later. "No. I told him he only has to stay for six months. After that, he's free to go."

"And you'll still be his wife even though you don't live together?"

"Yes. If I run into any trouble, he'll come help us."

Emilie's eyes saddened. "It doesn't make any sense, Lena, to live your life with no happiness."

"I'm fine."

Parchment stirred and Emilie brought the flyer out into the open. "Maybe you're content to stay as you are, but I'm not. I got this from the invitation committee. There's going to be a Candy Dance a week from tomorrow. Thomas said he could ride in from Placerville for the night. He asked me to go, Lena. I want to—"

"No."

"You're being unfair! You're not even listening to me."

Helena sized a wick next to a mold. "We're in mourning for our father. We cannot accept social engagements."

"If we're in such deep mourning, you never should have married while you're still wearing dark clothes."

"That's different."

"No, it's not. Last year we weren't in mourning for Father, and you didn't want to go then. You're just making up excuses. Well, I won't give you any. I can

236

cook the molasses candy and sugar candy. You wouldn't have to do a thing. You wouldn't even have to attend if you didn't want to. I could get Eliazer and Ignacia to be chaperons for me and—"

"It's not a good idea."

"Nothing fun is ever a good idea to you!" Emilie shot back. "You might as well be a prune-wrinkled old widow. You never want to do anything but stay here and make me look like a child! I'm a young woman, Lena," she implored. Straightening her posture, she proudly displayed the figure beneath the pinafore across her breasts. "Give me the same chance you had when you were my age."

The unveiled hope on Emilie's vibrant face made Helena reconsider. She couldn't keep staving off her sister's desire to be courted. To be a wife. That was what every woman sought. Emilie was no different and shouldn't have to be made to suffer for Helena's trial at that age. But still, sixteen was young. Too young for a serious beau. "Next year, Emilie," Helena said in compromise. "When you're seventeen, you can go to the Candy Dance."

"I don't want to wait a year! I want to dance with Thomas next week!" With that, she shoved the circular at Helena and left the stable in tears.

Helena held the paper, its dry crackle in her fingers making her spirits sink even lower. She'd thought negotiating the matter would be acceptable to Emilie. But it wasn't. Her heart was brimming with love for a gallant young man, and she wanted to dance in his arms now. Helena could understand that. Why couldn't she just let her sister go? She didn't like being so strict with her, but a part of Helena was afraid to be lenient. The painful reminder of what she had done was ever there in the back of her mind. She didn't want Emilie to feel such a bottomless void . . . but Emilie wasn't her. And it was time Helena started accepting that. Or she would lose her sister . . . just as Jake said.

The door opened on a gust, and Helena lifted her chin, hoping Emilie had returned. But it wasn't her sister. It was her husband.

On a dismayed sigh, Helena tried to focus on the candles, but her concentration had vanished. She quietly laid the circular on the counter and put her hands on the wooden edge.

"What's wrong with Emilie?" Jake asked. "She's crying."

Helena's own vision blurred, and she rapidly blinked her tears away. "She's upset with me because I don't want her to go to the Candy Dance."

Jake moved toward Helena. He stood by her, one hip butted against the side of the bench. Without reaching out to console her, he questioned, "Why not?"

"You know why not."

Picking up the circular, Jake skimmed through it while Helena watched his reaction. "It's not my idea of a good time, but I can see why a girl would want to go. I think you should let her."

"I can't," she whispered.

"You can."

"I said she could go next year. I meant it."

Jake folded his arms across his chest. "Next year she may not be your sister anymore."

Her chin lifted. "How can you say that?"

"Next year she'll resent you. Have you ever thought she might run away with McAllister and marry him?"

"No . . . no! She'd never do that . . . not my Emilie. She wouldn't go against my wishes. I'm her—"

"Sister," Jake finished. "Just her sister. Not her mother. I can't speak from a woman's point of view, but brothers are who a man turns to when he wants advice, not a fatherly lecture. If he wants a lick of the belt, he tells his father his honest thoughts. But brothers, and I'm assuming it's this way between sisters, are more likely to stand up for him. I have a sister, but I was never close to her. I wish I could go back and change that, but I can't. You still have a chance. You should think about it now. Before she doesn't come to you at all and does what she damn well pleases."

Helena mulled over Jake's words.

"I'm no philosopher, and you can tell me to go to hell and mind my own business if you want." He took off his hat, reshaped the brim with his fingers, then fit the crown over his head. "I just came in here to tell you Eliazer and I made peace."

"I was meaning to talk with him, but I've been so busy."

"No need to. I can take care of my own battles."

"What did you say to him?"

"I just told him the truth. And swore a lot when I did. That's a man thing you wouldn't have been able to convey. Real indignation comes from four-letter words, and I said enough to convince him I'm not to blame."

Helena didn't know what to say. At length she said, "Thank you."

"Don't thank me. Think about your sister instead."

Nodding, Helena vowed to lessen her restrictions on her sister. Starting with her clothing. No more child-length dresses, frilly aprons, and girlish shoes. From now on, Emilie would dress as a young woman. There were several nice bolts of blue gingham and small-patterned calico that would make suitable skirts. White poplin and cotton could be sewn into crisp, fashionable shirtwaists. Hopefully Emilie would see this as a beginning and be less inclined to fuss over the dance.

"I need to speak with Emilie," Helena announced, leaving the candle equipment behind as she went toward the door. She paused without turning around. "What you said about Emilie . . . it made a lot of sense. Thank you."

* * *

"I told you to stay out of town for a while," Bayard scoffed from the throne of his not-in-session courtroom. "I have no use for you right now."

The judge needed to think, therefore was sitting in his best thinking chair with its honeyed oak frame and worn burgundy velvet seat. It served as his throne of authority in lieu of a bench. He'd come to his office to weigh and balance his options like the scales of justice. The unexpected company not only threw Bayard off kilter, the other man's presence made him cautious. He didn't want anyone associating the two of them. The idea of being discovered made him apprehensive. Not that he feared this person who'd sprawled his rail-thin legs out before him when he'd sat down in the front row of empty seats. If anything, the unwanted spectator was offensive.

Bayard figured his visitor considered himself armed to the teeth with the ornate new gun he'd taken to wearing several weeks ago. His old piece had been a Smith & Wesson .36 in pitifully poor shape, that carried a bullet like a pea. Unless his aim was exact, it took a whole pod of them to make it worth shooting the gun. But the ill-kept revolver was gone, though not the bowie knife. Its handle projected from the top of his low-heeled boot. The cocksure tilt to his hip when he was standing said he was always itching for a fight. But he was so blatantly obscene about it, nobody would accommodate him who wasn't gone with liquor.

Observing him once in the Metropolitan Saloon, Bayard had noted the hayseed would try any method to ensnare unsuspecting gamblers into making insolent remarks toward him. But there was hardly ever a taker. His face would redden now and then like the color of plums when he fancied he was on the scent of a good fisticuff. But inevitably his pigeon would elude his carefully laid plans of a bloodied nose and worse. Then he would show a disappointment almost pathetic.

"I came to town to see what all the ruckus was with that fire yesterday. Saw the smoke way out on the ranch," the man remarked while crossing his legs at the knees. The star-spangled clatter of spurs sounded with his movement.

"If I didn't know any better, I'd say you started the fire just for the fun of it."

"I'm offended by that," he bristled, making a show out of being indignant. Breaking off a piece of chaw, he stuck it between his lips and spoke around the wad. "So what the hell happened?"

"The Paiutes started the blaze."

"Injuns." His blond brows pointed with interest. "Anyone going to fight 'em?"

"Brown at the Indian Affairs Bureau said he's calling in the military from Carson City."

Despite the man's tough gaze, he had a lot of bumpkin in him, which was evident in his whine. "I don't like military men."

"I could care less about the militia," Bayard snapped, feeling his patience running down faster than a cheap watch. "I govern Genoa, and the United States Army has no authority over me."

"They do if you interfere with them."

"I don't need your one-horse interpretation. You have no knowledge of law's writs, so quit imposing your opinion on me." Bayard sat straighter and hooked his fingers over the cushioned arms of the chair. "I want you out of here before someone comes and sees you."

"I'm going. To Carson City, as a matter of fact. I got in a fight with one of the hands and lost my job last night. Who the hell needs steers anyway? I'm going to be a professional gambler." A stream of beetle-brown spittle was aimed at a nearby spittoon and missed by a few inches. "But before I head out, I want to know what's being done about Carrigan. That son of a bitch is mine, and I'm tired of waiting around until you say

I can have a shot at him again. Why isn't he in your custody like you said he'd be?"

Bayard angrily kicked the leather Bible that was beneath his chair. "She wouldn't press charges against him."

"You said you'd convince her he was a horse thief."

"She didn't believe me."

The man laughed. "Some influence you are in her life."

The blood vessels in Bayard's head pounded his annoyance. He was tempted to rip the man from his seat and shake him until his teeth fell out like corn.

During moments such as this one, Bayard reconsidered his association with the likes of the degenerate sitting before him. But he'd been able to control the man with money, and in doing so, had been assured of his silence. For Bayard had made the threat early on. One slipup now, and he'd see himself swinging from a cottonwood. So far, his confidence had not been broken. And there had been plenty of opportunities for a loose tongue. No, the decision to involve him had been right. He'd done a good job of scaring Helena that day in the store. . . . If only she hadn't gone off in the wrong direction. And true to his word, he'd said he'd take care of Carrigan and had indeed shot him with the intent to kill. . . . If only Helena hadn't mended him.

Helena. She got in the way more than she sat idly by. But that was one of the things he admired about her. She stood up for law and order, wanting to do right by people. This latest being her offer of free mail service to those who lost their businesses to that fire. He'd found this out from Lewis, a man he'd been able to convince that a woman in business for herself was not a woman for Genoa. He'd spoken to Wyatt and Lewis about Helena running the Express right after her father's death. Though he hadn't come out and said it, he'd planted the seeds of doubt in both men, making them think it was in their best interest not to let a woman gain any kind of control in their town. Her being in charge of the Pony Express could have hurt them, seeing as, if she did well, she could secure her own feed and blacksmith and wouldn't need them. Wyatt and Lewis had bought in to this, and had withheld their services without Bayard ever saying it was his idea. But now Lewis was talking a little more generously about Helena since she'd come to the aid of those burned out, and it bothered Bayard.

Not only that, Helena kept doing right by Carrigan when she should have been denouncing him at every turn. But Bayard wouldn't give up. He loved Helena Gray. Plain and simple. He wanted her as his wife. His career demanded he have her. Thoughts of politics were ever in his plans, and he wasn't going to give up his want of the governorship. It made no difference how Helena came to him. Just so long as she did. But the prospect of having her after Carrigan left the taste of bile in his mouth.

"What are we going to do now?" The drawling voice intruded on Bayard's thoughts.

"I'm working on it." In fact, he'd found out more things about Carrigan he could use as ammunition without a gun. His inquiries into his past had turned up some interesting information. The Lord had been on his side when he'd done that favor for a judge up near the Yellowstone River. Bayard had hit pay dirt nearly his first letter out. He'd sent a dozen letters to different jurisdictions and had gotten one hell of a reply. All he had to do now was bank on Carrigan having told Helena what Bayard had found out. He would play them off of each other like two pawns, stand back, and watch them tear each other apart.

"I say you just let me shoot him," came the whine across from Bayard.

Bayard glared. "Once was enough. Twice, there would be inquiries. He's been in town long enough that a murder isn't as easily swept under the rug as I'd like. I'm still getting questions about August Gray's killing. And I don't need that dredged up. Especially not with the likelihood of Carrigan suspecting you in his shooting at the cabin. I cannot afford any connections between the two incidents. Do I make myself clear? I think moving on for a while is a good idea."

The man shrugged. "If I'm going to be a professional gambler, I need a stake to start me out."

Bayard sighed heavily while reaching into his coat for his billfold. "Hanrahan, you are a pain in my ass."

Seaton's smile was crooked. "But without me doing your dirty work, Judge, those clean white hands of yours would be as black as the bottom of the outhouse."

Helena sat outside making butter in a coopered churn. Sunlight caught the edge of her muslin skirt where the hem spilled from the shade of the smokehouse. The spot was a quiet one, a place to reflect and be outdoors while tending to an indoors task. Up and down, the dasher made the cream inside slosh, telling her she wasn't even close to thickening the liquid yet. The yard was peaceful, the hens and roosters clucking and scratching at the earth that had dried from the rain. Her thoughts drifted to Jake. Since their return, they'd resumed their prior sleeping arrangements. There were too many factors involved to switch rooms now. For one, Emilie's was directly across from hers. And for two, Helena was too cautious about her feelings for Jake to sleep with him for an entire night. Opening herself up to him while they'd been away had been difficult. If she allowed him into her bedroom here, she'd lose any ground she'd covered in keeping their arrangement cut-and-dried. But that certainly didn't prevent her from wanting to be with him again. . . .

Right now Jake was in the stables with Eliazer constructing new feed boxes to replace the ones the horses had gnawed down, and the temptation to walk away from the butter just so she could take a glimpse of him was a constant pull.

"Helena."

At the sound of her name, Helena turned and faced Bayard Kimball. He stood close with a beaver hat in hand and impeccable in a fine eastern suit. His hair was smoothed back and meticulously combed. Gray eyes gazed at her with remorse.

"Judge Kimball." She never missed a beat on her plunging, nor did she address him by the familiar name he was so insistent she call him.

"If you've a moment," he said in a humble tone, "I've come to make my sincere apologies and beg you to forgive my lack of manners the other day at the town meeting."

Helena stared across the stockyard at the garden where the seedlings were thickening in a verdant green carpet. She said nothing. What could she offer him? He'd wanted to hurt her, and he'd succeeded.

"I was totally out of line," Bayard went on. "It was inappropriate and unnecessary for me to make remarks about your husband when you clearly had come to a decision about his guilt or innocence. I didn't mean to offend you in any way, and I would beseech you to give me the opportunity to remain your friend. We were that once before, and I'm hoping that this matter hasn't killed any admiration, which I'd hoped was mutual." Her continued silence caused him to add, "Please say something before I make a bigger idiot out of myself."

Swallowing, Helena sighed before directly staring Bayard in the eyes. "You purposefully wanted to make my husband look like a criminal in front of the town. I was deeply hurt by that."

Bayard took a step closer. She could smell the bay rum on his person, a scent that was prominent yet inoffensive. "I will admit, I wanted him to appear guilty beyond a doubt in the town's estimation so you would see him as a . . . as less than deserving of you. But I can see I was wrong. You don't think he is capable of robbery, and I have to accept that."

"And you also have to accept that the person you thought you saw that night was not my husband, but some other man who you mistakenly identified as Jake."

"I will concede that you are right." Bayard twirled his hat in his lean fingers. "I've already confessed to being clouded with liquor. I must have erred in my fingering a culprit."

"Yes, you did."

The muscles on Bayard's neck visibly strained. "Would you like me to offer my direct apologies to your husband?"

Helena felt a moment's sympathy for Bayard. He wasn't a man who easily admitted he was wrong. In his courtroom he was always right, and no one else could question him otherwise. For him to offer he'd tell Jake in person that he'd falsely accused him took a lot. Helena saw no reason to draw out the matter further. "That won't be necessary."

"I appreciate that." The judge stepped closer, his face looking as relieved as if he'd just been given a stay of execution. She didn't want to persecute him. That had never been her intent. She'd just been very disappointed in his behavior. "Butter-making . . . are we?"

"Yes." Helena kept on with her rhythmic churning, her arms getting tired.

"Mind if I try?"

She gave Bayard a sidelong glance. "Have you ever churned butter before?"

"When I was a lad, on occasion my mother roped me into the chair and made me do a domestic duty of the house." Bayard put on his hat, removed his coat, then rolled up his pristine sleeves. "It's been years, but I believe I can hold a dasher without getting splinters."

Helena had to smile. She rose from the bench she'd been sitting on and allowed Bayard to sit in her place. Spreading his legs, he put the churn between them and took up where she left off. The content expression on his face was a recognizable one. This was the old Bayard. The Bayard her family had known and trusted. She couldn't stay angry with him, for he'd only lashed out because she'd married someone other than himself.

"How have you been faring?" he asked, the cream beginning to make less noise inside the churn. "I see you've been able to add feed to your yard, and I noticed all your horses are running."

"We've been fine." Helena didn't want to say, because Jake had come to her rescue.

"Good. Glad to hear it." Bayard kept on pumping his arms. "You know, should you ever need my counsel, please seek it. I would be wounded if you let this misunderstanding prevent you from coming to me with legal matters. Anything at all you'd require, I could help. Of course, there would be no fee either. Your father was a good man who, on more than one occasion, sought my advice, and I would hope to continue that with his daughters."

There was something she had to take care of, but Helena had been too involved with the station to begin the legal transaction. She had to sign the deed for the parcel over to Jake. She wanted him to have it so he could bank his future on knowing she would make good on her promise about the land. There was no reason to wait until fall for him to have it. Since Bayard had taken the first step at making amends, the least she could do was meet his efforts with a small token of her own.

"I do have a business settlement I need to transfer."

Bayard's gaze was receptive. "Certainly. I'll make sure you're well taken care of."

"It's the parcel of land my father bought for Emilie and myself."

"Yes. I remember that well."

"I'd like you to transfer the ownership of it to my husband."

For a split second, Bayard skipped a dash, but recovered so quickly, Helena thought she might have imagined his reaction. "Of course. I can make sure it gets listed in the Kinsey records. Is there anything else?"

"No. Just that."

"And you want this effective as of when?"

"There's no special hurry. In the next week if you have the time."

"All right." Bayard pushed harder on the paddle, his knuckles growing white from the tight grip he held on the slender pole. "Would you think me rude for asking if your husband has any plans for the land?"

Helena bit her lip. "No, I wouldn't." Just the same, she was wary to divulge too much about the intricacies of her marriage. "He's going to be building a paddock for the horses he'll be training for the Express."

"Very good." The judge's brows arched. "Would he be adding a dwelling onto the property as well? You see, the reason I ask is that the parcel is within legal city limits, and a permit will have to be filed. I can handle that when I transfer the deed."

Helena didn't want to reveal too much, but in all honesty had to reply, "Yes. He'll be putting a house up."

Bayard nodded. "I can see the sense in that. Two separate living quarters. It would be more convenient not to travel back and forth between both residences. I assume you'll be joining him there, and I can mention that to the census."

Becoming more and more uncomfortable, Helena said, "No. I have obligations that keep me here." She didn't want this conversation going any further and was grateful when Bayard stood.

"I believe you have butter." Rolling his sleeves

down and slipping into his coat, he tipped his hat to her. "I won't keep you any longer. I just wanted to settle things between us. We are back to the way we were, are we not . . . Mrs. Carrigan?"

Helena watched the hope filling his eyes and heard the sincerity marking his voice when he called her by her married name. She couldn't deny him her friendship. "We are, Judge Kimball. I'm sorry there ever had to be a falling out."

"So am I," he said while slightly bowing. "So am I. But I trust things between us will be all for the better in the future. Much better."

Chapter

→ 15 ←

The ensuing days were warm, but the nights that followed were cold enough to keep the extra blankets on beds. Despite the invasion of Company E, United States Cavalry, into Genoa, the Indian troubles still increased throughout the territory. The appearance of the troopers had Carrigan dredging up his past. After Jenny had been violated, he couldn't look a yellowlegs in the eye without the sharpness of hatred narrowing his gaze. His hostility toward them was durable, never wearing out or letting him go forward with his life. As soon as the blue-clad Indian fighters had taken over the town in a flashy exhibition of forage caps, epaulets, brass buckles, and yellow-striped pants, Carrigan had known the hate once again, keener than ever. These were the pompous men who wandered the countryside in so-called honor, but the only thing they seemed to do was spill Indian blood and rape women. Perhaps not a reasonable description since he'd once been a soldier himself, but it was the most generous Carrigan could offer. He stayed clear of them, not wanting to have to acknowledge them in any way.

While the troopers protected the streets, the Pony Express riders continued to come through town twice a week. Their supple, sinewy physiques and coolness in moments of great danger attested to their endurance and bravery. From what Carrigan had been able to learn in fleeting conversations with Thomas, the zigzag trails hugging precipices and the dark, narrow canyons were infested with watchful savages, eager for scalps. Only a man who could ride through the mountains swiftly could make it through without delay. Besides the trail being overrun with hostile Indians, road agents roamed the countryside in bands, preying on the mailbags and ready to murder for them.

During these passing words with Thomas McAllister, it became apparent to Carrigan, the young man possessed a strong will and persistence. Thomas was set on taking Emilie Gray to the Candy Dance. That much was evident in the way he talked about the upcoming Saturday night's entertainment without taking his eyes off the lovely Miss Gray whenever he was changing horses in Genoa.

Helena hadn't reconsidered about the dance. She'd told him she'd spoken to Emilie about the new clothes. Though the younger sister was appreciative, her disappointment over the dance didn't diminish. But surprisingly, after a few days, Emilie was taking her defeat rather well. It could have been because she was absorbed in her sewing, but Carrigan sensed there was more to the sudden change.

Thursday night, Carrigan had come into the sitting room late after supper and found Emilie sitting in the high-backed chair, with the blue calico he'd admired with Helena in mind pooled in her lap. Quickly she tried to hide it beneath her bottom, wincing when she must have sat on pins. She had guilt written all over her flushed face as she sat straighter.

"I thought everyone had gone to bed," she said in an urgent voice.

Carrigan strode into the room with its two sugar-covered sofas, wooden rocker, fireplace, and large picture window with the muslin curtains drawn. The light in the sitting room was the best in the house for reading or doing work requiring a fine eye. A high wheel—which was in actuality an old wagon sprocket—was anchored to the ceiling by several lengths of chain, and seven kerosene lamps could be lit at the same time. Emilie had four going, and the brightness was beneficial for using a needle and thread.

"I left my book in here," he replied. Carrigan had been voraciously reading ever since the lake, trying to occupy himself at bedtime with thoughts other than Helena. The intimacy that he and Helena had shared was left behind on the sandy shores. Not since the eve of their last night out had they made love.

It wasn't as if Carrigan didn't want to sleep in his wife's bed. There had been no invitation. And this was her house. Her domain. Her rules governed the space. He knew she was sensitive about Emilie knowing what went on between a man and a woman, but he doubted Emilie was ignorant.

Though he desired Helena, he couldn't afford to leave in love with her. Nor could he ask Helena to come with him. What could he offer her? Helena's plan for him to raise horses so no one would question their separate living arrangements had a major flaw. She hadn't considered the price for the horses' heads. He couldn't exactly sell his wife stock and expect her to live with him on the money she paid. That wouldn't be supporting her—that would be her supporting them. He could never take money from her again.

Besides, her place was here. She belonged. She fit in. He didn't. He felt caged in and shackled. There were days when he would stare beyond the stockade gates to the range of grasses that pressed downward toward the other side of the valley. He'd be halfway to saddling Boomerang for a ride when he realized he couldn't go. There were too many obligations for him to take off when he wanted. He was trapped.

Mostly, Helena worked by his side. She never complained about a nasty job, nor did she shy away from the domestic duties that went with the house. Each day he was falling . . . falling away from his resolve and his reason for being with her. And that was to help without becoming involved. Merely give her his name and be there for her in case she needed him to fight for her cause. That was all well and good, but it was killing him to be so close to her, yet feel as if they were miles apart.

Up at Lake Tahoe, they'd been on his terrain. He'd been comfortable and at ease. And he sensed Helena had been, too. For the first time, she'd let her guard down and taken what her body needed. But here, she'd pinned her hair up and was put in proper order once again. While she was at home, in her house and surroundings, she'd returned to her former self. Wary, cautious, afraid to get too close to him.

"Aren't you going to get your book?" Emilie asked, her face a grimace of pain as she shifted in the chair.

"In a minute." Carrigan had lost track of how long he'd stood there, his thoughts collecting inside his head. Before he picked up the volume, he sat on the edge of a sofa, his hands clasped between his knees. "I wanted you to know that when I made the arrangement with your sister for the parcel you shared, I didn't know you then. I didn't care whose land it was. I just wanted a piece of it to call my own." His knit fingers dangled together. "Still do. A deal is a deal, so I'm going to take it. But I didn't want you thinking I enjoy stealing it from you."

Emilie's eyes were wide and contemplative. "I never thought you were stealing it. My sister gave the parcel to you. There's nothing I can do about that."

"Well, it's good grounds to hate my guts."

She adjusted the wad of fabric at her hip. "I don't hate you . . . I just . . ." Clearing her throat, she said, "I don't hate you."

Carrigan nodded, passing on the subject for another. "Hold it up to your chin. Let me see."

"S-See what?" she stammered.

"What you're sewing."

"It's nothing."

"It's a dress, Emilie. Let me see it."

Hesitantly she lifted her thigh and removed the bunch of calico. With slow hands, she shook out the garment and put the bodice next to hers.

"Very lovely. And very mature."

"Th-Thank you."

"I'm sure Thomas will appreciate you in it at the Candy Dance."

"Why, I'm not going," she replied all too quickly.

"Of course you are. That's why you're sewing this dress in secret." Carrigan rose, taking the book with him that had been on the sofa cushion. "But you should be more careful. I could have been Helena."

"You won't tell . . . will you?" Emilie's glossy braids picked up fragments of the light, making the dual strands shimmer like ripe wheat.

"No." Carrigan stood in the doorway. "Because there won't be any need to keep it a secret. You'll go to that dance. Even if I have to take Helena there myself."

"You'd . . . stick up for me?"

"You're Helena's sister. And when I married her, you became my sister." Then he left before she could get sentimental on him.

As Carrigan climbed the stairs, he forced himself to put Helena and her sister from his head. At least for a little while. He had other things to deal with besides the Express. His mind naturally drifted to Seaton Hanrahan. Each time Carrigan went through town, he kept on looking for the man. Carrigan checked the Metropolitan Saloon every now and then. Taking calculated walks through the streets, he searched for a high-crowned black hat with snakeskin trimming. But congestion on the streets was thicker than axle grease, as the mountains had thawed enough so packtrains could pass through. The avenues were glutted with animals and wagons, making it difficult for him to conduct a thorough search.

Carrigan entered his room, read for a while, and was able to go to sleep after shoving Obsi off the bed. Into a sleep deep enough that his reaction was somewhat delayed, and the *pop-pop* didn't immediately register. But when it did, he was up and out of that bed with his Walker gripped in his hand.

Pop-pop!

Christ all Jesus, the noise was gunshots coming from the kitchen. With his Colt trained on the hallway, he met Helena and Emilie. It was a good thing he'd decided to sleep in his long underwear tonight due to the cold, because he wouldn't have had the foresight to dress before bolting out of his room. In the dim glow of a flickering wall lamp, the women huddled in their nightgowns, clearly frightened by the unknown attacker.

"Oh dear Lord, is it Indians?" Helena whispered, her hand at her throat. She held Emilie close.

"Don't know," Carrigan hissed. "Get back into your rooms and don't come out unless I tell you. Obsi, stay. Guard."

The black dog sat in the hallway, his hackles raised and teeth bared.

Carrigan took the stairs, cursing when the third riser from the bottom groaned from his weight. The gunfire had stopped, but he hadn't heard any doors open to let an intruder out or in, nor glass breaking to signify any windows had been broken.

His arm raised and eyes adjusting to the shadows,

Carrigan took the narrow hall that led to the kitchen. He was barefoot, his steps next to silent as he descended on the dark room.

Pressing his back against the interior wall, he yelled, "Drop your gun!" Then with one hand, he reached into the box of matches Ignacia kept on the stove and scratched the tip of one into a flame. The match gave off enough light that Carrigan could see he was in an empty room. Pushing off from the wall, he went to the back door and checked the latch. It was undisturbed and pulled in for the night.

The flame burned his fingers, and he quickly lit a lamp before blowing the match out. There was a sizzle-sizzle sound coming from the sideboard by the dry sink. Glass shards were littered on the counter and floor on the rug the cook kept in front of the sink.

"Oh, hell," Carrigan muttered. Then louder, "It's safe to come down."

In a moment the sisters appeared in the doorway, their matching blue eyes like delft saucers. Obsi stood between them.

Carrigan gestured to the counter. "Helena, your damn bottle of starter yeast exploded."

"What . . . ?" Helena moved closer, Emilie's hand in hers. When she saw what had happened, her mouth fell open.

Emilie began to laugh. "Lena! Why, you had us all petrified!"

The sizzle was the yeast running out of what remained of the bottle.

"And I was going to make bread tomorrow," Helena declared, her hand over her heart.

Carrigan put his gun down and picked up the prominent pieces of glass before he stepped on one. "You ladies ought not be in here without shoes on."

Emilie laid her hand on Helena's shoulder, her eyes shining in merriment. "This is the first time this has ever happened. What will Ignacia say when she sees what a mess you've made in her kitchen?"

"She won't see," Helena said, sniffing and reaching for the broom. "I'm going to clean it up so she can't find out. You go on back to bed, Emilie. The excitement's over."

Emilie gave Carrigan a light smile, then took off down the hall, her soft laugh filling the house.

Obsi went to the door and wanted to be let out for a while. Carrigan obliged, then faced Helena.

"I can't believe this," she said in an agitated tone. "Of all the things to happen." She took a step forward, but didn't get far. The starter yeast made a great hissing sound and spattered on a big gust of warm air. In a quick inventory, Carrigan saw that it was everywhere. Even on her nightgown and down the front of his underwear.

With her hair braided and falling down her back, her mouth open with astonishment, and despite her face spotted with doughy dots, Helena looked beautiful to him. Her gown was white as sugar, and just as sweet. Helena glanced at herself, brows furrowing while she inspected the speckles of gooey yeast that covered her. When she lifted her eyes to Carrigan, he met her gaze with a wry smile of his own.

"I'm . . . sorry," she said without much of a straight face. "This is terrible. . . ." Then she began laughing. Her voice, like sunshine, brought daylight into the room. He joined her, laughing deeply. It had been years since he'd given himself over to a good laugh.

Before long, Helena was tipsy with laughter, shaking her head and saying she had to clean it up before the rooster's first crow. "I've got to get a cloth," she said in between wiping the tears from the corners of her eyes. "Ignacia will have my hide if she sees what I've done."

Helena opened one of the cupboards and withdrew a stack of towels. "You may admonish me now or later for what I have to ask, but could you please go outside and pump some water?"

"It's cold out there."

"Yes, I know."

"And I'm barefoot."

"I'm aware of that. But you'll get the water for me?"

Carrigan shifted his weight off one hip. "I'll get it, but it's going to cost you." Before she could ask him what, he'd grabbed the bucket off the worktable and slipped outside. Dashing across the frigid ground to quickly prime the pump and fill the bucket, he ran back before his feet could get too numb. Once inside, he fended off the brittle cold and set the bucket down.

"Where do you want to start?"

"You'll help?"

"I'm awake. Why not?"

"I . . . I appreciate the offer. We'll start with ourselves." She wiped off her face, and as much of the sticky mess as she could from her nightgown. He did likewise, then they began on the room.

After numerous dunks into the water and wiping down walls, cupboards, the stove plates and pipe, and even taking the curtains from the rod and rinsing them as well, the place was cleaner than it had been before the yeast detonated.

Helena squeezed her cloth out and set it on the counter with the others. "She'll never know," she said on an exhausted sigh, crossing her arms beneath her breasts—an innocent gesture that pulled at his attention.

"Time to pay up," he reminded while enfolding her in the width of his arms. "You can either do me a favor or give me a kiss." He brought his mouth close to hers. "But I'll warn you now, I want them both."

Helena felt soft and yielding, her body warm next to his. Her chin tilted, the light in her gaze reflections of the lamp that burned behind him. "What kind of favor can I do for you?"

"Then you won't give me the kiss?"

Her smile was soulful. With eyes half-obscured by

the thick lashes of her lowered lids, she whispered, "Oh, Jake, you know I want to give you the kiss . . . for nothing."

The beat of his pulse a hot rhythm, he could only focus on her mouth when replying. "Then kiss me. Now."

She brought herself onto tiptoes. Lithe arms lifted over his shoulders, hands locked behind his neck, and her open mouth touched his with tantalizing persuasion. His fingers wove into the silky hair at the back of her head, and he thought it a waste she'd bound the glorious length from his exploring hands. Her hair was too pretty to plait, even at night.

Carrigan wanted her. There was no lying about that. It was desire, pure and simple. She'd been a responsive and gratifying lover, and she was his wife. No amount of convincing could talk him out of pushing her back on her feet. This was right. It felt right. Her kiss was sultry, invading his every sense.

His fingers tightened their hold in her hair as he kept her slender body to his with a hand moving down her back to press her pelvis closer. The scent of her, heated from passion, filled his head with a hundred poetic verses he'd read. Yet he could not quote a single one of them.

Her knees buckled, and he claimed her kiss with one of his own. An anxious, openmouthed kiss that had him thinking with his heart instead of reason. He was willing to take her on the kitchen table. Breaking the kiss, he thought it only fair to tell her what the favor was before he took things too far and she accused him of using her.

Passion-filled blue eyes gazed up at him while a lush mouth parted.

"I think you should know what I'd like you to indulge me in before we decide what we're going to do next."

Through her quickened breath, she asked, "What is it?"

"Let Emilie go to the dance."

The ardent expression on her face dimmed.

"Let her go, Lena. Let her go." He kissed her, hoping to recapture the languid gaze in her eyes. "I'll even go, too. We'll watch her, together, and make sure she's all right."

Helena's voice was a vibration against his lips. "You'd do that for my sister? For me?"

"Yes, I would."

Her lips nuzzled his. He pulled back a little to peer down at her. "What do you say? Let her go. . . . You'll have to sooner or later. Do it now, before it's too late."

She whimpered over the loss of his mouth. "I hope I'll never regret changing my mind." He gave her a soft kiss, her last words dying on his lips. "She can go."

Carrigan lifted her in his arms and spun her in a circle. Helena buried her face in his neck, kissing him in the curve and holding on to him as if she'd die if he let her go. He felt the same way, clinging to the satisfaction she gave him with a smile, a look, a laugh.

Urging her closer with a fervent kiss, he nibbled and bit the flesh of her lower lip with playful, thorough kisses. He would have bent her over the table, lifted her gown and taken what he so craved, but Helena had to say where. He didn't want to risk Emilie discovering them should she return downstairs. She was a young girl, and such an impression as the image of lovemaking was best left for her wedding night.

Helena's moist whisper raised the flesh on his arms. "We can't go upstairs. . . . Emilie might hear."

"Where do you want to go?"

Her forehead creased, then she took his hand while a half smile touched her mouth. "Would you think me debauched if I suggested the pantry?"

"Not at all."

She took his hand and they hid themselves in a

muted world of semidarkness behind the curtain of worn blankets. The cool fragrance of stored apples, spices, and the lingering tartness of preserves seeping through wax coverings filled the small space.

In this tiny cubicle of concealment, between feverish kisses, Carrigan undid the buttons on his drawers. Then he lifted her into his arms, kissing her soundly and without breath.

"Lift your hem and put your legs around my hips," he said in a ragged voice. "Hold on to me."

She did so, the outline of her breasts through the fabric of her nightgown searing into his partially covered chest. He found her wet entrance and plunged deep inside of her. His strong fingers cupped her buttocks as he thrust deep and rapid, her own body squirming against him in wild abandon. He was so close to climax, he had to slow things down. But when he did, Helena was digging the blunt ends of her fingers into his back.

"Don't stop."

His eyelids flew closed, and he let the release come when he felt her pulsating next to him. They clung to each other, their breathes mingled and the smells of dried fruits and herbs filling their lungs. The sex and been totally uninhibited, rapturous and satisfying.

With a tender kiss to his wife's mouth, Carrigan was reluctant to let her go. Now . . . and forever.

The Saturday of the dance was a beautiful spring day with a mild, pleasing temperature in the air, and an exquisite azure sky with clouds rolling calmly past a brilliant sun. Helena had spent her morning helping Emilie in the store, and her afternoon mucking the stables and taking stock of the root cellar. By the time the supper bell rang, she was a sight. Dirty from head to toe and in no condition to sit at a table. Washing up as best as she could from the rain barrel, she joined the others.

Jake didn't show up for the light meal. Earlier in the

day, she'd seen him mending one of the western fences. He'd had to go to the lumberyard for supplies and returned a while ago. But when she'd come into the house, she hadn't seen him in the far corner anymore.

"Has anyone seen Jake?" she asked nonchalantly.

"He said he had to go to his cabin for a few things," Eliazer supplied. "He'll be back before the dance."

Helena nodded, thoughtfully chewing a bite of hominy cake but wondering just the same. Jake didn't like crowds or town functions. Was he reconsidering putting in an appearance? She doubted that, as they'd just been together at sunrise out in the corncrib shed. Ever since the night in the pantry, they hadn't been able to keep their hands off each other. Secret rendezvous were daily. Kisses were stolen at every private opportunity, and a touch of hands whenever possible. Hours in each other's arms were spent beneath midnight stars or the scarlet mist of a sun just rising over the horizon.

Parting with Jake was going to be the hardest thing she ever did. She didn't want to watch him ride away, only to have him periodically come back into her life and make her wonder if the splendor had all been nothing but a dream. She'd been able to reconcile letting her parents go because she knew they weren't coming back. With Jake's leaving, it would be like a death, but he was free to return. It would be torture of the worst kind.

Because she'd fallen in love with him.

He'd come to mean more to her than all the flourishing Express stations, dowry parcels, and profitable general stores. Attaining success with material things wasn't enough anymore. She wanted Jake more. But he was bent on leaving, and she'd told him he could go.

Helena would have asked to go with him if she could work out a way to be in two places at once. Horses were her livelihood. She would gladly work

arter hour. Fifteen minutes to seven. It was
o go or they would be late. Jake hadn't shown
ce since leaving for his cabin, and Helena
n't quell the trepidation in her stomach.

ena glided toward the room's doorway and
, "Emilie, are you almost ready?"

e call in return was delayed, but came out as an
"Yes. Almost."

knock on the store's front door caused Helena to
n. They'd closed two hours ago. As she walked
rd the drawn shades of the windows, she had to
her skirts at an angle so she wouldn't snag the
ric on any sharp merchandise cluttering the aisle.
she minded her steps, she told herself whoever
ded anything would have to return tomorrow. As
e grasped the knob with her gloved hand, the bulb
un beneath her slick fingers.

"Oh . . ." she sighed, not accustomed to the sheer
oves. She gripped the knob with a steadfast hold and
wung the door open before lifting her gaze. "I'm
orry, but we're . . ." The words died in her throat as
he raised her eyes and met Jake's clean-shaven face.
"It's you." But she could say nothing more, as her
heartbeat was an endless pulse of flutters. Suddenly
she grew very insecure about her appearance. She
didn't want him to think she was unappealing, so she
couldn't meet his eyes just yet in case she saw he
thought she looked preposterous.

Standing next to Jake, Thomas McAllister held a
bouquet of vibrant prairie flowers in blues, violets,
and reds. He'd spruced and polished himself in such a
way, she almost didn't recognize him. With his blond
good looks and deeply tanned face, she could see why
her sister fancied him. Thomas was a very handsome
man in his black wool suit, crisp white shirt, and
ribbon tie.

Thomas doffed his hat and held it underneath his
arm. "Good evening, Mrs. Carrigan," he said politely
"I've come to call for Emilie."

hand in hand with Jake to capture and break them.
But there was Emilie. The Pony Express. And the
many responsibilities she couldn't just walk away
from, despite wanting to in the worst way. She was
duty-bound to her family and her business. They had
to come before anything else.

If only Jake would consider staying. She hadn't
asked him. From the beginning, she'd made it clear
she didn't want him to. She hadn't expected to fall in
love with him. Maybe if she explained how she felt, he
would remain. After the dance tonight, she'd tell him
she wanted him with her.

"Don't fret, Lena," Emilie said, her enthusiasm
spilling a bubbly tone into her voice. "He'll be back."

Helena smiled at her sister, taking comfort in the
fact that today Jake truly would come back for many
days to follow. And she intended to make the most of
them all. "I know he will," Helena replied.

Emilie was so excited, she was pushing her food
around her plate, unable to eat any of the soup and
corn cakes Ignacia had prepared. Emilie's face when
Helena had told her she could attend the dance after
all had been filled with pure joy. Her expression had
been so full of life and love, it had touched a note
inside Helena. She never should have said no in the
first place. It wasn't her right, and she was glad Emilie
could finally revel in the tunes of a fiddle while
twirling on a dance floor with the man she'd set her
sights on.

"I'll have Ignacia alter one of my Pennsylvania
dresses for you," Helena had offered that afternoon in
the store when she'd approached Emilie with her
change of heart. "There's not enough time to make a
new one."

"That won't be necessary, Lena," Emilie had replied in a breathless voice as sweet as a lark's. She'd
nearly dropped the bottles of elixirs she'd been inven-
torying. "I don't need anything new. I'm just happy to
be going. I . . . I can't believe you're letting me go."

Helena had nodded, feeling nothing but goodness well inside her. "Believe it, Emilie. You're really going."

Looking at her sister now, it was clear Helena had made the right choice. She wouldn't have done so without Jake's wisdom. Unburdening her secret had been the best thing for her. Jake understood where her fears rested. But he'd made her see the error of her ways and accept that holding Emilie back would only make her race forward. Perhaps by little steps, the two women would come together once again. And hopefully return to the camaraderie they'd had while growing up.

Attending the Candy Dance was as much of an event for Helena as it was for Emilie. Helena hadn't been to a dance since she was in the Kansas Territory. She wasn't even sure she recalled the fancy footwork necessary for quadrilles and schottisches. Did Jake know his way across a floor? Or would she embarrass the both of them?

After supper, Helena and Emilie made use of the bathtub, and Helena retired to her room to dress. Yesterday she'd gone through her trunk and unfolded several of the dresses she hadn't worn in years. These clothes had been so inappropriate for Genoa, they were ridiculous, and Helena had packed them away. There was nothing wrong with any of the dresses— they were just the ordinary clothes of a girl living in Pennsylvania. Her traveling dress was a dark blue camel's hair with a velvet jacket. The others were a black silk, a navy day dress with layers of flounces, a halfway sensible blue serge, and a white poplin gown trimmed with broad, black velvet bands. There had been the blue with the tiers that had worn out straightaway before she'd given up dressing in eastern clothes. These four had been stuffed in the trunk ever since without even a glimpse.

But this morning Helena had decided to have Ignacia iron the white poplin. It had been a long while

since she'd worn a light color. Ev[...] died, she'd worn somber colors [...] mother. She hoped her father's s[...] spect in her going against the dicta[...] was time she learned to live again.[...]

An hour later, Helena slowly des[...] feeling awkward and self-conscious [...] white skirt that brushed both sides [...] because of her wide crinoline. On her [...] of fashionable slippers trimmed with [...] pinched her instep in comparison to h[...] She'd heated her mother's curling iro[...] and had painstakingly tamed her curl[...] ringlets that she'd adorned with a headd[...] mingled with sprigs of leaves and whit[...] twice had she burned herself with the h[...] used to the confining entrapments of par[...] felt too frothy being dressed so fancy. The [...] nip of her satin corset—relaced ever so m[...] in order for her to fasten the front closu[...] dress—barely enabled her to breathe. She [...] be able to swallow one bite of food, which w[...] well since she was nervous beyond comprehe[...]

Once in the sitting room, she found no one t[...] a surprised lift of her brows, she realized she [...] first one ready. And it had taken her forever. E[...] she'd asked Emilie if she required help, but her [...] had said she could dress herself without aid. H[...] had given her a brand-new corset from the la[...] goods counter. She'd shown Emilie how to mol[...] without stretching the laces too tight; but Em[...] already knew how to fit the garment. Then Hele[...] proceeded through the store and gave her sister a pa[...] of lightweight stockings, lace petticoat with doubl[...] ruffles, pink-trimmed camisole, and kid leather shoes [...] of smooth, white hide. Emilie had asked if she could [...] take a bundle of the dried flowers. Helena had nodded in agreement.

The tiny, glass-domed clock on the mantel chimed

Helena smiled at his manners, stepping aside so that both men could enter. "She'll be ready in a moment. If you'll come this way, both of you."

The three of them couldn't exactly wait in the store, so Helena maneuvered her way back to the sitting room—thankfully without mishap. But getting there in one piece wouldn't solve the problem of taking a chair. Helena feared if she did, she'd snap in two. So neither man took an available seat. They stood in front of the fireplace, Thomas with his hat in his hands, and Jake wearing his. She wasn't offended, as she admired the light gray against the dark color of his hair. Jake hadn't said a word to her . . . but she hadn't been able to think of a coherent phrase to say to him. What was he thinking? Her own thoughts were filled with visions of her husband. He'd never looked finer. With wayward peeks in his direction, she couldn't keep from staring.

He cut quite a dash in a pair of foxed breeches. A heart-shaped piece of leather the color of off-white parchment had been sewn into the seat and extended down the inside seams of the legs. His broad chest and muscular arms filled out a cream-colored flannel shirt with a pinkish stripe woven into it. It didn't matter that he wore no suit jacket. He looked all the better without one. His freshly washed, inky hair was unruly at his forehead; the gray hat's brim with the thongs tapering to the bead in back made him all the more handsome.

Helena had never been so tongue-tied. She couldn't think of a single sensible thing to say. Some hostess she was. If Emilie hadn't appeared in the doorway just then, Helena might have made a fool out of herself and begun to jabber.

One look at her sister and Helena forgot to be nervous. Emilie looked beautiful. She wore a blue calico dress—fashioned from the fabric in the store—in a style that accentuated the slim curves of her figure. Helena had been unaware her sister had even sewn a dress with perfect stitches, puffed sleeves, and ribbon trim. The color on her was a perfect match with her sparkling eyes. She'd unbraided her hair and swept the length into a soft bun at the crown of her head, and she'd put dried flowers in the strands to highlight the golden color. Though she wore no cosmetics, her lashes were fuller, her eyes wider, her cheeks a subtle shade of rose, and her mouth a dusky pink. The natural beauty within Emilie had come out, and the girl before Helena was not her little sister anymore. She was a woman. A lovely, attractive woman.

"Why . . . Em . . . you're all . . ." Helena felt a pride in her well so strongly, she was too choked up to find the proper words to express her emotions. "You're beautiful," she whispered to her sister as she embraced her.

Emilie whispered back, "I wish we had a full mirror."

"You don't need a mirror, honey. You look just like Mother. So very pretty." Fighting the moisture in her eyes, Helena pressed a kiss to her sister's cheek. "I love you, Em. Have fun tonight."

"I will."

The two women drew apart and Thomas presented Emilie with his flowers. She went to the kitchen and returned with Ignacia and Eliazer, who'd donned their Sunday best clothing as well. The women carried trays of candy they'd made that week, and the six of them were ready. As the stars came forth in a twilight that wasn't lingering, they left the store for an evening of unbridled entertainment.

Chapter

⇀ 16 ↽

Singleton's Hall had been festooned with streamers and colorful decorations that hung from the ceiling and draperies. The strains of a fiddler tuning his instrument drifted through the noise of conversations, while the press of people holding punch cups and talking in loud voices bore down on Carrigan. He took everything in with a slight wince, telling himself that it was a small price to pay for being in the company of his wife.

When he'd first seen Helena, he'd been rendered speechless. He'd never seen her all done up before. Her hair was tamed into ringlets so perfect, he wondered if they'd feel as silky as they looked. The blush on her checks had been heightened with her throaty greeting upon finding him and Thomas at the store's door. When he'd stood back and taken in the entire picture she'd made framed in the doorway, he'd thought he was looking at a meticulous painting of a woman who was his wife, yet not the woman he'd married. He'd always known Helena was a beautiful woman, but seeing her this way was like seeing her for the first time.

The dress she wore was like none he'd ever seen. Either on her, or ready-made from the store. He didn't even think she carried a fine white material such as what she was wearing. It wasn't the exquisite fabric that caught his eyes as much as the color. She hadn't hidden herself in dark clothing. She was in a light style that showed off her figure to the fullest. The neckline fell in a modest curve, and a type of single ruffle hugged the swells of her breasts. Five black velvet bows ran down the middle of the bodice and met at a waist that was slender enough for his fingers to span and still meet at the tips. A belt of the same black velvet encircled the narrowness of her midriff, while the skirt fanned out in a wide bell of cloth that whispered seductively with each step she took. Though he hadn't been able to hear that scratch of lace from her underclothes as soon as they'd entered the noisy hall. Carrigan had a mind to take Helena outside so he could hear the provocative sound once again, and give her a kiss to hold him through the evening.

They'd been meeting, hungering, taking, enjoying each other, and he found when he wasn't near her, he was forever thinking of her.

Emilie and Thomas went off to the candy table to set down the sugar snap tray, Eliazer taking Helena's molasses brittle for her while Ignacia followed the younger couple. Alone, yet not alone, Carrigan leaned toward his wife and dipped his head to whisper in her ear. "I'd like you to introduce me to a woman I've never met before."

Helena's eyes caught his. There was a streak of curiosity and even an envious flint in the blueness. He knew he hadn't said a word about her appearance and figured she was agonizing over his silence. But the right words hadn't hit him until now.

"Who is she?" she asked in a tight voice, her puffy-sleeved arm still linked through his from the walk over.

With a smile that worked its way up the right side of his mouth, he said, "You."

"Me?"

"I've never seen you before, have I?"

"Of course you have."

"I don't think so. What's your name?"

A crease caught her forehead. "Helena. You know that."

"Helena what?"

"Helena Carrigan."

His mouth came very close to her fragrant skin, yet his lips didn't take what he sought. "You're my wife. I thought there was something familiar about you. But my wife has never looked as you do now."

"And that is?"

"Edible."

Her soft laughter curled around him, and he added, "You'll always be my wife, Lena, because you have my name. You've taken it and made it worth something."

A seriousness came over her. She touched his cheek with her gloved hand and gave him a smile that lovingly fell over him. "I always knew it was."

The musicians settled into their chairs on a raised platform, and tried to outdo each other once they struck up a polka. As couples formed and floated to the dance floor, they performed the lively dance to perfection. Skirts swirled and men's coattails swelled as the strains of the melody beckoned. Carrigan hadn't danced since his youth and wasn't sure how to move through a spirited polka anymore, as this seemed too complicated. A waltz, he could conquer, and would, as soon as one was played.

When he looked at Helena, she didn't appear upset that he hadn't asked her to dance right away. "I don't suppose you'd like to dance this one?"

"Do you know how to polka?"

"I did. Once. But I've forgotten."

She smiled. "Thank heaven you said that. I'm not certain I remember it exactly either. I didn't want to embarrass you."

Carrigan frowned. "You could never do that." Putting his hand on the small of her back, he said, "Let's watch for Emilie and wait for a waltz. Can you dance a waltz?"

"That's about all. I'm rusty with the rest. Shall we wait until they play one?"

"Save it especially for me."

They stood off to the side as the colorful couples spun by. When a flash of blue whirled in front of them, Helena rested her hand on Carrigan's forearm. "There she is. I'm so glad Eliazer practiced with her. She's dancing, Jake. Really dancing. And isn't she pretty?"

Carrigan noted the radiance on the younger girl's cheeks, the abandon in her merry smile. That Helena had relented and let Emilie attend with Thomas only strengthened his love for his wife. She was making sacrifices and changes. Whereas he was not the same man who'd walked down that mountain to be wed for a price, neither was she the same woman who'd asked for a protector. She stood on her own now, just as he was reconsidering his options for the future.

The harmonious and intoxicating tunes captivated the audience as the dancing continued. Carrigan ignored the presence of the military men who walked the room with domineering strides. Tonight wasn't for lingering on a dead past, so he put the troopers from his mind. Instead, he focused on the enchanting lady beside him, and Emilie and Thomas, who made an ideal pair moving in graceful sync.

A while later when a quadrille was complete, Carrigan said, "I'm going outside for a smoke. Do you want anything to drink?"

"No. I'm fine," Helena replied as Emilie and Thomas made their way toward them. Emilie was breathless and engaged Helena in a light conversation while Thomas departed for the refreshment stand. Carrigan took his leave since smoking wasn't permitted in the hall.

Once outside, he selected a tree-lined spot away from the other men who were speaking in groups with clouds of smoke above their heads. Rolling a cigarette, Carrigan lit the end. As he fanned the match out, he listened to the drone of crickets while enjoying the calming effects of tobacco. The tightly knit room seemed to amplify voices and raucous laughter to the point of irritation for Carrigan. He'd need to get a jolt of the quiet night before returning to endure several more hours of heady perfumes, the abundant smell of cedar oozing from suits that had been brought out of trunks, and hearty laughter that was more like guffaws.

Carrigan wasn't alone long when the crunch of bootheels came to him. Turning his attention in the direction of the visitor, he scowled.

A yellowlegs—a captain, from the insignia on his spotless blue coat—approached. The man was in his middle years, tall and well ironed like his clothing, with the cavalry emblem of crossed sabers stating his military affiliation on his hat, and a gleaming field sword at his hip.

"Good evening, sir," the captain greeted with an extension of his arm. "You are Mr. Carrigan?"

Carrigan made no reply, nor did he acknowledge the man's attempt at a handshake. Drawing on his cigarette, he glared at the captain, wishing to hell he'd never been found by the man.

"You are Mr. Carrigan, are you not?" The inquiry was repeated, this time with a note of reservation in his tone as he lowered his arm. "I was told you were Mr. Jake Carrigan of the Pony Express."

"What of it?"

"Then you are the man I'm looking for."

"Nobody's looking for me."

"I beg to differ with you. My name is Captain Eli Garrett. It's been said you've supplied the Express with swift mustangs. We're going to need fresh horses. Good horses that are up to the same speed as the Paiutes if we want to win this fight. The army would like to commission you to round up fifty head and—"

"Not interested."

A shadow of arrogance crossed the man's honed features. "We'd pay a substantial amount."

"I don't give a shit how much. I'm not wrangling horses for any cavalry."

Captain Garrett grew indignant, straightening his brass-clad shoulders to a stiff degree and putting his hand on the hilt of his sword. "You're making a grave mistake by not hearing me out."

Carrigan could face off with a weapon just as easily and curled his fingers around the butt of his Walker. "I've heard enough."

"I don't think you realize that it's your civic duty to serve your country by contributing—"

"I did my time. I fought in the Mexican War."

"That was years ago, and you are to be commended for your service. But now there's a new war and there are men who are risking their lives to save the women and children of this community. You do have a wife of your own to consider."

Carrigan came close to grabbing the man by his snappy collar. "You tell that to the men who—" The veins on his neck were pulsating with hot blood as his anger thrummed through his body. *Tell that to the men who raped Jenny.* "Tell your superiors there's no law that says I have to do anything for the U.S. Army."

Pitching the butt of his cigarette into the street, Carrigan left without any further comment. Feeling the captain's gaze burning a hole through his back,

Carrigan shrugged it off as he rounded the corner of the assembly hall and entered the building. The military man could kiss his bare backside. He wasn't obliged to provide a service to any troopers. His refusal had been founded on a matter of principle. It would be like aiding and abetting the enemy. He wouldn't. Not for anything. So he put the incident out of his mind as he sought Helena.

A square-dance caller on the platform was ripping out singsong directions for the partners. The climate in the room had grown as humid as a hothouse, and many collars were clinging to necks like wet rags. Some of the women were truly fine-looking in their latest gowns of rustic fashion, but none more so than his wife. She stood with a half dozen ladies in a tight circle, nodding her head and contributing to a conversation of which he couldn't hear the topic. That Helena had come out of her shell to address these women and make light conversation with them had him thinking she wasn't as closed off by women as she pretended. There was still that side in her, the part that wanted to share ideals and recipes. He didn't take it as a weakness; he thought the need to be included added new dimension to an already well-rounded personality.

Rather than intrude, he stood a ways back and folded his arms across his chest. Through a separation in the crowd, he saw Captain Garrett glaring at him. Carrigan moved his gaze. Was the son of a bitch going to sniff after him like a hound dog?

Just minutes after he'd put his cigarette out, Carrigan felt the need for another. Jumping to quick conclusions had never been one of his better traits. He'd made a fair number of rash decisions and had looked back on them with question. If pride hadn't gotten in the way, he might have asked the captain just how much money was involved. Too late, Carrigan realized he really needed the cash in a bad way. But to get it from the men who'd attacked Jenny—that was nothing short of being two-faced.

Jesus . . . payment for fifty head would be any-where between five hundred and a thousand dollars, depending on the quality of the horses. If he caught a few prime stallions, he could breed them with quality mares and . . . Hell, what was he thinking?

He was thinking of Helena.

Capturing and raising horses for the army would be a decent income. A cash resource he couldn't afford to refuse if he was to support his wife. Carrigan felt torn in half.

"Gents to the right! Ladies to the left! Promenade!" the caller twanged through the accompaniment of a banjo player and fiddler, who added much liveliness to the dance by vying to outdo each other with tricky bars. Carrigan hoped the next dance would be a waltz. He was aching to hold Helena in his arms and let the music flow while they embraced.

"Carrigan."

The greeting contained a strong suggestion of re-proach that he could easily identify. As he turned, he found he was in the company of Judge Bayard Kimball. The man offended him, not only because he wore a supreme righteousness on his expression, but because he had ties to Helena that went further back than his own.

"Kimball."

"You know who I am."

"I know."

"Ah, yes . . . from the fire."

"I didn't know your name then. I do now."

The man was attired in flawless black with gleaming diamond studs through the buttonholes of his silk shirt. A gem stickpin glinted from his tie, which disappeared into a bloodred vest with gold threads. The contrast of bold color against his subdued suit was startling, and in excellent taste. But Carrigan didn't give a rat's behind about the judge's fashion. In fact, he downright wanted to shoot the man for making a false accusation about him. Bayard Kimball saw him as a petty horse thief. And regardless that Carrigan had married the woman the judge had had his eyes on, that didn't necessitate trumping up charges to get revenge. Carrigan didn't like Kimball. And it was a good thing he didn't have to.

"You got something to say to me?" Carrigan asked in a tone cool enough to ice a branding iron.

"Are you enjoying yourself?" Bayard's gray eyes were forged with a purpose other than a general inquiry.

"I was."

The judge's gaze roamed toward Helena, and Carrigan didn't miss the open appreciation with which he studied her. "Your wife is looking quite becoming tonight. I'm surprised you got her to attend. I've tried to for some time, but she wouldn't accept my invitation. How did you convince her?"

"She's got her own mind. I don't have to convince her of anything."

"Yes, Helena is a very independent woman."

Carrigan didn't like the way Bayard said Helena's name so familiarly. Jealousy filled him. He would have walked away from Kimball if passersby hadn't trod in front of them. After nodding to the gentlemen, the judge redirected his gaze to Helena. "Even though she wed you, I'm glad she was able to continue our friendship in the manner that she has. Helena is a charming, warm person. From what she's told me, married life has been quite an adjustment for her."

This tidbit froze Carrigan in his tracks. What had Helena been telling Kimball about their marriage? His teeth gritted together, and no matter how badly he wanted to walk away, Bayard had piqued his interest just enough for Carrigan to grin and bear whatever else he had to say.

"She's had to adjust no more than any other woman would have had to," Carrigan offered.

"But she's had things somewhat harder, hasn't she?"

Carrigan's stomach twisted. Kimball knew something. It was deep, dark, and wicked, and he was going to reveal it with relish. That much was transparent on his face. "What are you getting at?"

"She's had to fill the shoes left vacant by your first wife. That's an imposition put on any woman, and it takes a strong one to come through." Bayard's lips lifted unkindly. "Unharmed."

The disclosure hit Carrigan hard enough for him to move back on his heels a short fraction. Helena had spoken to this man about Jenny? "Are you implying something?"

"Suicide."

The small word had a powerful impact on Carrigan, touching an unguarded spot. He feigned ignorance, hoping the other man was merely trying to bait him. "Suicide?"

But Bayard knew. His gray eyes smoldered like the ashes that had been the remains of his old home. "Helena said your first wife killed herself after she was repeatedly raped by cavalrymen. Such a horrible way to die," he tsked. "Suicide by setting herself on fire, burning the house down, and killing your father in the blaze. It must have been a difficult burial for you to attend. You have my condolences even now."

Treachery through a weakness was betrayal at its best. The knife cut sharp, and with such a poisoned blade, Carrigan could feel the sickness spreading through his insides like slow-pouring molasses. There was no worse a traitor than one who had been trusted with the truth. And he had trusted Helena. She was the only one in Genoa who knew about his past life. The hell he'd been through; the hell he lived in yet.

"I can see this is a sensitive subject for you," Bayard said with an unassuming tone. "You can rest assured I'll keep the details to myself, if you like.

Everything that Helena tells me—in private—I hold in the strictest confidence."

Resentment throbbed in Carrigan's skull. He didn't want to know, yet he had to. "What else did she tell you?"

"I've never made an itemization. . . ." Bayard conceded with a shrug. "There are many things we discuss. Too many to recall."

"About me."

"Nothing more than that your other wife killed herself after being raped." Bayard paused, the black slashes of his eyebrows raised as if he were deliberating what to impart next. "It may not be my place to tell you, but since I do care about her, I think you should know that Helena was very distraught over the news of a woman in your life being raped. Especially now that the Indians have begun attacks. She told me just the other day that she's worried about adequate protection in the stockade. About the possibility of being violated herself since you'd been gone when your previous wife was attacked."

Carrigan tasted bile, hot and stinging in his throat.

"But I assured Helena that the town is quite safe, and that in your absence, she may rely on me. As she always has."

"My absence?"

"She said you were going to be living separately in the near future." Bayard appeared somewhat uncomfortable, toying with the chain of his watch. "I was more than a little surprised by her statement that you intended to live away from her and that she was agreeable . . . actually very enthusiastic about this."

Enthusiastic? He'd known Helena wanted him to move out in the middle of October, but he'd thought in recent days that she'd changed her mind. There was only one clear-sighted reason why she was sticking by the original plan. She didn't love him. She never had, and never would. The deal had been basic from the beginning. She'd never strayed from it, until he'd pushed for intimacy. It had been her intention to live as man and wife in name only. And that was still her decision.

He had no reason to doubt Kimball. Helena herself had said she'd traded confidences with the man. She'd admitted to associating with him and made no effort to hide their friendship, even though she'd had a recent falling out with him. Obviously they'd overcome their grievances, and in the process, she'd unloaded her mind. In a big way. Whatever else she'd told Kimball went unsaid. In all likelihood, the judge knew it all. Carrigan's failure to find the men responsible for raping Jenny, his shame and guilt. Why stop at just divulging a woman's suicide? Why not impugn him with all the damaging material? Though the reason she saw fit to discuss private matters, Carrigan couldn't understand. She had stood up for him when Kimball accused him of thievery. That counted for a lot. But she'd always been close to the judge, and her discussion with him, even if Helena thought it an innocent exchange, was unforgivable.

"It's just as well you'll be living on the parcel alone," Bayard's voice intruded. "Helena needs security. You can see that her home and her station are her livelihood. You couldn't drag her away from that and expect her to be happy. It takes a strong man to admit his wife is better off without his constant guidance. But don't worry. I'll be here for her and make sure she is suitably looked after. I always have."

Carrigan could hear nothing else other than the fiddler, who threw all his powers into playing. The notes pounded in his head. Air seemed a precious commodity, and he suddenly couldn't get enough of it into his lungs. He was almost to the point of suffocation as the room seemed to devour what was left of his body, and he withdrew within himself.

Feeling dead, he walked out the doors to think.

* * *

Bayard could barely contain a victorious smile. He'd been right. His hunch had paid off. Carrigan *had* told Helena about his first wife. Because of that, Carrigan had consumed every word he'd fed him. He'd been able to poison him with his own venom— the disgusting truth of his own past. The ease with which he'd been able to manipulate him was almost laughable.

A man without a past to show always had a past to hide. And Bayard had tripped upon Carrigan's with practically no effort at all. The information had come without the difficulty of a long pursuit. He had the best wedge he could ever hope for to drive firmly between Carrigan and Helena.

Distrust.

Distrust could strip the flesh off a man, and make a woman never believe in him again. The first part of his plan had worked without a hitch. Now he would begin on the second.

He walked up to Helena, who was no longer talking to Mrs. Hunt, Mrs. Osterman, and the Mexican cook Helena kept on at the Express. Bowing slightly, he gave her a solicitous smile—a light smile she returned with a beauty that captivated him. He couldn't stop himself from taking one of her hands into his own and giving her gloved fingers a gentle squeeze.

"I am so glad to see you here tonight, Mrs. Carrigan." He hated calling her that man's name, but had to show his respect if he wanted to win her completely. "It's good to see you at one of Genoa's dances. I trust this won't be your one and only appearance."

"That will have to depend," she replied graciously, "if my husband is willing to come to another dance." Rather than look Bayard in the eyes, she scanned the crowd over his left shoulder. He found her search for Carrigan annoying, but didn't show her his anger.

The band, which had been forever belting out rambunctious melodies, began to strum a lilting waltz.

Bayard couldn't have asked for better timing. Crooking his arm, he addressed the woman of his heart. "This dance would be wasted without you."

Her soft gaze took a quick inventory of the room. "I can't. I promised the waltz to Jake."

Bayard conceded with a polite sigh, "Of course." Then he let his gaze follow hers. "Where is he?"

"I don't know. He said he was going outside for a moment to smoke, but I haven't seen him return."

"He's probably indulging in more than one cigarette. There are a group of men on the boardwalk who are discussing the fire, and how they're going to organize rebuilding the businesses that were destroyed. Perhaps he's offering his assistance."

"Perhaps . . ."

Bayard clasped his hands behind his back, nonchalance in his stance, as he forced himself to admire the dancers. He didn't want to pretend he was relaxed when he wasn't and only gave his artificial interest a scant minute before moving in on Helena. "We could join in the waltz until Mr. Carrigan returns. Then I'll gladly bow out for him to continue with you."

Hesitation marked her delicate brows. "But I promised."

"And you shall keep your promise. Just as soon as he comes back. That's *my* promise to you." Bayard gave her no further room to beg off, sweeping her into his arms and twirling her on the waxed floor.

She was like an elusive angel in his grasp. Light and effervescent, dressed in a virginal white. Feeling the way he did now, he could pardon her for sleeping with Carrigan. For Bayard would make her forget she'd ever known another man.

"He'll return very shortly, I'm sure," Bayard consoled when he observed the disquiet in her lovely blue eyes.

With masterful domination, he moved Helena through the waltz, feeling the stirrings of genuine rapture take hold of him. Earlier he'd spoken to Captain Eli Garrett and told him that he would be at his service should his company require any legal documentation drawn up during their stay. Keeping communication with the military open and friendly would be an asset. Things like that counted when it came time for political appointments. Everything was fitting into place. Now all he had to do was keep Helena in doubt about Carrigan's ability to take care of her.

"I dare to bring up a delicate subject—only because of the Indian trouble, mind you—about your husband's first wife."

Helena's face went pale. "How . . . ?"

"It wasn't hard to find out."

"You checked into my husband's past?"

"Only by accident. The details of how really aren't important." He hoped he'd appeased her with his vague answer, and rather than wait for her to grill him further, he continued in a tone riddled with sincerity, "As I said, I only bring the matter up because I don't want you to feel as if you're in the same kind of danger of attack. You needn't be afraid of the soldiers. Not all of them are rapists, and you know that if you have any trouble at the store, you may rely on me to deal with it with the heavy hand of the law."

"I don't anticipate any trouble," Helena said, her voice low. "I have Jake to protect me."

"But he won't always be there for you. Just like he wasn't there for his first wife."

Helena's cheeks colored.

"I'm only pointing out the truth. You know what happened and why it happened to that lovely young girl. Jake Carrigan wasn't around for her."

"I don't want to dance anymore," Helena said, trying to pull away.

Bayard wouldn't let her go. "My dear, my dear," he said in a calming voice. "I mean you no harm. I don't want you to feel like you have no one to turn to. That's why I mentioned this. I wanted you to know that you can count on me. Always."

Helena said nothing.

"I didn't mean to upset you." Bayard applied pressure on her back and attempted to pull her a scant inch closer. She barely moved, faltering in the beat of the music. "Nothing will happen. But if this war continues for an extended time, you'll be alone with Emilie, and I want you to feel secure."

"I do feel secure."

"Perhaps at the moment, but have you forgotten what it was like after your father's death? You were vulnerable."

"But I'm not anymore."

"Of course you're not. Not now. But you will be. You told me yourself. Times are changing. The town is growing. Hoodlums come and go. I am only one man trying to keep law and order in it all." He smiled at her, trying to get her to do the same. "If anything, think of Emilie. She's so young. Know that I'll be watching out for you from my window. I'll keep an eye on the station."

"That's not necessary."

"Of course it's necessary. Please . . . don't fret," he crooned. "Didn't your father tell you, you could trust me?"

She barely nodded.

"You can, because it's true." He tried to lighten the mood, now that he'd laid out his plans. "Smile. Just a little. For me. For old times' sake."

But Helena didn't, and he blamed it on Carrigan ruining her chances of true happiness.

Carrigan came back to the assembly after several smokes. He would have left for good, but he had to confront Helena and ask her why she'd seen fit to tell Kimball about his past. Carrigan had never asked her to keep the information to herself, but he'd figured it went unspoken that his disclosure was close to his heart—a secret he'd kept to himself for years, and something that he'd wanted to stay between them. He never would have revealed her affair with Kurt to anyone.

When Carrigan finally caught sight of Helena, she wasn't alone. She was dancing with Kimball. The image flared Carrigan's nostrils, and his eyes narrowed. Though she didn't look like she was enjoying herself overmuch, she was still dancing the waltz with the judge.

Seeing her with Bayard set off something in Carrigan. Helena looked like she should be a judge's wife. They complemented each other. He the dapper gentleman. She the gentile lady. Why hadn't he seen it before? That despite Helena downplaying her place in Genoa's society, she was one of them. And always would be.

The waltz ended without Carrigan moving a muscle to approach them. Helena's cheeks were an invigorated pink as she walked with Kimball to the refreshment table. He handed her a tiny glass of punch. She never once saw Carrigan watching her. Drinking the beverage, she conversed with Bayard, her gaze skimming the doorway every few seconds, dutifully watching for her husband.

When her eyes finally did connect with Carrigan's, she smiled brightly. But Carrigan could only return a cool gaze. She seemed puzzled by his reaction and even distraught. But with Kimball standing there, Carrigan wasn't about to ask for any explanations.

Not allowing the situation to dictate to him, Carrigan went to Helena and gave the judge a stiff glare.

"I was worried about you," Helena said, leaving Bayard's side and crossing over to his.

"If you'll excuse me," the judge said. "I'll leave you two alone."

Carrigan refused to touch Helena. He stood with-

out flinching, his joints tensely knotted. "I was outside having a smoke," he replied in a tone burdened
with tightness.

"That's what you said you were going to do. But
when you didn't come back for so long, I wondered."

Carrigan couldn't meet her eyes. "Felt like having a
few," he said.

The musicians, who had taken a short intermission,
returned to the platform. "Last dance before the
bidding on the candy starts!" shouted the harmonica
player. "Form your squares!"

"I . . ." Helena chewed on her lower lip and looked
over at him. "They played a waltz while you were
gone. I waited, but Bayard insisted I dance with him
until you came back. I was hoping you'd find me
before the music ended."

"I saw you."

"Why didn't you cut in?"

"It's no big deal."

The fiddler's bow plucked the inviting notes. A man
who'd been the designated caller turned up his
sleeves, bent his knees, and started slapping them in
time to the beat with the palms of his hands. Women
were light on their feet. Men were huffing for air. All
were smiling and having a good time.

Carrigan wanted to leave, but was obligated to stay
for the remainder of the evening. Which was probably
several more hours.

"When they play another waltz, we'll dance to
that," Helena offered.

"We'll see," he replied noncommittally. Then he
took in a breath and asked, "You have a nice talk with
Kimball?"

Helena's eyes met his. "We made polite conversation."

"Just like you always do?"

"What are you getting at?"

He leaned his head closer toward hers. "I don't like

my private life being discussed with anyone. Especially with a man I don't like."

"Your private life?"

"Do you deny talking to him about Jenny?"

She was silent for a minute. "No, I don't. But how would you know?"

"I trusted you, Helena," was his tight reply.

"I didn't say anything."

"The hell you didn't."

She put her hand on his shoulder. "I never betrayed you. What you told me in confidence, I would never tell. Bayard didn't hear it from me."

"Then how could he know?"

"I couldn't say."

Carrigan was disappointed that he'd actually trusted her. Even if there was an excuse Helena could offer in her behalf, he couldn't accept it right now, or whatever else she wanted to say. He just couldn't see a good reason for her to talk about Jenny's suicide with Kimball. He should have known something like this would happen. He'd been feeling too right in the relationship. Things that felt too comfortable made him uncomfortable. And perhaps he'd been waiting for the opportunity to end the relationship before it got out of hand and he was in love with her. . . . But was he already too late to stop his feelings?

The song ended and people began milling toward the candy tables to bid on the confections.

"Don't shut me out, Jake. We need to discuss this. You're thinking I've done something and I haven't. We could leave if you're upset. But Emilie . . ." Helena was clearly at odds. "I feel like I should stay."

"We'll stay. I'm not going to ruin her night. Forget about it."

"But—"

"I said, forget about it."

Then he took her arm and went through the motions of partaking in the festivities, giving her no opportunity to break through to him. Her talk with Kimball had left the door wide open. It was a way out if he wanted to leave. Even though he knew in his heart she hadn't done anything wrong, he was scared to admit he'd gotten too close to her. Thoughts about working for the military had done it. He'd known at that instant that he was willing to cross the line for Helena and put convictions behind him. That he was willing to make her the most important thing in his life. Nothing and no one else mattered. It was a hell of an option to consider, seeing as he felt the way he did about soldiers.

Being with Helena felt so right, it had to be wrong. So he'd decided to take the door and throw himself out before Helena could beat him to the punch. He had land waiting for him. And that had been the prime objective for him marrying her. For a while, he'd forgotten that. But now it became his goal once again.

Chapter

➤ **17** ➤

The weekend was passed in near silence between Helena and Jake. Gone were the unguarded moments of intimacy. She couldn't understand why he'd felt it necessary to block her out. She'd told him that she hadn't said anything to Bayard. Why hadn't he believed her? Each time she tried to speak to him, he talked over her and cut her off with an abrupt tone and went to work in another part of the stockade or stables. She wanted to scream her frustration. She had her pride, too, and gave him his space for a time. Father had been that way. When he was upset or angry, Mother had stayed away from him, giving him time to cool down and realize that what he was angry about was nothing to be angry about at all. After several days without Jake's willingness to talk to her, Helena was exasperated and said enough was enough. They were going to have it out even if she had to yell for everyone to hear.

She began her search in the yard, her thoughts trailing for a few minutes to the other topic constantly on her mind. The Indian war had blossomed into a full-fledged battle. Like hot spots from a fire, skirmishes blazed across the territory. News came in with the Express riders, who were edgy and high-strung. James Whalen had been thrown off his horse when an arrow shot through the sky. Luckily, he'd been able to remount and make it to Busby's. But James's leg had been broken in the fall, so the eastern run was short a man. This put added pressure on those who were already taxed from the demands of breakneck speed and unfaltering endurance.

Telegraph lines were constantly being cut by the Paiutes in a show of contempt for the white man's singing wires. Communication was severed between several stations, and the only way words were traded was by the reliability of the mail. Descriptions of braves streaked with paint, their bodies greased, were offered by the thirsty riders as they halted in clouds of dust at their stations.

Well-armed dragoons patrolled Genoa's streets, keeping order in their imposing blue uniforms. Yet that didn't take the edge off the fear the citizens were feeling. Especially Emilie.

Thomas had made one run to Gray's station since the Candy Dance, and was due in to town within the hour. Emilie was a bundle of nerves waiting for his appearance. When he'd come by Monday, unharmed and coated with trail grit, Emilie had broken into tears on the heels of his departure, praying she would see him again. Helena had felt helpless to comfort her sister. There was no guarantee that she could give Emilie that Thomas would stay safe. But Helena held on to her mother's cross that encircled her neck, and said a prayer of Godspeed for the young man.

Since Emilie had already fallen in love with Thomas, there was nothing Helena could do to stop her sister. Emilie was growing up and would have her own choices to make. It was a horrible suffering for any woman to go through, unsure if her man would still be hers in the days to come. Helena knew how Emilie was feeling. Though she and Jake were bound together as husband and wife, she was more of an outsider in his life than his partner.

As Helena crossed the yard, she saw no glimpses of Jake in the corral, or in the stables when she entered. Eliazer was alone.

"Where's Jake?" she asked.

"Left."

The word sliced through Helena. "Left?" All she could think of was he'd left for good, and a panic flared in her so great, she almost couldn't breathe. But she calmed when she saw Traveler in his stall. Jake wouldn't leave one of his horses behind. Boomerang was missing. "Where?"

"Said he was going up to the ridge." Eliazer pointed out the open doors toward the northeast.

The land.

"Could you help me saddle Maria Jane?" Helena picked out a striped wool blanket while Eliazer selected a saddle. "I'll try and be back before Thomas McAllister comes in. But if I'm not in time to help you with his mount, saddle Columbiana."

"Yes, Miss Lena. I'll make sure she's ready."

Helena's horse was equipped, and she mounted. Riding out the tall stockade doors, she headed east. As she climbed to higher ground and approached the one-hundred-sixty-acre parcel, she spotted Jake's roan and Obsi streaking through the high grass with his tail twitching. When she neared, the dog barked and Jake turned on her with his Colt drawn and aimed at her chest. Seeing her, he paused and reholstered his revolver. The expression on his face was anything but welcoming when she dismounted.

Tethering the horse's reins to a chaparral, Helena removed her rawhide gloves and stuffed them into her belt. She scanned the land, seeing in it the splendor that was so appealing. The ground was rich and verdant, the trees spired and thick, while a cross section of the Carson River fed the parcel with endless water. Jake stood in an area devoid of trees, a natural meadow surrounded by pines and edged with cotton-woods toward the south. There was a slight slant to the terrain, but with it came an expansive view of the valley to the south.

"It's pretty here. I've always liked this spot." Her observance caused Jake to frown.

Without answering, he strode toward her on the thick heels of his boots. He was attired in worn black pants and a checkered cotton shirt with the sleeve cuffs turned up once, and his rugged appearance made her pulse beat at the base of her throat. His face was tanned a burnished brown, while his gray hat kept his blunt hair away from his brows. The brim and crown had been molded and shaped to suit him. Weather permitted him to go without a vest, but a bandanna was tied in a knot at his throat.

"What are you doing here?" he challenged. "You change your mind?"

Confusion filled her. "About what?"

"This. The land."

"No, I haven't." Why would he think she did? "Since you keep running away from me, I came to talk to you."

Jake reached into his pocket, took out a drawstring bag and papers, and rolled a cigarette. Lighting it, he inhaled and the smell of smoke drifted on the breeze. She hadn't realized how much she'd missed the scent of tobacco in his presence. Putting her hands behind her back, she bit her lip and walked to where he stood. The strain in him was evident, as the muscles in his neck were taut. He was so very angry with her—angrier now than the night of the dance. Had she made a mistake by leaving him alone for so long? Did he think she didn't care?

"You have to listen to my explanation about the dance," she began in a rush so he couldn't stop her. "I didn't want to dance with Bayard. He suggested we do—only until you came back into the assembly.

Then I would finish the waltz with you. I'm sorry if you find that so offensive. I never meant to hurt you just by dancing with Bayard. It meant nothing to me. As for Jenny, Bayard brought her up, not me. I still don't know how he found out. I asked him yesterday to tell me how, but he wouldn't. He kept going around the issue and wouldn't say."

Holding his cigarette between his thumb and forefinger, he watched it burn in his grasp, then lifted his gaze toward the high-domed cape of blue sky. "You don't need me anymore."

"Of course I need you!" she exclaimed.

Ignoring her plea, he went on. "You can stand on your own now. No one is going to go up against you." Jake lifted the cigarette to his mouth and pulled in the smoke until the end burned red. "I think it's time we end this. We've played the charade out."

Shock and dismay clutched her.

"I want the land. You've given it to me. It's legally mine." His eyes were cold and unfeeling when he said, "Let's not prolong the inevitable. I always said I'd leave, and you knew that."

Hurt drew a deep line in her. She'd wanted him to stay. Would have asked him to stay. Then something hit her as sure as if she'd been physically struck. "How do you know this land is legally yours?"

His forehead dented into a scowl. "That's fairly obvious. Your name was in the Kinsey book I signed this morning. Right there in ink, says you transferred this land to me as of yesterday. Don't know why you couldn't have told me instead of that goddamn judge."

Helena was sick. Bayard had spoken to Jake about the turnover on the parcel? How could he? The only reason she'd told him he could begin proceedings was to give him a show of faith. Demonstrate that she was willing to let bygones be bygones. But Bayard had abused her once again. He'd gone to Jake. And now Jake thought she was trying to get rid of him.

"I'm sorry, I didn't mean to make it appear that I wanted you out of the station."

"Could've fooled me."

"Jake," she implored, "you've got to listen to me. I only told Bayard to transfer the deed because—"

"Doesn't matter." Jake ground his cigarette beneath his boot. "It's over." He began walking toward his horse.

"It's not over," she called, chasing after him. "It's not!"

Sharply he turned on her. "It is when I'm singled out off the goddamn street by a man I don't like and am told my wife wanted me to have this land as soon as possible so she could get me the hell out of her life."

"I never said anything of the kind!" Terror made her weak. "You've got to believe me. I would *never* say such a thing to Bayard."

"No? But you talked to him about Jenny."

Helena's breasts rose and fell with her anger. This had nothing to do with Jenny, or the deed, or even Bayard. "Jake Carrigan, you're being totally unreasonable. This is all just an excuse for you. It's a way for you to leave me."

"I never said I'd stay."

"But things changed between us, and you know that." She knew that her admission would sound like a ploy to get him to stay, but she went ahead with it anyway. He had to know before he went off without her. "Jake, I love you."

He froze, one foot in the stirrup of his saddle. She waited long minutes for him to say something. Anything. Even if he called her a liar, it would be better than his silence. At last, all he offered was, "You better mount up. I can't leave you here alone."

Helena stared at him. "You're scared. At least admit it to yourself if you won't admit it to me."

Jake leaned forward and put his elbow on the saddle horn. "I don't know what you're talking about." His gaze was unmoving as granite, his mouth a fixed line of fury.

"Well, I'll say it, then. I'm scared, too. I won't deny I wanted you to have the parcel, regardless of what happens in our relationship . . . where you live . . . or don't, I wanted you to feel secure in knowing I would make good on my promise to give you the acreage." She looked into his eyes, seeing the flecks of gold against green. Seeing the pain and indecision he wouldn't acknowledge. "I want you to come back to the station. Don't say the charade is over."

"Too late. This is mine."

Desperate, she lashed out at him with whatever ammunition she had to hold him to her until she could figure out what to do next. "But we had an agreement. You were to stay with me for six months."

"Things change."

"They don't. And if you don't stay, I'll consider you a liar."

Jake merely laughed. A terrible, insincere sound. "I've always told you I was a liar, Lena. That's the one thing I've never lied to you about."

Carrigan rode behind Helena, watching the line of her shoulders as she stiffly held the reins of the mustang. How he hated hurting her.

She'd said she loved him. The words had cut right through him. She'd admitted her feelings so easily, he'd fought against really believing her. But Helena wouldn't have said it if it weren't true.

She loved him.

He didn't know how to deal with her love. It was more of a burden to him than a blessing. Because in return, he couldn't say the same. Even though it was true. Or almost true. Hell, it was true, but he was too much of a realist to deny that loving her wouldn't be the best thing for her.

Even while he was telling himself he'd be better off without her, he'd been thinking a lot about Captain

Garrett's offer. This not only had him in knots, it had him wondering if he was making the biggest mistake of his life by pushing Helena away.

It wasn't too late to hunt down Captain Garrett and tell him he'd changed his mind. Carrigan had been rationalizing rounding up horses that would, in a sense, be used to kill part of his heritage. There were no shades of gray. It was a war drawn in black and white. Either you fought back, or you were killed. There was no disrespect to his mother's band of people, yet there was no loyalty to any tribe of Indian just because his blood was part Choctaw. He'd been raised a white man, and he had to take their side. If he didn't, people could get hurt. Helena could get hurt. By rounding up horses for the cavalry, he'd be helping her. Them. With the income off the horses, Carrigan could hire an extra man to help at the station while Helena was with him while he began building a house. Their house. He was going to ask her where she wanted the windows, and how many rooms she'd fancy . . . and if she liked porches . . . and porch swings.

Jesus, he couldn't afford to dream such dreams.

She loved him. Carrigan couldn't get the words out of his head. She loved him. And he'd hurt her.

A distant horse nickered, and Carrigan grew alert. Helena sat straighter and looked over her shoulder at him. He waved her back. She lightened the reins and had Maria Jane fall into step next to Boomerang. Carrigan withdrew his Colt and trained the barrel on a dense thicket of poplars. Within a moment, color came into view. Clothing of blue and red, swatches that were familiar to Jake.

Carrigan's first thought had been that the rider was a lone Indian, but the man astride a slow-loping mustang wore trousers and a shirt, with a slouch hat. He was slumped over the saddle horn, his body swaying with the jarring movements of the horse.

"Oh, dear God," Helena gasped.

Carrigan heard her cry in his ear just as he recognized the rider. The mustang cleared the trees and plodded over a sheet of granite on his way toward Genoa. The rider, in the uniform of the Pony Express, had an arrow sticking out of his back.

It was Thomas McAllister.

They guided the horse across Fifth Street with Thomas's crippled body hunched in the saddle. He was alive, but just barely. His crumpled appearance drew a hasty crowd, and someone ran to the Indian Affairs office to notify the authorities. Since there was no physician, Helena and Jake brought Thomas to the station. As soon as they entered the wide gates, Emilie was dashing out of the store with her fist to her mouth in an effort to stop her screams from coming. But they did, and the sorrowful sounds caused even Obsi to sit back and howl his sadness.

Eliazer arrived to help with the horse, and as soon as Jake had Thomas off the saddle, he hoisted him over his shoulder and carried him toward the rear entrance to the house. Down the hall and up the stairs, the pattern brought an agonizing sense of déjà vu to Helena. She'd made this crossing once before . . . with the man she'd fallen in love with. Then, she hadn't known how she would come to feel about him. But for Emilie, the emotions were already there. Her sister was suffering immensely.

Once Jake reached the top of the stairs, he headed for his room, but Emilie cried out, "Put him in my bedroom."

Helena would have made a comment, but the tone in Emilie's voice, despite her outward appearance, was calm and insistent. "I'll take care of him. Just tell me what to do."

She led the way and pulled the coverlet off her bed so Jake could lay Thomas down on his stomach. A wide circle of blood had spread across the back of his shirt, the arrow's feathered end almost unbearable to view. Its sight was gruesome and merciless, making Helena want to close her eyes. But cowering and falling into tears would not help Thomas. Emilie must have seen the prudence in this as well, for her sobs had ceased, and she was standing over Thomas with determination holding her fair face captive.

"How do we get the arrow out?" She addressed Jake, who had taken the knife from his boot and was slicing down the middle of Thomas's shirt with the blade.

"Carefully."

Once the shirt was free, Helena had to swallow the saliva gathering in her throat. For some reason, she'd been more equipped to handle Jake's injury than Thomas's. She'd taken charge without blinking, knowing that Jake had no one else to count on to see him through other than her. With Thomas . . . she couldn't explain why she was falling apart. Perhaps because Emilie was being so brave. It gave Helena some leeway to feel her discomfort and fear.

Jake wiped his palms down the sides of his trousers, then gave Emilie a level glance. "If I don't pull it out straight, the tip could break off inside of him. Many men have lived with an arrowhead in their bodies, but it's painful. I'll try and go slowly. It's going to hurt him like hell. If he yells, don't panic. I'm not killing him. I have no choice."

Emilie nodded, taking one of Thomas's hands into her own and squeezing so tightly, her knuckles whitened. "Do what you have to do to save him."

Jake grasped the shaft and began to twist his wrist very slightly as he pulled. The slight movement had Thomas screaming out in his unconscious state. Emilie bit her lip so hard, she trembled from the pain.

Helena felt the beginnings of sickness slap her. Wave after wave, until she knew she would be sick unless she left the room. "I'll have Ignacia heat some water." But that was just an excuse. Surely Ignacia would have the water hot and ready without being told. But Helena had to escape.

She swiftly went into the hallway, gasping for air as she did and pressing her hands on the walls as she went toward the stairwell. Once there, she sat on the top riser, put her face in her hands, and wept. Of all the things she'd worried Emilie might experience with her first love, they didn't include having to cope with the death of a beloved as Helena had. She'd never thought Emilie would have to live through losing the man she loved to an accident, or an act of war. It hadn't seemed possible for two sisters to have to bear the same thing, but it was happening. She saw herself up in that room, and she couldn't bear it if Emilie had to feel the pain of letting go of Thomas. It wasn't fair.

Helena lifted her chin as Ignacia came up the stairs with a basin, kettle of steaming water, and towels draped over her arm.

"It doesn't seem real," Ignacia said. "I just did this for Mr. Carrigan. Poor, dear Emilie."

Wiping her tears from her eyes, Helena forced herself to pull together. Emilie needed her. She couldn't desert her now. So she stood, blotted her face with the hem of her dress, and went into Jake's room to pilfer his whiskey. She came up empty-handed. Of all the times for him to quit.

Running downstairs with the intent of snatching a bottle from the counter, she was faced with a throng of curious well-wishers who'd flooded the store.

"How is young McAllister?" Mr. Mayhew inquired, his face sober with serious regard.

"Mr. Carrigan is doing what he can for him," Helena replied. "He's removing the arrow."

Mrs. Doyle, her cheeks apple red, stepped forward. The stiffening in her petticoats crackled as she walked. "We are very concerned about him. Is there anything I can offer?"

"Certainly not your husband's services," Helena

said, unable to stop herself from the biting comment. Only too late, she realized Mrs. Doyle was being sincere. "I'm sorry, ma'am. It's just that things are very trying right now. If you all wouldn't mind leaving, I think quiet would be the best thing for the household right now. We'll inform you tomorrow how Thomas fared through the night."

On that note, she shuffled the gathering out the door with a nod of her head that said indeed, she would let them all know about Thomas's condition in the morning. Turning the key in the lock and drawing the shades, she retreated for the upstairs with the whiskey bottle firmly grasped in her hand.

When she reached Emilie's bedroom, Thomas was moaning softly as Emilie cleansed his wound with warm towels. Jake had gotten the arrow out, or what appeared to be the entire arrowhead.

"Were you able to remove it all?" she asked, putting aside the tension between them, and glad Jake was doing the same.

"I got it all out. But the sharp edges really cut him up. He's going to need a good poultice."

"Eliazer has begun one," Ignacia supplied, her reed-thin body looking frail and overwrought. "Why does the Lord see fit to keep sending us disasters?"

Helena could not reply, for Thomas wasn't the only disaster to hit the station today. But she wouldn't spend time dwelling on the argument she and Jake had had when Thomas lay with his life in the balance.

Emilie was careful to be very gentle with Thomas, each stroke of the cloth a loving and careful blot. His face was toward Helena and Jake when his eyes fluttered open, and he mumbled something incoherent.

Rounding the bed, Emilie bent down in front of him and put her face next to his. "Thomas, you're safe. You're with me. Emilie. At my house in my room. I'll take care of you."

"Mmmmmmmm," he exhaled with a rasp.

"Don't talk." Emilie put her hand on his forehead and smoothed his blond hair from his brows.

"Mmmmmmmm," he said once again. "Mmmmaaaaaa."

"Ma?" Emilie questioned. "You want me to tell your mother something?"

"Not," he spoke through cracked lips. "Nnnnot Ma. Mail."

"Don't worry about the mail. You need to get better."

"Got." He licked his parched mouth. "Got to get through. Mail."

Helena handed Jake the whiskey. "I think he needs something to sedate him."

Jake shook his head as he set the bottle on the short-mirrored cherry-wood bureau. "Laudanum first. It'll be more effective against the pain right now."

"Mail," Thomas repeated. "Got to get through." This time he tried to rise, but Jake was at the bed and put his hand on Thomas's shoulder.

"You're not going anywhere, Thomas. You've been hit with an arrow."

"I know." Thomas's eyes closed halfway. "Happened . . . by Yank's station. Didn't see the Indians . . . till it was too late."

"Save your strength." Emilie laid a warm towel on Thomas's back and continued to smooth his hair. "You need to rest and let me take care of you. I love you, Thomas."

That her sister could speak the words so unabashedly had Helena a little envious. Even more so when Thomas returned them.

"Love you too, Em. But the mail . . . got to get it to Carson."

Jake shoved his hands into his pockets and said, "I'll go."

Helena shot him a surprised stare. "You'll go?"

"I'll ride the mail. I know where Carson City is. I passed through there several years back. Just follow the river."

"Yes," Thomas hissed through his pain. "Station's down on Carson Street . . . between Fourth and Fifth."

"All right." Jake slid the bead up his hat strings. "I'll get it there."

"Thanks."

Jake turned and left the room. Helena went after him. She caught up with Jake on the landing. "You can't go."

"Why not?"

"Because. It's dangerous. You could get killed."

"I gave you your legitimacy. You're all set. If something happens to me, take good care of my dog and horses. You can have whatever you want out of my cabin, but nothing's worth a whole hell of a lot."

"Don't talk like that!" she exclaimed. "Like you don't care."

"Don't you see, Lena? I have nothing to lose." Then he departed from her sight, and her heart was broken in two.

It was sometime around two in the morning when Helena finally convinced Emilie to leave Thomas's bedside and go into the kitchen for a cup of coffee. Thomas had been sleeping comfortably, and soundly, for the past five hours with no threat of complications. Emilie had been by him the entire time. She'd shown a maturity beyond her years, bathing his wound, applying the poultice, binding him, giving him the proper dosage of laudanum, and seeing to it he was resting peacefully. Helena was proud beyond measure.

In the deserted kitchen, she waited on Emilie and served her a steaming cup of black coffee. Her sister's hair had come loose from its bun and fell around her tired face. She sipped on the hot liquid, toying with the spoon Helena had used in the sugar.

"I think he'll be all right, Emilie." Helena let the coffee soothe her throat. "You've done a wonderful job taking care of him. Mother and Father would be proud of you. I am."

Emilie smiled weakly. "I thought that I'd be too scared to help him. But there's something about loving someone that makes you strong."

Helena squeezed back her tears, mutely nodding.

"I remembered how it was with you and Kurt. How in love with him you were. And how brave you were when they told you he died. I couldn't have been like you, Lena. I would have . . ." Emilie's tears fell freely. "I wouldn't want to live if Thomas were to die."

Helena reached out and took Emilie's hand. "He won't."

Her sister held on to her with a firm grasp, a lifeline of compassion and understanding. Helena made a decision in that split second. It had been a long time since they'd confided in one another. And an even longer time since Helena had told Emilie the truth.

"I'm in love with Jake," she whispered.

Emilie's chin lifted. "I suspected you were. And he loves you?"

"I thought he did . . . but . . . it's very complicated." Helena took in an unsteady breath.

"What do you mean?"

Helena lowered her head, then met Emilie's gaze. "There's something I've never told anyone. Only Jake. And Mother knew. Maybe I should have told you before now. Then you'd see why I've treated you the way I have."

"What is it, Lena?"

"You'll . . . think of me differently once you know."

"I would never."

"Perhaps . . ." Helena released Emilie's hand and

sat straighter in the chair. Gathering her thoughts, she began at the beginning. The day she'd first met Kurt. She left nothing out, revealing everything to Emilie and telling her why she'd raised her the way she had after their mother had died. When she was finished, Emilie stood, went around the table, and held Helena in her arms. The two girls cried for lost years, for years of doubt and hurting.

As the last tears were shed, Emilie put her hands on Helena's face. "You have another chance, Lena. With Jake. You have to make him believe you love him."

"I will." Helena nodded, her emotions in shreds. Jake had to be safe. He had to come back tomorrow. "If I get another chance."

Chapter

⋗ 18 ⋖

Carrigan had taken a plain room at the King Street
Hotel in Carson City. He'd been trying to catch a few
hours of shut-eye before riding back to Genoa, but all
he could do was stare at the fingers of shadow on the
ceiling. The cracked lantern had been extinguished a
while ago, and he lay on the springy bed fully clothed
with his Walker still strapped to his hip. Maybe he'd
known he wouldn't be able to sleep with the way
things were between him and Helena. The way things
could have ended with his death and her burying
him . . .

On the precarious ride along the river, he'd been
watchful for Indians. Galloping headlong over the
terrain, he'd run into an ambush of some twenty
Paiutes. Calmly he'd removed his Colt as he approached them, the barrel sited on a few. There was
no way he could have taken them all down, but he
could have died picking off at least six of them. With
his shoulders low and head down, he'd ridden reck-
lessly toward them with his revolver raised. Bows

were in hand and arrows trained on Carrigan's chest, but at the last second, the leader had let him pass without an altercation. Perhaps out of reverence for his daring. But Carrigan knew his courage hadn't come from bravado. He'd gone ahead with no heed for the danger and the fear of them taking his life because he'd already been defeated in spirit. He'd lost the woman he loved.

Or maybe not.

Maybe it wasn't too late to fight for her. Her words had been soaking into his head for the past few hours. She loved him. It would be enough. It could be. If he'd let it. And he wanted to. He'd been a stubborn ass, running when he'd been home all the time. No matter where they lived, it would suit him because it had to. Because he wanted to be with Helena. But right now, she was there and he was here. There wasn't a hell of a lot he could do at the moment.

Reining in to Carson, he'd found the Express station where Thomas had described and handed over the *mochila*. After he told the master what had happened, a telegram had been sent to alert Russell, Majors and Waddell, though there was some question whether or not it would make it through the lines. Carrigan had left and boarded his horse for the night at a nearby livery on the corner of Third and Curry, then he'd checked into the King Street. Buying an overpriced supper in the dining room, he'd eaten the meal before going upstairs to his room. He'd thought he was tired enough to close his eyes and get in a few hours before heading out, but sleep had been elusive. There were people he cared about. People he was lying here thinking about. Thomas, if he would make it through the night. Emilie, if she could handle the situation. Eliazer, if the old Mexican was looking after Obsi. Ignacia, if she had enough firewood for the box, or if in all the confusion of Thomas's injury, she'd have to get more herself.

And Helena. She'd never left his thoughts from the

second he'd ridden out of Genoa. He couldn't sleep without hearing her in the next room. Without being assured she was there in her lawn nightgown with her braid tumbling down her back.

Not knowing the answers to the questions that plagued him, and wanting to set things right between him and Helena, Carrigan sat up and collected the key and handful of coins from the scratched table at the bed's metal headboard. Pocketing the silver, he took his hat from the hook on the wall and went into the hallway. He locked the door and headed out for the nearest saloon. After several cups of strong coffee and a few smokes, he'd be up to sitting in the saddle with as much alertness as he had in him.

He was going back to Genoa before the sun hit the tops of the eastern pines.

Outside, the dark air finally hinted of summer. The usual briskness of spring was absent, and the promise of parching heat in the months to come rode the current. A drowsy smell of grass and flowers overtook the pungent odors of animals, saloons, the old bricks of buildings, and the dry wood of weathered stables. Walking two blocks west and turning the corner, Carrigan entered the Division Saloon through its swinging doors with wickerwork on the tops.

The sawdust on the floor muffled his steps as he strode to a table in the corner near the front. Sitting with his back to the wall decorated with miners' tools and sportive nudes, he surveyed the barroom's interior. The lighting was dim. What little of it there was coming from the flaming cluster of lamps suspended from the ceiling was reflected off the vast backbar mirror. Colored labels of stacked bottles residing on the counter behind the bar lent a bit of cheer to the gloomy ambience. An upright piano was at the bar's left, but wasn't being played.

A handful of men sat at an oblong table covered with black oilcloth near the rear exit. They were playing cards and smoking cigars. On a glance, Carrigan could make out five of them—the fifth member of the game, just his shoulder. The rest of him was obstructed by the dented stovepipe hat of the man sitting across from him.

The bartender, with the face of a bulldog and a body just as squat, asked in a friendly tone that contradicted his appearance, "What'll it be?"

"Coffee." Carrigan slumped lower in his chair, kicking up his boot on the chair opposite his. "Black and hot."

Adjusting the wristbands that protected his calico cuffs, the bartender said, "Bring some right over."

Carrigan brought out his cigarette makings, rolled one, and lit up. As he was waving the match out, the bartender came over with his coffee. Nodding, Carrigan accepted the cup and set it down to let the steam blow off.

Once again, his attention was drawn to the other men in the saloon. A voice above the rest sounded commonplace, but he couldn't figure out where he'd heard it before. There was a laugh, the clink of coins as they were pitched in as antes, then cards shuffling. After a pause while each studied his hand, that voice spoke up.

"Newt, how many you going to take?"

"Two."

"Vern?" came the drawl.

"Three."

"Horace?"

"One."

"Ike?"

"Four."

"Four," the dealer laughed over the jingle of spurs as feet were crossed at the ankles. Carrigan's gaze had lowered to the floor where the man had moved his legs. Now, lifting his eyes level with the tabletop, he was disappointed he still couldn't see a face. "You might as well fold right now, Ike."

Ike shook his head and began arranging his cards.

Carrigan took a pacifying drink of coffee before inhaling on his smoke. He couldn't explain it, but his fingers were tingling. Itching with a kind of antsiness he hadn't felt since he was down in Mexico looking through the sight of his rifle waiting for the enemy to advance. He'd felt it then, and not many times since, this indication of impending danger. Back then, he'd also felt a fear of being sucked up, much as one does before a tornado strikes. Only this time, the premonition wasn't a signal that he could be swallowed whole or had to ward off would-be attackers. The instinct was to attack. That man talking. Carrigan felt it. Running deep inside. He knew him. Had been waiting on him for some time.

Carrigan put his hand on his gun, slowly removed the weapon, and, without causing undue interest toward himself, checked the chambers. He knew there'd be six bullets. Always was. But he had to make sure before reholstering the Colt .44.

Hooking his finger around the handle of his cup, he drank his coffee. And waited. To make certain that the man with the drawl was indeed the one.

"Full house, tens high," the dealer announced while slapping his cards on the table. Carrigan still couldn't see his face, but if he slid over toward the left, he could make out a shoulder encased in a black shirt with embroidery.

"Out."

"Me, too."

"You win again."

"Your game," was the stilted remark of the fourth. "I'd rather play faro for a while."

"Now, why would I want to buck the tiger when I'm on a hot streak with poker?" As the dealer rose, spurs made a noise like the bartender's tips being plunked in a jar. "Got to take a whiz, boys. Back in a minute."

Carrigan tensed tighter than bed ropes. But he didn't move a muscle as the man slipped out the back door to use the privy in the alley.

Seaton Hanrahan had taken to sporting a new look. Slick and sophisticated was the attempt, but the end result was not. He'd parted his hair in the middle and festooned his bangs into two distinct spit curls that were like commas facing each other over his sandy brows. His clothing was flashy, the boots new, but the cocky voice was there, and the high-crowned hat. That same black hat banded with snakeskin he'd been looking for in Genoa with no luck.

Draining the coffee from his cup, Carrigan stood and walked quietly to the table.

"Gentlemen." He put a finger to his hat and tipped the brim. "Have you got room for one more?"

Several shrugged. "Why not?"

Carrigan slid a hardwood chair away from the table behind him, brought it directly across from Hanrahan's vacant one, and took a seat. "What are you playing?"

"Poker," Newt advised. He was spindly as a fencing post, with a toothpick rolling at the corner of his mouth.

"A good game."

The one named Horace, who had a buckshot hole in his stovepipe hat, remarked, "For Hanrahan, not us, this evening."

"He'll come back, won't he, so I have a chance against him?" Carrigan asked, lighting another smoke. He would have gone after Hanrahan if he'd thought Seaton would quit while he was ahead. But men like him never learned to walk away when the pot was theirs.

"He'll come back," Vern, with his heavily oiled hair and thick fingers marked up by scrapes and bruises, supplied. "He's here every night. The whole livelong night."

"Bum a smoke, mister?" Newt mooched.

Carrigan obliged and was just twisting off the ends when Seaton returned, still buttoning the fly of his trousers, those little iron clogs and chains of his spurs jingling with every step. When he looked up and saw Carrigan at the table, he stopped dead in his tracks. Then a slow smile crept over his mouth.

He snorted, "Well I'll be a sumbitch, if it isn't Carrigan."

Carrigan's unmoving gaze held Seaton's. "Small world."

"It is indeed."

Seaton's hand fell to the back of his chair just before he yanked the legs out. The metal end-grip of his pistol caught in the light of Newt's flared match. Carrigan's eyes took in the handsomely carved .32, his gut burning much like that flame that lit Newt's cigarette. Seaton had his gun. The gun that had been missing from his cabin after he'd been shot.

If there had been any doubt in Carrigan's mind as to who had pulled the trigger on him, it was blown up in the smoke clouding the barroom. Hanrahan had knocked him down in cold blood and left him to freeze up like a water pump in the dead of winter.

"You two know each other?" Ike frowned. "Ain't going to be any funny business, is there?"

"Hell no," Carrigan assured, crushing his cigarette in the bowl of butts off to Horace's side. Glasses of drinks, full and empty, left water rings on the ash-strewn table covering. He hadn't had a drink since that night at his cabin after the fire when he'd had that horrible dream, and he didn't plan on starting up again. But if he were of a mind to take a drink in hand, now would be that time. But Carrigan wanted to stay stone-cold sober.

As Seaton slouched into his chair, Carrigan wanted to know, "What happened to that .36 you used to arm yourself with?"

"Got stolen." His brown eyes were full of unintimidated swagger. "Had to get me this new one here. You like it?"

"Used to have one myself. Exactly like that. Mine got stolen, too."

"Damn shame. Thieves ought to be hanged. Every last one."

Carrigan's voice was as dry as a bourbon cork. "Or be shot."

Seaton gave off a single guffaw before taking up the cards and dealing out six hands. "I've always liked a good shooting myself. Ain't been one in Carson tonight that I know of." He began sorting his five cards. "Yet."

"Night's still young," Carrigan said offhandedly.

The men played cards for close to two hours, the hard liquor continuing to come to the table on the barkeep's circular tray. Carrigan stuck to black coffee, taking heckles from Seaton about him being too sissified to splash back rotgut like a real man. He was being baited, and he knew it. But Carrigan wasn't going to snap over some two-bit insult.

"Ante up," Seaton harped as he dug into his pockets for more money. He flipped several pieces of silver into the pot with the blunt nail of his thumb. Carrigan wouldn't have paid the half dime any attention if there hadn't been etchings on it just below the flag. When he leaned forward slightly to study the coin closer, Seaton slapped his palm over the Lady Liberty just as Carrigan had made out the inscription.

"That's my lucky coin. Not going to give that up. It's my Jesus-God coin." He slipped the half dime back into the slash of his pocket and pulled out a wad of small bills.

"Jesus-God? You don't strike me as a devout man, Hanrahan."

"Never said I was. It's the initials on the coin's face. J for Jesus and G for God. That sure as hell is a sign from above. Haven't had me any bad luck since I got it."

Carrigan kept his features deceptively calm, but his heart was pumping with the squeeze of a fist. There was a suggestion of something deeper, more sinister, surrounding Hanrahan than a bullet through

Carrigan's chest. It was pointing to another murder. A murder that was senseless and criminal, and had torn a family in two. Hanrahan could have been August Gray's killer. Carrigan was almost certain of it. That coin had the letters J.G. Helena had told him about the half dime. Told him that August had scratched her mother's initials on the face as a commemorative to their first sale. Hanrahan had the coin. Sure, he could have come by it secondhand. But secondhand wouldn't be a prize or lucky to a man who hadn't gone through a cash box in search of trinkets. Coming by the coin accidentally would be ordinary, and wouldn't encourage a second look before passing it on again.

"Where'd you get your Jesus-God coin?" Carrigan questioned.

"Picked it up somewhere in Genoa." His mouth turned up on one side into a warped smile. "In Gray's store, as a matter of fact."

That Seaton wouldn't lie only made Carrigan more set on killing him. It was coming down to that. A killing. There was no other way.

"We going to play cards, or are you two going to jaw all night?" Horace whined.

Carrigan didn't want to play poker. He hadn't since he sat down. "I'm finished playing games."

Seaton took a cigar from his breast pocket. He stuck the cheroot between his lips and flamed the end. Puffing, he tapped the deck of cards. "Think I'm finished, too."

"You're finished," Carrigan countered, but Seaton didn't flinch. "I want to know where you got that .32."

"I think you know the answer to that." He indolently leaned against the back of his chair and blew a smoke ring toward the ceiling. "When I'm done with this seegar, I'm going to have to kill you, Carrigan. This time there's nobody around to patch you up. Your girlie is in Genoa all by her lonesome. Imagine she's going to need some consoling when she hears what happened to you."

Carrigan didn't lower his hand to grip his gun. As long as Seaton's were both in view, he wasn't going to make any moves.

Newt, Horace, Ike, and Vern started scooting their chairs back by long inches until they were up on their feet and heading toward the protection offered behind the bar. They stood there with their mouths agape. The bartender reached under the counter and took out a burly rifle.

"Ain't going to be no trouble in my place." He put his hand across the stock.

"No trouble, a'tall, Remie." Hanrahan swallowed a gulp of whiskey. "I'm just sitting here."

"And blowing a lot of smoke," Remie shot back.

Carrigan began counting seconds in his head. Two and a half to draw, one to fire, one for impact. That hand-bored .32 had a stiff trigger when the workings weren't oiled properly, and leaned a hairsbreadth toward the left when fired. All told, when the user knew what he was doing, from holster to impact took six seconds. That was, if the gun wasn't performing properly. If Hanrahan had taken care of it, the time was cut to five. He'd have the man up by a half second. Not too damn much when the end result was a slam in the chest with a shell of lead.

"Since you seem set on killing me," Carrigan said to Seaton's affirmative nod, "you might as well tell me why you killed August Gray."

Hanrahan didn't even blink or try and cover his tracks. "Never meant to, but he was threatening me. Said he'd get that Sharps off the wall above the door and hunt me down. Knew who I was even though I wore a scarf." Hanrahan took short puffs on the cigar. "Supposed to be a robbery to scare them. Make that girlie run to the boss for help. He tried to take my gun away, so I shot him. But things don't always work out, do they? Like tonight. You was probably thinking to sit a spell, have some muddy water, play a little cards, never thinking that tomorrow you'd be laid out on the undertaker's table."

"What makes you so sure it'll be me and not you?"

"I'm good." He tapped the ash onto the floor. "I got you once before. No problem."

"So you did." Carrigan was wasting away the time, getting Hanrahan to talk. "Who's the boss?"

"Wouldn't you like to know?" he chuckled. "I'm not stupid. Never going to get that out of me."

Carrigan's eyes narrowed. "I suppose I would, but whoever you're working for isn't too bright. He's gone and hired you." Seaton's confidence cracked. "You're nothing but a screwup, Hanrahan. You didn't pull the robbery off right—you said so yourself. Didn't succeed in getting rid of Gray's horses, either. Did you?"

"I sure as hell did succeed. They all got out, didn't they?"

"Yeah, but I got them back."

"You should have been hanged."

"Kimball wanted it that way. Said he saw me." Carrigan kept a close watch on Seaton to make sure he didn't do any sudden moves. "Now, how in the hell do you suppose he could have mistaken you for me? I'm a lot bigger than you."

"Not stronger. I could whip your ass if we were to fight."

Carrigan shrugged, unimpressed. "Kimball tell you to go kiss Helena Gray? Make her want to run to him if you pretended like you were going to rape her?"

"I never had to rape no woman in all my life. The judge isn't so smart as he thinks." Hanrahan lifted his glass to his lips. "Thinks he knows how to handle women. I could have told him she wouldn't go to him. He's too old for her, but he said he had to have that one."

"You were working for Bayard Kimball."

"I was . . . ah, shit." Lowering his glass, Seaton took a taste of his cheroot again. "What the hell difference does it make if you know it was Kimball or not? You're a dead man come the next few minutes anyway."

"Ike! Horace!" Remie shouted, his rifle raised to his beefy shoulder. "You go get the vigilante committee. Tell them to get their butts over here. Now! We got big trouble." Then to Seaton. "I'm telling you, Hanrahan, I don't want no shootings in my place. That wallpaper come from Salt Lake, and I ain't putting up a new piece if you put a hole in it."

"Don't you worry about your wallpaper, Remie. The bullet'll be stopped by his heart."

Carrigan didn't find Hanrahan's boastful picture amusing. It was all going to be over, but not for him. Dueling wasn't one of his sports, but that's what this was going to end up being. There'd be no paces to walk. Face-to-face, each of them would draw his gun and fire. It was a cold-blooded way to be on the offense, but Carrigan saw no other choice. He'd never killed a man while looking into his eyes. Watching the life being blown out of a body. It wasn't going to be something he'd relish, but alternate options weren't on his menu. When he thought of Helena, what she'd been through because of Bayard, Carrigan knew he had to do this. To kill Seaton and get back to Genoa to tell Helena how she'd been deceived by that bastard judge. How they'd both been deceived by him.

Seaton enjoyed a final puff of the cigar before he tamped the ashen tip out in the bowl. "Well, I guess this is it," he said without a single note of fear in his voice. "You've been a pain in my ass, Carrigan. This time I intend to put your lights out for good."

But the words were the last Seaton would ever speak. Before Hanrahan's arm was down at his side to grip his gun, Carrigan had drawn and fired. The close proximity of the shot blew Seaton from his chair. He fell backward, tumbling onto the floor with a thwack that raised the sawdust.

The swinging doors busted inward, and Ike and

Horace came panting in on shaky feet. Behind them was a group of six gentlemen in nightshirts that fell to their calves. They were a sober bunch—like a half dozen jurists coming in to proclaim their sentence. Taking one look at Carrigan with the smoking gun in his hand, they hoisted their weapons—a mixture of shotguns and pistols. With Hanrahan sprawled on the floor, a crimson stain barely visible on the front of his shirt, it looked bad. Real bad. Vigilante committees weren't known for their honesty. A hanged man was better than a released man. It looked more like they were doing their jobs when they slipped a rope around a neck instead of waving good-bye as the offender rode out of town.

"We're going to have to talk with you, mister," the man standing in the forefront said. "Drop the gun on the table, nice and slow."

Carrigan did as he was instructed, then lowered himself into the chair and hoped to God he wasn't a dead man yet.

Helena left Emilie's room, quietly closing the door. Thomas had come through his ordeal, and it appeared as if he would make a full recovery. Emilie had sat with him all night, making sure he was comfortable. Since that late hour of reflection when the two sisters had shared cups of coffee in the kitchen, they'd been more in tune with one another. A hand on a shoulder, or a kiss on the cheek. Helena hadn't realized how much she'd distanced herself from Emilie. From everyone. But she was beyond that now. Life moved on, her with it. There would be no more tears, no more looking back with sadness. The future was what loomed ahead. But without Jake, what happiness would there be for her?

Helena descended the stairs, the sharp smells of coffee and bacon coming from the kitchen as Ignacia prepared breakfast. Not altogether hungry, Helena had had enough coffee to keep her up all day. But a little food would help settle the nerves in her stomach. There was someone she had to see, and now was as good a time as any. She wanted to clear something off her conscience. A confrontation was the only way. No matter that the sun hadn't been in the sky for very long. She knew that Bayard Kimball went to his office very early in the morning.

Sitting at the table, Helena ate what she could. After washing a biscuit down with milk, she stood from her chair.

"Ignacia, I'm going to the judge's office. If there's any change in Thomas, or if Emilie needs me, please send Eliazer."

"Yes, Miss Lena." Ignacia was fixing a tray for Thomas in case he wanted to eat when he woke. "I don't think Mr. McAllister will take a turn, though. Your sister is a good doctor. Much like yourself."

"Let's hope we won't have to doctor anyone else for a long time."

Ignacia nodded with a heartening smile.

Helena took her leave with a glance at the clock on the sitting room mantel. She had one hour before the store needed to be open. But if things went bad at Bayard's and she was too upset, she wasn't going to open today. Emilie needn't be pressed into working behind the counter, and Ignacia had enough to do without the extra work. Today things could just fall apart. Helena didn't care.

As she stepped out of the store, she thought it ironic that almost two months ago, she would have done anything and everything to keep the store and station operating. No matter the price. But now she'd learned that nothing was as important as the people she loved. Emilie . . . she should have always come first for Helena, but she hadn't. Helena intended to make that up to her sister. Ignacia and Eliazer . . . they were due for some quiet days of rest in which they could do whatever they chose. Jake . . . he was the most deserving of all. And that was a second chance. Even if he wanted to leave, he had to realize that she truly loved him with all her heart, and that she'd be forever grateful for everything he'd done for her.

Why hadn't he come back?

The lament was a constant fixture in her mind. He should have been in Genoa by now. That he wasn't only increased her fears that something had happened to him. Something . . . No, she didn't want to think it because she had no means to do anything right now to bring him back. She had to rely on her faith, and pray he would be all right. That he was taking his time, that he was being cautious, that he would return to her and she could have one last chance to tell him . . . to finally speak the words she'd been hiding in her heart.

"Mrs. Carrigan."

Helena looked up to find Mr. Van Sickle coming down the boardwalk.

"Glad I caught you," he said. "Word came into my station that as of today, the Express is shut down."

"All of it?"

"Everything. From Sacramento to St. Joe. It's been suspended."

Helena wished she had her shawl. She suddenly needed the warmth. If the Express was closed, that meant that the dangers were far greater than anyone had anticipated. That meant that Jake was out there unprotected. . . .

Van Sickle scratched the underside of his chin. "One of the owners, Alexander Majors, was the one to stop it. Said until adequate military protection could be offered his riders and the stations, it's the end of a legend in the making."

Her father's dream of seeing the West connected to the East via a trail where letters were exchanged was dying, and all Helena could think about was how she could save Jake—not the dream. Had she come to love him so much that nothing else mattered but his well-being, whether he was with her or not? Was this what it was like to love someone unconditionally?

"Heard there was some trouble with one of the riders." Mr. Van Sickle's voice broke into her thoughts. "McAllister, wasn't it? He's a nice kid. Will he be all right?"

"Yes, my sister is staying with him, and I think he's going to be fine."

"Mind if I go check on him?"

"Not at all. Ignacia's there to let you in."

Van Sickle tipped his hat and strode by.

Helena proceeded, crossing the street and walking toward the courthouse. Fear got the best of her. It gripped her, took hold, and shook. She couldn't help shivering, not wanting to imagine the worst had happened to Jake . . . but sensing that it had. Otherwise, he would have come back. Even angry at her, he would have wanted to see how Thomas was doing. And see Traveler . . . and Obsi.

When she reached the outside steps, she was on the verge of tears. Blinking them back, she held the railing and went up. Her heart was thundering in her ribs as she finalized in her mind the lecture she would give Bayard. First, she would demand to know why he told Jake about the deed. She didn't like being hostile to anyone. But enough was enough. There was no call for Bayard to speak to Jake in the manner in which he had about the land. That was business between herself and Bayard as an officer of the court. It had been easily misconstrued by her husband as her wanting him out of her life. Well, Bayard wasn't stupid. He must have known how it would appear, and had taken great pleasure in making Jake look like a fool. She wasn't going to accept Bayard's conduct. Calling him on it, and splitting any ties between them, was the only way.

Knocking on the door, she waited for footfalls to reach her. At length, they came. When Bayard swung the door open, it was apparent he hadn't been too involved with his work. His tailored black suit was minus its tie, his vest hung open, and he wasn't wearing his coat.

"Mrs. Carrigan, what a pleasure." He stood back. "Please come in."

She did so.

"Excuse my appearance. I was reading some files. I don't normally receive callers at this hour, but for you, I can always make an exception."

She followed him toward his desk and took a seat opposite him. There was the usual stack of papers and folios on the top, as well as opened letters and writing implements. Once he was facing her, he rolled himself forward in his chair. Putting his hand on the pile of papers at his left—the Kinsey recorder's book that chronicled Genoa's transactions on top—he dumped the stack into the open drawer below. With a shove, he closed it. There must have been a key dangling from the lock, because he withdrew one and let it fall into his vest pocket.

"What can I do for you?"

Her pulse was like the tattoo of a telegraph, but there was no help for the rage she was feeling. It would do no good to come right out and lash at him in a biting tone, but that was precisely what was on the tip of her tongue.

Since she could be very good at disguising her feelings, she forced herself to remain composed, folding her hands on her lap and giving him a smile she didn't feel like giving. "I was wondering if you've had the opportunity to legalize the transfer of my parcel into my husband's name."

"Yes, of course."

"Then I'll have him come by and sign the register." She waited for Bayard to say something to the contrary. When he didn't, she wanted to scream. He was sitting here with every opportunity to explain himself to her, and he wasn't.

"I'll make sure—" A knock on the door interrupted

his sentence. "Pardon me." Rising, he went to the door and answered it.

Helena turned in her chair to see who was there. It was Mr. Lewis.

"Excuse me," he said, glancing between the two of them. "But we needed the permit application for the buildings."

Helena gazed at her lap, then at Mr. Lewis. He was looking at her as if he thought she shouldn't be here. She couldn't hear the rest of their words, but soon Bayard was closing the door and walking back to her.

"Excuse me, but I need to speak with Mr. Lewis downstairs." Bayard buttoned his vest, retrieved the coat from the back of his chair, and picked up several blank forms from his desk. "I won't be gone but a minute. Please stay so we can continue our talk."

Nodding, Helena watched as Bayard let himself out the door. As soon as it was closed, she sat for a long moment, indecision skittering through her. Her mind made up, she rose from her chair and went around to the front of Bayard's desk. She scanned the contents of the desktop. Documents of the territory, depositions, fine bills, letters that looked unimportant. Nothing of interest caught her attention.

Her gaze fell to the drawer Bayard had put the Kinsey book in. She wanted to see Jake's signature herself, but knew that drawer was locked. What was in there that had to be put under lock and key in her presence? Didn't Bayard trust her? She had to laugh. Of course not. Bayard didn't trust anyone.

Helena resolved she would never see that register as she turned to resume her seat. But when she did, the new angle afforded her a different view of the drawer. It wasn't pushed in straight. Holding her breath, she put her hand on the handle and pulled. It opened! The lock hadn't caught.

She quickly lifted the book and flipped to the page with recent recordings. There was Jake's signature, and everything appeared legally entered. Helena had hoped that Bayard had somehow misrepresented himself. But it all seemed to be in order.

When Helena put the book back, the papers beneath it shifted. She caught the edge of a daguerreotype. Her fingers fell to the corner, and she slipped it away from the documents obstructing her view. As she brought the photo toward her, her hand began to tremble.

The picture was a sliver of a whole. There had once been four members of a family on it, but now there was just one.

Her.

"My God . . ." Helena whispered, staring at the reflection of herself that last day in New Providence. Bayard had the photo that had been in the cash box.

The door slammed shut, startling Helena from her shock. She raised her gaze, only to see Bayard bearing down on her with an anger in his eyes that made her blood run cold.

Chapter

⇒ 19 ⇐

"What are you doing?" Bayard demanded.

Helena wouldn't give him an answer. He wasn't owed one. Not when he was in possession of something that he should have given her long ago. He'd known about the photograph. She'd told him it had been in the cash box. That the picture had ended up in his drawer without his knowledge was highly unlikely. That he hadn't come to her with the evidence made him very suspect. Only someone who was guilty of something would have kept this from her.

When she found her voice, the words rushed past her lips. "How did you get this?"

Bayard stepped around the desk and attempted to pull the picture from her fingers. Jerking her arm back, she wouldn't let him have it.

"Helena, don't play games with me."

"You've been the one playing them with me." She retreated from his reach and stood a good distance away from the desk. "I want to know why you have my picture. Where is the other part of it?"

Bayard's expression went flat. "I don't have the other part."

"Why do you have any of it at all?"

"I came upon the daguerreotype by accident and saw no reason to tell you." Bayard sat down, seemingly no longer affected by her discovery. That he could be so blunt with his answer galled her. He knew how much the picture meant to her and Emilie. It was the last likeness taken of her parents. There was no photographer in Genoa, so a more recent photo had never been taken. "Where is the other part?" she repeated firmly.

"I told you, I don't have it."

"How did you get this by accident?" Her tone was dark, an edge of hostility to it that she couldn't suppress. He was toying with her, not fully giving her what she asked. She would not be appeased by little crumbs and excuses. The whole answer was all she would accept. "How? You know who killed my father. Was it you?"

Bayard inhaled, knit his fingers together, and stared toward the window where sunlight streamed through the portieres that were pulled back by silken cords. "I did not kill him, and that is the truth."

"Would you swear it under oath?" she shot back.

"I would swear it to you."

To Helena, that now meant nothing. "If you didn't kill my father, who did?"

"I don't know."

"You're lying."

"I'm not." A vein at his temple visibly pulsed with the ire he had suddenly checked. "If I had known who murdered August, I would have apprehended him and sentenced him to death. But I don't know." He put the Kinsey book away and closed the drawer, this time without attempting to lock it. "I found the photograph in the alley behind Main Street. It was in a pile of rubbish, along with the cash box minus the money.

The picture was damaged, and only your side was salvageable. I didn't tell you because I didn't want to upset you. You were grieving for August, and I felt that your seeing the ruined picture would serve no purpose other than causing you further duress."

Helena gazed at the film paper in her hand. If the daguerreotype had been blemished, why wasn't all of it ruined? This section looked fine. There were no dirt smudges, no residues of garbage, and no scratches on the surface. It looked as if someone had taken the original and neatly cut a third of it cleanly away from the rest.

Her mind worked to put the pieces together. It wasn't adding up. Something was wrong. There was a lie. A collection of lie upon lie, until nothing was distinguishable. There was nothing she could pinpoint. She had to talk to Jake. To tell him what she feared. That Bayard was somehow involved with her father's death. That perhaps he had not pulled the trigger, but had initiated the killing. That was Jake's theory . . . that whoever was responsible for letting her horses out was working for someone. A higher power. A man of influence. Bayard fit the mold without a doubt. He'd gotten the photograph from the killer. A sick memento to be kept in his drawer under lock and key.

She was in a sea of confusion, one word repeating itself in her brain: Why? Why had Bayard felt it necessary to have such a brutal crime committed? Why had he wanted to hurt her? Why did he want her picture?

"I have to go," she murmured, suddenly quite afraid and wanting to be away from Bayard. She wanted to be safe at the station with Emilie. And be with Jake. He'd have to be there by now. She wanted to be in the haven of his arms so badly, she could cry.

"No," came Bayard's denial.

Helena began walking, not listening. "I have to go."

"You will not!" Bayard was out of the chair and painfully gripped her arm before she'd taken three steps. "Helena, don't leave me. Please, I have to talk to you."

"I don't want to. . ." she moaned as his fingers constricted around her sensitive muscles.

"You have to. And you will." Bayard's eyes were angry orbs of gray. "You need to hear how I feel about you. Once you understand, you'll know that you can't possibly stay married to Carrigan. It was a mistake, and I forgive you for it."

"Forgive me?" she whispered. "I have done nothing for you to forgive. How dare you say such a thing?"

"Because I love you," he declared, but the fierceness of his confession had no influence on her. She didn't care how he felt. She wanted to get away from him. "I have from the minute I first saw you. You should have been my wife, and you would have been if you hadn't run to Carrigan." Bayard's brows were black slashes of fury. "You were supposed to run to me! To me!"

Helena couldn't swallow. She couldn't move. Amid all the confusion, there came a dawning so powerful, she knew that it was the one absolute truth. "You had my father killed so I would be alone and turn to you for help . . . just like I had on other occasions."

"I didn't have him killed!" He shook her just a little. "Stop saying that I did."

She didn't believe him. His denial was too vehement, his secrecy about the photograph not credible. Given a change in their positions, she would have gone to him with the ruined daguerreotype and handed it to him in whatever condition she'd found it in, knowing how much it would have meant to him. But Bayard hadn't seen things like that because he was hiding something.

A darkness threatened to engulf Helena. She had never fainted in her life, but the overwhelming need to surrender to oblivion so she could escape the man who held her pulled strong. The need to be free, in whatever way possible, had a hold on her just as surely as Bayard did.

"If you love me, let me go," she asked once more, her words even and from the heart. If she could appeal to his distorted infatuation for her, maybe he would release her.

"I cannot." He shook his head. "Not now . . . not ever. I love you too much."

A despair welled in her so great, she knew instantly how her mother had felt when she'd sunk into the endless blades of prairie grass. Hopeless . . . and alone.

Just after nine o'clock, Carrigan reined his lathered horse in to the stockade and jumped down from Boomerang as Obsi's bark signaled his arrival. The dog ran toward him, tail vigorously wagging while he jumped to Carrigan's thigh for a pat on the head. The smells of breakfast were left over in the yard as he walked into the stable, hoping to find Helena and tell her to stay clear of Kimball until he could have charges of conspiracy for murder brought against the judge. Carrigan knew now that Bayard had been trying to drive a wedge between them from the start. He'd almost succeeded. Carrigan had doubted himself and the strength of his relationship with Helena. But no more.

Carrigan hadn't been able to avenge Jenny and had to reconcile himself to the fact that he would never find the men responsible for her pain. That part of his past was like dust blowing in the desert. Shifted and gone. But he could help Helena. Despite how things stood between them, he was going to do everything in his power to keep her safe from Bayard Kimball's clutches. He'd make sure the judge paid for his criminal actions. Kimball was nothing short of a murderer himself for having given the order to kill

August Gray. Carrigan intended on making everyone in Genoa see that they'd been duped by a fancy suit of clothes. Given his horrendous night, Carrigan had almost lost that chance altogether.

He'd had one hell of a time explaining the circumstances of Hanrahan's death to the vigilante committee. Despite the bartender, Remie, and the card-players backing his story that Hanrahan had been itching for a fight, he'd still had to convince the committee that he'd acted in self-defense. That if he hadn't fired first, it would have been Seaton they were talking to instead of him. An hour after sunup, the six men had finally relented and said that they'd never liked Hanrahan anyway. That he'd been on the verge of being run out of town because of his card-playing practices. Everyone knew he was a cheat, but thus far, no one had been able to catch him at it.

The undertaker had intruded on Carrigan's interrogation, which had taken place in one of the members' parlors, and informed the group that when he'd examined Seaton's body, he'd found several unaccountable cards on his person. Hearing that, the committee huddled together, and when they broke up, told Carrigan he could ride out of Carson, but stay clear of it in the future. The news of Seaton's double-dealing had cinched Carrigan's freedom, and he'd ridden like the wind to get back to Genoa. And Helena.

The nickers of horses sounded on Carrigan's entrance into the stables. He found Eliazer and immediately addressed him.

"Where's Helena?"

Eliazer turned from the work bench. "She's not in here." The stock tender's face brightened. "But she will be glad to see you have safely returned. She didn't sleep all night worrying over you and Thomas."

"How is Thomas?"

"Better," Eliazer said. "He'll recover."

"Good to hear that. I have to see Helena right away.

Do you think you could cool my horse?" Carrigan asked as he headed toward the doors.

"I'll take care of him."

"Thanks."

Carrigan ran across the yard and vaulted for the back steps, Obsi on his heels. He swung the door open and entered the kitchen, startling Ignacia, who was at the dry sink washing the dishes.

Rather than greet her, he blurted, "Where's Helena?"

Ignacia put a thin hand to her meager bosom. "Why, she's not here. Mr. Carrigan, my prayers have been answered. I asked God for your safe return."

Though he appreciated the woman's concern, he couldn't stay and reassure her he was all right. "Where is she?"

"She went to Judge Kimball's office."

"Jesus," he swore. "How long ago?"

"About a half hour. Why? Is something wrong?"

Yelling at Obsi to stay, Carrigan was halfway down the hall.

Carrigan ran into J. H. Lewis on the courthouse steps. His ear was pressed to the door's window. When he saw Carrigan, he straightened with a jump. Carrigan practically yanked him by the collar, leading him quietly away from the door.

"What are you doing?"

The eyes behind the man's glasses were wide. "I . . ."

"Is my wife in there?"

"Yes." Lewis swallowed. "With the judge."

"Why are you listening?"

"Because I was worried about her."

"You weren't before," Carrigan hissed.

"That was then. Now we've come to realize that Mrs. Carrigan isn't such a bad woman."

Carrigan frowned.

"You see . . . the judge made us think that she'd be bad for Genoa; that's why me and Wyatt denied her the service. But now . . . well, I don't trust the judge," Lewis whispered as if Kimball was going to come out at any second. "I was at the door earlier, and he and Mrs. Carrigan were having a talk. . . . Judge Kimball . . . I don't know . . . there was something in his tone when he came downstairs with the forms for the building permits. He's doing something wrong. . . . I can't say what."

Carrigan shoved the man aside. "He is doing something wrong. He had August Gray murdered."

Mr. Lewis's Adam's apple bobbed. "Dear God."

"Go get a group of men together and get them back here."

J. H. Lewis nodded and dashed down the steps, barely making a noise.

The faded window shade on the door to the courthouse was drawn, but Carrigan could hear voices inside. Bayard's and Helena's. The judge was doing most of the talking. Through the muffling pane of glass, Kimball's tone was distorted but appeared to be aggressive.

Without knocking, Carrigan let himself in. When he saw that Helena was captured in the judge's hold, his hand went reflexively to his gun as he strode heavily on his heels.

"Take your hands off my wife."

Bayard didn't move an inch. Undaunted, he remained exactly how he stood. With two hands on Helena's shoulders, with his face close to hers, yet turned in Carrigan's direction.

Carrigan automatically withdrew the revolver when his direction went unheeded. "I said to remove your hands from my wife, Kimball."

The judge glanced slowly at Helena, then at Carrigan, before stepping away from her. His expression was indolent, as if he had no concern for his welfare. As soon as Helena was free, she ran to Carrigan. He put his arm around her, her face pressing into the front of his shirt.

Her soft and terrified voice vibrated against his chest as she spoke into the fabric. "He has my picture, Jake. The one that was in our cash box. I'm sure he had my father killed."

The deadly threat of the Walker's steady barrel trained on Kimball never wavered as Carrigan replied, "He did."

Helena's face lifted to his. "How do you know?"

"Seaton Hanrahan told me."

Kimball snorted. "The man's a liar."

"The man is dead," Carrigan said in a level voice.

"Good riddance," was Bayard's only comment.

"So you don't have to pay him anymore to do your dirty work? He told me how you paid him to scare August in the holdup. But things got out of control when August tried to disarm Hanrahan, so Hanrahan fired."

Helena's tears intruded on Carrigan's words. He hated having her hear it this way. Sitting her down in the privacy of her room would have been better, but there was no help for the turn of events. He would have held her tighter and comforted her, but he had to watch Bayard for any sudden moves.

"I never told Seaton Hanrahan to do such a thing. Whatever he did, he took it upon himself," Bayard charged. "I can't help it if he was a petty thief."

"That's not all he was," Carrigan said. "He was your henchman in an effort to win Helena. Well, it didn't work. Not even when you sent Hanrahan to threaten Helena by touching her . . . kissing her," Carrigan ground out.

Kimball attempted to fold his arms across his chest, but Carrigan yelled, "Don't move! You move once more, and I'll shoot."

"You shoot me, Carrigan, and you'll not see the

sunset. You'd be strung up so fast, you wouldn't even feel the rope around your neck."

Carrigan shifted Helena to stand behind him. "I want you to leave, Lena."

Her eyes were rimmed with tears. "No . . . I can't leave you."

"Go."

Kimball's nostrils flared. "How touching, Helena. But you must leave."

She shook her head. Carrigan walked backwards, taking her to the door. Once there, he fingered the knob and twisted it. Without taking his eyes off Kimball, he said, "I told Lewis to get some men together. You explain what's happening when they come. Tell them they're going to be a vigilante group. It's time the citizens of Genoa took the law into their own hands."

Nodding, she sniffed. "But I don't want to leave you. . . ."

Disregarding her plea, he declared, "I won't shoot him. I don't want him dead. He's going to have to stand trial for what he's done to you and your family."

"But it's your word against his," she whispered. "He'll make everyone believe you're lying."

"No he won't." But Carrigan knew she had a valid point. It was his word against the judge's. Hanrahan was dead. The only witness who could prove Bayard's involvement. But the picture might be enough. And the coin. Carrigan had it in his pocket. Between the two, he would have to convince the townspeople that Kimball was behind everything. Were it not for Helena, he would have shot the man in cold blood and damned the consequences. But that she had been this man's friend at one time, that she had divulged pieces of his life to Kimball, made him important to her. Perhaps not anymore, but killing Kimball to satisfy his own taste of revenge wasn't the way to go.

"Leave, Lena. Now."

Helena gave him a soulful look, then slipped out the door. He heard her footsteps hurrying down the weathered risers, then nothing. Shutting the door, he squared off with Kimball.

"Well, now it's just you and me and my Colt."

"And this." With the speed of lightning, Bayard had dipped his hand into his trouser pocket and come out with a small but lethal derringer.

The explosion of a gun could be heard from Main. Helena hadn't even crossed the street when the sound erupted from Bayard's office. Mr. Lewis, Mr. Mayhew, Mr. Wyatt, and a group of six other businessmen had been running down the street. Their gazes locked on the second-story window.

"Jake is in there!" she screamed. "Please, you've got to help him. Bayard . . . he had Bayard at gunpoint and . . ."

Mr. Lewis was bounding up the stairs, Helena close on his heels. When he reached the top, he crashed the door inward, and Helena practically slammed against his back. Jake was standing over Bayard, who was holding on to his arm while moaning and cursing his pain. Blood dripped from the wound in his upper arm, his fingers growing red from where he held his injury. A small gun glinted in the sun where it had been kicked toward the window.

"Lewis!" he wailed. "The bastard shot me! Get his gun!"

But J. H. Lewis didn't move. Neither did any of the other men.

"We're putting you under a citizen's arrest," Wyatt declared. "I don't take kindly to having my mind made up for me without me knowing it's being made up."

"What are you talking about?" Bayard asked.

"You making me think that doing business with

Mrs. Carrigan wouldn't be a good thing for Genoa. You were wrong."

Helena felt the blood drain from her face. All the anger, frustration, and fear took hold of her until she wanted to scream at Bayard and tell him what an indecent human being he was. That he had fooled her, used her, manipulated her. Taken them all in, and done a lot of damage to a lot of people in the process.

But no more. He was going to be stopped. Because there were enough people to testify against him. From now on, he couldn't hurt anyone, anymore.

Bayard rolled to his side. "You don't know what you're talking about. Helena, don't listen to him."

Jake still kept his gun on Bayard. "I didn't want to shoot him, Lena. I gave you my word. But he came out with that derringer, and I had no choice. I hit him in the arm to get the gun away from him."

She felt sick and numb and cold. Nothing seemed real. It was all a horrible nightmare. She didn't blame Jake. She would have done the same thing. In fact, she probably would have killed Bayard dead.

Mr. Mayhew went toward the judge with Mr. Wyatt. "Some of you go unlock the cell downstairs and we'll put him in it."

"If the lines are up, a message should be sent to Salt Lake City so we can notify the authorities what's happened," Helena said.

"Helena, you don't know what you're doing!" Bayard coughed. "It's all a fabrication. Everything. You know me."

"I don't know you." Her voice lowered sadly. "I never did."

After Judge Kimball had been removed by the delegation of business owners who had rallied together, Carrigan led Helena away. He'd taken her hand and they'd walked across the street to the store, which had yet to be opened for the day.

"Don't open," Carrigan said as he let her pass by him through the doorway. "Not yet."

She nodded.

Closing the door and locking it, Carrigan followed Helena to the counter, where she leaned against it with her palms pressed on the surface. "I can't believe that Bayard had this . . . and never told me." Helena was looking at the photograph. "I hate him. Hate him for destroying what was left of my family. For taking my father, and even taking my mother by cutting the picture and probably destroying the other half. I know he did it. He was lying. Just like he lied about everything." She lifted her gaze and looked at him. "How did you find Seaton?"

"In a saloon, quite by accident."

"You killed him. . . ."

"It was him or me."

Carrigan shoved his hand into his pocket and came out with the half dime. "Hanrahan had this."

Helena took the coin and examined the initials. "Thank you."

Leaning into the counter with his back, Carrigan put his elbows on the worn planks. A pause lengthened the silence stretching through the cramped room. Outside, the noises of civilization bore down on the quiet air, but Carrigan failed to be bothered by it. Perhaps he was coming to accept that having Helena could mean he'd have to make an adjustment. The big question was, did she still want him?

"I'm sorry. For everything." Swallowing the ache in his throat, Carrigan said, "When you told me you loved me, did you mean it? Do you still?"

"Yes," she whispered. "I couldn't stop loving you even if I wanted to."

"I should have told you then how I was feeling, but you guessed. I was scared. And I was running. Using what you and Kimball talked about was just an excuse. He could have found out by writing to the area sheriffs. He must have gotten lucky when he inquired to Libertyville. That's all I can think of. But however he found out isn't important. I know you didn't betray me. You'd never do that."

"No . . . I wouldn't."

Carrigan pressed the heel of his boot against the underframe of the counter. "I haven't been honest with you because I haven't wanted to be honest with myself."

Their eyes held. No more pretending he didn't care when he did. He couldn't stop himself from pulling her into his embrace and holding her tight. Helena's arms circled his neck, and her cheek met his chest. The sweet rose smell of her hair filled his lungs, the soft feel of her body made him think that a life without her wouldn't be a life at all. Christ all Jesus, he'd stay here, if that's what she wanted. He'd be with her.

"Lena . . ."

She broke away to stare into his face. When he told her, he wanted to see her eyes. To be able to read into her soul and see if what he was feeling was mirrored there.

"Lena . . . I never thought I would want to be with a woman after Jenny. Never thought that I'd be worth a damn to anyone. So I hid. Up there on that mountain. Feeling useless . . . and alone. But with you, I found my heart again. I remembered what it was like to want to please another person . . . to be with them night and day . . . talk with them . . . smile at them . . . kiss them." Moisture shimmered in her eyes as he lowered his mouth to her fluttering lashes and kissed away the tears. "I love you, Lena."

Trembling, her hands fitted behind his head, and she brought his mouth to hers. The kiss was long and deep, lingering and searching. She felt his heartbeat, for his was racing with hers. Her lips were a joy to him, a new beginning. A start that would make him look beyond the horizon to a new day.

Breathing next to his mouth, she said, "I love you,

too, Jake." She pulled back, and the reflection in her eyes was one of sorrow. "But I can't ask you to stay here. You wouldn't be happy."

"I could be happy with you no matter where we are."

"What about the land?"

"I don't care."

"Yes, you do."

Carrigan splayed his fingers over her slender back. "I wouldn't want to live there without you. So it's out of the question."

"There could be a solution. . . ."

He waited.

"The Express has shut down until adequate military help can manage the Indian attacks. With Thomas here, and unable to ride, he could be with Emilie, and you and I—"

"Does that mean you'll let Emilie have him?"

Helena softly smiled. "How could I not? She loves him so." She sighed. "With only the store to manage, I wouldn't be needed. And when the Express starts up again . . . well, then . . . we could round up mustangs together."

"But you wouldn't make any money."

"I don't care. We'd manage. . . ."

"I do care. I'll support my wife, and her family." He brushed his lips against hers. "Your idea is no good. We'll have to use mine."

"What is it?"

"I'll tell you later. Right now I have a better idea." His mouth took possession of hers, and he kissed away any fears. For them, what was to come would be the best part of both of their lives. Because they would be together.

Now and always.

→ Epilogue ←

October 1860

It was a double wedding, with both sisters wearing gowns of white silk. Helena's fabric was shipped in from California and made with definite modifications from her normal patterns. Emilie wore the wedding dress their mother had worn. The younger sister held a bouquet of colorful prairie flowers, while the older sister clutched a bundle of dried woolly violets that she'd preserved in June. The crisp mountain air carried the new judge's voice with perfect clarity as the couples stood before him at the site of the nearly complete house that was to be Helena and Jake's new residence.

Judge Ulysses Douglas had been in office going on two months now. He was a plain man, not taken to flashing his position of power by the mode of his clothing. To him, his success was his wife and their seven children, ages two to sixteen. His personality was friendly and open. His record was clear. The town had checked into his background before wiring their approval to Salt Lake City. He'd run a clean court, was fair, and exceedingly honest with his verdicts.

"I now pronounce you husband and wife," Judge Douglas proclaimed to Emilie and Thomas. Then to Helena and Jake with a broad smile, "I now pronounce you husband and wife. Again."

The small crowd of well-wishers laughed. Helena and Jake had decided to retie the knot, as their first wedding had been nothing more than a filing of papers. This new ceremony brought with it everything a marriage should. Honor, hope, and love.

Helena lifted herself on tiptoes and kissed Jake softly on the mouth. While Thomas took her sister into his arms and gave her a thorough kissing that had several in attendance whooping with cheers. Congratulatory claps followed as Helena and Emilie greeted those who stood around them.

It was a lovely October day. The kind that had leaves falling in golden hues and swirling around the pristine hems of their gowns. Helena had never thought there would come a time when she would see herself so utterly contented that she wanted to laugh and cry at the same time.

She looked up and saw Jake talking to Captain Garrett and several other men from the company. Beyond the group was a paddock of mustangs. Two of the mares would foal in the spring. With the army in constant need of horses, she and Jake would make a decent living. His idea had been the better one, and the most practical for all parties involved. She'd known what a sacrifice it had been for him to make the arrangement with Captain Garrett. She was proud of him for it and told him so.

Gazing at Thomas, she smiled. He'd healed, but hadn't returned to riding when the Express started up again in late June. He'd stayed on at the station, running it now with the seasoned eye of a veteran who knew the terrain and had the utmost respect for those men who risked their lives on a daily basis. Helena and Jake had given Thomas six new mustangs as a wedding gift. Helena loved her brother-in-law as if he were the brother she'd never had. He was a good, competent man, and Emilie had done well for herself.

Things had turned, much like the leaves as the seasons had progressed. Life was treating them well, and as for the past, it was not often in Helena's mind. There was that one moment when Bayard had stolen into her thoughts when she'd found out what happened to him, but that had been months ago. He hadn't stood up against the charges brought on him. The military had issued an escort for him to the capital of the Utah Territory, but en route, the coach and its conveyance had been ambushed by Paiutes. Bayard had been killed along with three other men. Helena had felt a fleeting remorse. She hadn't wanted him dead . . . she'd wanted him to have to address his crimes and pay for them.

But she couldn't look back. . . . There was no more of that. Time went forward. So did she. There were so many things to rejoice over. Her husband, just for starters.

Jake drew up to her side. "Let's say we slip away."

"From our guests?"

"Sure. The kitchen to our house is almost finished." Her gaze fell on the log cabin behind Jake. "I wanted to show you the view."

Her brows arched as he took her hand in his. "I've seen the view. It looks out at the valley, just like I told you I wanted it to."

"But today it looks better."

"I think you're just trying to get me away from everyone."

"I think you're right."

He led her up the split-log steps that climbed to a covered porch spanning the length of the cabin's front. There was a swing suspended by thick rope, a single potted plant next to it with a ruby-colored geranium, and a horseshoe nailed above the front door for luck. Obsi lay on the planks, his head on his paws. He'd run himself down some hours earlier when all the guests had arrived with baskets of food to stock the larder of the new house.

Once at the door, Jake wouldn't let her pass.

"What are you doing?" she asked.

"You can't walk through there."

"Why not?"

"Because I'm going to carry you."

"Oh, really," she scoffed. "That's silly. I can—"

He scooped her into his arms, and Obsi threw his head back and grinned while she giggled.

Jake made a huffing noise from his throat. "You're getting heavy. But not too heavy for me."

The secret within made her smile with love and tenderness. The impossible had happened, and she still couldn't believe that fortune knew there was a place for them. "Because there are two of us."

"I know that." He dropped a kiss on her cheek. "Come February, you think it'll be a boy or girl I get to hold?"

"I told you, I don't know."

"My mother said in her letter, it sounds like a boy."

Helena smiled. "Well, when she and your sister, Sarah, arrive next week, I'll let them both figure it all out."

Giving her a gentle squeeze, Jake whispered, "I love you, you know."

"I love you, too."

Then he bumped the door open with his foot and made the traditional crossing over the threshold with his bride.

Author's Notes

There's something to be said about being known as a writer who tends to write humor. It's hard to be serious! But with *Crossings,* the group of misfit western characters that usually come to my fingertips at the keyboard all went into hiding. Carrigan and Helena, and the people of Genoa, were not my normal, colorful mixture of characters. I hope that you, the readers and booksellers, will feel comfortable with the change of tone and style and enjoy this story as much as you have my prior books.

As usual, I haven't done this alone. I want to thank Dorine Taggart, a fellow mom and neighbor here in this rural area we live in. As a transplant from the city, I just assumed that when mares foaled, you had high drama. You had to be in the barn with the lantern burning bright and biting your nails awaiting the big event as if the mare weren't capable of this feat on her own. Dorine set this citified girl straight—quick. She's offered to let me learn about horses via her minis. A good choice for this chicken, as I'm scared to death of anything with hooves and bigger than me.

I have to say that I could not have written this story as it is without the help of a very dear friend, Barbara Ankrum. Her insight with conflict and plotting was pivotal to me, without which *Crossings* would have taken a completely different turn—for the worse.

My sister, Michele, and her husband, Joe, were helpful in filling in the holes about Genoa and its history. Thank you so much for extending your hospitality to our family this past summer.

And lastly, a moment of praise for the best editor in the business. Without Caroline Tolley, none of you would be able to read my books in the quality she demands of me—nothing less than I am capable of. Her willingness to listen to my stories before they are developed, and give me constructive advice, is what makes writing worth it for me.

Thank you to the booksellers who continue to voice their generous opinions of my books. Without you, none of us would be here.

For those readers who are wondering about what's up and coming . . . it's back to the funny side once again, with a dash of intrigue, a look at the West around the turn of the century, and a repertoire of the most whimsical characters I've done yet. Coming soon from Pocket Star Books is *Portraits*. I hope you'll watch for it.

As always, I enjoy hearing from readers. Drop me a note and let me know what you thought of *Crossings*. A self-addressed stamped envelope is helpful and speeds up my reply.

Happy trails,

Stef Ann Holm
P.O. Box 121
Meridian, ID 83680-0121

POCKET STAR BOOKS
PROUDLY PRESENTS

PORTRAITS

STEF ANN HOLM

Coming soon
in paperback from
Pocket Star Books

The following is a preview of
Portraits. . . .

Eternity, Colorado

Wyatt Holloway stood on a rubble pile in the shadow of the towering cross, some hundred feet down from its base, not feeling the least bit spiritual. Instead, he was giving the mountainside some of his best blasphemous words.

Encountering the landslide was a hell of a note to end the trip on, but what had he expected? That things would have been as he'd left them seventeen years ago? That he'd retrieve $60,000 in twenty-dollar gold pieces, with five- and ten-dollar coins and a balance in currency? Buy a ranch, settle down and get married so he could have some kids? Nothing in life fell into place that easily. He should have learned that by now.

Lowering himself to a crouch, Wyatt ran the palm of his hand over the loose stone. There were smaller rocks and big chunks of light yellowish-pink sandstone. It would have to be sandstone. As if he hadn't had enough of it.

Wyatt shaded his eyes and looked up, gauging the

distance to the cross, hoping that he'd miscalculated. No. He was in the right spot. But the crevice and its markings were gone. Years and years of nature had taken their toll. Heavy snows had probably done the most damage. The spring thaws hadn't helped any, either. From the looks of the terrain, the landslide wasn't recent.

Standing, Wyatt removed his hat and rubbed the sweat off his brow with the back of his duster sleeve. At least the cross was still here. Without it, finding the gold would be like searching for a calf lost on a thousand acres of mesquite—if indeed the money was still here. Could be that some lucky miner unearthed the bags years ago. Then where would he be? He didn't want to accept the possibility that the gold wasn't here. Because without it, his fresh start was no start.

Wyatt was thoughtful, considering his next move. Buying his horse, the saddle, gear and tack had set him back. All he had to his name was twenty-two dollars and eighty-seven cents. He'd been planning on using the gold to buy himself a fine woman and a few nights of unbridled pleasure. To really live it up for a couple of weeks, then claim some prime acreage and settle down. Now he couldn't even spare a quarter for a kiss. He'd have to purchase tools—a pick, ax, shovel, chisel and hammer, to name a few. Tools that fit his hands like second nature.

Wyatt took in his surroundings, thinking that if he had to stay put for a while, this wasn't too bad a place, considering where he'd been. The air was soft and warm and drowsy. Perennial streams, as pure as crystal, came dancing down from the high peaks. The foothills were thick with cottonwood, piñon, juniper and aspens. And from his position on the mountain, he could see all four boundaries of the town.

Eternity.

Well, it hadn't stayed eternally the same. Back in '87, it had been nothing but a tent city with not more than four hundred miners and nary a woman in sight. From his vantage point, Wyatt could see four streets running north and south, and seven running east and west. False-fronts, what looked to be native stone, and wooden structures made up the town now. The streets were wide enough for two-way traffic. But at least there wasn't a single one of those skunk-smelling automobiles scaring the hell out of the horses and leaving a trail of smoke to choke a person. The roads being as narrow and twisting as they were, four tires and four thousand pounds of working mechanical strength couldn't beat four legs and a thousand pounds of horseflesh to access this place, which suited Wyatt fine. Though Ford's Boss of the Road and the Model B Cadillacs weren't present, the electrical wires were. Wyatt had seen them so thick in Boise City that there was hardly a visible piece of sky left.

Eternity was a regular civilized place, yet still looked like one of the sleepy little Western towns he was used to from the old days—except for the wires. The absence of present-day vices could most likely be attributed to the fact that the city was in a deep valley, fifty miles from anyplace, and surrounded by ranges—notably the San Juan.

Glancing up, Wyatt estimated the time. Several hours past noon. The sky was like a blue bowl of soup: clear, with cloud dumplings casting slow-moving shadows over him. When the clouds hit, he was given a few minutes' respite from the shimmering August sun, but when they moved on, he was reminded of how hot it was.

He could use a cool drink. One of those Coca-Colas would have been just the ticket. That was just about the only thing of importance that the new century had to offer him. All the rest was nothing but trappings and useless gadgets.

Wyatt went to his horse, a well-put-together black that had a lot of bottom to him. He'd been lucky to pick the gelding up for twelve dollars. After untying the lead rope, Wyatt mounted and nudged July down the winding trail of the mountain. As he entered the town, he passed a fancy house with music drifting through the diaphanous curtains flitting through the open sashes. A man was singing with an orchestra, but Wyatt couldn't understand a word. The singer wasn't from around these parts. He sounded like a foreigner. There must have been some kind of important concert going on, though there didn't seem to be an audience. The curb was empty of buggies. The white-and-blue stone residence itself was decorated with gables, dormer windows and scalloped trim that made it look like a gingerbread house. The placard planted in the grass read "Leah Kirkland, Photography Gallery."

Wyatt had never heard of a female photographer before. He shied away from cameras and the people behind them.

As he approached the center of the town, an oddity caught his attention. Different-colored beer bottles were strung out on a tree like Christmas ornaments. Next to the tree was an office.

Usually Wyatt could spot a lawman about as far as he could see one. They had a way of conducting themselves in an official manner that was like a red flag. But in this instance, it was the sign nailed to the building front that tipped him off that the man in the shade was a lawman: United States Marshal Benard Scudder. That and the slice of sun—just enough to cut across the man's chest—flickering off the badge pinned to his fishing vest. He sat beneath the awning on an overturned apple crate drinking a High Hog beer—a cold one, from the looks of the water droplets sliding down the bottle and dribbling onto his pants leg.

A vague pang for a drink of liquor hit Wyatt, but it was gone before the old need came to fruition. He'd had his last taste on September 18, 1887. He'd gone too long without it to start up again. Liquor was nothing but trouble for him. It always had been.

Lifting his gaze to the marshal's face, Wyatt gave his craggy features a cursory look. Nothing stood out more than the handlebar mustache, which appeared to have been given a good grooming with a heavy coat of pomatum wax. The russet twist of facial hair was a whopper the biggest growth Wyatt had ever seen on an upper lip.

In Wyatt's experience, lawmen weren't always worth what they were paid. There were those who liked doing nothing at all. And those who liked to detain a person for doing nothing just so they could throw their weight around. From the bulge of Scudder's stomach, and the glint of purpose in his eyes, Wyatt sensed this man was a combination of both.

Wyatt was just about to avert his gaze—eye contact with the marshal would spell challenge—but he was too late. Scudder saw him and pursed his lips. Standing, he hitched his pants with his left hand, though his suspenders were doing most of the work. Scudder's stomach started at his celluloid collar and didn't end until his belt, where it flowed over his buckle like bread dough left to rise too long.

"You there!" he sternly called to Wyatt. "Get off of that horse and come on over here, boy!"

Wyatt hadn't been a boy in over two decades, and he resented the degrading remark. But he wasn't in a position to argue about it. He wanted to go about his business as soon as possible, and cooperation was his best chance. So he dismounted and led July to the sidewalk.

Stepping down the few steps of the porch, Marshal Scudder swaggered to the decorated tree and placed the High Hog bottle on one of the empty branches. He took two steps toward Wyatt, then stopped as if to say, "You'll come to me, not me come to you."

Wyatt moved in as far as he could without putting his horse on the walkway. Even standing in the street, he had the lawman by a good head and a half.

"What's your name, boy?" Scudder asked, his hand slipping onto his revolver butt to emphasize his authority.

Wyatt's answer wasn't short in coming. "Wyatt Holloway."

"Wyatt Holloway." Scudder tapped his temple with a pudgy finger as if to get things working. "Wyatt Holloway." The repetition of his name made Wyatt think the gears in the marshal's brain were spinning, arbitrarily trying to connect him with some unsolved criminal act and make the lawman look like a hero for apprehending the culprit right in front of the city jail. Well, it wasn't going to happen. Wyatt Holloway's record was so clean, it was invisible. "Doesn't sound familiar."

"It wouldn't."

"Where you from?"

Scudder was really pressing his appointed duty. There was no law saying Wyatt had to give up that information if he wasn't under arrest, so he figured a lie was in order. "Billings."

"What in the hell are you doing so far away from Montana?"

"Checking out possibilities further south."

The marshal gave him a stern going-over with a narrowed gaze. "Where'd you get that antique gun?"

Wyatt glanced at the '79 Remington-Rider .44-caliber double-action revolver at his hip. He didn't favor the newfangled automatic pistols. This was the gun he'd been trained to sharp-shoot with. He knew how it operated, and it compensated for its kick with perfect accuracy. "Picked it up in a secondhand shop."

Scudder cracked a snide smile. "Does it still work?"

"Last I fired it."

The corners of the lawman's mouth went grim. "You won't be needing to fire it in my town. Just how long do you think you'll be checking out prospects in Eternity?"

Wyatt couldn't say. No one needed to know his business, especially that he'd be mining. Someone might have already made a claim on that land, not knowing that Wyatt had a claim on what was buried beneath the rocks. And he couldn't exactly say he was passing through. If the digging was slow to bring results, he may be here for a couple of weeks. He'd have to come to town if he ran out of food, and he couldn't sneak around.

"I can't rightly say how long I'll be."

"Then you need for me to set you straight. If you stay, you got twenty-four hours to get yourself a job. You don't have one by"—Scudder checked the time on his pocket watch—"four-thirty-nine tomorrow, you'll be run out of my town, Mr. Holloway. I'll be considering you a vagrant at precisely four-forty." The marshal snapped the lid on his watch and shoved the timepiece into his tight pants. "Seeing as there's only one opening in town, I suggest you act on it. Quick. Before someone else snaps up the position."

Wyatt didn't have the opportunity to ask Marshal Scudder what it was. A woman holding a small envelope approached them. She was tall and slim, wearing one of those shirtwaists with a man's tie at the throat. He couldn't get used to a woman strapping on an article of man's attire. Her skirt was narrow, accentuating the slender shape of her thighs, yet she wore one of those bustles that gave a man a false image of a lady's derriere. The rest of the skirt fabric flowed to a wider hem at the bottom, where her lace-up shoes—which were laced up only halfway—peeked from beneath the cotton print. One of the laces was untied, though she apparently didn't care. She stepped on the black ribbon without putting a hitch in her purposeful stride.

"Excuse me, Marshal Scudder, but I have your documentation ready." She handed the lawman the flat envelope, then gazed in Wyatt's direction. "Pardon the interruption."

She had straight brunette hair that was messed up beneath her straw hat and its plum-colored ribbon. Wispy strands fell into her golden brown eyes. Her flyaway hair made her look like a woman who'd just been in bed . . . and not alone.

Wyatt checked himself before he thought further on that. It was broad daylight, and a lady like this wouldn't have been doing something like that. It was his need for a woman that had him thinking along those lines. But still . . . she did have that look about her. That radiance—like she was content about something. He made a quick search of her left hand. No wedding ring. Could be she had herself a lover. . . .

A dark smudge was at the hollow of her cheek, but he passed that by, gazing at her mouth, the lips full and pink. Her eyebrows arched with a slight pitch. He found that attractive in a woman. Especially when her complexion was pale and her brows darker.

"Benard!" a shrill female voice called from around the corner. Wyatt cringed. "Benard Scudder!"

The marshal turned to the woman with a grumble. "What is it, LaRaine?"

"Your fried chicken is going to be on the table in fifteen minutes. You'll be home then if you want to eat it while it's hot."

Scudder's face brightened. "Why, yes, sugar puss. I'm on my way just as soon as I give Moon his orders." Then he said to the lady, "Thank you for the fast work. I'll have Deputy Moon log it while he's on his night-shift duty."

The marshal turned toward the office, but Wyatt's inquiry slowed him down. "You didn't say what that job was."

Calling over his shoulder, Scudder said, "Dishwasher at the Happy City Chinese Restaurant. Like I said, you don't have lawful employment in twenty-four hours, I've got a cell with your name on it, boy." The marshal's parting comment was spoken through a snicker that Wyatt didn't appreciate.

The lady cleared her throat, startling Wyatt, and he turned toward her. "He's not kidding, you know." She stood pretty close—despite his being a stranger, she was not in the least bit giddy or afraid around him. "I'd suggest you do as he says, or he *will* lock you up. He's had a bad day. A drunk shot six bottles off this tree."

Wyatt lifted his brows. Her friendly advice invited

him to flirt with her. He hadn't flirted in a long time, and decided to test the waters. He used to be able to send the ladies into bashful giggles. "You've got a cute smudge on your cheek, darlin'."

"Oh, do I?"

But that was it. She made no coy attempt to wipe it off—nor did she ask him for a kerchief to do so.

Wyatt knew he'd changed physically, but he'd hoped he could still charm a woman. Maybe it was because he was big now. Not the same lanky kid he used to be. His body had hardened like the sandstone. Years of back-breaking labor had cut and chiseled his muscles into well-defined slabs of flesh. He'd had his nose broken, so his face wasn't that of a pretty boy anymore. And his hands were too large, with the knuckles bulky from abuse. He didn't think much of his appearance these days. He wasn't ugly, but he wasn't that willowy young man who could mount a horse by making a running leap and landing squarely on its back.

In short, he was thirty-eight and beginning to feel his age.

"Leo opens at five," she was saying, snapping Wyatt out of his thoughts. "I doubt there'll be a line for the job, but you never know."

Then she went scurrying up Eighth Avenue, sometimes stepping on that shoe ribbon, and disappeared from his view.

Wyatt refused to believe that the only job to be had in Eternity was that of a dishwasher. Since he had some blacksmithing experience, he checked at the Anvil and Forge first, talking there with a man named Casswell Tinhorn. But Tinhorn didn't need any help, and he directed Wyatt to the Happy City. Wyatt made arrangements to put July up for the night in a stall in the livery, then set out on foot.

He spent all of ten minutes walking both sides of Main Street, making inquiries that were shot down within seconds. He'd had hard-luck jobs before. He'd done worse than dishwashing—and without pay. But only because he'd had no choice. Cannery work, and washing and pressing laundry, were low on the list. Breaking rock in the quarry had looked a lot better afterward.

As Wyatt ended his full circle, one of the last establishments on this side of the street was the Happy City. It stuck out like a sore thumb with its twin carvings in front of two fat guys in underwear. There was a short tower over the entry door that had an upward-curving roof over each story. Its paint was peeling red in sore need of a fresh coat. From outward appearances, it looked like the owner didn't have a buck to his name.

Wyatt wandered over to have a better look—not because he was considering the job, but because of the sign in the window that looked invitingly familiar. It was that same red sign he'd seen throughout the countryside at various eateries:

REFRESHING AND DELICIOUS
COCA-COLA .05¢

That made Wyatt pause and deliberate. He was thirsty, and could go in and have a glass to think over his options. Opening the door, he was met with some of the strangest aromas he'd ever had the displeasure of smelling. He hadn't a clue as to what Chinese food was.

The place wasn't well lit, but he clearly saw the porcelain cat, with fangs and a grin to put a laughing madam to shame. It sat in the vestibule, almost as if to deter customers from coming in. Hanging on the wall were Chinese watercolors of tradesmen and an oil portrait of a guy in a black cap who looked like he was important. There were many colorful silk screens, and a red lacquered cabinet with brass hardware that appeared out of place with all the plain pine tables.

A man parted the curtain of beads separating the kitchen from the dining area. He was a good-looking fellow. Not too short, and with a pleasant face that thwarted any attempt Wyatt would have made to guess his age. His almond-shaped eyes were as black as his hair. He squinted against the smoke curling from the cigarette clamped in his mouth.

"We don't open till five for supper."

Wyatt wasn't sure how he'd expected the man to sound, but a prominent Eastern accent was entirely unexpected.

"Wasn't looking to get supper. I just wanted a cola."

The man gave him a tentative glance, then shrugged. "Sit down."

Wyatt sat in the rawhide-bottomed chair he'd been pointed to. He took his hat off and ran his hand through his windblown hair. The table was situated at one of the front windows, where wooden shutters had been pushed open to allow lingering sunlight in. A fat candle was on the table, making Wyatt glance at the ceiling. No electric lights.

The man had gone into the kitchen, the beads stirring behind him. Wyatt saw a younger fellow at a square butcher's table. Holding a cleaver, he was whacking a raw chicken into parts faster than a roper hog-tying a calf in a contest.

Returning with two cola bottles, the man gave one to Wyatt, then sat down opposite him. Using an opener, he flipped the caps off each bottle and slid one over to Wyatt.

"You aren't from around here," the man remarked as he took a sip. His cigarette still dangled in his fingers.

"No," Wyatt replied.

"You look like you're out of place, mister."

Wyatt did feel sort of out of place, only he didn't want to admit it. "I could say the same about you. You're no Westerner."

"No Far-Easterner either," he said as he lifted his chin a notch. "Born and raised in Brooklyn, New York."

Wyatt hadn't taken a drink yet, uncertain if he wanted

to share a conversation and a Coca-Cola with a stranger. But as soon as the man replied with blunt candor, Wyatt warmed up to him a little.

"Leo Wang," the restaurateur offered with an extended hand.

Wyatt took it. "Wyatt Holloway."

"Where you from, Mr. Holloway?"

"Wyatt," he amended. "Up north."

"Ah, a man who doesn't want people to know too much about him. I'll respect that." Leo drank again, noticed Wyatt hadn't, and frowned. "You don't want your Coca-Cola?"

Wyatt lifted the bottle and drank that first sugary sip that always slid down his throat better than fine bourbon. There was something about this cola stuff that really appealed to him. He couldn't say exactly what. He'd had sarsaparilla before, so he'd known the texture of carbonation in his mouth. But this was just like the sign said. Delicious and refreshing.

A face appeared in the window. It was Scudder. He tapped on the glass with his gun tip. Leo gave him a big smile, and Wyatt had to at least acknowledge him with a nod. Then the marshal chuckled before walking off. It annoyed the hell out of Wyatt to think he was being followed, or made to do something he didn't really want to do.

In the marshal's wake, Leo's smile fell, and he muttered, "What a pain in the tail butt."

Wyatt laughed. "You don't like the local law officer?"

"About as much as I like hot dogs."

Wyatt didn't know what a hot dog was, and took it to be some kind of Chinese food, but he didn't want to insult Leo by asking him if he really ate dogs. A good feeling was finally settling over him. He didn't want to ruin the moment.

The front door opened, and two kids—a girl about the age of nine and a boy no older than four—wove their way around the tables, a woman not far behind them. She was the one from in front of the marshal's office.

Leo stood and took his bottle with him. "The cola is on me since we both think Bean Scudder is a windbag." Then to the children, who were scraping chairs back, he said, "Hey, Rosalure and Tug. Have you been behaving yourselves today?"

The girl smiled. She looked a lot like the woman, and Wyatt quickly deduced these were her children. "We were at Nanna's house making candy. Tug ate too much. He says he's got a stomachache."

The boy didn't say anything. He slid his chair out and slipped onto the seat, his face not much higher than the table. He made fists out of his dirty hands, stacked them, and plopped his chin on the top.

"I'll bring you a glass of milk, Tug," Leo offered, and went through the beads into the kitchen.

Wyatt glanced at the woman.

"Hello, again," she greeted. Before sitting, she paused, indecision on her face and in her eyes. Then she squared her shoulders and walked directly toward him. "I suppose on a chance meeting it isn't necessary to introduce ourselves, but since we've met twice within the half hour, I believe we should." She extended her hand, and he was late on taking her smooth fingers into his own. Never had a woman who wasn't up for sale made the first move to touch him. Though this lady was definitely not a sporting-row gal. "Leah Kirkland," she said in that brisk voice of hers.

"Wyatt Holloway," he countered.

She lightly pumped his hand, then pulled away. A faint tint of a blush was on her cheeks, but she managed to tamp it down before it colored her face. He noticed the smudge was gone. "Well . . . enjoy your dinner. I recommend the Yen Ching Chow Mein." She took her seat without a backward glance and reprimanded the boy for poking his finger into the candle wax and making shavings out of it.

Leah Kirkland . . .

Oh, hell, she was that female photographer. One of those infernal picture-takers. It had been a photograph that caused many of the miserable things in his life. He never wanted one snapped of him again, so he was going to have to avoid her like the plague. Because a reprint of his likeness would be lethal. If the picture ever circulated, they'd know where to find him.

And Wyatt Holloway was a man who didn't want to be found.

Look for
Portraits
Wherever Paperback Books
Are Sold
mid-August 1996